SWINGBOATS ON THE SAND

*The second title in the
Holidays and Homes series.*

The Castles have owcned Piper's Cafe
on the beach at St. David's Well fur
three generations and, in 1940, business is booming. But not everyone in
the family is happy. Bethan Castle
becomes engaged to Freddy Clements,
but he longs for excitement before
being called up and his indiscretions
soon cause Beth sleepless nights.

SWINGBOATS ON THE SAND

Grace Thompson

Severn House Large Print
London & New York

This first large print edition published in Great Britain 2002 by
SEVERN HOUSE LARGE PRINT BOOKS LTD of
9-15, High Street, Sutton, Surrey, SM1 1DF.
First world regular print edition published 2001 by
Severn House Publishers, London and New York.
This first large print edition published in the USA 2002 by
SEVERN HOUSE PUBLISHERS INC., of
595 Madison Avenue, New York, NY 10022

British Library Cataloguing in Publication Data

Thompson, Grace
    Swingboats on the sand. - Large print ed.
    1. World War, 1939-1945 - Social aspects - Wales - Fiction
    2. Domestic Fiction
    3. Large type books
    I. Title
    823.9'14 [F]

ISBN 0-7278-7133-1

All characters are fictional and bear no relation to any living person.
Wartime episodes are, in the main, factual.

Printed and bound in Great Britain by
MPG Books Ltd, Bodmin, Cornwall.

One

At Piper's Café close to the sandy beach in the small town of St David's Well, the Piper family were all busily engaged in preparation for the new season. It was 1940 and the effects of the war were beginning to be felt, but for the people who worked on the sands at St David's Well, it was soon to be business as usual. Beth Castle and her sister Lilly were helping their mother Marged to clean the café after opening its doors and windows for the first time in months. Beth Castle's brothers, Eynon and Ronnie, and her cousins, Taff and Johnny Castle, were putting the finishing touches to the paint-work of the helter-skelter and the swing-boats, ready to erect them on the sand.

The small beach was still dressed for winter, with the shops and stalls boarded up and with no more than a few people en-joying the golden sands. But soon the place would be transformed, as the day-trippers and the holiday-makers arrived in ever-increasing numbers.

Through the café doorway Beth could look down on to the beach where Ronnie, Eynon and her father Huw stood in deep conversation, punctuated occasionally by her father pointing up at the roof of the café. She climbed up on to a café chair and leaned out of the window to wave, but they were too intent on their work to see her. She saw her brothers leave, shrugging on jackets and heading for the bus stop.

Beth was excited. Her dark brown eyes shone and a smile was ever constant on her generous mouth. Her black hair looked like a polished cap; always neat, it was cut in a short bob with a fringe that just touched her eyebrows. Her mother often told her she looked like the beautiful film star Anna May Wong. She was just under five feet tall, a half-inch that she regretted; four feet eleven and a half sounded so childlike. But being a bouncy, happy person, rarely critical of anyone, a friend to every person she met, the lack of height added to her air of innocence and was an enhancement rather than a disadvantage.

She loved the summer season with its lively crowds intent on having fun. The days were hectic and she knew from previous years that she would sink into bed each night exhausted, but happy. Only a few more days and the place would be open for business. War or no war, St David's Well Bay would attract the crowds.

Looking across the sand to where the waves were lit by the early sun, she watched as her Uncle Bleddyn set out his pitch ready for the boat trips he would run on the following day. He launched his twenty-seven-foot, clinker-built boat, registered to take twelve passengers, with his son, Johnny beside him and put-putted gently around the area of bay they were allowed to use. Further out there were barricades and mines, and soldiers ready to shoot to kill, a grim reminder of what was happening in France.

Beth's brother Ronnie, who at nineteen was just a year older than herself, greeted the start of the summer season with as much happy anticipation as herself. For Eynon who was a surly seventeen, and her sister Lilly who was twenty-six, the prospect was gloomy.

"All the hours we have to work and for a wage most of my friends would laugh at," Lilly grumbled as she lifted the cover off a display cabinet behind the counter in the café and began to pile up the assorted bars of Cadbury's and Fry's chocolate.

"But it's such fun," her sister replied. "What other job could we do that would give us such fun?"

"I can't see the fun. Only months of hard slog. A waste of the summer. Everyone on holiday except us. We'd be better off working for someone else. Family loyalty is all very well, but I want to earn real money. Don't you?"

"This year will be a good one for me." Beth's eyes shone. "A time to remember. There's my engagement party on my eighteenth birthday for a start. Only three weeks away."

"Marrying that Freddy Clements isn't something to celebrate," Lilly warned. "I'm telling you now that if you marry him you'll regret it. Too fond of himself, that one."

"Come on, you're only jealous. Twenty-six you are, Lilly, and no sign of a fiancé for you yet, is there?"

"That's all you know. I don't share my private life with the whole town like you do."

"Still seeing this secret lover-boy then? Hard to believe in someone you keep so well hidden, mind."

"Shut up about a secret lover or you'll get a thump. Right?"

Their mother Marged walked in then, staggering under the weight of a long shelf, recently painted a cheerful blue, on which the glasses for the popular ice-cream sundaes would stand.

"Give me a hand, Lilly, you're a bit taller than our Beth."

"Oh Mam, I'm just finishing this."

8

With a barely audible sigh, Beth put down the glass shelf she had been polishing and went to help her mother.

Beth's soon-to-be fiancé, Freddy Clements, worked as "third sales" in a gents' outfitters in the town. As this was Wednesday, a day on which the shop closed at lunchtime, he went home to change out of the formal suit he wore for business, having promised to go and see Beth. He wore another suit, one reduced to second best since it was no longer smart enough for work. As he straightened his tie and admired himself in his wardrobe mirror, he wondered whether he dare raid the savings account he and Beth had started a year ago and buy another suit and a few shirts. If rumours of clothes rationing became fact, then he would need a good stock. He didn't think Beth, who wore white overalls over any old thing, would understand this.

Freddy himself was not tall, measuring only an inch and a half more than Beth. He jokingly told her that he would never marry her if she grew that extra inch and a half as she'd shame him. He was as fair as Beth was dark; he used to try and flatten his hair, which was a bit longer than most and deeply waved, with Brylcreem, but now allowed it to move freely around his ears. His boss was constantly complaining about it but Freddy knew that girls liked it and he preferred to please girls than his boss any day.

Aware of his lack of height, he walked with his shoulders well back and his neck stretched to hold his head high. Giving himself one last look in the mirror and seeing that his collar wasn't sitting flat, he called to his mother.

"Mam, can you give this shirt one more go? The collar isn't up to your usual standard, and I know you'd hate me to go out looking sloppy."

Twenty minutes later, declaring himself satisfied, he set off for the bus stop. He was a bit late, but he knew Beth would be waiting. Confidence widened his smile.

Beth left her cleaning and went to the bus stop to wait for him. She leaned on the sea wall and studied the groups of people dotted around the sand. Several families were painting their stalls, small wooden shacks in which they would offer for sale everything needed for a day on the beach. She waved to the people she knew, rivals but still friends.

Her cousins Taff and Johnny were helping to paint the swingboats and the helter-skelter in bright red and yellow stripes. Now, before the summer season began, the magic was yet to come. All there was to be seen were rather shabby wooden structures being disguised by cheerful paint, touched here and there with gold. Bright colours and glitter were essential elements of the seaside.

Many stretches of the coast, both isolated areas and a number of once popular beaches, were now inaccessible to the public, having been surrounded with barbed wire and concrete blocks to prevent invasion forces landing. In the more isolated places they had been heavily mined and flags and notices gave stark warnings of the dangers to those who thought of trespassing. It had been decided to leave St David's Well Bay relatively open, however, apart from defences further out to sea, to offer families a chance to forget the worries of the war for a week, or a day or even a few hours. Holidays at home were encouraged and every town, not only those on the coast, were providing entertainments to persuade people against travelling. "Is Your Journey Really Necessary?" asked the posters.

She saw the bus making its way around the funfair and turned to watch its approach. It was two o'clock and this was the third bus she had seen arrive. Freddy was sure to be on it, smiling, warming her with his obvious delight at seeing her. She walked towards the bus stop but the only passengers to alight were her two brothers, Ronnie and Eynon, struggling with a piece of glass and assorted packages. They explained they had been sent home for some tools, glass and putty to fix a loose window.

"Tell Mam I'll wait for one more bus," she told them, turning once more to look at the busy people on the sands.

Piper's Café had been started by Joseph and Harriet Piper, her Granny Moll's grandparents. Joseph and Harriet had actually been Moll's husband's grandparents, but she always referred to them as her own. It was tucked into the curve of the cliffs on the eastern side of the bay and could be reached from the path along the headland or, when the tide allowed, by climbing metal steps leading up from the sand.

Some distance below the level of high tide, in front of the café steps, some council workmen were scrubbing the pool built from rocks that was filled regularly by the incoming tide. As the tide ebbed, it would slowly empty to await the next high tide, leaving small crustaceans, which colonised the cracks and hollows throughout the winter. These were now being evicted for the summer by men wearing waders and carrying brushes and spades, who were filling buckets with the winter residents, intent on making it more comfortable for the bare-footed children who would soon fill the place.

With hope slowly fading, Beth glanced towards the bus stop where a few people were waiting to return to the town. He wasn't coming, she thought sadly. Sitting once again on the strong sea wall she watched the activities below as the traders made the last-minute adjustments to their stalls and rides. A few people wandered around, idly watching others at work, intrigued perhaps at the sight of the flat boards and sections of corrugated iron that, by tomorrow, would be bright, cheerful, overloaded stalls.

She saw a bus in the distance, travelling up to turn and come down to the stop where she stood. This was her last chance. If Freddy wasn't on board she would have to get back to the café and finish the job she had started. Her sister Lilly was right – Freddy *wasn't* reliable – but they understood each other. After growing up only a street apart and spending most of their time together, they understood each other's failings better than most. She knew that love wasn't perfection. There were cracks in the best relationships; you only had to think about Mam and Dad to know that. Always arguing they were.

When the next bus spilled out its passengers, Freddy Clements was the first to alight and he hurried towards her, a smile to match hers on his handsome face.

"You look nice," she said shyly. "Not dressed for work, though. Painting it is today, mind."

"Not for me," he said, pulling a face, persuading her to laugh with him. "Wearing a good suit is my way of avoiding the jobs I hate."

"What are you planning to do, then?" she asked. "I thought you promised to help?"

"Windows?" he offered. "I don't mind cleaning windows."

They walked hand in hand along the promenade, their height practically the same, her dark head close to his fair one. They did not look like a couple; Beth was dressed in a skirt and blouse, both damp and stained from her work, while Freddy was dressed immaculately in his navy suit and white shirt. Beth was suddenly self-conscious, aware of the difference in their appearance, unable to excuse herself on the strength of eight hours' work in the café that day.

On the promenade they passed the shop also owned by the Castle family, although still bearing the Piper name after Moll's grandfather who had begun it. Like the rest of the shops and small cafés it was freshly painted. Beth was surprised to see that it had been decorated with stripes of pink and pale green and that on the window was written "Piper's Peppermint Rock".

"That's smart," Beth said, "but I'm surprised Granny Moll agreed. Adamant she was that it should be blue like the café. It looks much better, don't you think, Freddy?"

"Much better. More suitable than blue. Blue isn't a colour for eating, is it?" he agreed. "What can you eat that's blue? No, pink and peppermint green is much better." He looked in through the window. The shop was empty and the stands holding postcards were just inside the door.

"I wonder if someone has persuaded your gran to sell saucy postcards as well?" he grinned. Then his face sobered and he asked, "Why don't you forget the café and run this little seaside rock shop? Tidy little job that'll be, with no overalls and no messy cleaning to do. You could dress smart working here, couldn't you?"

Beth blushed then, even more aware of her untidy appearance. She knew Freddy hated her looking like a skivvy, despite the fact that cleaning was a part of her work.

"Cleaning is as important to the entertainments business as smiling and waving flags and selling sticks of rock, Freddy," she retorted. "And besides, Auntie Audrey's in charge of it."

"Auntie Audrey spends more time at the café, getting someone to take over for her here. It's obvious she prefers it there, so why don't you ask her if you can run the shop?"

"Because I like the café and being on the beach. Piper's is a family affair, remember, and we all have to do whatever's needed."

"Your dad and his brother don't think so, do they? Granny Moll never listens to them. In fact I'm amazed she let them have their way over the colour of the rock shop."

"She does listen! But we have to do what's best for the business, and sometimes Granny Moll has to disagree with Dad and Uncle Bleddyn."

"Sometimes?" Freddy said with a laugh. "Uncle Bleddyn and your dad have been trying to make some changes for a long time, but Granny Moll never listens to them, family or not."

She led him in silence to where her father and her brothers were preparing to climb a tall ladder to fix the loose window.

"Afternoon, Mr Castle," Freddy said and in reply was asked to help fix the window. "I've got a good suit on," he began to protest, looking at Beth for support.

"For God's sake someone, get him an overall," Huw ordered, and after borrowing an overall from Eynon, removing his jacket and placing it carefully over a chair, Freddy resignedly climbed the ladder after Huw to help him deal with the task.

They worked for most of the afternoon making sure everything looked its best, the

16

men outside putting the finishing touches to the paintwork, cheerful reds, blues and yellows chosen to attract the customers. Beth and her mother Marged were both very tired as they put the finishing touches to the inside, decorating the fresh clean shelves with doilies and checked shelf-paper before filling them with glasses, cups, saucers and plates. Teapots and jugs were piled conveniently close to the small trays they would need, everything in readiness for the following day.

Their last task was to place a few artificial ice-cream sundaes in the window and hang pictures on the wall. A formal portrait of Granny Moll's grandparents looked down on the customers as they queued at the till, and there were old photographs of the beach in past years which showed the changes in dress to amuse the customers as they waited to be served.

Beth's grandmother, Molly Piper, no longer worked every day in the café. When she had reached seventy, she had decided that it was time to relinquish her role and allow her daughter Marged and son-in-law Huw to run things their way. Although now, at seventy-four, she still liked to think her opinion was respected, as she told everyone who asked her about retirement. The truth was that she couldn't relinquish her position as head of the family to Huw and his brother and, for them, this refusal to "let go" was frustrating.

She arrived as Huw was locking the door and they were gathering up their tools and cleaning materials to go home for a well-earned meal.

"Hang about, hang about," she called as she hurried along the path towards them. "Let me get my breath."

"What d'you want, our Mam?" Marged asked, trying not to sigh. "Finished we have and off home for something to eat. I thought you were going home from the wholesaler on the bus with Audrey?"

"I came down to look at things after I'd been to the wholesaler and just as well I did. Have you seen what your Huw and that brother of his have done to the shop?"

Huw and Marged exchanged a look that told of their expectation of argument.

"I have, Granny Moll, and Freddy and I think it looks wonderful." Beth looked at Freddy for his agreement but he was half smiling, looking from one to the other, expecting fireworks.

"Stripes! And in green and pink! This will delay the opening, mind. We can't open it looking like that. You'll have to get it changed. I won't have it looking like a – a—" "A seaside shop selling seaside rock?" Huw said threateningly.

Bleddyn arrived having made the boat safe

18

and heard Moll's comments. He spoke in support of his brother. "All the others along there are painted either brown or dark green. It stands out and shows clearly what it sells, Moll."

"It won't open until you've changed it back to how it was!"

"Can we discuss this at home? I'm sinking for a cup of tea," Freddy said, winking at Beth. "This could go on all night and I'd rather be sitting down, eh?"

They started to move away again but Moll stopped them. "Hang about! I want to check that everything looks right for the first day," the elderly lady insisted, taking out her key and reopening the café door.

While no one was looking, Beth and Freddy held hands. Huw exchanged a glance of irritation with Marged, Bleddyn stood head down waiting for a decision to be made and the two boys groaned and asked if they could walk on home. Beth's sister Lilly drooped her shoulders and complained loudly that she had done enough. She was going to the pictures and didn't want to miss the beginning.

"You can all wait," Moll insisted. "This business was started by my grandparents and they had high standards. I don't want those standards slipping." She looked around her, an expression on her face suggesting disapproval, then she nodded. "It'll do," she said, touching a shelf, straightening a display. "Now, are you sure everything is ordered for the morning, Huw?"

Patiently, Huw and Marged went through the list of bread, cakes, milk and the rest until Moll announced she was satisfied. Thankfully, they all turned and walked towards the van, which bore the Piper name, with Moll mentioned as proprietor below.

"An' it's time that was changed, too," Huw muttered, before being shushed by Marged.

The ladders and benches and heavier tools were already on board and the rest was thrown casually on top of them. Huw drove with his mother-in-law next to him, and as the rest squeezed themselves among the tools they set off home.

"And don't think I've forgotten about what you did to the shop. Tomorrow you'll have to repaint it in the blue, like always. Right?"

"Fine, if you don't mind closing the café as well as the shop. If Bleddyn and I have painting to do we can't deal with the café."

"Or the boat trips," Bleddyn added quietly.

"I suppose it will have to stay for the moment – unless," she added, glowering at them, "the council sends someone to close us down!"

Two hours later, fully recovered from the

hard work and fortified by a good meal of fish and chips from their Uncle Bleddyn's shop, Eynon and Ronnie were out with friends, Beth and Freddy were sitting hand in hand listening to the wireless, Huw was snoring, and Lilly had slipped away to see Phil Martin.

Phil was waiting as arranged at the corner of Garth Row and Angel Villas, a place where few were likely to see him. Both roads had few houses, just a few privately-built detached properties with high walls and gardens filled with shrubberies and tall trees.

"Oh, Phil." Lilly sighed as they hugged each other passionately. "I'm so glad you could get away. I've had the most awful day and you're the only one to make me forget it."

"You're opening Piper's Café and the stalls tomorrow, then?" he said. "It'll be more difficult for us to meet now the season's starting, what with your long hours and my wife wanting to go out and about. I hate the summer."

"I hate it because we can't see each other as easily, but I'd dread the season anyway. Why should I have to work in the family business when they won't give me a say in the way it's run? Mam and Dad and Granny Moll have all made it clear that I'll never be in charge. Only my brothers are good

21

enough to run it. No matter that I'm the eldest and I've worked there since I grew tall enough to see over the counter. No, unless they can promise me one of the businesses to run as I want it run, then I'm going to tell them I'm finished."

"Best to hang on a bit longer, Lilly love. I don't think your Eynon is too keen to take it on and Ronnie, well, he's due for call-up soon and if he's in the forces fighting Hitler, then they'll need you proper, won't they? No, best you hang on."

"I hate it."

"What about the rock shop on the promenade? There's a tidy little back room there that would be handy on a quiet afternoon, eh?"

"I don't think Auntie Audrey will part with that job. Oh, have you seen what our Dad and Uncle Bleddyn did to it? Granny Moll asked them to touch up the dark blue paint and guess what they did? Painted it in stripes." They laughed as she described the various faces when her grandmother arrived at the café to complain, then grew serious once more.

"If I leave, show them I can be independent, then I could come back when they need me and make my own conditions."

"That's a clever thought. Bright girl you are, no mistake, Lilly Castle. But come here and forget it for an hour. I daren't stay longer; my wife will be back from her sister's by nine o'clock and we shouldn't waste valuable time on all this. Oh Lilly, if only things were different. You and I would make a wonderful team, we could do anything. If only—" His words were silenced by her kiss.

As the big clock on the church chimed the half-hour he walked her back to the corner of Sidney Street where she lived. Arms around each other, pressed as tightly together as possible yet still able to walk, they strolled through the dark lanes behind the houses, stopping for just one more kiss, a few murmured endearments and regrets, seeking privacy until the last moment, when they would step out into King Edward Street where they would part.

"I think I could persuade our Mam to let me find a job in a shop where the hours aren't so long and the work easier, but it's Granny Moll. She won't hear of it."

Stopping for a final kiss before going their separate ways, they were half hidden, having pressed themselves deep into an overgrown privet hedge. When they heard footsteps approaching they turned away, hiding their faces in the thick foliage and waited for the person to pass. To their consternation, the footsteps faltered and a female voice said, "Evening, Lilly."

Lilly froze and didn't reply, but once the footsteps began to fade she pulled away from Phil and looked along the quiet unmade road to see who had spoken. There was no one in sight. Whoever it was had disappeared into one of the houses on King Edward Street.

"Damn it all, Lilly," Phil muttered, "I hope whoever it was didn't recognise me. If my wife hears about us we're finished."

Lilly said nothing. She knew that forcing their relationship out into the open was her only chance of ever becoming more than a secret love, the one hope of a satisfactory end to all this. She wondered who had spoken, hope rising in a flood of excitement.

Beth was at home going over the endless lists that were an essential part of arranging an engagement party. The list of guests was growing by the minute and Marged glanced at it and shuddered. Beth was the first of her daughters to become engaged and she was determined to have a real good do but, with rationing already limiting her plans for a generous meal, she was doubtful of the wisdom of inviting so many.

"What about making it a late evening do instead of starting at teatime? That way we'd cut out the children and invite only the adults. We'd be able to give a better meal if we cut the numbers," she suggested. She and Beth discussed this idea for a few minutes but when Beth turned to ask Freddy how he felt, he looked bored.

"Let's leave it for now, Mam, is it?" Beth said, hiding her disappointment. "We've all had a busy day and we're tired."

"Great," Freddy said, jumping up enthusiastically. "Let's go to the pictures."

"Sorry, but I feel too tired, love. I want an early night."

"That's okay," he quickly agreed. "I'll get off home. An early night isn't a bad idea." He gave her a chaste kiss and left. But he didn't go home. He went to the Chain and Locker for a pint, then to catch the last showing at the pictures. Boring, that was what Beth had become. She talked about nothing but the engagement party or Piper's damned Café. When would she have time for him?

The picture house wasn't full. Most people came for the earlier performances and he chose a seat a few rows from the back and threw his coat across the seat next to his.

A few moments later someone lifted up his coat and put it on the arm and sat beside him. He took no notice as he was involved in the film, trying to work out the plot, which was difficult as it had been well under way when he had arrived. He didn't try to see who it was until a voice said, "Want a toffee, Freddy Clements? Or a marsh-mallow or a hard-boiled?"

Shirley Downs worked in a shop near the gentlemen's outfitters, selling newspapers and magazines and sweets. Freddy often stopped for a chat when he called for his paper. Shirley was taller than him by several inches and to compensate she usually leaned on the counter, or kicked off her high heels.

Sitting down, they were much of a height, but she slid down in her seat and lolled against the arm as she spoke. She held out a large paper bag and he smiled in the darkness and riffled around in it until she closed her hand and locked his among the sweets.

"Ooh, 'elp! Let go of me, Shirley Downs," he said in mock alarm. "Grip like a set of pliers you've got!"

Amid demands to "hush" she allowed him to choose a sweet and they laughed as they settled down to watch the film. They whispered as they each tried to work out the story and an irate patron warned that he would speak to the manager and have them thrown out if they didn't stop talking. So they moved places and sat in the back row.

Shirley usually wore her long hair fastened in a tight "sausage" around her head, rolled around a ribbon and held in place with clips, but tonight she had allowed it to fall about her shoulders and Freddy enjoyed the sensation of its fluttering touches as they leaned towards each other to whisper observations about the plot. He realised with some surprise that he didn't remember ever touching Beth's hair. He wondered whether the effect of caressing the short, orderly bob would be the same as running his fingers through the tempting tresses so close to him.

They watched the end of the main film and sat through the "B" offering, plus the news and all the shorts. Then they watched the main one again, hardly taking in what they saw.

At eleven o'clock, Freddy said, "I can't let you go home alone at this time of night. Where d'you live, Shirley?"

"Above the shop. Mam and I work there and live in the flat above. It's handy, but I've no excuse for being late for work, mind, and I start at five thirty. So get me home quick, so I can get some sleep."

"Fancy you living above the newsagent. All this time and I never knew."

"There's a lot you don't know about me, Freddy Clements."

"I might spend a bit of time finding out," he said, flirting with his eyes, receiving a promising response.

Crossing the park on his way home, Freddy sat on a bench for a long time, thinking a little about Beth and a lot about Shirley. As the day of his and Beth's engagement drew close, he had become less and less excited. Surely there should be more than lists and more lists?

The romance that had slowly grown out of friendship had vanished almost as soon as he had proposed. He remembered their most recent discussion on the subject, when he had failed to convince Beth of his plan.

"I know we've agreed that we'll live with your Granny Moll and your Auntie Audrey," he had said, "but it isn't too late to change our minds. Why can't we do what we originally planned and get rooms of our own?"

"We'll be fine with Granny Moll. She has such a big house it seems a waste of money to spend on rent while she has rooms empty. Oh Freddy, we'll be so happy with her to look after us. And we'll be only a few doors away from Mam and Dad."

He shuddered. Why couldn't Marged and Huw set them up in a flat? It wasn't difficult to rent a place and furnishing wouldn't cost much if they bought second hand.

"I want us to start out on our own," he had said, trying to provoke an argument.

"We can't afford it, Freddy."

"Yes we can, if your mam and dad would help and if we buy second hand. My mam and dad have a lot of spare stuff they want to give us. I want us to be free to do what we want, lock our door and go out when we choose to, come in with the milk if we like, without having to tell Granny Moll where we're going and what time we'll be back."

As he remembered, his frustration grew. He walked on until he was at his gate. It was almost midnight and his parents were in bed, trusting him to go in quietly and lock the door. It would be a return to childhood to be "looked after" by Granny Moll Piper.

Was becoming a part of the Piper family and the seaside café, shop and stalls what he really wanted? Or had he thought of it as an easy way to earn his keep? Was he ready to settle down? He wasn't yet eighteen and he and Beth had been together since their first day at school.

His thoughts returned to Shirley Downs and the way they had laughed together. He had felt more alive after talking to her for a few hours than he had felt for months.

Guilt touched him then, but he shrugged it off. Was he wrong to want a bit of fun before settling down with Beth and becoming a part of the Piper family's business? Security and money had been and still were the attraction, he admitted, as he leaned on his front gate and stared at the sky, but the thought of being married to the earnest and kindly Beth was losing its appeal.

Beth and Lilly didn't have a peaceful night but it wasn't thoughts of Freddy that kept

29

Beth from sleep, it was the argument between her mam and dad, a shouting match that quickly woke Lilly and Eynon too. Huw and Marged had been late going to bed and by the time they had done so their low murmuring had grown into an enormous row.

Lilly covered her head with a pillow and, after wriggling about and complaining, fell back to sleep, but Beth was upset. Mam and Dad frequently argued and with the beginning of the season making everyone tired and edgy, their rowing was becoming worse by the day.

The morning of the opening of the summer season broke fair and Marged and Huw were up before six and on the sands by half-past. Everywhere was frantic activity as owners opened up the serving areas of their stalls and displayed their wares. Balloons and windmills on sticks were fixed all around the brightly painted stalls. Flags caught the morning breeze and waved a welcome to the crowds who were expected to come and buy.

In the café high above the sands, Marged and Huw were setting out the food, turning on the chip-fryer and filling the boiler for making tea. Occasionally they looked out to see their sons setting up.

Even from a distance, Marged could see

the lack of enthusiasm in their younger son, Eynon. He stood looking towards the edge of the waves where their Uncle Bleddyn, their father's brother, was fixing the painted sign that advertised boat trips. Ignoring Ronnie's need for help, he stared while Ronnie climbed up on the helter-skelter to fill the spaces with the last of the flags, and only did something to help when chivvied by his brother.

Marged watched and wondered how long they would keep him working the beach. There was no doubt that his heart wasn't in it.

Huw looked over her shoulder and, guessing her thoughts, said succinctly, "Lazy sod."

Ronnie, who was nineteen, tried to encourage his younger brother.

"Do you want to finish off here, Eynon, or go and fetch the ice-cream with Dad?"

"I don't want to do either. I want to join the army and get away from this boring beach for ever!"

"Come on, you know the call-up isn't to take you on a picnic. I'm two years older than you and I'll have to go before long and believe me, I'd rather stay here than face guns and tanks and bombs and God knows what all, over in France."

"At least it won't be boring." Eynon kicked at the sand which had settled around the base of the round wooden stall, making it appear to have been there for ever.

"You're right there. You damned fool, haven't you seen Eddie Powell who's lost a leg? Or heard of the fathers who won't be coming back? Stop pretending and be thankful that you're here and safe!"

"Until they start bombing us!"

"Oh, go and fetch the ice-cream!" Ronnie snapped.

"No I won't! I'm going to find my mates."

"You'd better serve these kids first," Ronnie warned him.

"Any pop, mister?" the first customer requested.

"Waiting for it to come."

"Do you sell Snowfruits?"

"No, that's Wall's. We make our own."

"Is that the biggest balloon you've got?"

"Yes, and you can't have it, so clear off before I thump you."

Every request received a short and irritable response until Ronnie lost his temper with his brother. "Eynon, for heaven's sake, boy, these people are here to have fun, not to be shouted at by a misery-guts like you!"

"I hate this stupid stall. I'm off!" He reached for his jacket and slung it over his shoulder.

"Too late to slope off, boy, here's our Dad."

"Ronnie, d'you think you could help in

the fish-and-chip shop this dinnertime? Your Uncle Bleddyn needs to get the boat ready; there are quite a few passengers waiting and he can't be in two places at once."

"Why can't I do that?" Eynon moaned.

"Because he asked for Ronnie. You'll stay here and serve on the stall, right?"

"Not much point without ice-cream or pop."

"They're on the way. Your cousin Johnny is bringing it all. He's been on the job since five o'clock this morning."

"More fool him," Eynon muttered.

"What about the shop?" Ronnie queried. "Did Granny Moll mean it when she said she wouldn't open it till the paint was changed?"

"Auntie Audrey is opening it later."

"I could open it now," Eynon said hopefully. Anywhere away from Mam and Dad and Granny Moll's eagle eyes. There would be a chance of a bit of flirting, and he might arrange a date for himself for later with a bit of luck.

"Gran's determined that Dad changes it back to blue, mind," Ronnie told him.

"Pity. Our Dad ought to get his own way sometimes. I wouldn't allow a woman to boss me around, would you? Oh," Eynon added cheekily, "I forgot. You already have Olive, haven't you!" He darted away to avoid the cuff aimed at his ear.

The café was busy that first day. Although it was not warm enough for bathing, several families had settled for the afternoon and the sand was dotted with deckchairs and brightly coloured towels. Buckets and spades were in action as the tide approached and children, mothers and a few grandfathers made channels inviting the water to flow in and fill the moats around castles. Using the iron steps, mothers climbed up to the café and ordered teas. Beth and Marged were kept busy serving meals and filling trays with cups and saucers and teapots and milk jugs for people to take down on to the sands, while Granny Moll and her youngest daughter Audrey made sandwiches, cut and filled scones and baked Welsh cakes on the heavy metal bakestone.

Beth's Uncle Bleddyn was not like her father even though they were brothers. Huw was small and slim, whereas Bleddyn was taller and heavier with a beard that disappeared during the winter and grew again in the spring to give passengers the romantic impression that he was a seasoned sailor – which he was not. He looked powerful and strong however, which he was. At forty-six, Bleddyn Castle, with his dark hair scattered with grey and skin toughened by summers spent in the open air, was still a handsome man. His recently widowed status had added to his appeal to the ladies of St

David's Well.

The beach was far from crowded, but his boat set off several times. The passengers were few, but he didn't like disappointing them and took the sturdy flag-bedecked boat out as far as restrictions allowed, pointing out the various landmarks and the beauty of the headlands proudly, as though they were of his own making.

At five o'clock the stall-holders began to close. They would extend the hours of opening as the season progressed, but the summer visitors were yet to come in their thousands and they were content with the little they had done.

At the end of the day Bleddyn moored the boat and locked it securely before going to open the fish-and-chip shop and the small café behind. After accepting the last of the trays returned from families who had picnicked on the sands, Beth and her Auntie Audrey began packing up the remainder of the food. Everything not sold would be discarded and fresh food bought for the following day. It was a matter of pride that they never sold food that was stale. The chip-fryer and pans would be emptied, the fat cooled and the utensils thoroughly scoured. Beth smiled as she saw Granny Moll's suspicious eyes on her.

"Don't think you can get away with a quick wipe around, my girl," the old lady admonished her. "Good shiny pans are what I want to see before I go home."

"I'll do the greasy old fryer and all that," Auntie Audrey told her. "You get ready to meet that young man of yours. I'm in no hurry tonight."

Gratefully, Beth accepted her aunt's help and hurried home. Freddy was coming over and they were going to write out the invitations to their engagement party.

"Do we have to do it tonight?" Freddy asked, as he watched her start to prepare the table for the family supper. "I don't feel like doing anything tonight. And," he added solicitously, "I bet you're tired, it being your first day on the sands and you up so early. Let's forget it for tonight and you have an early night, is it?"

As he spoke, his words, so low and sympathetic, had the effect of reminding her of the long day she had worked. She was aware of tiredness which a moment ago she would have denied. Her legs ached and she felt a stiffness across her shoulders.

"Perhaps that is a good idea," she agreed. "The party isn't for another fortnight, we can do them another time."

"Tell you what, why don't I take them to work and do some in my dinner hour?" he offered and, taking the list, the pile of envelopes and the writing pad, he kissed her and left.

Out of sight of the house where Beth lived with her parents and her sister and brothers he broke into a run. If he hurried, he might be in time to catch Shirley Downs before she and her mother closed the shop.

Before the start of the season Audrey had found an assistant for the shop, Alice Potter. The young girl was willing to help out when necessary and seemed amenable to irregular hours. After a few instructions, Audrey felt able to leave the girl in charge, calling once or twice during the day to see that everything was running smoothly. Meanwhile Eynon worked the swingboats and Taff and Johnny managed the helter-skelter and the stall selling ice-creams and items for the beach.

The stalls set up on the sand were very busy, with newcomers wanting buckets and spades and flags and windmills and water-wings. Dippers – the local name for bathing costumes – had to be measured for size, and beach balls blown up with a sense of fun. As visitors arrived they set themselves to enjoy the day, and everything – even the exhausting effort of filling a beach ball or changing into dippers covered by an inadequate towel – was accompanied with laughter.

Bleddyn's boys swopped occasionally to share the work evenly, as the stall was more hectic than the helter-skelter. It was truly a family affair with everyone capable of doing any job, although each of them had their favourites – except Eynon, who constantly told the others that he hated it all!

Business increased over the first weekend and the Castle family were forced to work non-stop from dawn to dusk making food and attending to the queues waiting for the helter-skelter and the ever popular swing-boats. Even Eynon forgot to be miserable as groups of young girls began to flirt in the hope of a longer ride. He didn't mind help-ing on the swingboats. All he had to do was time the rides and take the money.

Marged sighed with relief to see her youngest smiling and enjoying his work – until Ronnie left the ice-cream stall and insisted it was time for a change. He wanted his turn at the swingboat ride. Eynon refused to change and an argument quickly ensued. When it was finally sorted, Marged sighed.

"When will our Eynon grow up?" she asked Huw.

"Will he ever?"

"I hope it isn't the army that does it. The time for our Ronnie to sign up is getting close and unless Hitler gives up quick our Eynon will soon follow."

In spite of the sun and the laughing crowds, the day grew suddenly grey.

Lilly was determined to show her parents and grandmother how efficient she was and she spoke briskly to the customers in the café as they hesitated about what they wanted. Twice Beth had to push her sister aside and deal with customers herself because Lilly had made them so flustered.

"Talk to her, Mam," Beth pleaded. "She's making the customers feel they're a nuisance."

When the café was quiet, Marged took Lilly to one side.

"Even when the café is full and they're queueing down the steps and as far as the swimming pool, you give them all the time they need to decide what to order. Right? It's their holiday and we're here to make sure they enjoy it."

Turning away from her mother, Lilly poked a tongue out at Beth, who said softly, "Oh, very grown up and responsible, aren't we?"

At the end of the first weekend Granny Moll gave two shillings to Beth.

"What's this for, Gran?"

"Hush an' don't tell your sister. It's for your savings. Put it away quick."

"Gran, you're very generous. You've given us so many ten-shilling notes already. I'm sure you can't really spare it."

"Between now and when you get married, I'll help when I can. I know you're doing

39

without things to put a bit by. Just a few shillings now and then. I want you to have a nice little nest-egg when you start off on your own."

"Thanks, Gran." Beth kissed her and they hugged.

That evening as she and Freddy were walking home from the pictures, where he had had to sit through the film he had already seen twice, she handed him the two-shilling piece. "Another gift from Granny Moll," she said. "She helps us a lot, doesn't she? How much have we got now, about forty pounds or more? We'll be able to buy our own house at this rate, specially if we live with her and Auntie Audrey for a while. Just think of it, Freddy, a house of our own, just you and me."

Freddy kissed her to avoid the need to reply. The savings had been reduced recently. With the rumour of clothes rationing, he had ordered a suit and a pair of trousers and a sports jacket. It wasn't really extravagant. He wouldn't have to buy any others for a while and he had to look smart in his position.

"When are we going to choose the ring?" she asked, as they hugged in the shadows of the fruit-and-veg warehouse. "You've been saving for that separately, haven't you?"

"It's difficult, me working in a shop and having the same half-day as the jeweller."

40

"What about me getting a few hours off and meeting you one dinnertime? I'm sure Mam and Dad won't mind, seeing as it's for such an important reason."

Evasion failed to work and Freddy arranged to meet her the following Tuesday.

Beth chose a double-twist diamond ring that cost seven pounds. She walked to the door as Freddy dealt with the transaction, her eyes shining. It was really happening. She was really going to marry Freddy Clements.

When they got outside she asked to look at it again.

"Sorry, but I've left it in the shop," he said, hurrying her down the street towards the café where they were going to eat. "The salesman wasn't satisfied with the fit, he wants to take it in just a half-size to make sure you don't lose it."

The engagement of Bethan Castle and Frederick Clements was displayed on a banner in the café a week later. The party was to be held there on Saturday after the trippers had gone home and the café closed.

Moll Piper and her two daughters were already setting out the food when Beth took the final few trays from the families leaving the beach and dealt with the last of the dishes. Lilly had gone early, insisting she had to have her hair set. Eynon was chatting up a couple of girls as he locked the swing-boats and fastened the gate of the helter-skelter.

Beth had realised she would have no time to go home and had brought her new dress so she could change in the toilet when the work was finally done. She combed her dark hair and brushed it until it shone, then pulled the taffeta dress over her shoulders. It was coppery brown and had a full skirt. The wide belt showed her trim figure off perfectly.

Freddy forced a smile when he saw her and asked quietly why she had chosen such a dull colour for their celebration. She felt uneasy for the rest of the evening, especially as there was no sign of the ring.

Most of the guests were family. There were fewer than she had expected and the café was far from full. She missed a few faces she had expected to see but didn't have time to dwell on their absence as she greeted the newest arrivals.

Her father's brother Bleddyn and his sons burst in and filled the room with their size and their loud voices but they soon subsided into silence as though the smallness of the crowd inhibited them. Taff, whose real name was Arthur Brian, was twenty-six and large like his father. He was about to enlist. He and his wife, Evelyn, sat looking away from each other and almost back to back,

42

and argued all evening. Johnny, who was twenty-two, had come with his girlfriend Hannah. She was thirty, divorced and had two children, and felt ill at ease meeting the family *en masse* for the first time.

As her brother Eynon came and slumped in a chair, fist under chin, obviously not wanting to be there, Beth's heart dropped like a stone. This was not a good start to the evening.

There were few of Freddy's family present when the time came to cut the rich fruit cake that Marged had robbed the café's store cupboard to make. His parents sat apart from the rest and made little effort to join in the chatter, the teasing or even, Beth thought sadly, the congratulations.

Once the cake was cut and distributed, Beth and Freddy opened the many gifts that had arrived for them. Tea-towels and towels, china and cutlery piled up. There were egg-cups and spoons, a tin kettle and a brown teapot and several ornaments. The largest gift was from her parents, a hearth tidy to place near the fire. It was in the shape of a cloaked figure with hooks around it on which hung a small shovel, a brush, poker and tongs.

Beth thanked them all and rubbed her wedding finger disconsolately. Somehow the excitement hadn't happened. "Where's the ring?" she whispered anxiously to Freddy.

Freddy led her into the kitchen. "Sorry I am, Beth, love, but the jeweller let me down proper. Not ready till next week he said. Shortages are already causing problems, he told me."

"He had to make it smaller, that's all. He didn't need to add anything, so how could shortages—"

Once again Freddy stopped her tearful protest with a kiss. Fumbling in his pocket he produced a tiny brass curtain ring. "We have to make our special day somehow, love, so will you wear this for a week until I get the ring and we can do it all proper? I'll go down on one knee an' all, mind."

He was rewarded with a smile and he placed the tawdry object on her slim hand and kissed it, and then her lips, slowly, and with a groan of passion that made her forget her disappointment.

They made a huge joke of the substitute ring and only Huw and Marged looked less than amused.

"There's another gift here," Beth's Auntie Audrey called, handing them a small box. It contained a china clock painted with roses and forget-me-nots and was quite the nicest present of all. It was from Bernard Gregory, the man who kept the donkeys that gave rides to children, and Beth suddenly realised that, although he had been on her list, he hadn't appeared.

"I wonder why he didn't come?" Beth frowned. Then, as she thought of those who had turned up, she realised how few of the people on her list had actually been there. Counting on her fingers, she began to list the people from the beach, people she had known all her life, who had not shown up. "None from the cafés and none from the other stalls. I hope I haven't offended them. Not even Sarah the fortune teller, and she never misses a party. And the two from the wholesaler didn't come. Neither did Alice, the new girl from the rock and sweet shop, or Granny Moll's friend Greta."

The list went on. Freddy felt a twinge of guilt. He had only written invitations to half the names on his list before getting fed up with the whole thing and throwing the list away. He covered up his concern at Beth's dismay, however, laughing to try to ease her disappointment that people whom she thought of as friends hadn't bothered to come and wish them luck. Who needed them?

That night when Beth was undressing, hanging up the lovely dress that had been ruined for her by Freddy's remark, she looked down at the brass curtain ring and a tear dropped into her small hand. When she went into the bathroom to clean her teeth and wash her face, the ring slipped from her finger and disappeared down the drain.

Two

Belgium and Holland surrendered to the German army at the end of May and a week later the British Army became caught between the sea and the determined attackers. The call went out for the owners of boats of thirty feet and over to go to their rescue. Bleddyn had already registered his boat, but as it was only twenty-seven feet he wasn't needed, although like many others he would have attempted to join in had he been near enough to respond to the call in time. What was being asked of them seemed an impossible task, but determination was a strong weapon.

In horror the audiences in cinemas all over the country watched the newsreels that showed the bravery of the rescuers as they lifted thousands of men from the beaches of Dunkirk under the persistent fire of Hitler's army. Fear filled the hearts of everyone and it was to the beaches they went: some to feel closer to their loved ones, others to help their family relax and forget, even momentarily, the dramatic events taking place across the water that could be changing history.

"Laughter always was good medicine," Moll told her family, "and it's our duty to provide it. The war effort isn't just making bombs and bullets, remember."

Huw was sent to repaint the rock and sweet shop and with ill grace he set off with the cans of dark blue paint to restore it to its previous dullness. He was just about to start rubbing down when Moll appeared.

"I need you to go to the wholesaler, Huw," she said.

"Can't. Sorry. Got this painting to do."

Moll looked undeniably shifty, Huw told Bleddyn later, as she said, "Perhaps we could leave it. Several people have remarked on its cheerfulness."

Huw dropped the sandpaper he was using and stared at her, enjoying her humiliation at having to back down.

"You mean I was right for once, Ma?" he grinned.

"No, you weren't!" she snapped. "Doing it without discussing it with the rest of us! This is a family business, Huw, and don't forget it!"

"As if I could," he retorted. "But it's the Castle family, no longer Piper's."

"Piper's it will always be."

"Face it, Ma, Bleddyn and I run it and we have for years. Bleddyn and me, Marged and our children. All Castles, not a Piper among us except you."

Muttering insults not intended for his ears, she scuttled off. Huw loaded the painting equipment back into his van and drove to Sidney Street, smiling. She'd give in eventually, she'd have to; she knew the business depended on Bleddyn and himself to survive, especially now with so many of the young men being called up to fight Hitler.

Presuming Huw was repainting the rock shop, Marged asked Ronnie to go to the wholesaler for more supplies. "You'll have to go on the bike, mind, your father's got the van."

"No thanks!" Ronnie replied. "I'll walk to the rock shop and borrow the van."

He walked up on to the promenade and along past the assorted shops and cafés but when he reached the rock shop, it was open for business with Auntie Audrey smiling behind the counter. There was no sign of his father's van.

After hearing Audrey's brief explanation Ronnie set off to walk to Sidney Street, where he joined his father in a sandwich and a cup of tea before setting off. He went first to Goose Lane where Mr Gregory kept chickens and ducks as well as his donkeys.

The house looked empty and Ronnie was writing a note asking Mr Gregory to deliver four dozen eggs the following day when a tall figure dressed in a heavy sweater and corduroy trousers came around the corner.

"Peter Gregory?" Ronnie said hesitatingly. "It is you, isn't it?"

"Ronnie Castle. How delightful to see you," Peter said, his voice lacking the local accent, the words formal and very polite. He held out a rather grubby hand. "Not called up yet, I see? Or are you on leave?"

"Not yet, but I'm expecting it any time. I can't wait to get stuck in. Still working on the beach until they want me, with Mam and Dad and the rest of them." He wondered why he was apologising, and lying about wanting to go. There was nothing he wanted more than another deferment. But seeing Peter Gregory, who had volunteered as soon as the word "conscription" was mooted, made him feel ashamed of being a civilian, especially after the tragedy of Dunkirk. "All set to go I am, but they know what's best, they'll send for me when they want me, eh?"

He paid for the eggs and placed them in the van.

"How are the family?" Peter asked. "Is your sister Beth still working the beach too?"

"We're all there, Uncle Bleddyn and my cousins Taff and Johnny, and Beth and Lilly and our Eynon and me. And Granny Moll

49

of course, still thinks she's in charge she does."

"Perhaps I'll call and see you all. I sometimes walk down to help Father bring the donkeys back to their field."

Driving off Ronnie chuckled. Posh voice; "Father" instead of "Dad": what a boring bloke he'd turned out to be. Different from when they used to go out looking for apple orchards and helping themselves to the fruit, scrumping they called it. Now he'd probably call it "depriving the owners of their property by illegal means", he chuckled.

The weather turned nasty and the days at the beach consisted of bedraggled families coming into Piper's Café for shelter more than food. The place smelled of damp clothing as people who had booked into a bed and breakfast filled the hours before they could return to their accommodation, change their clothes and make themselves comfortable.

Marged and Huw felt sorry for them and initially allowed them to stay longer than the amount of money spent would justify. Many more arrived as the season moved towards the main holiday period, however, and they realised they couldn't fill the place with unprofitable bodies and exclude those who might spend money and eat the food they

50

had prepared. Some of the stalls on the sand closed and Mr Gregory walked his patient donkeys home earlier than usual.

The cafés stayed open but few did more than cover their expenses, throwing left-over food away each evening. Mr Gregory might have taken the discarded food for his pigs but it was too far to travel for a few cakes and sandwiches. Buses and trains continued to bring people but fewer and fewer left the town and braved the dampened splendour of the seaside. The weekdays were very quiet and Beth and Lilly were given time off to enjoy as they wished, though at the weekend the whole family turned out, the stalls were opened and even a few flags were set to wave and help create the illusion of enjoyment.

One evening as Beth, draped in her father's mac, had put the left-over food in the bins at the side of the café, she saw a young girl, who looked about eight, search through the rubbish and take several packages before running off, scuttling through the wet grass away from the headland and down towards the fields beyond.

It wasn't the first time Beth had seen the girl and she felt a growing concern. A child hungry enough to steal food from a bin? She made up her mind that in future she would make sure the best of the left-over food was wrapped carefully and left on the top. She mentioned the incident to her mother and Marged agreed to do the same.

There was more waste than usual during those two wet weeks and towards the end of each day they gave any customers they had more generous portions than usual rather than throwing the food away. Each evening, however, a couple of cleanly wrapped packages were placed at the top of the bin, and Beth waited until she saw the small child run out and take them. All the stale food that went into the bin was well wrapped in newspaper so she didn't feel too worried about the child eating any other food she might take.

On the days when she wasn't needed, Beth had been spending a few hours working on a rug she was making for the house she and Freddy would one day own. Taking an idea from a friend who had begun to build a business making rugs, but using the method of weaving scraps of material into sacking, she used old coats and skirts she was given and a backing made from a potato sack. With so many oddments of material, she worked with only the slightest attempt at a pattern. Most of the colours were either navy or brown. Drab, Freddy would call it, she thought with a stab of pain, remembering his unkind remarks about her engagement party dress.

At that moment she heard the wailing call

of the rag-and-bone man, who wandered
the streets of St David's Well with his horse
and flat cart, begging for rags which he
would later sell. On impulse she gathered
the bags of material, all dark, practical
colours, took the partly made rug with the
hook she used to pull the scraps through,
and gave them all to the surprised old man.
She refused his offer of a mechanical
singing bird or a goldfish and as she closed
the door she saw he was examining her gift
with interest. His wife might like to finish
that; it would be better than putting it with
the rest and getting a few pence. Pleased
with the result of his day, he ambled slowly
home.

"I brought this old skirt from Auntie Audrey," her mother said as she came through
the door, shaking the rain from her umbrella. "Dark brown it is, just what you need
for the border."

"I've thrown the rug away. I didn't want to
finish it," Beth said, taking the baskets from
her mother and beginning to sort out the
tea-towels and tablecloths for the wash.
"Dull, it was; boring."

"You can hardly want pale colours to put
on the floor, love." Marged frowned.
"What's the matter, fach?"

"The truth is, Mam, I don't feel engaged.
I can't see that Freddy and I will ever get
married if I don't even have a ring to show

we're engaged."

"Two weeks and he still hasn't collected it from the jeweller?"

"Why don't you go in tomorrow and see what the trouble is?" Huw suggested, following Marged into the house. "Lord knows we aren't busy, what with this rain an' all, so get yourself down there first thing and sort him out, is it?"

Freddy didn't call that evening so Beth wasn't able to discuss it with him. She imagined going to the jeweller and then calling into the gents' outfitters and surprising him by wearing it. Or perhaps she would just give him the box so he could choose a romantic moment and place it on her finger. She was dreamily imagining it all as she walked to the jeweller's shop next morning.

The shop was being opened as she reached the door and she tentatively asked the rather haughty-looking young man if her ring was ready. The man was formally dressed in a three-piece suit, his hair slicked back severely, his mouth pursed in disapproval. Pimples in abundance failed to reduce the self-confidence that his position clearly gave him. He paused after she posed her question as though deciding whether or not she was a suitable person to enter, then he stood back for her to walk in.

She had never been inside a jeweller's shop before going with Freddy to choose the ring, and there was something intimidating about entering the sparkling shop where so many expensive items were on display, items she would never be able to afford. She waited, feeling like an interloper who was about to be thrown out.

There was much discussion going on behind the half-closed door and then the assistant came out and shook his head offhandedly. "I'm very sorry, Miss Castle, but we have nothing reserved or under repair in your name."

She began to leave, embarrassment colouring her cheeks, wondering how she could have made a mistake. Then the assistant was brushed rudely aside and the proprietor came forward, a kindly expression on his face.

"I'm very sorry, Miss Castle, but there is nothing reserved for you. Could you have perhaps made a mistake about the shop? There are other jewellers, and..." He smiled kindly.

Feeling marginally better she smiled and began to leave. Had she come into the wrong jewellery shop? Then she turned back. "Of course! It would be under the name of my fiancé, Mr Frederick Clements." She smiled.

"I'm sorry, Miss Castle, but Mr Clements didn't buy that ring after all. I understood you had changed your mind."

"Oh, no. Er, there must be some mistake."

The man felt sorry for her and said kindly, "If the mistake is ours, I apologise sincerely, Miss Castle. We will do everything we can to put things right."

She almost ran from the sympathetic voice, the knowing eyes, fumbling her way out, unable to see for humiliating tears.

Lilly's way of spending her spare time as the rain continued and the beach was quiet was to lie on her bed and read. Phil Martin worked in the back room of a wireless shop, on the outskirts of the town, repairing wireless sets and gramophones. The fact that he was married meant she couldn't go and see him, even as a customer. She had already done so twice and another visit in the guise of a customer was out of the question. With other members of staff there, she would soon be noticed; remarks would fly and Phil's wife would get suspicious. That would mean disaster. Or would it? Again she felt that impish desire to confront the woman, make her face the fact that Phil no longer loved her. Then she would have to let Phil go. It was an intoxicating prospect.

Why had she been unlucky in love? She comforted herself with the thought that her sister Beth wasn't any better off marrying Freddy Clements. Liked himself too much, that one. She threw down the book and stared at the ceiling. If only she had met Phil a couple of years earlier, she would be the one celebrating an engagement. She didn't think Phil would spend the money for the ring by putting clothes on his back, which was what Mam and Dad suspected Freddy Clements of doing. No, Phil Martin would buy her a beautiful ring and then the wedding ring to snuggle up beside it and they'd be so happy. If only he hadn't married so soon.

At four o'clock Auntie Audrey was due to call to pick up the freshly laundered gingham tablecloths for the next day. Regardless of how quiet the café was, the white tablecloths were washed daily and the gingham ones underneath were changed twice a week. Over-fussy Mam was. Lilly wouldn't waste time on unnecessary washing if she were in charge.

She heard the knock at the door and, picking up a duster and a tin of polish to make herself look busy, she went down to let her aunt in.

"Was that Phil Martin or whatever he calls himself that you were kissing in King Edward Street the other night?" Audrey demanded. "Want your head read you do, my girl."

"Phil who?" Lilly blustered.

"You know who I mean. What are you thinking of, carrying on with a bloke like that? Notorious he is, that one!"

"I didn't – we aren't—" Seeing the glare of confidence in her aunt's beady eyes, Lilly lowered her head, giving up trying to bluff her way out of the accusation. "You won't tell Mam, will you?"

"Best we forget it and you keep away from him. D'you hear? Or I'll have a little chat with your mam and your dad. Right?"

The fear that churned in Lilly gradually turned to excitement. Notorious! She was the reason for him being called notorious. There's romantic! An illicit affair! That was what she had just been reading about. It was so thrilling, and it was her story too. A deep and forbidden love. She couldn't wait to see Phil and tell him again how much she loved him. She smiled at her aunt and tried to look contrite.

Audrey saw the gleam of excitement in Lilly's eyes and sighed. Her nieces didn't seem to be any luckier in love than she was.

Audrey Piper and Wilf Thomas had been courting for more than twenty years. Audrey lived with her mother and, she explained to anyone who asked, by the time she and Wilf began thinking about marriage she had felt unable to leave her. Wilf lived with his aged mother too and he didn't see how he could leave home and live with Audrey and Moll. The situation could have been resolved in the early days of their courtship, but there seemed to be plenty of time and now, with Wilf's mother in a wheelchair and Moll so dependent on Audrey, they were trapped.

Audrey had told the story so often she almost believed it herself – except at night, alone in her white counterpaned bed, when she imagined how it could have been.

Every New Year's Eve, she and Wilf opened a bottle of port and drank to the coming year, convinced that somehow their trap would be sprung and they would be free to marry. There was always a tinge of guilt in their eyes as they looked at each other and clinked glasses. The only solution to their dilemma was for both Wilf's mother and Granny Moll to die.

Bleddyn Castle had worked with his brother Huw since they were children, first running messages and helping out with a few chores for Moll and her husband Joseph, earning a few pennies, then, when they left school, coming to work for the Pipers full time, doing odd jobs in the winter and spending wonderful summers on the sands.

He had married Irene and they had had two sons. Taff and Johnny had taken to the beach and their life seemed set to continue into the foreseeable future, but Irene had died and for a while everything had changed. Nothing had seemed worth doing. But after a short time of mourning and regrets and guilt, Bleddyn revived his interest and his summer began as so many others had done, working happily among the holiday crowds.

Now Johnny and Taff seemed content to follow in the family tradition, with only Taff's wife Evelyn breaking out and refusing to take a share of the responsibility during the summer. At twenty-five, two years younger than Taff, Evelyn was basically very shy and hated the beach trade. The crowds embarrassed her and she was unhappy serving on the stall or in the café, fumbling with the change and getting flustered when orders came thick and fast. So the family had accepted her decision and she now worked as a supervisor and inspector in a factory that had once made enamel saucepans, washing-up bowls, food canisters and other kitchen equipment, but had changed to making items for the war machine. In this role she was efficient and well liked. On the beach, dealing with the public at play, she had felt like a stupid child.

Bleddyn's other son Johnny also loved the beach and dreaded the end of the season. He wasn't married but was seeing a divorced woman called Hannah. He didn't bring her home to meet the family very often as he sensed that it was an ordeal for her. At thirty, she was eight years older than him and although he wasn't concerned

60

about the age difference or the fact that she had two daughters, Hannah was inhibited by it all. Occasionally she would bring the girls to the beach when she knew Johnny was working on the swingboats and he would give rides to the girls and spend a little time with them. But mostly they went for walks in the park or travelled into the next town to go to the cinema there. The outings always included the four of them, as Hannah's parents refused to help her, accusing her of bringing shame to the family by leaving her husband and having no sympathy for her difficulties.

Hannah and the girls, Josie who was four and Marie who was three, lived in two rooms in her mother's house but were not allowed to have any visitors. To earn money to keep herself and the children she worked as a cleaner, getting to offices very early in the mornings, when her mother grudgingly agreed to listen for the children waking, or during the evenings once they were asleep. She was an accomplished needlewoman, and she supplemented this small income with dressmaking. She loved Johnny dearly, but the children, the divorce and the age difference made her afraid. She left all the running to him and prayed he wouldn't grow tired of her hesitancy, mistaking it for lack of love.

Marged and Huw's son, Ronnie, loved the

beach and looked forward to the opening of the holiday season with great joy. But his happiness was tempered by the discontent on his wife's face. Like Taff's wife Evelyn, Olive hated the summer. As the weeks passed, leaving winter behind, she had begun her campaign. Reasons why Ronnie should not join his family for the summer poured out in a steady stream. As the days grew longer, her frustration grew stronger.

"I have to give up my job and help out, and it just isn't fair," she complained one Wednesday morning as Ronnie gathered his white jacket and hat ready to work on the ice-cream stall.

"The money's regular and if we have a good season we all get a bonus; what's wrong with that? Your job will be waiting for you when the beach closes." Ronnie spoke calmly but he was tired of the constant battle. He had worked on the beach with his family since he was six, standing on a pop-bottle box to see over the counter as soon as he was capable of serving. He had been doing the job when he and Olive met, and she had joined in with enthusiasm then, so he couldn't understand why she now wanted him to change.

"I want your family to keep Piper's fish-and-chip restaurant open all year. You know it would pay for itself."

"Uncle Bleddyn runs the chip shop and he

closes the café part for the summer. It's the way it's always been done, love, you know that."

"Because it's always been done doesn't make it right!"

"Look, I've got to go." He kissed her lightly then went to the door. "Don't forget you're taking over from Eynon at three so he can go to the pool. He's taking swimming lessons for some life-saving badge, him and Freddy, remember?"

"Just an excuse to get out of his shift if you ask me," she muttered.

"Who d'you mean, our Eynon or Freddy Clements?"

"Both! Your Eynon hates the beach as much as I do."

"Rubbish. Born to Piper's Café and the stalls he was." But Ronnie looked doubtful as he got on his bicycle to leave their rooms in Curtis Road and head for the beach.

Olive put down the hearth brush and ignored the mess of ashes from last night's fire. Granny Moll would be at home today; it might be worth trying once more to talk to her.

The day was dry but the sun was reluctant to show itself so she put a short jacket over her cotton dress, slipped her feet out of slippers and into sandals and went to get the bus.

Moll answered the door and smiled a

63

welcome. "Come in and stay for a bite to eat, Olive, we don't often get the chance to chat now summer's here. You aren't on till three, are you?" she continued as she led the way down the passage to the kitchen at the back of the house. She bustled about making sandwiches, grating cheese and mixing it with salad cream and chopped onion and adding a leaf or two of lettuce. "The thinnings," she said, to explain the smallness of the lettuce leaves. "Auntie Audrey and I thinned the row of lettuce plants and it's a pity to waste them."

"Granny Moll, don't you think it would be a good idea for me to keep the chip-shop café open? I'm not much use on the beach, am I? I don't like it and I find it hard to be polite some days. If I had one assistant I could run the café and it would bring in more than having me helping out on the beach, now wouldn't it?"

"Bleddyn has to close the café part so he can do the season with the boat trips, you know that."

"He could still do the boat trips, Granny Moll. All it would mean is that the man he employs to fry the fish would have to work a bit harder. I'd see to that." Olive smiled. "That café is popular with people coming out of the pictures and there'll be extra people in the summer months, won't there? The town is full of trippers and they all look

64

for somewhere to eat that's good and reasonably priced and quickly served."

"We've always closed the café part for the summer, Olive love. It's tradition."

Moll's arguments were becoming weaker, Olive noted. "Things are changing, Granny Moll, and we have to change with them. A lot of the cafés are staying open till nine o'clock for the busiest weeks. I heard them discussing it last week."

"They can't do that!"

"They can, Granny Moll. There's a war on!"

When Olive left to walk to the beach at two thirty, Moll had agreed to think about it and discuss it with Bleddyn. Her last words were, "Fair play, Olive, I can see the sense in it."

Beth was waiting for five o'clock, when her brother Eynon and Freddy were due back from their swimming lesson. She had to find out what Freddy had to say about the non-existent engagement ring.

She was serving three young girls with chips and bread and butter – a scrape of margarine, in fact, but butter sounded better – when Freddy arrived.

"I passed with distinction," he told her as he walked in, fresh faced, his eyes glowing. "Fastest, calmest and with the highest marks in first aid; what do you think of that, then?" he boasted happily.

"How many marks did you lose for dishonesty, Freddy?" she asked quietly. Then she turned to her brother and congratulated him, having been told that he too had passed the exam. "Well done, Eynon. You'll be even more useful on the beach now, with a life-saving qualification."

"Wait a minute, Beth, you don't think I cheated on the exam?" Freddy demanded.

"No, just on me."

His thoughts fled to Shirley Downs, but there had been nothing to that. A chat in the pictures, that was all. "Who's been talking?" He added quickly, "And what about? I haven't cheated on anything." He stared at her, willing her not to have found out about the missing money in their savings account.

"I went to the jeweller today," she said, taking the one shilling and sixpence for the servings of chips.

"Oh, there's been a bit of a mix-up. I should have told you. I've been meaning to, mind."

Taking off her apron, she went into the small kitchen and turned to him. "Well? I'm waiting."

"Truth is, Beth, I didn't have enough money. I didn't expect you to choose one that cost seven pounds, see, and I only had four pounds ten shillings."

"Only four pounds – but you've been

66

saving for the ring for months and months."

"I am sorry, love. I didn't know how to tell you, did I? Shall we go in next week and choose another one?"

"No, Freddy. I've already chosen the ring I want. It's up to you whether or not you buy it for me."

They were interrupted by Eynon. "Beth, I didn't do the life-saving to help on the beach. I've been offered a job in the pool. Every afternoon. Not much money, mind, but I want to take it. Anything to get away from Granny Moll and our Mam."

"Ask Mam," Beth said irritably. Pushing Freddy unnecessarily out of the way, she went back into the café.

The following day Freddy took his dinner hour early. The jeweller's assistant was at lunch and the proprietor was not very understanding. He remembered the embarrassment the pretty, dark-haired girl, Miss Castle, had suffered. After a stilted discussion, it was agreed that Freddy could pay for the ring by instalments.

"That will be two pounds ten shillings deposit, Mr Clements, and, er, five shillings a week?"

Freddy agreed, wondering how he would manage to survive while it was being paid off. It also crossed his mind that the money could have paid for a weekend away with the easy-going Shirley Downs. He tried to push the thought away but as he handed over the two pound notes and the ten shillings in half-crowns, he begrudged every penny, paying as it did for a closer tie with Beth, whom he was no longer sure he wanted to marry.

Unaware of Freddy's feelings, Beth too felt a certain unease as he kissed her and slipped the pretty, sparkling ring on her finger that evening. He said all the usual loving words and promised everything she wanted to hear. But something was missing and she couldn't explain, even to herself, what it was. Whatever the reason, the future as Mrs Fredrick Clements did not seem as rosy as it once had. The ring looked odd set on her finger, even cheap and garish, whereas in the shop and in her dreams it had glowed beautifully as a symbol of all she had ever wanted.

The young girl searching for food became a regular visitor to the café refuse bin, and although the food was well wrapped and left on the bin for only a short period, Beth wished she could help further. Granny Moll was so fussy about wrapping everything there wasn't much risk of contamination, but it was a sad way for such a young girl to have to live.

She wondered where she did actually live. It couldn't be in any kind of home or food would be provided. She must be living out-side society, probably in a derelict house or a barn. All right now, with the summer ahead of them, but what did she do in winter? Where did she find food then? And where did she find clothes?

She said nothing to her parents, but she still had a few coats given to her for her famous rug. She took them to the café and left them draped across the bin after putting the food where the girl could find it.

Hiding in the kitchen, now spotlessly clean and ready for the following day, she looked through the window and saw the girl come, pick up one of the coats and examine it.

It was tempting to shout, to tell her it was all right and she could take them all if she wished, but Beth knew that if she did the girl would run away and might not come back. The food must be keeping the girl alive and she couldn't risk her losing it.

As Beth watched, the girl tucked the coat under her arm and, taking the two packages of food, ran down from the headland and disappeared once again into the fields.

Olive was closing down the ice-cream stall on the sands. She scraped the last of the ice-cream from the tin, and piled it dangerously high on to a double cornet for a small boy. "Lucky you are, that's the last of it and we're just closing down."

Half of the boy's face disappeared as he tucked into the soft, runny confection.

"Ta, missis," he said as he came up for air.

Olive was smiling as Moll and Marged walked towards her but the smile soon faded.

"Have you asked Uncle Bleddyn about the fish-and-chip café?" she asked, crossing two sticky fingers out of sight below the counter.

"Sorry, Olive dear, but Bleddyn won't change his mind about the café," Moll lied. In fact she hadn't mentioned the suggestion. Bleddyn might have agreed and she couldn't have that. The family dictating to her? That was something she couldn't allow! "He thinks we'll be spreading ourselves too thin if we keep it open," she told the disappointed girl.

"That's nonsense. We manage really well, plenty of people to help."

"We'd only need a bout of flu or summer colds to hit us and we'd be going round like headless chickens trying to keep it all going. No, love, he's right, best we keep it closed and concentrate on the beach in the summer, like we always do. The Pipers have been here for a long time, we don't want to risk losing our place, do we?"

"If the family can't manage, there's a pool of casual workers looking for summer jobs," Olive pointed out.

"We like to keep it in the family, you know

70

that," Moll replied. "Good idea, mind, shows you're thinking of the business now you're a part of the Piper family."

"I'm a Castle, Granny Moll. I married Ronnie Castle."

"But the business is called Piper's and always will be, you know that. And we keep it in the family, so the café has to close. You understand, don't you, dear?"

Olive didn't look convinced – in fact, Moll thought, she looked rebellious. "Now come on," she said in an effort to change the subject to a less contentious one, "it's our Ronnie's birthday next week; what shall we get for him? New shirt? That's always handy, specially if the clothes rationing happens like they're warning us."

Olive didn't reply. She gathered the tools for serving ice-cream and dropped them into one of the empty ice-cream tins ready to be cleaned. The serving counter flap was wiped and closed for the night and Moll helped lock everything away before she followed her granddaughter-in-law over the sand and up on to the promenade to the café.

Aware of the girl's disappointment, Moll said, "Go on home, Olive, love. I'll see to the rest."

Thankfully, Olive turned and went to stand at the bus stop. She saw Ronnie closing up the helter-skelter and flirting

71

with a group of giggling girls. She didn't wait for him; she was in no mood to talk to any of the family for a while, not even her husband.

Marged watched her go and wondered if Ronnie would be wise to forget his dream of working alongside his wife during the summers.

"I think we'll lose Olive soon, Mam," she said to Moll as they approached the café high above the beach.

"She ought to do what her husband wants, Marged. If she'd been brought up proper she'd know that, wouldn't she?"

"Olive isn't a Piper, she married a Castle. I think we're being unfair to expect her to feel the same as us."

"Nonsense, Marged. A woman has to do her duty and follow her husband's wishes."

Marged wondered how much longer people would talk that way. The war, less than a year old, had already reminded women that they had choices. Factories paid better wages than shops and seaside stalls and Olive knew it. Who could blame her? she reasoned silently, as she walked into the café with the empty tins and utensils.

When Ronnie had closed up the swing-boats and helter-skelter, she took the keys from him and said, "Go home, Ronnie, and talk to your wife – or, more important, listen to her."

"What's the matter?" Ronnie stared at Marged in alarm.

"Nothing's the matter, boy, but she needs a bit of maldod, a bit of spoiling. Not happy working the beach? Wanting something different, perhaps?"

"Oh, that old story. She knows what I do and she's always known, so why is she being so awkward?"

"She prefers working in the chip-shop café and Granny Moll won't agree to it staying open. Fed up she is, bach, and needs a sympathetic ear, that's all."

Lilly, whose turn it was to stay and load up the van, had slipped out of the door while attention was distracted and it was Beth and a reluctant Freddy who were left to finish the day's work. Beth closed the doors of the café, having watched the departure of her sister with dismay.

"It's not fair," Beth began, as Granny Moll tried to hush her. "Our Lilly gets away with it every time."

"Never does as good a job as you and me, Beth. Slapdash our Lilly is, and there's her expecting to share the running of the business one day. What a hope, eh?"

Huw stood looking up at the window they had replaced a few weeks before. A crack had appeared and was slowly moving down from the corner, and he knew that it would soon be unsafe. "One good storm and it'll blow in," he said to Marged. "We must have cut the glass a fraction bigger than we should and it's giving under the strain."

"We'll ask our Ronnie to get a new piece and fix it, shall we?" Moll said as Ronnie prepared to leave.

"No, the boy needs more time to talk to that wife of his, not less. We'll get it done tomorrow."

"Ronnie, I don't want to discuss it any more," Olive said irritably as she set the table for their evening meal. "I don't want to work on the beach and you won't accept it. There's no point talking about it; you never listen! I asked Granny Moll if she'd consider keeping the chip-shop café open, but she said Uncle Bleddyn refused. I don't believe she even mentioned it to him. She's that strong, she always does things her way and I don't know how you and the others stand it."

"What was her reason?"

"The usual, we've always done it that way and there's no reason to change."

"Is that all?"

"Oh, she said we'd be overstretched."

"Perhaps she's right. We do need you help-ing on the sands during the busiest weeks at least."

"Well, you'll have to find a way to manage

without me. I'm going to look for a job in another café or perhaps a shop."

"Olive, we can't do without you. The family has to pull together; you know Granny Moll is against employing strangers. Piper's is a family concern."

"What about Taff's wife? Evelyn doesn't work for the family. Everyone accepted that."

"She had a career before Taff married her and he didn't expect her to give it up."

"Evelyn works as a clerk in a factory! Hardly 'career', Ronnie!"

"It was different with Evelyn, she didn't want to belong. And we have enough people, so long as you help. Granny Moll docsn't want to employ strangers; you know how strongly she feels about that."

"What about the call-up? How will you Pipers manage when half of you are in the army? It'll be down to your mam and dad and Beth and me. She'll have to agree to strangers working for her then. Your Lilly isn't keen on work, is she? Why won't Granny Moll listen to reason? With food rationing already tight and threatening to get worse, people will depend on cafés to eke out their food. It's bound to be a better investment."

"You've thought about this seriously, haven't you?"

"Ronnie, love, if you have to go into the

forces, I don't want to be stuck all day in a job I hate then come home to these empty rooms. Misery all day and loneliness all night, that isn't much of a life, now is it?"

"I'll have another talk with Granny Moll."

"I mean it, mind. Tomorrow I'm starting to look for a job. There's plenty of factory work now, and good pay too I'm told."

"Not a factory. If I have to go away, I'd feel happier knowing you're with Mam and Dad and the rest. You'd be safer somehow than working in some factory."

"Munitions are part of the war effort and I might not have a choice." She hugged him, pressing her cheek against his. "I couldn't bear it, Ronnie, and you might as well face it. I'm dreading you going away to face such danger, and the only way I can survive is by getting involved in something I enjoy."

"And you enjoy serving chips?" He grinned at the stupidity and was rewarded by Olive returning his smile.

"All right, I know it sounds ridiculous, but it's better than the Pipers and their 'everyone having jolly fun' beach days. Uncle Bleddyn's fish-and-chip café will do for now, until I find out what I really want to do."

Ronnie was concerned. Olive had never really taken to the family business, but he hadn't realised just how strongly she resented having to be a part of it.

When the café closed the following day, Beth hid just inside the door while her mother and Auntie Audrey cleaned the oven and washed the floor. She didn't have to wait long before the little girl came around the corner of the path and strolled nonchalantly towards the bins. Beth held her breath as if afraid the girl would hear her. She intended following the girl and finding out where she lived that made the theft of food so important.

Meanwhile Huw collected putty and knife, pliers and tacks and a small hammer, all of which he stuffed into the pockets of his dungarees. Whistling cheerfully he climbed up the ladder to replace the pane of glass he had removed earlier. To his relief the new piece of glass fitted perfectly and, after working around the frame to make the bed of putty which would hold it firm, he pressed the glass in place. He was feeling in his pocket for the tacks when a movement caught his eye and he turned to see his daughter creeping across the grass heading for the fields.

"Where the 'ell's she off to?" he muttered. Stretching his neck and leaning away from the ladder, he saw the small figure just ahead of her. She was following someone, but why? Not a thief; everything would be locked up by now, surely.

He stretched a bit further and to his alarm felt the ladder move sideways. "Ronnie, hang on to the the flamin' ladder, boy!"

He dared to look down and saw that Ronnie had abandoned his job of putting weight on the bottom of the ladder and was playing football with a group of children further down the beach on the wet sand. He swore loudly and with feeling as the ladder slid further and further to one side. He tried to make a jump for it as it increased speed after sliding past the corner, but his foot was stuck and he landed heavily with his hands still foolishly gripping the hammer.

Marged was emptying a bucket of soapy water at the sink and saw the figure of her husband, his mouth in a rictus of fear, slide past the window. Calling the others with a scream of panic, she ran out.

Beth was unaware of the accident as she hurried after the fleeing figure of the young girl. But the girl was perfectly aware of Beth. Knowing she was followed, she darted on through the back streets and lanes, past the overgrown path leading to the abandoned stable where she lived. Amused at the unexpected fun, she led Beth to a field further on. Hiding one precious package under her coat, she opened the other and fed the contents to the horses who stood hopefully at the hedge.

Surprised, but amused and heartened by the young girl's kindness, Beth turned and went back to the café.

The girl waited until she felt safe from being followed and made her way slowly back to the stable. Lying in a corner, covered by Beth's gift of a coat, was another girl, aged about fifteen but looking younger.

The older girl sat up slowly and greeted her sister.

"Myrtle, you're late. I was wondering where you'd got to. No trouble, was there?"

"No trouble, but I'm afraid we've got half rations today. The girl from the café followed me so I gave one package to the horses." They tucked in to the sandwiches and cakes Beth had packed and Myrtle told the story of the chase again, with many exaggerations, before they both settled under the assorted covers to sleep.

When Beth returned to the café, hoping the family were still there to give her a lift home, voices led her to the crowd around her father. Seeing him on the ground, surrounded by the rest of the family and several onlookers, she ran down to investigate.

"It's your dad; he's fallen and I think his ankle's gone and broke," Granny Moll wailed. "Fixing that window he was, mind, when he should have left it till he had some help."

"Our Ronnie was supposed to be holding

the ladder and he went off to play football," Marged sobbed.

"And that wife of his will have to put an end to whatever plans she's making to work somewhere else!" Moll added firmly.

It was late before Huw was comfortable in hospital and the family had dispersed to their various homes. Beth was tearful, convinced that her father's curiosity about what she had been doing had been the cause. All this was her fault. And all because a shy little girl liked to feed the horses.

Olive was silent as she and Ronnie left the hospital. Sorry as she was for her poor father-in-law, this would be another reason for Ronnie to want her to stay at the beach and help the Pipers and Castles with the café and stalls. She knew she should support them, but the fear of living alone and working on the beach all hours while he was away was daunting. If she could earn more money, then as soon as the war ended they could get themselves a better place than the two rooms they rented in Curtis Road.

She said nothing further. Today was not the right time to bring up the subject, not while Huw was in hospital and they were having to face managing without him for a while. Thank goodness Ronnie's calling-up papers hadn't been delivered; that would really have made life difficult for them all.

Letting themselves into their rooms, Olive picked up the post and gave a cry of dismay. She was trembling as she handed the OHMS envelope to her husband.

"Your papers; they've come," she said in a tight voice. Then she burst into tears.

Three

With Huw out of action as far as helping on the sands was concerned, Eynon was taken off the swingboats and made to help in Piper's Café, a job which he hated. The beach gave opportunities for flirting and making dates for later. In the café, even if attractive girls did come in, with his parents watching he had no chance for any fun.

Few of the Castle boys were above average height. Huw, Ronnie and Eynon were five feet four inches tall and all were of slim build. Ronnie was like his father, rather serious. He had married young and had settled down with Olive in their rooms in Curtis Street with no regrets. He pretended to flirt with girls on the beach knowing that was a part of the entertainment, but he was content with Olive, living with the hope that one day they would have children to follow him and work on the sands.

Eynon, with his wide-apart guileless brown eyes, had an air of confidence and boldness that was appealing to all ages. On first sight he appeared younger than his almost seventeen years, and the gleam in his eyes when he saw girls he liked first surprised then intrigued them. He had perfected the skill of revealing to them that although he looked young, he was no longer a child.

So far he had got nothing more than kisses and some gentle fondling, but he had hopes of celebrating his seventeenth in the best possible way. With any luck, he would have the willing assistance of Alice Potter, Auntie Audrey's assistant in the rock and sweet shop.

Huw Castle's brother Bleddyn was the exception to the rest by being both heavily built and tall. At five feet eleven, weighing about fourteen stone, and with a rather pugnacious jaw, he sometimes gave the erroneous impression of being aggressive. The heavy jaw had reappeared in Taff, who, although tall and powerful like his father, was also amiable and rarely roused to anger. Like his cousin Ronnie, Taff had married a girl who disliked working on the sands. Stronger and more determined that Olive, Evelyn stubbornly refused to help in the business.

With his leg in plaster, Huw wished the two young women were more amenable. The family was stretched severely and the situation would be even worse once the boys were called into the forces. He spent his days propped up near the till in the café, taking money and joking with the customers. It was obvious that he couldn't help with much else and, to avoid frustration, he spent a lot of time thinking about ways of improving the place, although his suggestions were usually quashed by either his wife or his mother-in-law.

"What about doing lots of different meals? Chips all the time is boring."

"No room, no time and too wasteful."

"What about salads like the posh hotels along Old Village Road? Them hotels make a packet. Their owners go abroad for holidays every October."

"Not now they don't! And salads aren't popular with our beach families. The kids complain."

"What about—"

"What about you getting on putting the small change into bank bags and letting us be?" Marged grumbled irritably, before turning to smile at a harrassed young woman with a brood of young children hanging around her skirts, shouting for crisps and chocolate and cakes.

"Rissole and chips for six," the woman

ordered. She looked at Huw nervously. "Er – no salad, the children won't eat it," she added.

Marged gave Huw a "told you so" look and went on serving. Huw went on thinking, this time about his daughter Beth.

He had serious doubts about young Freddy Clements. He'd noticed the boy was wearing new clothes again, and wondered where he was finding the money to pay for them when he was too short of the readies to pay for his fiancée's ring.

"Pity he works in a clothes shop, it's making him one of the best-dressed people around. Better if he changed his job and worked for a bank," he told Marged during a lull. "Then he might think about saving. Or an ironmonger, so he could start getting interested in tools, and think about things for their bottom drawer!"

"I've tried to warn Beth that he isn't doing all he could," Marged said. "But will she listen? No."

"She's like you there, then!"

Ignoring his remark, Marged said, "Too vain that boy is, for sure."

"At least they have some savings, so when they get married they'll have a good start. And if he joins Piper's we can keep an eye on him."

"You don't think he's using their savings to pay for all these clothes he keeps buying, do you?" Marged looked alarmed at the thought.

"Never. He wouldn't do that, Marged, love. That would almost be stealing, wouldn't it?" But he didn't look as convinced as he sounded and when Beth called in to fill a basket with food for a picnic she was planning, he brought up the subject of savings.

"Savings are building up nice, then?" It was a question rather than a statement. "Reached your first hundred yet, have you?"

"No, Dad. But," she said, frowning thoughtfully, "we can't be far off forty, mind."

"Check with Freddy and if you're close, perhaps your mam and I can top it up. You'll have enough to buy your own house. Wouldn't that be great?"

"Thanks, Dad." She smiled. "I'll ask Freddy this afternoon."

She was puzzled by the strange look in her father's eyes as he replied, "Yes, my lovely girl, you do just that."

It was a Wednesday, Freddy's half-day, and Marged had given Beth the afternoon off so that she and Freddy could go out. Beth had packed a picnic that included a bottle of Tizer, which was Freddy's favourite, and they walked to the pebbly beach with the beautiful park close by.

"I can't think why you choose to spend

85

your day off at a beach when you work on the sands seven days a week," Freddy grumbled, changing the basket from one hand to the other with exaggerated discomfort. "Damn me, this basket's heavy. What you got in there, table and chairs?"

"I thought you'd like a picnic."

"I hoped we'd go into town, do a bit of shopping and see a film."

"That's as far as your imagination goes, the pictures," Beth said, a smile disguising the edge of irritation in her words. She wanted to talk, make plans, share their thoughts and dreams, but he preferred to blank her out with soundtrack music and other people's words.

"Better than sitting on an uncomfortable beach surrounded by yelling kids."

"All right, we'll eat our food then go back and see what's on. OK?"

"It doesn't matter. I promised Mam I'd start decorating the kitchen. I'd better not be late," he said.

Beth hid her disappointment. Some day off this was turning out to be.

They found a comfortable place, built a wall of stones to protect them from the breeze and stripped to their bathers – or dippers, as they called them.

"Teas for trippers, donkeys and dippers, Sunhats, hoopla and rides, Piper's kingdom, cloths of fresh gingham, Fortunes, windmills and tides," Beth said softly.

"Did you make that up?" Freddy asked with a smile.

"No. It used to be printed on the window of Piper's Café when Granny Moll's grandparents first opened it."

"Piper's Café is important to you, isn't it?"

"Very. It will be to you too when we're married and you're part of the Piper family."

"Yes," he said without enthusiasm. "Lovely it'll be."

"Us married with a home of our own, and working together," she said dreamily.

"God 'elp, I don't have to change my name to Piper, do I?"

"Mr and Mrs Freddy Clements we'll be," she said, kissing him.

It wasn't warm but they braved the waves and swam a little.

Beth knew she had to talk to him about their future and she waited until they were dry and warm and were stretched out on their towels.

"How much have we got saved now, Freddy?" she asked, staring up at the sky.

"Don't remember for certain sure. We're doing all right, though. By the time we marry in a couple of years, we'll have the deposit for a house. Won't that be great? Just you and me in our own little home?"

"Yes, it'll be wonderful, Freddy love. I can

hardly wait." She raised herself up on her elbow and looked down at him. "But how much do we have now, this minute?"

He frowned as though trying to think, not meeting her gaze. "Tell you what, I'll check in the book when I get home and tell you tomorrow, is it?"

"Fifty pounds?" she persisted, exaggerating to make him answer.

"Never! Nothing near fifty pounds!"

"Granny Moll has been good, giving us two shillings a couple of times a month, beside them all starting us off with twenty pounds, the same as they did for our Ronnie. Then there were gifts of money as part of our engagement presents from Mam and Dad and Uncle Bleddyn, and Auntie Audrey gave us two pounds ten shillings. So generous they've been."

"The Pipers can afford it, mind," Freddy added ungraciously. "Plenty of money they've got."

"Gifts from your mam and dad too. They gave what they could. We must be heading for forty at least."

"You dream on," he laughed.

He was being evasive. Beth knew that where money was concerned, Freddy was never this casual. He probably knew right down to the last penny piece. "I'll walk home with you and we can check it together," she said, watching his face, sad to be doubting him.

"No, don't let's waste this precious time together. Come here and let me show you how much I love you."

Hidden from the few others on the almost deserted beach, they kissed and apparently forgot their discussion, giggling when an elderly couple approached and separating quickly in case they were seen.

It was only five o'clock when they reached Sidney Street, having walked arm in arm back through the lanes behind the terraced houses of the old part of the town.

"We ate our picnic so early I bet you can do with something more to eat. Stay for supper?" she suggested. "Ham, salad and potatoes, without the ham," she added, only half joking. With fresh meat rationed and only three ounces of cooked meat per week allowed, meatless meals were becoming the norm.

Freddy made his excuses. "Best I go. Mam's expecting me back."

"How could she be? You thought we were going to the pictures!"

"Sorry, love. To be honest, I just don't feel like listening to your mam and dad talking about their day. The beach isn't my favourite topic."

"But Freddy, I thought you were keen to join Piper's when we get married?"

"I am. But it's a long way off and there are

other more important things happening. I like the pictures because of the newsreels. This war is something that won't go away, love. While we're standing here safe as safe, people in the big cities are preparing the underground shelters, knowing that soon they're in for uncomfortable and dangerous nights with bombs falling all around them. Day after day our soldiers, sailors and flyers are fighting, young boys facing terrible dangers like we could never imagine, and we shouldn't forget it just because we're safe down here and spending our days playing on the sands." He hugged her and added, "We can't make no plans until Hitler is beaten."

"You still want to marry me, Freddy?"

"I do, of course I do. But unless this war ends miraculously quick, I might have to think about being called up. It's frightening, Beth. I can't concentrate on much else, specially now I'm eighteen. A turning point my birthday was. I'm liable for call-up at any time now, and I can't forget it for a moment."

He succeeded in making her feel selfish and uncaring. "Of course you're worried, Freddy, love. I didn't think. I should have realised."

"There you are, there's more to life than Piper's Café. You've seen the injured arriving in the town, young men only months older that me. I could be one of them soon."

"But," Beth insisted, still feeling guilty but determined he shouldn't forget, "you will let me know how our savings are doing. We ought to transfer them into National Savings; that would help the war effort a little, wouldn't it?"

He lowered his head, hesitating. Beth held her breath, not knowing what he was about to say, but certain it would be something she did not want to hear.

"Look, Beth love, I might as well tell you. I've used some of our savings. I've drawn out some to buy some clothes which, because of my position, and being promoted to second sales now another of the salesmen has been called up, I really need. I've got to look smart, Beth, it's essential for my job."

Beth's mind flashed back to the rather quizzical expression on her father's face when he mentioned their savings. In that moment she understood that he had guessed. Why was she so naïve?

"You shouldn't have! Not without telling me."

"I am telling you. I think you should spend a few pounds too, get yourself some decent clothes before we lose the chance. Then we'll start again and nothing will make me part with a penny. We'll get that house and have a big wedding, a honeymoon, everything you want. And," he added quickly to appease her, "I took out enough to buy you a brooch. That one with daffodils you admired when we were looking at engagement rings. I couldn't bear to see you without it. You work so hard and get so few treats, I had to buy it for you. Beth, love, I want to buy everything for you. I want you to be the most cherished wife in St David's Well. I want you to look at the brooch when I'm away and know how much I love you." He held her tight, kissing her with more passion than ever before. "I've got it at home and I intended to give it to you on the day I left. There, now you know the truth."

She found herself apologising for his cheating and spending the money they had saved, most of which had come from her family. She went inside, delirious with happiness. She could hardly remember the daffodil brooch. But he must have seen her looking at it and had seen the way she had admired it, and had bought it for her. She put aside the niggling dismay at the loss of their savings. Freddy loved her and that was the most important thing.

She went to her room and sat for a long time imagining the loving letters he would write and how close they would remain even though he would be miles away from her. She had a chocolate box in which she kept pressed flowers. Emptying it, she put it in a drawer, ready for Freddy's letters.

After leaving Beth, Freddy went to a call box and telephoned his boss to ask if he could be an hour or so late the following morning, as he needed to go to the bank and to the jeweller.

He didn't feel like going home. It was not quite six and he ran to the newsagent just in time to catch Shirley closing the shop door.

"Come to the pictures?" he invited, and stood around the corner in a doorway until she came. He felt a bit mean paying for Shirley when he should have been with Beth, but then, he comforted himself, Beth wasn't very keen on the cinema.

It was eleven o'clock when they came out, having shared a bag of hard-boiled and a brief cuddle in the back row.

"I'll walk you back," he said as they set off towards the newsagent.

"Thanks," Shirley said. "But why don't you come in? Mam will be up and she'll make us a sandwich and a cup of cocoa."

"I don't think so," Freddy hesitated. "Up early I am, and—"

"Not as early as me! Mam and I do the morning papers, remember." She smiled at him and said shyly, "Don't think I'm trying to steal you from your girlfriend. I know you're engaged to Beth Castle and so does our Mam."

"OK, why not? Go down a treat a cup of cocoa will."

Shirley's mother, a small, thin woman dressed in the overalls she wore in the shop, greeted them with little enthusiasm. After a nod, she went into the kitchen and began to fill the kettle and stir the cocoa and sugar and milk in the cups. "Nothing fancy, mind," she warned as she reappeared with a plateful of sandwiches. "Meat paste or bloater."

"Thank you, Mrs Downs. Very kind." Feeling a little uneasy, Freddy was glad when Shirley leaned across him and turned on the wireless. Dance band music issued forth and Shirley stood up and persuaded Freddy to dance.

Mrs Downs looked on and smiled. "My Shirley never could keep still when there's music to dance to," she chuckled.

"Beth doesn't dance," Freddy said. "So I'm not very good. I like it, mind. I just don't get no practice."

"Soon put that right," Shirley replied. "So long as you've got rhythm."

Freddy was surprised at how enjoyable it was to hold Shirley in his arms. She pressed close to him and, being slightly taller, leaned towards him until her head touched his. Her cheek was warm against his own, the illicit contact far more exciting than he would have imagined, and he didn't want the music to stop. He continued to hold her when the Sid Philips number came to an end; and the look in her eyes disturbed and excited him.

When they sat to enjoy their supper, Mrs Downs said, "Engaged to that Castle girl, aren't you?"

"Yes; we're getting married in a couple of years, if the war doesn't stop us."

"You don't sound very sure," Shirley said, looking at him quizzically, her head tilted to one side. "How can the war stop you?"

"Old enough for call-up, I am."

"So? If you want to marry Beth, then you will."

"Best you don't!" Mrs Downs said, unexpectedly fiercely. "Dishonest, deccitful family they are. Not a decent one among the lot of 'em."

"What d'you mean?" Freddy asked.

"No, Mam," Shirley pleaded. "Don't start on all that. Not tonight."

"All what? If there's something I should know, then you have to tell me," Freddy said.

"Stole that business of theirs from my grandfather, that's what."

"Your grandfather? A hell of a long time ago, then."

"The Pipers, Joseph and Harriet Piper, Moll's grandparents they were, put in a complaint about the state of the place, got a bunch of thugs to knock it about a bit, and bought it off him cheap. They built that

95

place you see today by deceit and dishonesty, that's what."

"And when is all this supposed to have happened, Mrs Downs?"

"Don't matter when. It happened, and that's all you need to know before you tie yourself to that family."

It was only then that Freddy realised that Shirley's mother had been drinking. Soon afterwards he excused himself and left. That was a lot of ol' rot she was talking. As if the Pipers would do anything like that. Decent they were, and well known for their generosity.

As he let himself into his parents' house he made a decision. If Shirley's mother drank, then she might not always guard her tongue. Tomorrow he would tell Beth about going to the pictures and meeting Shirley there, and walking her home. She'd understand, probably admire him for his thoughtfulness. Best to cover the situation before it jumped up and knocked him between the eyes. Best too if he didn't see Shirley again, innocent or not. He closed his eyes and danced with Shirley blissfully, bewitched, into his dreams.

The following evening, he told Beth an edited version of his meeting with Shirley and her mother.

"I was miserable, Beth. I knew I'd let you down, so I went to the pictures."

"Oh, Freddy, I'm sorry. I should have gone with you."

"You wouldn't have enjoyed it, it wasn't much of a film. Gangster stories aren't your favourite, are they? Anyway, Shirley Downs was near by and as she had a big huge bag of sweets, I sat next to her and shared them," he grinned. "I walked her back to the shop after. It was late, see, after eleven. I didn't think she should walk back on her own."

"That was kind of you, Freddy."

"Well, I'd like to think someone would do it for you when I'm not here to look after you, love." He handed her the velvet-lined jeweller's box. She seemed oblivious to what he was saying as he placed the dainty, sparkling brooch in her hand. "I had to buy you a ring, it's convention, isn't it? But this was something different. I bought this not because it was expected of me, but because I wanted to." He lowered his voice, adding, "Because I love you."

She choked on tears of joy and, speechless, she hugged him. Then as she calmed down she told him he was marvellous, thoughtful, romantic and that she was the luckiest girl in St David's Well.

He felt euphoric at her reaction, his body fired with love, and this lasted until he left to walk home. As he walked past the news-agent and looked up at the blacked-out window above, he remembered the dance he had shared with Shirley Downs and despondency fell over him like a threatening shadow, an augury of a future without joy.

Beth proudly showed the brooch to her sister, but Lilly was far from impressed. She had just got home from a very unsatisfactory meeting with Phil Martin, and she was miserably aware that for her life was far from perfect. Then her stupid sister had come in boasting about some boring present from that cheat Freddy Clements, and she was supposed to be pleased? Fat chance. "It was probably your money he was spending anyway!" she snapped.

"The trouble with you, Lilly Castle, is that you're jealous! No one ever buys you presents!" Beth retorted and soon they were arguing as only sisters can.

Eynon came in after a while and said, "Stop it you two! I could hear you halfway up the street. It's bad enough our Mam and our Dad rowing all the time without you two joining in. Honestly, I'll be glad when I can sign on and join the army. It can't be much worse than living here!"

Slamming the door he ran upstairs and flopped on the bed. Through the wall, he could hear the subdued mutterings of his parents. They were not as loud as his sisters, but the tone told quite clearly that they were arguing.

Coming home from a date with Alice Potter he had felt great. Then, as soon as he stepped inside the front door, his mood had changed. He thought of leaving home with greater anticipation. If it weren't for the war he would be facing living here until he married, years ahead. At least the army was an escape available to him. Even if it meant danger it would be an improvement, he thought, as the voices downstairs rose to a crescendo, in counterpoint with the increasing volume from the next room.

A note pushed through Olive's door that evening asked her to call in to see Granny Moll on the way to the beach next morning. Curious, and preparing to stand her ground if there had been any complaints, she called and stepped into the large, three-storey house in Sidney Street a few doors up from the smaller one owned by Marged and Huw.

After the usual offer of a cup of tea from the blackened metal pot on the hearth, Granny Moll said, "We've been thinking about what you said about keeping the fish-and-chip café open. Do you think you could manage it without calling for help and expecting some of us to leave the beach and rescue you if you got into difficulties?" She handed Olive a cup of tea that was as thick as paint and waited for the girl's first polite sip.

"You really mean it? I can run the café instead of working on the beach?"

"You'll have a month's trial. Fair play, you should know all about it, working there all winter like you do, but we'll need to be sure. It will be different from working under Bleddyn. You'd have to organise the staff and deal with orders; it's a lot of responsibility."

"I won't have any problems. Just give me a girl to serve tables and some help with the dishes and you won't need to do anything more."

"What's wrong with your tea? I can spare another spoonful of sugar if it isn't sweet enough."

"Sorry, Granny Moll, but I find it a bit strong."

"Not expecting, are you?" The old lady looked hopeful.

"No, it's just too strong for me."

"I've been trying an experiment. Instead of emptying the pot, I put a small sprinkling of tea leaves on top, just to see if it saves on the tea. Now it's going to be rationed we have to try and save a bit."

"I think I'd rather drink hot water," Olive said, making a face.

"Shall we start next Monday then?" Moll suggested and Olive thankfully discarded the tea and nodded agreement.

"I know Ronnie wants to tell you himself, but he had his calling-up papers a couple of days ago."

"What? I thought he'd applied for deferment on account of the business?"

"Turned him down it seems."

They discussed their fears for a while, both trying not to remember the steady stream of injured young men returning to the town and the increasingly long list of the missing and killed.

"The best way of helping Ronnie is to appear matter of fact about it. We'll talk about it when he comes home, plan for the future as though it's only around the corner," Moll said, holding Olive's trembling hands.

They comforted each other and with their fears talked out honestly and fully, they agreed to try not to think about the dangers Ronnie would undoubtedly face. They agreed to take it for granted that he would return, soon and unharmed, to take his place once more within the Piper family.

"There is one thing, Olive, love," Moll said sadly. "This news changes things. I think our plans to reopen the café will have to wait or at least be reconsidered. We'll need you to replace Ronnie on the stalls."

Thinking of Ronnie leaving her, at that moment Olive was too distressed to care.

Telling Granny Moll the news, saying it aloud, had been almost as shocking as when she saw that dreaded envelope with OHMS on the corner.

For the next couple of weeks Ronnie concentrated on "training" his wife to run the two stalls for which he was mainly responsible, which sold everything needed for the beach, including ices and pop, plus the swingboats and helter-skelter.

Disappointment over the refusal to run the café was given greater emphasis, a cover for her real distress at Ronnie having to leave her. She tried to hide the true cause of her unhappiness, instead being as difficult as she knew how when Ronnie and the others tried to encourage her to take an interest in the beach. How could she admit that her real reason for hating the business was that she was shy? Even a light-hearted joke from a customer made her colour up and want to run. She was being forced into something for which she was totally unsuitable.

"Eynon will give a hand when you're busy, and when you aren't he'll deal with the helter-skelter," Ronnie told her one afternoon, when the cloudy weather had brought disappointingly few people in search of fun. "There's no set job for any of us. We all muck in where we're most needed."

"I know that, Ronnie. I'm not stupid!"

"You'll be fine, love," he said, hugging her. "It's only till I come back and then you can give it up. Keep it all going for me, will you?"

"It seems fine on a day like today when most of the trippers have stayed in the cafés and shops. But when there's a queue and I'm running out of ice-cream, or short of change, what d'you expect me to do then?"

"Taff's job is to keep an eye on us all and help where needed, you know that." He was beginning to become concerned by Olive's obvious reluctance to learn. Then he sighed. "Look, love, I know you're disappointed not to be running the café, but—"

"Restaurant! It would have been a restaurant." She turned away so he couldn't see tears. How could she tell him that she was crying for him?

A group of young girls walked up, chiffon scarves in their hair, sand on their feet where they had been walking along the edge of the tide, blue with cold in their bathing suits but determined to have fun. Olive watched as he turned to present them with his special smile.

"You need something more than dippers on today, girls," he said. "I'm not complaining, mind." He served them generously with top-heavy cornets and when he turned to speak to Olive she was on her way up the metal steps to Piper's Café.

He couldn't understand her attitude. Knowing he was going away any day, he had expected these last hours to be special, but instead of being more loving, she was more prickly and bad-tempered.

He was appeased a little when she returned ten minutes later with a tray of tea and sandwiches for them both.

"Sorry I've been awkward, Ronnie," she said, staring down into her teacup. "I'm finding it hard to accept that you're going away and I won't know what you're doing or even where you are. Since we married we haven't been apart for more than a few hours."

"I'll write, love. I'll write as often as I can, although from what I understand there won't be much time in the first weeks; they really put us through a grilling. I promise I'll write but don't be upset if you don't hear for a while. The training is important, see. Our lives depend on knowing what to do in any situation. But I'll be all right, I just know it. You have to believe that. It'll help me to cope, knowing you're here with the family. I'm the lucky one. I will know what you're doing and where you'll be."

"I'll keep the stalls going as well as I can. I know you'll need a job to come back to and no other job will do." She smiled and, forgetting their tea, they kissed, much to the amusement of the girls who had returned for another ice.

"Make the most of it, ladies," Ronnie said as he served them. "There isn't much more where that came from, thanks to Adolf, rot his socks."

Beth watched each evening as the young girl casually walked up to the bins outside Piper's Café and took the parcels of food. She saw her run off over the path, across the headland and through the fields. One day she failed to arrive and Beth wondered if she were ill, or had just got tired of feeding the horses. The following evening she was there early and hovered around until the food was placed in the bin. Beth stopped her cleaning and watched as the girl went only as far as the grass and, with her back to the café, opened the packet and began to eat.

So the food *was* for herself! Beth was glad she hadn't altered her habit of putting out only the best food for her, and had not decided that the horse might not be very fussy. She tried to follow, but the girl easily evaded her and she walked disconsolately back to the café. The following night she tried again, then, realising that the girl was well aware of her intentions, decided it was best to do nothing for a while and hope the girl would regain her confidence and allow her the chance to get close.

Beth had told her parents nothing about Freddy using their savings. She proudly showed them her beautiful daffodil brooch and boasted about how well their savings were growing. If Marged, Huw and Moll had their doubts, they said nothing to her. There was plenty of time before they would be married and everything could change before a wedding took place.

There were evenings when she and Freddy didn't meet and on those, Beth worked at making tablecloths and embroidering cushion covers for her future home. She had three large boxes in her bedroom, boxes in which the local shop received its five-weekly orders of cigarettes and tobacco. Strong and roomy, they were gradually filling up with the necessities for beginning to build a home.

Occasionally Freddy would contribute something. His mother found a pair of pillow cases she had never used, a saucepan that she no longer needed. In spite of the fun of watching the collection grow, Beth sometimes felt a melancholy surround her as she took out the items and listed them, writing down items they still needed and planning how they would be used.

On the day Ronnie left, a travel warrant and a small suitcase his only possessions, she stood with the rest of the family outside the family home and wondered how long it would be before Freddy went off in the same way.

"I wish I was going with him, don't you, Freddy?" her youngest brother Eynon said.

"Shut up, you damned fool!" Lilly said. "No one in their right mind would want to go and fight in a war!" She was tearful. Phil had told her the previous day that he too was waiting to be called up.

"Yes, use your sense," Marged scolded him. "Can't you see how upset we all are? Especially Olive, seeing him go like this."

As the others tried to hush him for Olive's sake, Freddy agreed with Eynon.

"I can't say I'll be sorry to go, Eynon. This waiting around is terrible when we want to go and help fight."

Surprised, Beth turned to him and asked, "You really want to go and fight in a war?"

"I don't want to leave you, Beth, love, you know that, but I can understand the excitement Eynon's feeling."

"You're the only one, then."

"Wearing a uniform and carrying a gun and hand grenades; I'll show 'em," Eynon said. "I can't wait till I'm old enough."

"The way it's going over there, you'll have your chance," Huw said gruffly, as Bleddyn put the clutch in and began to move off with Ronnie and Olive inside the van. "Me an' all, perhaps, even though I'm past fifty." He dragged himself inside with the aid of crutches, the reason why he hadn't driven his son to the station.

As the van moved off, taking Ronnie and Olive to the railway station, and the rest of them stood in the road waving until they disappeared around the corner, Moll said sadly, "Your brother's boys will be going next, Huw. I don't know how we'll manage without Taff and Johnny."

"We'll all have to work that much harder, that's all," Huw said, his voice choked with fear at the thought of the danger Ronnie would soon be facing. "We'll work hard to keep everything going till they come home."

"You don't really want to go away, do you, Freddy?" Beth asked as they made their way back into the house.

"Of course not, love. Specially now I've been made second sales," he joked.

When he went into the shop the following morning, wearing his newest suit and a crisp white shirt, he was told his services were no longer required.

"What? I've just spent a hell of a lot of money on new clothes, and for why? So I can look my best for you, that's for why! You can't tell me you're sacking me. With men being called up you'll need me to keep the business running." He was red in the face, disbelief in his blue eyes. This couldn't be happening. What would Beth say? How could he tell her he'd just spent another ten pounds on three pairs of shoes, a dozen pairs of socks and a new trilby hat?

"One of the men who was called up has come back, with part of his hand missing. We have to find him a place. It's only fair and proper when he's been fighting for us all," the manager said. He handed Freddy his cards and pay packet and thanking him formally for his work for the company, opened the door for Freddy to leave.

Lilly's reaction to her brother joining up was to burst into tears every time he was mentioned. She wrote to him twice in the first week.

"I don't know what's got into our Lilly," Marged said one day as she prepared toffee apples for the sweet and rock shop. "Her and our Ronnie have always quarrelled and now it's as though he was her greatest friend."

"Had a row with this mysterious boyfriend probably. Who is he, d'you know?" Huw asked.

"No, and I don't intend to question her. She'll tell us when she's ready."

"You're her mother, she should talk to you," he complained. "You should know what's going on."

"I can't interfere. God 'elp, Huw, she's twenty-six."

"And without the sense she was born

with!" Huw heaved his heavy leg off a stool and walked to the door. Making sure it was closed, he asked Marged, "Has our Beth said anything about Freddy's savings? I bet you anything you like he's spent them."

"She's said nothing to me."

"Then we should make her talk to us, warn her about him. Take everything that's going, he will."

"We can't say anything. Mam says she has to learn for herself."

"Oh, Mam says, does she?" There was incipient argument in the words. "That's typical of you, Marged! Bury your head, pretend nothing's happening! God alone knows who our Lilly's carrying on with, and there's our Beth being cheated on by young Freddy. You know he's been seen in the pictures with that Shirley Downs, don't you? Or are you pretending that isn't happening too? Mam says this, Mam says that! You're their mother and it's up to you to look after them!"

Tightening her lips, Marged said, "There isn't much of the Luxona ice-cream powder left. Shall we use it, or save some for a celebration at the end of the war?"

"What are you asking me for? When do you ever listen to my opinion? Ask Mam; she's in charge of this house as well as her own!" Thumping down heavily on his

110

plaster-encased leg he stormed out and went to join some friends for a drink.

Beth tried a new tactic in her determination to discover where the young girl who stole the food was living. Instead of waiting in the café kitchen, she finished early with her mother's willing permission and hid in the field through which the girl regularly ran. She waited until the girl was running well ahead and had stopped glancing behind her, obviously free from worries about being followed, then set off after her.

Beth was led through back lanes, pausing at each corner before catching up with her quarry. They were in the poorer part of St David's Well, where houses had fallen into neglect and many were abandoned and beginning to fall down. Beth would never normally have ventured into this part of town, where broken-down stables and ware-houses made it an alien landscape, where danger lurked in the shadows and the fallen buildings leaned towards her, daring her to enter. Even though the evening was still light, her heart raced and her body was tense, prepared for flight. She felt a presence behind her and her skin tingled with fear of an imminent attack. She felt that vulner-ability between her shoulder blades but was afraid to look around.

Wondering how best to make her retreat,

she was startled by a loud noise. She froze and waited for long seconds, expecting discovery, before slowly easing herself around the corner of a building. She looked along a back lane where weeds and saplings were growing out of the broken concrete. A drainpipe had fallen and was still rolling a little. Beth wondered if the girl had knocked it as she passed.

Looking down the length of the narrow lane with its crooked buildings and air of menace, there was no sign of the girl, or of anyone else. The broken and distorted doors leading to once smart stables and warehouses were still and there was no sound other than the pipe that still moved slightly, its weight giving it momentum for longer than Beth had expected.

A shiver of fear twisted her shoulders as she turned and retraced her steps. There was no point in searching through the desolate buildings. Once away from the area she walked hurriedly, trying to tell herself it was common sense and not cowardice that had persuaded her to leave without investigating.

Ronnie wrote regularly both to his wife, Olive, and to his mother. Olive wrote back assuring him that she was happy and managing well on the stalls, but it was not the truth.

"Granny Moll," she said one day, "I'm sorry, but I can't carry on working the stalls. I hate it and although I promised Ronnie I'd help while he's away, I just can't."

"Give it time," Moll began, but Olive interrupted.

"If you don't let me work in the chip-shop café or the sweet and rock shop, there's plenty of call for factory hands. I might have to go soon anyway. At least that way we'll have some money when Ronnie comes home, enough to get out of our two miserable rooms in Curtis Road and into a place of our own."

"Take these toffee apples down to the shop, will you, dear? I promise I'll talk it over with Marged, see what we can sort out, is it?"

Audrey was serving a family with seaside rock to take back after their holiday and, placing the toffee apples and some slabs of coconut ice on the counter, Olive waited until Audrey had finished. Before she could ask Ronnie's aunt what she thought of her working there, Lilly came in.

"Mam says I've got to stay here while you go and get some lunch," she said sulkily.

"It's all right, I'll stay if you like," Olive offered.

"No, you go back and fetch me a few sandwiches and a pot of tea, Lilly, I'll eat here. Wilf is coming to share it with me."

Lilly wandered slowly along the promenade, looking over the sea wall, down to where the Punch and Judy man was about to begin his midday performance in front of a group of children who were sitting cross-legged on the sand. To her surprise she saw Phil walking towards her. She ran towards him but to her shock and dismay he pushed her aside as though he didn't know her and hurried on.

She stared after him in disbelief. Had he seen someone he knew, someone who might tell his wife he was talking to a woman? Tears welled up. This was no way to live, she thought sadly. She watched as he went past where the audience of the Punch and Judy theatre were sending up shouts and laughter, enjoying the fun. Every eye was turned to the puppet swinging the string of sausages and she approached him again.

"Phil, I—" He glanced at her, then stopped and began to turn away once again. She darted around until she was facing him. At that moment the beach photographer jumped out in front of them and snapped. Walking backwards beside Phil, he tried to persuade him to buy the photograph. So that was why he was so cautious. He was unwilling to have his photograph taken, although she had tried to persuade him on several occasions.

"Keep away," Phil hissed and Lilly stood

114

back and watched as he strode towards the road.

Almost without thinking, Lilly ran to the photographer who had given up and was looking around for a better prospect.

"That last photograph you took. Can I have a print, please?" she asked.

The small triumph was short lived. As she turned to go back to Piper's Café, she began to feel angry. She tried to fuel the anger, telling herself she would finish it, that Phil was treating her badly and she deserved better, but the emotion flared only briefly and was done, stifled by the achingly empty thought of life without him. She tried to tell herself that any hopes of his eventually marrying her were nothing more than foolish dreams, but while there was a chance, however slim, she had to cling to it. She knew she was being a fool, but hope flowered through her humiliation and disappointment. At least she would have a photograph, around which she could spin fantasies. A picture of them together. That would be something to help her pretend that one day everything would be perfect.

Four

The town was awash with posters warning about careless talk, unnecessary travel and the need to save fuel and food and paper and almost everything else. Besides these posters there were others telling mothers to let their sons and daughters go to war. Men walked around with feelings of guilt if they were not in uniform and informed everyone who would listen that they were exempt either on health grounds or age, or because their work was of national importance; excusing themselves for being there and not on some distant battlefield.

The men who were called up to serve in the armed forces put on a brave expression and told their family that they couldn't wait to get stuck in. Any fears they had were hidden behind confident smiles and light-hearted words.

It was not only the men who were worried. Wives, girlfriends and sisters, besides being frightened for their men's safety, were concerned about their own ability to cope alone. For Olive, the suggestion that she give up the two rooms where she and Ronnie had lived since their wedding seemed the end of everything.

"It's our home, Ronnie," she said sadly when on his first leave he suggested she went back to live with her parents until he came home.

They stood together looking around the small, over-filled room with its basic furniture and the clutter of their own belongings with which they had tried to create a place that was clearly theirs and couldn't belong to anyone else.

"Perhaps Mam and Dad could find room for it all in the store room at the ice-cream factory?" he suggested.

"I want to stay, be here when you come back and we can pretend nothing's happened."

"Think about it, Olive, love. I'd be happier knowing you were with your mam and dad and not on your own. What if there's an air raid? We've already had a few. What if the town gets bombed? Please, love, think about it."

Later that day, while they were counting up the takings on the stall, Granny Moll came across the sand, pausing to speak to them. Huw was struggling to close up the helter-skelter with one of Bleddyn's sons. He limped across to speak to her but she waved him away.

"It's amazing how quickly this war is changing things," Ronnie said. "We won't be selling ice-cream, the sweets and crisps will be on allocation if not rationed. What are we going to give the trippers when we can't give them those things, Granny Moll?"

"We'll think of something," Moll smiled. "And in the mean time, Olive dear, what about you? Ronnie's right. You can't stay in those rooms on your own, can you?"

"Why not? I'm married. I can't run home to Mam when things get difficult, Granny Moll."

"That's what Ronnie wants you to do, isn't it? Happier he'd be, knowing you weren't on your own."

"I can't go back to live with Mam and Dad. Not after running my own home. I've got used to doing things my way."

"Then I've got a suggestion. What about coming to live with me and our Audrey? The house is too big for just Audrey and me. And," she went on quickly as she saw that Olive was about to refuse, "with all my spare rooms, I'll be having soldiers or evacuees billeted on me if you don't come and use a couple of them."

The suggestion was discussed all that day, Moll and Audrey deciding which rooms would be best for Olive, Olive asking Ronnie if he thought he would be able to accept not having a place of their own when he came on leave.

"I'll put up with that knowing you're not on your own," he replied, then he looked at her with a suspicious grin on his face. "There's something else stopping you, isn't there? You're thinking you'll be unable to refuse to work on the sands if you take two rooms with Granny Moll?" He hugged her and asked, "What if I make sure she knows you aren't willing?"

Moll promised she wouldn't try and persuade Olive. "Just give me a couple of weeks when I can call on you if I'm real desperate at weekends and when you're not working, and as soon as I can find some extra help I won't ask you again, right?" To add further persuasion, she added, "And think of how much cheaper it will be, easier for you to save for a place of your own, better than two rooms, eh?"

So it was arranged and before Ronnie left, he saw their possessions packed away and his wife settled into two rooms in his grandmother's house.

At first Olive spent the evenings with Moll and, when she was in, with Audrey. But she gradually spent more time in her own room. She couldn't write to Ronnie in the loving way she wanted to with Granny Moll there. Moll's presence inhibited her from expressing her feelings.

Audrey was out several evenings each

week. She had joined the Air Raid Precaution group who met in the school, learning ways of dealing with the air raids they were sure would come. She had also started organising weekly sales of unwanted items to raise money for servicemen's comforts. Using a wooden barrow she walked the streets knocking on doors collecting items for sale, and every Saturday afternoon she set up a stall on the pavement outside Woolworths to sell them all.

Olive thought that having to live without her husband's presence and suffering the occasional session on the beach stall was enough support of the war effort for her to give, and ignored Audrey's attempts at persuading her to help with these activities.

Huw, with an ankle almost healed, but still using a stick, had joined the Local Defence Volunteers which many had joined at its conception in May. They had been promised weapons and a uniform and a new title in the near future and in July, Churchill gave them the more impressive title of the Home Guard. Their ages varied from seventeen to over sixty – although most were in the upper age limits – and they quickly earned the nickname "Dad's Army".

Everyone seemed to be doing something to support their country on the home front when they couldn't help further afield.

★ ★ ★

Freddy quickly recovered from the shock of losing his job. Perhaps he would be lucky and find himself a position in a reserved occupation and evade call-up, he thought hopefully. He was not as keen to serve as he pretended and had nightmares of himself in battles surrounded by faces filled with hatred and hands threatening him with guns.

He went to the Labour Exchange straight away, hoping to find a position that would exclude him from call-up. There were plenty of reserved occupations, although he didn't think that experience working for a gents' outfitters qualified him for many.

"Certain farm workers are exempt," the man in the labour exchange told him. "But without experience I doubt that you'd qualify."

"Thank God for that!" Freddy replied fervently. He thought of all that mud – and worse – and large smelly animals and decided he'd rather take his chances against Hitler's army.

Prospective employers always began an interview by asking his age and, knowing he was ripe for call-up, were unwilling to take him on.

"Hardly worth our time training you, see," he was told. "You'll be off before you can be any use to us."

There were vacancies at one of the

factories that had changed from con-
structing machinery to making munitions
and aeroplane parts. When Freddy arrived
for an interview he was offered work on the
bench with a lot of women, for which he
would wear greasy overalls, or an office job
with less money but for which he could
dress in a tidy suit. He chose the office job
and was determined to become so indispen-
sible he would evade conscription.

Moll called Beth aside one morning and
handed her a pound note. "Here, love, put
this with the rest. Best to save while you
can."

"Granny Moll, it's too much. A whole
pound! Freddy earns less that in a week!"

"Take it and start building on it."

"Thank you, Gran," Beth said, hugging
her.

"There won't be much for him when he
gets army pay."

"He isn't getting much now, Granny
Moll."

"I thought the pay was good at the munitions?"

"Yes, but he's in the office and the pay is
less than he was earning in the shop." She
shrugged. "Not everyone will make money
out of the war. Although I'm sure there's
some who will, mind."

"Didn't fancy dirtying his hands? Don't

be shamed by that," she added as Beth was about to protest. "Freddy is who he is. Don't be one of those girls who marry someone they want to change." She opened her purse. "Here, love, put this with the rest." She handed Beth another ten-shilling note. Ignoring her granddaughter's protest, she pushed it into her pocket. "Piper's is a good business and you should benefit from all the work you do. I want you to have a real good start. Put it in a savings book in your name. Keep it as a surprise for Freddy when this lot is over and you can plan your wedding, is it?"

When Beth met Freddy later that evening she had the money in her handbag to give to him. Granny Moll had advised her to put it into a savings account of her own, and add to it regularly every week, but Beth felt she had to show Freddy she still trusted him after his confession about taking money from their joint savings. It had given her so much pride, knowing they had a bank account with a real bank and not a post office book like most of her friends. Surely he wouldn't take from it again?

"Here you are, Freddy, this is to start our savings for our own house." She handed it to him and felt only the briefest of doubts as he took it and put it in his inside pocket.

"Marvellous she is, your Granny Moll. I wish I could contribute more, but my wages are worse than before. Fancy me being given the push. Just when I was promoted to second sales too. I've been there since I left school at fourteen, and that's the way they treated me. I wouldn't mind if I'd been called up, but just to be told to go – insulting it is, Beth. Damned insulting."

"Think of the chaos there'll be when the war's over. All the men coming back and wanting to return to their jobs and the replacements told they're no longer needed."

"Doesn't bear thinking about. I hope I can stay where I am for the duration. Small pay is better than none, eh?"

"You don't think you'll be called up, then? Thank goodness for that."

"Couldn't bear to leave you, Bethan." He kissed her firm little mouth and thought of the soft generous lips of Shirley Downs and the sensations she created with a kiss. He held Beth close to hide the disappointment in his blue eyes.

Lilly still met Phil whenever he could get away from his family. During the summer months, with the evening too light for concealment, they had been desperate for a safe place to meet. On one occasion they shared a shed with a couple of sheep, on another they jumped over a farm gate for an hour's privacy, burrowing deep into haystacks when the weather was kind. Back lanes, shop doorways and certain places in the woods all had their uses, but with the end of summer in sight they needed to find a sheltered place to meet. Then Lilly had an idea.

"Piper's Café closes about eight," she said excitedly. "I've got keys, so why don't we meet there?"

The beach was never as busy in the evenings, although some of the cafés stayed open and the fairground was still packed with those looking for thrills. As the evening wore on the lights from the rides grew brighter, until the time for blackout came and they were all snuffed out. The voices became more shrill for a while as young people held out before setting off back home, but fewer and fewer stayed to stroll along the beach. The bay gradually became shrouded in darkness and was abandoned. Seagulls strutted along the edge of the sea looking for food left by the trippers. A few older children searched for empty pop bottles which they could return and claim a few pennies for. An elderly man stacked the last of the deckchairs under the promenade where he was supposed to lock them up for the night, though he never actually bothered to find the chains and padlocks.

Wardens were strutting about warning people not to show a light. A man struck a match to light his pipe and the warden ran after him shouting angrily, "Oi, put that light out! Don't you know there's a war on and you can be fined for striking an unguarded match?"

Lilly watched with amusement. She wondered whether the warden really thought a match flame could be seen by a German pilot as he flew over or whether he was just being officious. Although, she remembered, there had been a fine for that offence in the paper recently. What a farce. They'd never be bombed; the Germans wouldn't waste effort on a small town like St David's Well.

She watched as the pipe-smoking man walked slowly up the slope leading to the promenade and headed for a pint of beer to celebrate the end of his long day. She was sitting at the bottom of the rocks in the shadows at the end of the promenade, the smell of the warm wet sand redolent of a thousand summer days. When she felt it was safe to do so, she crossed the sand, climbed the metal steps up to the café on the cliff path and unlocked the door. She went through the seated area and as she opened the main door, Phil slipped inside and took her in his arms.

The chairs were hard and too small for comfort, entwined as they were, so they sat on the floor in the corner near the door, where passers-by wouldn't see them. They held each other close, spoke in whispers and thought they were in heaven.

"What did you tell your wife so you could get away?" Lilly asked when they were sitting smoking a cigarette, the glow lighting their faces at intervals and lighting up their expressions of love.

"I'm walking the dog," he grinned.

"Where is it then?"

"Left it with a mate."

That evening visit was the first of many. They left no evidence of having been there, even disposing of the rubbish that was sometimes pushed through the letter box by passers-by too lazy to find a rubbish bin. No one guessed the café had nightly visitors.

As weeks went by, Lilly persuaded Phil to reveal more about his unhappy marriage.

"She's out all the time, see," Phil explained when Lilly asked why he worked such long hours. "Never home to get my tea. I usually go in to find something keeping warm on top of a saucepan of hot water."

"That's terrible." Lilly longed to help him, spoil him, look after him as a wife should.

"I might as well stay at work and earn a bit extra," he went on. "Putting it away in secret I am; she's a bit extravagant and always short of cash. I need to have a bit put by to dig her out when she gets into debt."

"You deserve better treatment," Lilly said, knowing she was the one to provide it. If only he would face the fact that his marriage was a terrible disaster, a mistake to be recti-fied.

"I hope to be running Piper's one day," she said, hoping he would understand what she was offering him. "Our Beth and my brothers and cousins will stay in the busi-ness of course, but it needs a strong person in charge. I'm like my Granny Moll, and I'm the one to do it after her time. Plenty of money then. If I marry, my husband won't have to work such long hours."

"And your husband will have something to hurry home to," he whispered. "Lucky he'll be, no mistake."

Lilly was better tempered now she and Phil were meeting regularly and had reached a new level of understanding. They seemed able to talk about anything now the barriers were down and he had told her about his unhappy marriage. She began to believe that he would one day leave his wife and, far into the future, would marry her.

She worked a little harder on the beach and didn't complain about the various jobs she disliked. She was anxious to show her father and mother how much she deserved to be given more responsibility, building up to the time when they would retire and leave the business in her hands. Me and Phil running Piper's, she dreamed. Handyman he was, good at fixing things; he'd be an asset to Piper's with its almost continuous maintenance problems. Yes, life looked good. If only she could persuade him to leave his uncaring wife.

Beth continued to pursue the little girl who came each evening to take the food. The girl was now well aware of being followed and easily evaded Beth's attempt to follow. Beth tried leaving Piper's early and waiting near the lane to which she had been led, the place where she suspected her quarry lived, but although she waited long after the girl should have returned, she didn't appear.

With the familiarity of several visits, the run-down places had lost some of their terror but it still wasn't a place where she liked to dawdle. The semi-derelict buildings seemed to hold unseen dangers, their interiors dark and threatening. She saw a door move occasionally as though someone was watching, hidden behind its rotten wood. A cat paused to look at her as it slunk along the gutter about its business and a rat sat for a while, watching her with beady, intelligent eyes, but there was no sign or sound to suggest human habitation.

She tried putting a note with the food, but saw it flutter to the ground and dance away on the breeze. It seemed she needed some assistance if she were to find out more and be able to help the child further. She decided to ask her family.

Lilly told her she was stupid, and Eynon said he hadn't the time. Both were involved in their love lives and when they weren't meeting their loved ones they were dreaming about meeting them. Eynon had met a girl who was holidaying in the town, and he was determined to pursue her during the few days left. She lived about sixty miles away so the romance was unlikely to continue after the holiday, but at seventeen he found that an advantage rather than a problem. Beth pleaded with them both to no avail.

Ronnie came home on embarkation leave and Beth asked him to help. When the situation had been explained, he agreed. On the following evening he went to the field near the café and settled down in a spot from where he could see the café bins. Olive was with him, lying down in the tall ripe summer grass. They were inseparable during those precious days and Beth had to accept the help of both of them or neither.

They saw the girl take the food, which Beth now left on top of the bin, the packages having increased in size and the contents more varied. Olive spoke aloud to Ronnie, who replied as though angry and stayed where he was. Olive walked off in the same direction taken by the girl, making sure she had the girl's attention. A lover's tiff would reassure her as to their presence there. She wouldn't see them as a threat.

Ronnie waited until they were both out of sight then darted through the lanes to the area Beth had described. Beth waited at the far side of the field but was careful not to show herself.

As the girl reached the lane behind the run-down houses, she paused and looked around her. Feeling safe from curious eyes she ran softly up the worn concrete with its immature forest of weeds and saplings. She gave another brief look around before she darted in through a stable door and closed it softly behind her.

Half an hour later, the three conspirators met and discussed their next move.

On the following day, Beth did not put out the usual bundle. She watched as the girl came and searched through the bin, which Beth had filled with unwrapped fish leftovers to discourage her. She was crying when she ran off and Beth's eyes filled with guilt at the way she had made the girl suffer disappointment.

An hour later she took a generous packet of food, which included fresh fruit and some chocolate, and made her way to the stable. Ronnie and Olive met her and together they went in. Darkness and silence greeted them and they stood for a long time while their eyes grew accustomed to the poor light. Then they made out a mound in one corner and on investigation discovered a child who looked about twelve lying, obviously ill, under a heap of old coats.

"Who are you?" the girl asked, her voice low and wheezing as though with a heavy cold.

"Friends," Ronnie said. "Come to help you we have."

"Please, go away."

"You have to see a doctor."

"No need for a doctor, my sister is looking after me."

"So is *my* sister, though you don't know it," Ronnie replied.

"It's you who puts out the food?" The girl turned her head slowly to look at Beth, who nodded. "Thank you." She lowered her head as though the weight of it was too much for her slender neck.

"We can't leave you here like this," Olive said, compassion softening her voice.

"We manage fine," the breathless voice insisted.

"We could take you to the hospital," Ronnie offered. "When you're well again maybe you will manage fine, but you have to be fit to live rough like this."

"And what about school?" Beth asked. "Doesn't someone at school try to help you both?"

"None of your business!" a voice shouted and they turned to see the small figure of the younger sister silhouetted against the open door. "Go away and leave us alone. We don't want no interfering busybodies!"

"Either you accept our help or two of us will stay here and the other will go and fetch the police," Ronnie said firmly. "The choice is yours and you have one minute to decide." He deliberately panicked the girl, knowing that if they went away, allowing them time to consider, the girls would have moved on before they could return, even though the older one looked too sick to be moved.

"No police, please, and no hospitals," the elder girl pleaded between coughing.

"They'll send us back, see," her sister added. "We can't go back; we're trying to find our brother." She crouched down beside her sister in a protective way.

"Back where?" Ronnie asked, bending down to talk to them. "Do you have a mother somewhere? We'll help you find your brother if we can," he offered encouragingly. "Or take you back to your mother."

"Dead, she is, and our dad. We were put in a home, see, and our brother was sent somewhere else, and we can't find him. He'd look after us if we could find him."

"Take them to Granny Moll," Olive suggested. "She'll know what to do."

With Ronnie half carrying the sick sister and the other fussing around her like a distraught mother hen with a solitary chick, they made their way through the lanes towards Sidney Street.

Before they were halfway there, Ronnie had to lift the girl and carry her. She smelled unpleasantly of perspiration and the dampness of the bedding in which she was wrapped. She felt very light and he wondered how long they had been surviving on what the younger sister could steal. They were both so thin and gaunt, he didn't think they had had sufficient food for a long time.

Olive opened the door and called to Granny Moll. She was convinced that Moll would get the two girls into hospital and back into the care of the council as soon as they explained, but Moll had different ideas.

"Food and some cough medicine, that's all they need," she said when she had heard the impassioned pleading of the two girls not to send them back to the home. "We'll see if a bit of maldod will put them right, then we can think again."

Somewhat doubtfully, Ronnie, Olive and Beth agreed.

Moll rang the police later and rather evasively explained the situation.

"They aren't criminals – and they aren't running away from conscription," she joked. "Two children in need of a home, they are. I'll keep an eye on them and you say nothing to your superiors or the authorities till I tell you, right?"

"If they're runaways, I need to—"

"You didn't find them, you don't know where they are, so how can you tell anyone?"

"But it's my duty to—"

"Forty-eight hours, that's all I'm asking."

"I have to see them and find out where they're from. You can't just casually take on someone else's children."

Moll could hear a lot of noise in the background, people talking, shouting, arguing, laughing. She guessed the man was in the middle of something important. Depending on it, she added more weight to her argument. "I'll take responsibility for them, and you've got plenty of other things to see to with this war an' all. So give me a couple of days, right?"

"All right," the constable agreed reluctantly, knowing he was wrong but too harassed by the local residents classed as aliens to argue. The front desk was crowded with Italians and Germans who had lived in the town for many years, many of them sailors who had liked the town and found work and stayed. These foreign residents now had to report weekly to be checked, or risk being imprisoned. After being kept waiting, they were becoming restless and noisy and he gave up. "Keep them for tonight and I'll be over first thing tomorrow. And make sure you're there," he warned as a pretence that he was in control.

"Oi! Where d'you think you're going?" Moll demanded of Beth and Olive as they went towards the kitchen door. "Staying here you are, the three of you. I'm not doing this on my own."

"We were going to make some tea and get them some hot food," Olive explained.

"Washing comes first," Moll said firmly. "A wash and a clean bed is what these two want most. Then we'll see about cawl and a cwlff. Right?" "Cawl and a cwlff" was a bowl of home-made soup and a thick slice off the loaf. Once the two girls were settled between Moll's clean white sheets, Olive and Ronnie were allowed to relax and eat their own share of the food, and Beth was allowed to go home.

Moll smiled. The house had felt empty for years. Once Marged had left, she and Audrey had rattled around in the three-storey building. Now, with Olive and Ronnie staying there and these two children desperate for a home, the place was filling up nicely.

The sergeant came the following morning and after numerous phone calls it was agreed that the children would stay with her until something else could be arranged. Myrtle and Maude burst into tears at the policeman's words.

"We don't want to go back."

"We have to find our brother," Maude wailed.

"Don't worry, trust Granny Moll," the old woman promised. "You won't go anywhere you don't want to go. The sergeant is too busy with important things to worry about a couple of tiddlers like you."

Before July ended, Bleddyn's two sons received their call-up papers. Marged and Huw wondered how they were going to cope with the severe shortage of staff. Marged asked Freddy to help by giving up his job at the factory and joining them, but he refused. He didn't explain that he hoped to avoid being sent into the army; instead, he told them that the factory desperately needed his organising skills and war work was more important that holidays on the beach.

"That's where you're wrong, boy," Huw replied. "Wars aren't only fought on the battlefields, it's on the home front too that wars are won or lost! Morale is important and we have to do everything we can to keep it high."

"Selling ice-creams and making money from rides?" Freddy was sarcastic, almost believing his story about the importance of his position. "Bullets and bombs we need, not ice-cream."

In spite of several enquiries, Moll could find
no information about the family of Maude
and Myrtle. The girls insisted that they had
a brother whom they had never met, but the
matron of the Children's Home – where
they had been taken after several attempts at
finding them a foster home had ended in
failure – knew nothing about any relations
apart from an aunt, who had since died.

Moll called a family conference and everyone attended, including Freddy. It was held
at Moll's house as it was the largest, and
they all squeezed into the parlour, even
Bleddyn, Johnny – who arrived with
Hannah and her two daughters – and Taff
with his wife Evelyn. The idea was to decide
on the best way of dealing with the shortage
of help now the army was taking the young
men. Moll also hoped they might come up
with some ideas for extending the search for
the girls' family. They had been surprised to
learn that Maude, who was recovering well
from her illness, was fifteen, and Myrtle,
whom they had guessed was eight, was in
fact twelve.

With regard to the beach, Freddy offered
to help when he could, but reminded them
with importance that with the factory
working around the clock with different
shifts, he might not be reliable. Bleddyn

decided to cut out the boat trips. "I can't go very far out and they'll soon be stopping me altogether I expect," he said gloomily. "So I'll deal with the chip shop full time." Huw and Marged insisted they were unable to do more than run Piper's Café, and they needed Beth's assistance to do it properly.

"Can I help?" Maude asked. "I can take the money for the swingboats or the helter-skelter. Love that we would, me and Myrtle could do that easy."

"Threepenny ride, how much change from half a crown?" Huw asked and neither girl could work it out. "All right, try this. You're given a shilling, how much change for a threepenny ride from that?"

Maude felt her fingers as she counted and came up with the answer eventually but Myrtle looked as blank as before.

"You have been to school?" Marged asked them.

"Not much," Maude admitted. "We didn't go much after Mam and Dad died, then we went for a while when we lived with Auntie Hazel and again when we were with Auntie Rita and—"

"When did you last go to school?" Moll asked Myrtle, who shrugged and looked at her sister for an answer.

"You're too old for school, Maude, we'll have to get you some help from somewhere else, but you, Myrtle, you'll go back to school as soon as the new term starts, right?"

Myrtle looked frightened and hugged her sister. "I can't. They laughed at me before, for not knowing how to read," she said. "I can't go back."

"I'll help you," Beth said, feeling a sense of responsibility for the two girls she had rescued from dire poverty. "We all will."

Huw emptied his pockets and began at once to teach the girls the names of the various coins.

"It seems like we're stuck with you two until we find that brother of yours," Moll said, smiling at the two thin, pale children. "Best we do what we can for you while you're here."

The two girls settled in happily with Granny Moll and Auntie Audrey. With decent food and proper care their skin glowed with health and their hair shone. But their insecurity was still clearly shown by the way they clung to each other in sleep. Moll and her daughter Audrey always looked in on them before they went to their beds and they were touched by the sight of the two little girls tightly clasped in each other's arms, using only a fraction of the big feather bed. Sometimes one of them would cry out in her sleep and the other would whisper soothingly to reassure her that everything was all right and they were safe.

Enquiries went on to try and discover any relations or friends who could give them some information about their early years, but so far nothing had been learnt. Moll repeatedly discussed the situation with her family and others and most were of the opinion that they would never find any relations as they did not want to be found.

"Best we don't tell Maude and Myrtle how hopeless it is, mind," Moll warned. "We don't want them to give up hope, or run off again. Not now, when they're beginning to settle down and build a life for themselves with us."

Audrey, and on occasion Wilf, spent time with the girls helping them to master reading skills and basic adding and subtraction. Myrtle, who at first had understood nothing about reading, was a quick learner and one day Moll was amused to see that the younger sister was helping the older one with a task set her by Audrey.

Hannah came to see the girls sometimes, bringing her two small children, Josie aged four who was already at school, and Marie who was three. Using the books bought for her own girls, Hannah patiently encouraged the four girls to play "schools", thereby adding to the development of them all.

"Great with the kids, isn't she, Granny Moll?" Johnny whispered when they were watching Hannah playing a counting game with the children. "Endlessly patient and so gentle when she has to correct them."

Moll looked at Bleddyn's son fondly. "Besotted you are, young Johnny."

"You do like her, don't you, Granny Moll?"

"How could anyone not like Hannah?" Moll replied. "She's beautiful inside and out." Johnny smiled at her until she spoilt it by adding, "Too old for you to think of marrying, mind."

"I loved her long before I knew her age," Johnny said. Moll recognised a quiet determination in his young face and said nothing more.

Johnny left her and went to join the game of I Spy, which Hannah had changed into a more beneficial game by telling them the object they chose had to be written down. Moll watched them and her eyes softened. Hannah was beautiful and she had helped generously in the teaching of Maude and Myrtle. Bleddyn would be fortunate to have her as a daughter-in-law.

The girls were excellent pupils, she thought, as she watched them laboriously writing on the paper she had supplied, Hannah helping her own two and ready to assist the others when necessary.

Everyone needs an incentive to persuade them to work at a new skill, and for both Maude and Myrtle the urgency was to acquire sufficient ability to be allowed to help on the beach. Moll's motives weren't entirely selfless. With the boys all likely to go to help the fight against Germany, she knew that two other members of the family, even though temporary, would be a valuable asset.

The first week of August was the busiest of the beach season and the family asked friends, neighbours and even a small band of children to help out. Little boys standing on pop crates, wearing outsized shirts back to front in place of overalls, stretched over the small counter to reach for the pennies, which they counted carefully into the biscuit tin which served as a till. Arms waved like frantic jellyfish as everyone tried to be served at once. Ice-cream melted and ran down chubby arms to be licked off when no one was looking, leaving faces sticky as well as rosy in the warm sun, and causing havoc when wasps were attracted by the delicious confection.

The beach filled up until there was hardly any sand to be seen when the tide was high. Screams filled the air as children splashed in the sea and performed wobbly walks both around the edge and inside the beach pool. The uneven surface hurt their feet, adding to the excuses to shout and scream.

More and more day-trippers came: mums,

dads, aunties, grandmothers and grandads, arriving by train, bus, bicycle or on foot. They were mostly loaded with heavy baskets and bags filled with whatever they considered necessary for a good day out.

Besides the increasing number of visitors, more vendors came in the hope of a successful day, and Beth noticed that the men who came were generally older than usual, fathers and uncles and brothers with things to sell, services to offer, taking the place of those gone to serve their country, trying to keep the business alive for when their loved ones returned.

Cyril the Snap, the street photographer, abandoned his occasional pitch in the centre of a large city and came for his annual "holiday", smiling hopefully at young girls, flattering them and persuading them that, "Not to take your photographs, beautiful girls that you are, Duw, it would be a crime."

They accepted his words willingly, laughing, half believing him, and he thanked them, told them they were adorable, blew kisses and went to look for more prospective customers.

Mystical, Magical, All-Seeing, All-Knowing Sarah, the Gypsy Princess, advertised her psychic powers on her booth on the promenade. An exotic addition to the rest, her tent was decorated in bold colours and bedecked with gold and silver, attracting some and frightening others. She would sometimes appear, draped in layer after layer of dark-coloured skirts and shawls edged with sparkling designs, and smiled to herself when some hurried past, afraid of those dark, intelligent eyes, which sometimes looked at them boldly and sometimes softened into a wink.

Candy floss failed to appear, obviously a victim of sugar rationing, but Moll dug into her store cupboard and continued to offer coconut ice, Turkish delight and toffee apples made from the last of her stock, selling it in the rock shop run by Audrey, as well as on the stalls where ice-creams were still the favourite.

Bernard Gregory was kept busy with his team of donkeys and the small cart, decorated with flags and pulled by his pony, which gave rides to children. Bernard had retired from the sands several years previously and left the happy business to his son, Peter, but with Peter previously studying for better things and now serving in the forces, Bernard had returned to enjoy his summer with the children.

During a particularly busy day, Beth stood at the top of the café steps, after having been down to the sands to make sure there was no crockery left abandoned, and looked at the scene below. Colour and noise was everywhere: children yelling, mothers shouting louder to attract their attention, and, in many cases, surprisingly, being heard. Every colour imaginable was shown in the summer dresses and dippers and towels, and tablecloths too, as families set out picnic meals. The only dull spots were the men, most of whom sat wearing their suits, sporting a handkerchief on their heads, the only concession to summer being the few inches they exposed of their ankles by rolling up their navy serge trousers. Some had removed their jackets which were folded neatly beside them, but most still wore shirts and ties; loosened, but still respectably in place.

Beth thought of Freddy working in that stuffy factory and felt sorry for him missing these wonderful days.

Freddy had worked a morning shift, finishing at two p.m. and at five o'clock he called to see Shirley.

"Decision day today," he told her when she had finished serving a customer and was free. "Today I'll know whether or not my application for deferment will be approved."

"Good luck," Shirley said, but she sounded far from interested.

"Is everything all right?" Freddy asked, slightly offended. "I thought you'd want to know."

"I might be signing up myself," she said.

"You, signing up? Leaving your mam to cope on her own? You can't do that."

"The shop has been sold and the new owner will let us stay in the flat but we're losing our jobs."

"Sorry I am, Shirley. There's me worrying about my own problems and you're facing this." He was still unappeased, thinking she should have been more concerned for him, but he bravely ignored his own worries and suggested, "Tell you what, I know that Piper's are looking for staff, for the last weeks of summer at least. Shall I put in a word for you and your mam?"

"Lovely – I don't think! With Mam convinced that the Pipers stole the business and it should rightly be hers, she'd love working for them, wouldn't she?"

"Sorry, I didn't think."

"I wouldn't say no to working on the beach," Shirley's mother surprised them by saying. "And I'd be good at it. It's in my blood after all – not that they'd think so, the thieving lot!"

"No, no, no!" Huw was adamant. "I don't want that woman working for us."

"We're desperate, Huw. I don't think we can refuse," Marged said.

"She's trouble. She might think I've forgotten, but I remember the way she called us everything she could lay her tongue to and that's plenty, telling everyone your grandparents stole the business from her grandparents."

"Load of ol' rubbish that was," Moll said, agreeing with Huw for once. "We don't want her sort here, cause trouble she would for sure."

Marged argued and finally threatened to go on strike. "I can't do all the cooking and serve tables with only our Beth to help. Lilly is worse than useless, half the time she doesn't turn up and when she does she's only in the way. I have to have help until the end of summer and this Mrs Downs is all we've found."

"You're right, Marged," Moll conceded eventually. "It's only for the last few weeks, so what harm can she do?"

"Damn it all, Marged, when am I going to have some say in what happens at Piper's?" cried Huw. "Never listen to me, none of you. I make suggestions and you throw them out without discussion, you employ the staff without consulting me, but on this I'm determined. Mrs Downs will be trouble and I don't want her here, right?"

"What about starting her daughter Shirley as well?" Freddy suggested, a flutter of amusement in his throat.

"No, no, no!" Huw shouted angrily, but the idea was discussed as though he hadn't spoken.

"Let's see how Mrs Downs gets on first," Moll said.

"We're not taking on either of them. I forbid it." Huw's voice was losing its power, knowing he was making no impression on the others.

"We'll have a vote," Marged said, realising that she was on safe ground. Huw was outvoted and Mrs Downs arrived the following morning to start work at Piper's Café.

Some of the boats were still managing to give short rides when the tide was high and the barricades built to deter invaders far out to sea. Bleddyn had put his boat in storage for the duration, however, sadly covering her with tarpaulin after giving her an extra coat of paint to protect her.

It was sad to see the small craft hugging the shore and giving a pretence of danger to a few passengers, while others looked on and patiently waited their turn. Bleddyn preferred not to look.

On the morning of Mrs Downs's first day, she collected the rubbish that had been pushed through the letter box during the night and sniffed disapprovingly.

"Don't you clean up before you go home?"

"Yes we do," Marged retorted. "Everything here is shining spotless and all the leftover food is thrown away. You know how fussy we are about quality and cleanliness. This cigarette packet is what some idle creature has pushed through after we've closed. Don't think you can tell me anything about cleanliness, Mrs Downs."

It was not an auspicious start. With another busy day, there was little time for point-scoring though, and Marged had to admit that Mrs Downs – Hetty, as she chose to be called – worked as hard as any of the others, needing little instruction, seeming to understand what was needed, and to learn quickly where everything was kept. When she mentioned this to Huw he only grunted.

Freddy turned up at five o'clock and offered to help clear the tables and stack dishes for washing. He had been to the swimming baths in his occasional role of lifeguard, which meant a free swim after he had kept watch for a few hours. His towel and dippers were in his bag, which he put on a chair near the door. He thought he might get a swim in the sea later, although he was never very keen, preferring the more orderly pool with its changing rooms and lockers and no waves to worry about. The waves were rough that day, and increasing in size as the tide grew towards its highest point. Perhaps he wouldn't bother. He wouldn't admit it but he never felt easy about sea bathing, in spite of his training as a lifeguard. He preferred to have a safety rail handy and near enough to grab.

He kissed Beth when Marged wasn't looking, then stood beside Shirley's mother and settled to the routine work of cleaning up. The day had been a very busy one, with a continuous queue of people wanting food, partly to save on their rations by eating out. The sea was too rough for most people to enjoy bathing and the sand was being blown about by a frivolous wind, making picnics less pleasant, so instead many trippers had found their way into the café to eat in comfort.

Beth felt a slight twinge of jealousy when Mrs Downs's daughter Shirley arrived to meet her mother. She saw Freddy invite her to join them in the kitchen and shortly afterwards laughter swelled out interspersed by whispered conversation. She went in once to find them doubled over with mirth and asked what the joke was.

"Too complicated to explain," Mrs Downs said, and this increased the laughter as Beth walked away.

It was fast approaching closing time but still the people came and still Marged and Huw and Beth served meals.

"More plates, please," Beth called, popping her head into the kitchen. Shirley and

151

Freddy were wiping plates and stacking them, laughing at something Shirley's mother was saying, and she felt again that surge of jealousy, a sensation of being left out, pushed aside by the girl and her mother. Perhaps her father had been right, and they shouldn't have invited Mrs Downs to help, she thought, although honesty made her admit to herself that the woman worked hard and didn't need constant reminders of what was expected of her.

Bleddyn called unexpectedly to borrow some cooking fat, since he was running low at the fish-and-chip shop, and as he left, carrying the white slab in its greaseproof wrapping, a roar was heard coming from below them. Beth and her parents ran to the window and, looking down, saw that there had been an accident. A crowd was gathered and more people were running towards the edge of the tide. Some were pointing to where one of the small pleasure boats had overturned.

"Freddy!" Beth called. "There's been an accident! Quick, you'll have to help!"

Freddy ran to see what had happened and his heart began to thud painfully. The sea had turned quite rough and he couldn't face diving in and swimming out to where people struggled in the water far beyond the surf, where breakers rose and fell in giant peaks and valleys. The sea was rising and falling like some great boiling cauldron. How could he swim out through that? He was afraid of the sea. Panic set in and his mind whirred. How could he get out of helping without disgracing himself in the eyes of Beth and her whole family?

He glanced at Shirley and knew at once that she understood. She could offer no help, though, and he grabbed his towel, hid in a corner and struggled into his wet bathers. He appeared to rush but many precious seconds passed before he stepped out and began to go down the metal steps to the beach.

"Two children and two women there are," Beth shouted to him as she ran beside him, "besides the boatman."

"I think I'd do better to run to the first-aid hut and ask them to phone for help," he said, slowing down and standing near the edge of the tide. "I can't go out there and bring five people back! What can I do?"

"Do what you can, just get out there," Beth pleaded, thinking of the people in such danger only yards from where they stood. "Someone has already gone for help. We can't stand here and watch them drown!"

He dived in and began to swim but was making little progress, faking cramp, when Bleddyn, who had just realised what had happened, stormed down the beach and dived in. He swam strongly and was soon overtaking Freddy.

The children were crying, the women close to collapse. After talking to them briefly and making sure they had something to hold, he supported each child with a hand under their heads, coaxing them, encouraging them when he realised they could actually swim a little but had been terrified out of trying by their distance from the shore and by the danger represented by the barricades and the mines frighteningly close.

He hadn't wanted to leave one behind while he helped the other. He had thought the women and the boatman would be able to cope but it would have taken only one extra strong wave to have sent the child way beyond the beach and out of reach. Their being able to float enabled him to bring them both in together, kicking strongly with his legs until he could touch the bottom, then wading out, carrying them one under each arm, laughing, persuading them it had been an adventure, something to relate to their friends.

The owner of the boat had persuaded the two distressed women to hold on to the upturned boat, assuring them that the children were safe, and he waited with them while Bleddyn swam to safety with his precious charges and handed them over before swimming back to help the man bring the two women ashore. Like Bleddyn, he had been afraid to leave one of them for fear of them relaxing their tenuous hold and being swept out beyond help.

Bleddyn looked with utter disgust at Freddy when he walked past the younger man. He was carrying one of the women and was followed by the boat owner carrying the other.

Freddy turned to Beth and mouthed silently, "What's up with him? I was on my way, wasn't I?"

"Were you, Freddy? Or were you waiting for someone else to do what you're supposed to be trained to do?"

"Beth, be fair. I did try but I got cramp and—" But Beth was running up the beach beside her uncle, hoping the reason for her tears would be presumed to be relief and not shame.

Five

Beth looked at the ring on her third finger and thought it had lost its sparkle. How could Freddy have been so useless when five people were in danger? She had hardly spoken to him since the accident. Thank goodness nobody had been hurt. He could have been responsible for someone's death, she kept reminding herself. Trained in life saving and too cowardly to swim out when he was needed.

It was early morning and she had been awake since five thirty, the brightness of the day making it impossible to chase sleep any longer. Hearing sounds from above her, she went into the kitchen and filled the kettle. Mam was usually first to rise and would be glad of a cup of tea.

"How long have you been up?" Marged asked as she came into the kitchen in her ancient woollen dressing gown. "Couldn't you sleep?"

"I keep thinking of that boat overturning and Freddy pretending he had cramp. Mam, what would have happened if one of those people had drowned? I couldn't ever have forgiven him."

"You won't be a very suppportive wife then, will you?" Marged said sharply. "The minute he makes a mistake or loses his nerve, you'll stop loving him, is it? Fine start to an engagement that is. I love your father and that means I forgive him whatever he does and support him when he's done something foolish. And he'd do the same for me. I only have to reach out a hand and I know he'll be there. That's what love is, not being so sure of your own perfection. It's knowing you'll give, and have, understanding and forgiveness."

"Mam!"

"All right, I don't like the boy very much and I'd hoped you'd choose to marry someone else, to be honest. But you chose him and you should honour your decision."

As they cleared up after breakfast and prepared to leave for the beach, Beth said, "Can I come over later? There's something I want to do."

Marged only nodded.

The factory worked shifts, but recently Freddy had worked days only, starting at nine and finishing at six o'clock. Instead of the usual stream of people rushing in to clock on before they were late and would miss a quarter of an hour's pay, that morning at ten minutes to nine there were only seven people strolling through the entrance. Beth saw Freddy immediately, and ran up to him before he could disappear through the heavy reinforced metal gates with their barbed wire mounting.

"Freddy? I'm sorry I've been so upset with you."

"I'm sorry too. I should have been braver. But I was so scared. I didn't know what to do; my brain seized up. I couldn't think how to deal with it, how I could possibly rescue five people when I got out there. I had no idea what to do. Ashamed I am, and I don't blame you for hating me."

"I don't hate you, you know that. My shame is that I reacted like I did."

Freddy pulled her round to face him and took her hands in his. People were calling him from the gate but he ignored them. "I'm no film-star hero, am I?" he said sadly.

"None of us are. I don't know how I'd react when faced with sudden danger."

A security man came towards them looking angry.

"For God's sake, come in if you're coming, boy! Lost your shift work because you were always late for shift and now you can't even be on time at nine o'clock!"

"What does he mean, Freddy? You moved to a more important job, didn't you?"

"I missed the six a.m. start a few times, that's all, and the foreman's got it in for me,

Beth." He gave her a quick kiss and hurried inside the factory.

Beth wandered back through the town, heading for the small railway station. She would need to catch a train since she'd missed her ride to work. Mam had been right about her lack of loyalty, but she was more unsettled than ever after her attempt to make amends. Freddy had told her he'd been promoted to a more important job, but that wasn't true. He'd lost his position because he was often late. Just how important had his job been, she wondered? Just how well did she know Freddy? They had been togcthcr since they were four years old, but she was beginning to think he was a stranger.

The reason the boat had overturned was that the boatman had gone too close to the defences and it had become caught on a metal spike. Held in place, the next wave partly filled it. That it had overturned rather than sank was pure good fortune.

A few days after the incident, the army came and blew up the boat; a frightening reminder that they were at war.

Under Moll's tuition, helped by other members of the family, Maude and Myrtle quickly improved their ability to handle money. To encourage them, Marged allowed them to work on the stalls taking money and giving change under supervision. The knowledge that they were useful was like magic medicine and as their abilities developed so their health improved. A nurse attached to the welfare department of the council visited them at intervals and declared herself satisfied that they were being cared for adequately.

"I think a family environment is what most of these abandoned children need, Mrs Piper," Nurse Francis told Moll one morning. "Pity is that there aren't enough families for them all." She sighed gently. "With any spare spaces being used by evacuees, there are fewer than usual."

"And things will be far worse in the big cities, Miss Francis, with bombing taking away so many houses, and families separated by evacuation as well as everything else. How will it ever get sorted once we've seen an end to it? Lucky we are, to live in a small unimportant place like St David's Well."

"Indeed," Miss Francis agreed. "Now, have you learned anything to suggest there might be some truth in this story about them having a brother?"

"They insist that they have a sister-in-law, which presumably means they have a brother somewhere, but nothing we've discovered gives any clue to where this sister-in-law might be, or even if she exists. Could they have invented her?"

"It's possible. Children who have no one of their own have been known to dream about discovering a long-lost aunt or invent a story that their mother isn't really dead and one day will come back to find them. Sometimes they come to believe it."

"Poor dabs," Moll said sadly. "Never mind, they've got us Pipers now and we'll look after them like they're our own."

"In the circumstances Maude and Myrtle are lucky girls."

Beth's younger brother, Eynon, resented the beach. As far back as he could remember he had been made to help on the stalls or doing menial jobs in Piper's Café. As a child he had enjoyed it – he'd made his friends envious when he described his days on the sands – but now he wanted something different, something that didn't take so much of his time. He had discovered the joy of girls.

Today he had sloped off when his cousin Taff had come to repair a wooden support, and he had no intention of going back. Let them find someone else. The day was warm, summer was coming to its end, the girls were out in force and he was free.

He wandered aimlessly through the busy little town, where shops had filled their windows with patriotic displays supporting

161

the soldiers and sailors and airmen. A pretty, dark-haired girl was standing looking at a tobacconist's window and he strolled casually up and offered her a cigarette from his gold-coloured case, "borrowed" from his father's drawer.

"No thanks, I don't smoke. I think it's a filthy, smelly thing to do," she said, tilting her pert little nose.

"Neither do I," Eynon said, hiding the cigarette he had taken out. "I just keep some on me and offer them to any soldiers I see. Got it hard they have, not much money an' that."

"You are kind," she purred and as he stretched up to his full height and smiled modestly, she added brightly, "Here's my boyfriend, perhaps he'd like one."

With a forced smile, Eynon opened his cigarette case and invited the soldier to help himself. "Greedy bugger needn't have taken two," he muttered as he walked away.

From then on, every likely girl he saw was either with her parents or had a member of the armed forces on her arm. When he met Freddy coming out of the factory at six o'clock, they agreed immediately about the boredom of working for the Pipers.

"Granny Moll thinks that as I'm family I'm bound to love working the beach, but I hate it," Eynon moaned.

"I think it's madness you wasting your

talents serving kids with buckets and spades or helping them on and off the swingboats," Freddy said. "Your Beth wants me to work for the Pipers when I come back from the services, but I don't think I'll settle for that, not when I've travelled the world."

"Travel the world?" Eynon said, his mouth open in awe. "Is that what you do in the army? I thought you'd go no further than France, stay a while blasting away at the enemy until you got wounded, them come back home."

"Of course I'll travel. They can send you anywhere they like – and you can bet it won't be anywhere near St David's Well Bay! It's the RAF for me, Eynon. Smart uniform and plenty of girls." Freddy suddenly realised he probably shouldn't be talking to Beth's brother about other women. Never mind; Eynon was a kindred spirit. He'd understand.

Eynon looked starry-eyed. "Just think, Freddy, you might be a pilot! Imagine that, skimming over the towns in France and Germany." He smiled dreamily at the thought of himself wearing his wings proudly on his sleeve and having girls pleading for his attention.

"I'm thinking of enlisting," Freddy told him. "Not waiting for my papers, but signing on for a few years, official like. Then I'll be able to choose which service I join.

That's got to be better than waiting to be called up. They can put you where they like then. So I'm told, mind."

"I'm not eighteen till next year, Freddy. I wish I was old enough to go with you."

"They'll take you as a regular, won't they? You're old enough for that. Grab a fine lad like you without hesitation they will. You sign on for five years and you'll come out smarter than you'd be after five years working on the sands. What can you possibly learn on the sands?"

Freddy didn't tell the gullible young boy he had recently learned that his application for deferment had been turned down and that he was expecting his papers any day. "Come on, Eynon, let's see what they tell us at the recruitment office, is it?"

"Is there a place for Royal Navy volunteers, Freddy? I fancy that uniform more than the RAF, don't you?"

"No, I fancy that forage cap. Racy that looks, mind."

During the busy weeks when factories and employments of all kinds normally closed to allow their workforce to take a week's holiday, most continued working. But the beach was still packed and the café had a continuous queue from the moment it opened until the family thankfully closed the door and fell exhausted into the kitchen chairs.

People who didn't usually take a holiday away from home were making the most of the short time before their sons or husbands went into the forces and the atmosphere was lively, with a kind of forced gaiety.

Maude and Myrtle were learning fast and were already very useful members of the Piper team. Lilly had found a new way of avoiding the tasks she hated, insisting she was teaching the youngsters the basics of working on the sands. She also realised that with the place so busy, Marged and Huw didn't have time to check on what she was doing and she became adept at looking busy whenever they approached.

Beth was aware of her sister's idleness but after complaining several times and having nothing done about it, she ignored Lilly and got on with her work. She knew that Lilly wasn't the only one of the family who wasn't doing their fair share, although for the past week her younger brother had seemed much more cheerful.

Eynon stood near the swingboats and was smiling and helpful to the steady stream of customers. Marged and Huw were relieved at his change of attitude. That he was especially charming to the young girls just made them smile. He was growing up. Huw and Marged were just thankful for the effort he was making at this particularly busy time.

Freddy came every evening in time to help, and even Lilly seemed willing to join in with the cleaning at the café when it came to the end of the day, so they could get off a little bit quicker. The family were unaware that she would soon be back there. Marged sighed contentedly as she told Moll that the family were pulling together and everyone seemed to be content despite the long, tiring days.

Audrey's assistant at the rock shop, Alice Potter, worked for several hours each day, though she couldn't work regular shifts as she was needed to look after her father. Colin Potter was an ex-boxer who had been injured in a fight. He couldn't stand without support as he kept losing his balance and he was also deaf.

Alice found looking after him a thankless occupation. No praise was given, however well she managed. They lived in a building that had once been a shop. The room at the front, with its once grand entrance, was empty. The windows were streaked with dirt, and the whole place had a neglected air. Many rooms were unused, since they could afford to furnish and heat only a few.

Eynon saw Alice serving novelty rock when he was on his way to collect more crisps from the store room in Moll's house and he went in to talk to her. That evening, when the rock and sweet shop closed and

Audrey came to deal with the money, he was there to walk her home.

Alice was small and very thin, and dark haired like most of the Castle family. Audrey remarked that they could be mistaken for brother and sister. Eynon laughed and winked at Alice. He wasn't feeling at all brotherly.

Alice and her father lived in a dingy lane and the back entrance to their home was blocked with abandoned shelving from the shop. Immediately behind it was another similar terrace. The place was dark and gloomy and from what Eynon could see when he glanced inside, the long passage leading through to the back door, past the hollow space of the shop area, was bare of lino. The walls were in serious need of fresh wallpaper.

On impulse, when he was on his way home, he went to the shops, which were just closing, bought a bunch of chrysanthemums, and returned to Alice's house. When she opened the door her smile was rewarding, and he was about to invite her to go with him to the pictures when another figure appeared.

Leaning on the wall, Colin Potter came down the passageway in a series of jerking paces, angled oddly and using the walls for support. He demanded to know what Eynon wanted.

"Just to thank your daughter for helping my aunt out today, sir," Eynon said politely and after a sly wink for Alice, he went home.

War or no war, Marged still insisted on throwing away what hadn't been used, and starting each morning with clean shelves and fresh food. A man called Richards arranged to collect the discarded foodstuffs and he came every evening and emptied the separate bins containing food, which he took back to his farm and boiled up for his ever-hungry pigs.

Maude and Myrtle often stood for long periods, staring up into the faces of passersby.

"I'm sure I'd know our brother if I saw him," Maude would say repeatedly. "He must look like us."

"And Dad used to talk about St David's Well Bay, didn't he?" Myrtle said, never tiring of the stories her sister told about what she remembered of their parents.

"Yes, he did, and that's why we came here, because this is where we'll find our sister-in-law and our brother."

The business during those last few weeks of that first season of wartime increased instead of slowly fading. Even with the whole family working all the hours of daylight,

Marged and Huw had difficulty coping. Alice was invited to work as often as possible, releasing Audrey to assist in Piper's Café. Lilly was given clearly defined tasks to do, much to Beth's satisfaction. Freddy helped out as and when he could, spending a lot of his spare time on the sands working the helter-skelter and the swingboats with her brother Eynon, with whom he had developed a kinship not previously apparent. Beth also suspected that the pair of them sloped off early some evenings to go to the pictures. Still they needed extra hands, and small children known to Marged and Huw, who were on holiday from school, were occasionally employed to help serve.

The youngsters tried to outdo other stall-holders, shouting to attract customers and having a wonderful time, with the added bonus of getting some pocket money at the end of each day. Tin buckets and spades, flags and balloons were in constant demand. There had been no sign so far of the shortages they had been warned to expect, so stocks were not conserved. There seemed no need when there was an apparently endless supply. The war would surely be over before they need worry about supplies for the next season, eight whole months away.

The summer was one of the busiest and happiest they could remember. The youngest assistants hoped the men wouldn't come home too soon and spoil their fun. As the family's confidence in them grew and the stalls were at their busiest, they were each wrapped around several times with a white aprons and, wearing saucy hats pinned to size, they were soon selling ice-cream. They tried not to be seen licking their hands or the scoops too often, because Moll had threatened them with a cut in their pocket money if they were caught.

Youngsters ran with the donkeys too. Old Bernard Gregory walked sedately with the older patrons but when children wanted a more daring ride, one of the band of enthusiastic helpers would run behind the patient donkeys, urging them into a gallop. All the beach people were sunburnt and happiness shone in every eye. It was with surprise, therefore, that the family greeted Freddy's words one Saturday night when they were making their way homewards.

"I won't be able to help you after next week."

"Why not?" Beth demanded. "Don't tell me you're fed up with the beach already?"

Making the most out of the situation, lying with ease, Freddy said sadly, "I was devastated at my cowardice when that boat overturned, and, well, I had to prove to myself that I'm not a coward, so I ignored the fact that I'm in a reserve occupation, getting the bombs and bullets out to our boys. Sorry, Beth, but I've enlisted. It's the army uniform for me instead of a white jacket." Dramatically, he opened his arms to Beth to be hugged, and they clung together, oblivious of Huw and Marged's stare.

"Joined up voluntary, like?" Huw said, amazed.

"When you didn't have to go?" Marged asked with a frown.

"Oh Freddy, I wish you hadn't," Beth said. "Why didn't you discuss it with me? I am your fiancée."

"I knew you'd try and talk me out of it, and this is something I have to do," he said emotionally.

Moll just stared at him enigmatically. This wasn't what she had heard from others who worked at the factory. She said nothing. Perhaps her information was wrong.

"There is something I'd like to suggest," Freddy went on. "I know how desperate you are for help, so I asked Shirley Downs if she'd be willing to give up the job she found at the café in town and come here to help you. She's experienced now, waiting table at that café."

"No! We've got her mother against my wishes. That's bad enough," Huw complained. "Why should we give them work when they call us names? Just let me see her mother drunk, just once, and she goes,

171

right? So we don't want no Shirley Downs, right?"

"Wrong," Marged said. "We're too desperate to argue. Bleddyn's boys are off in two weeks' time and we'll take who we can."

Huw appealed to Moll, but she agreed with her daughter. "It's only through these next few weeks, the busiest times will be over by then. Not worth making a fuss about, Huw."

Huw walked a little way past the van and stared out across the slowly emptying promenade. He wondered how Marged could accept help from Hetty Downs after all the accusations she had made about Marged's great-grandparents cheating her family. The woman must be exaggerating about the dishonesty of Moll's parents. There was certain to be a grain of truth in the story, there usually was, but that would be all.

He ignored the struggles of the women as they put all the tablecloths and other washing into the van and fitted themselves around it. He didn't try to help, and he drove home in silence. Why did no one ever listen to his opinion? He was the man of the family, its head, yet it was as though he were invisible. He wasn't a Piper, he seethed, he was a Castle, and one day he'd remind them of that fact.

The Castle family had a party the night

before Bleddyn's two sons left for the forces. As Freddy was due to go soon afterwards, he was included in the capacity of departing friend as well as part of the family and Beth's fiancé.

Moll's house was the largest so it was there they all gathered, each wondering how to set the tone for the evening. Although it was an excuse for a family get-together, the occasion had sombre undertones as they were saying farewell to those they loved as they left to face untold dangers.

Music was the way they set the mood, Huw playing piano and Bleddyn on mandolin. They started with comic, music-hall songs, laughter a release from the inhibitions of not being sure of what role they should play. The conversation was stilted for a while, but as the flagons emptied and the singing began, the mood swiftly passed through the usual stages of laughter, nonsense and into the sentimental or downright maudlin as they sang the melodies of years ago.

Bleddyn spoke very rarely to Hannah. He didn't like the closeness she and Johnny were showing. The glances they shared were very revealing. She was too old and too worldly, with a divorce behind her. The fact of her parents being unwilling to support her told of some other event to discredit her and he didn't want his son to become embroiled in anything sordid.

Hannah sensed his disapproval and was saddened by it, but she didn't push Johnny away when he took advantage of a quiet moment and kissed her. Then he sang a love song, smiling towards the corner where she sat with a sleepy Josie and Marie. Taff looked shyly at his wife Evelyn and slid his hand into hers. Beth glanced at Freddy, but he was looking across the room towards Eynon as though they shared a secret.

It was when this late stage had been reached that Moll suddenly realised that Lilly had failed to appear. Before she could remark on the fact, Lilly came in, apologising none too sincerely for being late.

Moll looked at her, assessing her granddaughter's mood. Lilly's eyes were shining, her hair dishevelled, her face aglow with intoxication that had nothing to do with alcohol. Moll knew the signs of love-making; she had seen it on her own face many years before and on the face of her daughter. Her granddaughter had been with a man, not a casual friend either, someone to whom she was strongly attracted and she showed the headiness of having that love returned.

In Piper's Café, where Phil and Lilly had spent a blissful two hours, a cigarette burned slowly in a corner near the door. It glowed with one last burst of energy before guttering out.

Bleddyn was at a loss. He no longer ran boat trips, and the fish-and-chip shop was easily managed with the competent staff he had. Time hung heavily, and with his sons gone he had little heart for the beach. He kept looking up, expecting one of them to come and relieve him. He knew he should spend more time talking to Taff's Evelyn and Johnny's Hannah, comforting them, discussing their plans, offering help where needed, but when he met them he had nothing to say.

Subliminally he blamed them for his sons' leaving, as if by looking after them better they could somehow have prevented it. They came to see him as often as they could and sometimes stayed at the beach all day, wanting to help, to lose themselves in work. He should have been grateful, but distress and fear obliterated all compassion for them.

One morning, after heavy rain during the night, they even managed to remove the stiff and awkward covers from the swingboats and the helter-skelter by themselves. Although he didn't want to help, he was offended by their unwillingness to ask for it.

He took over the ice-cream making, using the last of their stock of powder, and spent time in the pop factory dealing with the jobs no one else wanted to do, clearing out corners, painting areas that were looking shabby, seaching for tasks he could do alone. He relieved his brother Huw of the ordering and checking the deliveries of foodstuffs, but all without any joy. It was as though he had presumed the deaths of his sons, knew they would never survive and was already in mourning.

As Marged and Beth were setting the tables with the freshly laundered gingham cloths one morning, Marged complained that the floor hadn't been washed properly the evening before.

"Look at this, there's dirty ol' ash down in this corner. Whose job was it to mop the floor?" she demanded angrily.

"Lilly's, I think," Beth said as she straightened the cutlery.

"She never does anything proper and still thinks she could take over from me," Moll added, outraged at the negligence. She collected brush and dustpan and dealt with the ash and cigarette ends. "Imagine if our first customers came and saw that," she tutted.

"I did the floor last night and I didn't miss that corner," Mrs Downs said, having overheard. "However it got there, it wasn't there when I washed the floor." Her eyes were bright as she prepared to defend herself.

Seeing her mother about to argue, Beth said curiously, "Mam, the same thing happened a few days ago. I'd done the floors the day before, and I didn't skimp on the cleaning either. I think someone pushes rubbish through for a joke or because they're too lazy."

"That's likely," Mrs Downs agreed.

Marged disagreed. "I don't think so. It isn't in the right spot to have fallen through the letter box."

With customers already banging on the door, they didn't discuss it further, but they were all puzzled about the overnight appearance of the cigarette ash. Could someone be using the place after they left? It seemed impossible. The place was firmly locked each evening and nothing had changed when they arrived in the morning, except the occasional appearance of cigarette ash. Moll sighed and put it down to tiredness. It was not surprising that after a long busy day they were less than fussy over the final cleaning job.

Aware that they were in danger of being found out, Lilly and Phil still used the café, but were more careful not to leave behind any evidence of their nocturnal visits.

Because he had been employed to work in the parks during most of the summer, it was for two weeks only that the Punch and Judy man joined the other entertainers on the sands. Twice every morning and three times every afternoon, a crowd of children and adults would gather, sitting cross-legged on the sand to watch the performance. Boos for the villain, cheers for the hero, sympathy with the victims were all interspersed with laughter. Nothing changed from year to year and it was the repetition, the knowing what came next, that gave the performance its special delight.

Audrey Castle did very little on the beach these days. Leaving Alice Potter in charge more and more often, she cleaned and ran her mother's home, leaving Moll free to help where she was needed. Besides looking after her own mother's place, Audrey also spent a lot of time helping Wilf's mother run hers.

Geraldine Thomas was a semi-invalid, rising late, going to bed early and taking a rest each afternoon. Wilf worked as a storeman in a wholesale fruiterers and besides working at the early morning market, he was training as an auxiliary fireman with special emphasis on how to deal with incendiary bombs in case of air raids.

Audrey went up to King Edward Street after she had dealt with breakfast for her mother, Maude, Myrtle, Olive and herself, and prepared a late breakfast for Mrs

Thomas. When the rush of early customers had slowed, Wilf cycled home to join her. Audrey went shopping then, shopping for her own meals as well as food for Wilf and his mother. Wilf went with her and this was the longest time during their busy days that they spent together. This was the extent of their "courting". Sometimes they went into a café and enjoyed a cup of tea, although instead of personal conversation, Audrey usual whispered criticisms on the way the place was run, comparing it unfavourably with Piper's.

She did a little housework, although most was dealt with by Mrs Thomas and Wilf, and usually stayed to get their midday meal on the table before going back home in time to cook the evening meal for her family.

"One day, my dear. One day," Wilf always whispered as they parted.

"Yes, dear, one day," she would whisper back. The remark and response were automatic, having lost their excitement over the years they had been repeated. She had almost stopped dreaming about being married to Wilf and having a home of their own. Being needed, flattered and complimented, she was content.

Despite local enquiries, the Castle family had failed to learn anything about the girls they had taken under their wing. Maude was fully recovered and Myrtle was preparing, somewhat nervously, to return to school.

Both girls were able to read simple stories, although understanding arithmetic had come easier. Huw had been right: having a reason to learn – their desire to help more fully on the beach stalls – had given them the incentive they needed to understand the mathematics of money.

Eynon was talking to the donkey man, Bernard Gregory, one day and the old man thought he remembered the family. "Maude and Myrtle are easily remembered," he told Eynon. "They sound like a music-hall act. If you call round the house one evening, I'll let you see the snapshot album, old snaps taken years ago. I've got a feeling that Maude and Myrtle are in some of them. If I'm right, then the family used to work the beach, but I can't remember what they did."

Eynon told Beth and they arranged to go to see the man together.

Bernard Gregory lived in an area just outside the town, where he had a couple of fields for his donkeys and hen houses as well as a pond for ducks. Beth and her brother Eynon walked down there one Sunday evening and found the old man carrying a bucket of warm mash to feed the chickens.

They walked around the smallholding with him, admiring the ducks as they were

180

locked up for the night and the hens and the thirty cockerels – which, he informed them, were being fattened up for Christmas. Beth shuddered. Even though she ate chicken with as much relish as the rest of her family did, she didn't like looking at the beautiful creatures and being aware of their purpose.

They went inside the cosy, over-furnished living room and Mr Gregory handed them three battered photograph albums. He pointed out the children, then very young, whom he thought were the sisters and invited Beth and Eynon to take the albums home in the hope that they might trigger some memories. But as to who Maude and Myrtle were, he insisted he could not remember.

Beth came away convinced he knew more, that his memories of the children were clearer than he admitted.

"Perhaps it's not his story to tell," Beth said thoughtfully.

"Or it might involve a juicy bit of scandal," Eynon said.

"You don't think Granny Moll or Mam and Dad are pretending not to know, do you?"

"Why not? You can't imagine they're connected to St David's Well, without someone recognising them, can you?"

Eynon had persuaded Alice to go to the

pictures with him several times and had managed a few brief kisses. One rainy evening when they had run from the picture house and were very wet, she invited him in to dry his hair.

"What about your Dad?" he asked

"Fast asleep by this time, don't worry," she whispered as she opened the front door.

They walked on tiptoe along the dark passage and went into the kitchen beyond. As Alice filled the kettle and set it to boil, upstairs her father stirred. He could barely hear a sound, but some sixth sense told him there was someone in the house. Not bothering to find anything for his feet and not possessing a dressing gown, he moved quietly down the stairs, walking with his body slanted, his shoulders leaning against the grimy walls.

Eynon turned off the gas under the kettle and said, "Why don't we go upstairs, Alice?" She took his hand and they had actually begun to climb the stairs when they saw Mr Potter on his way down. "Who's there with you, Alice?" he shouted and Eynon tried to leave.

The door was stiff and the man was moving very fast. Eynon abandoned the door and ran down the passage. There might be a high wall, but the approach of Alice's father promised him wings!

The uneven footsteps scurrying along the

bare floor behind him were frightening. The man ran leaning against the wall to stay upright but it didn't slow him down and he reached out and gripped Eynon's shoulder painfully tight.

"I only came in for a moment," Eynon said. "I wanted the lav, see."

"The lav's out the back, not upstairs like the posh Piper family."

"I'm a Castle," Eynon said weakly. For someone supposed to be deaf, this one was quick to understand what was being said, Eynon thought. He hadn't seen Alice repeat the words slowly so her father could lip-read. Confused by the pain, he struggled to escape the man's firm grasp.

"It's all right, Dad." Alice tried to pull her father's fingers free. She could see that Eynon was in pain.

Mr Potter gave Eynon a powerful push before letting him go and he slithered along the passage, fell but immediately recovered and made for the door. Alice opened the door and whispered, "See you tomorrow," before he was out in the night and running down the road. His shoulders hurt, but before he reached the corner he was laughing.

Marged and Moll looked through the albums sent by Mr Gregory but saw no one they recognised. Marged showed several of

183

the snaps to Huw but he was clearly not interested – although she did see him looking through the tattered pages once, when he thought she wasn't looking.

"See anyone you know?" she asked and he shook his head and threw the book down.

The girls browsed through the pages time after time, refusing to give up hope of finding someone they knew, but eventually the albums were put aside, another dead end.

Eynon considered himself one of Freddy's closest friends since their talk regarding conscription. When he spoke of him he referred to him as "my butty", the local name for a close friend. So when he was walking along the main road with his sister late one evening, after a second visit to Mr Gregory to return the albums, and saw Freddy coming out of the picture house with another girl, he quickly led Beth away so she wouldn't see them. He was bubbling with barely controlled laughter, which eventually exploded as they turned a corner and left the main road behind, along with any possibility of the couple being seen by his puzzled sister.

"Eynon? What's struck you as so funny?" Beth asked with a frown. "You're always laughing these days." The frown faded and she began to smile, amused by his helpless laughter. They were soon sharing the merriment even though Beth still didn't know the reason.

"That Bernard Gregory, he's got them long teeth and miserable eyes," Eynon spluttered between bouts of laughter. "He's beginning to look like one of his donkeys."

At any other time Beth would have been angry with her young brother for being so unkind, but with laughter already irresistibly out of control, she giggled louder. They went home in a cheerful mood but with no news for the two girls searching for their brother.

"He found a few more photos of them but couldn't remember a thing," Beth giggled.

"We'd have done better to ask his donkeys," Eynon gasped, his eyes full of tears.

Irritated with their stupid behaviour, Marged told them to "be'ave", and got on with her knitting.

"Eh up, boy," Eynon said when he and Freddy met the following day. "You owe me a favour."

"What's that, then?"

"Saw you and some girl coming out of the pictures and I made sure our Beth didn't see you, that's what! I dragged her round that corner so quick she must have thought Hitler was coming!"

"Oh, that was only Shirley Downs. Her mam works for your mam and dad. I met

185

her inside and we walked out chatting, that's all. Tell Beth if you like, but she won't be very bothered," Freddy said. He hoped Eynon wouldn't tell, however. He and Beth were supposed to be careful with their money and visits to the pictures were forbidden as unnecessary extravagances. He felt a surge of resentment. He enjoyed the pictures, Beth didn't, so it was easy for her to give up going, pretending she was depriving herself of a treat!

Shirley was different. She loved the glamour of the beautiful women and the grand houses and the suggestions of wealth portrayed. She loved dancing too and twice they had slipped into the local dance hall, pretended surprise at meeting and danced happily for several hours. Beth and he never went dancing and she worked rather anonymously in the beach café, hidden away in the kitchen most of the time, so it was unlikely she would be told. He was recognised, of course, having worked in the town's main gentlemen's outfitters until recently, but Shirley Downs was such a good dancer and such lively company, he thought it worth the risk.

With news of the war shown on the Gaumont British News every day, many went just to see a pictorial version of the latest events. The next day Beth decided she would like to go, since the newsreel was said to contain pictures of the new Home Guard. Huw and Uncle Bleddyn had joined and she had a fanciful idea that they might be shown. Once again, Freddy had to pay to see a programme he had already seen right through. It was as they were coming out that someone remarked on his enthusiasm for the film.

"So good you've seen it twice?" one of his friends called. Quickly, Freddy hustled Beth out on to the street, but the young man followed. "Oh, aye, a different girl too. You old devil, Freddy Clements!"

"Get lost! You've mixed me up with someone else."

Beth stared back at the young man as Freddy hurried her along pavements which were wet after several days of rain.

"Ignore him, Beth. Stirring up trouble is his idea of fun. Start a war he could with his so-called 'only joking'!"

He was irritable when Beth tried to question him and when they got back to Sidney Street, Beth didn't invite him in. She was frowning as she went into the living room, where her brother Eynon was the only occupant.

"He's always bumping into that Shirley Downs," she said half to herself.

"He told you then, did he?" Eynon said. He was studying the evening paper, quite unconcerned, and didn't see the shock that crossed his sister's face. "I told him I wouldn't split as you'd be sure to get the wrong idea. Met her inside he did, nothing suspicious about that, is there?"

"Nothing," she said, the words forced out of tight lips. "Except that we're trying to save and he'd promised not to go without me." Memories of their laughter the previous evening returned and she glared at her brother, who was trying to read the newspaper, with suspicion in her dark eyes. "You saw them, didn't you?"

"Yes, I did, and he was upset, afraid I'd tell you, so he must have decided to tell you himself." He tutted and looked superior. "Fancy getting married to a bloke and not trusting him. Asking for trouble that is, sis. He's all right, our Freddy. Real butties we are."

Freddy walked around the town, restless and unable to face going home, getting to bed and trying to sleep. Having signed on for the armed forces was no longer an adventure, a bit of fun. It was frightening. Now he was on the edge of losing his job again, and being made to do something about which he had no choice until he was called up, all because the foreman had it in for him and complained about his time-keeping. He felt cut off from everything that had once seemed normal. He was detached from Beth too: his happiest moments had been spent with Shirley during the past weeks and instead of feeling guilty about that, he felt trapped.

He no longer felt safe and secure. A door was opening and hc was going to step through with no idea what was on the other side. When he tried to analyse how he felt, he had a premonition of death. There was no one he could talk to. Perhaps his thoughts were usual at such a time and everyone went through a period of morbid imagination? He needed someone to tell him this was so, and that he would feel different once he met others and found companionship and confidence from the numbers involved. He wouldn't be alone, he kept telling himself, and alone was how he felt at the moment.

The following morning he went to the bank and withdrew the remainer of his and Beth's savings. What was the point of leaving it there if he was going to die?

Mrs Downs again found a small amount of tobacco ash in the corner of the café one morning and she told Moll. "This time it couldn't have been pushed through the letter box. It's too far away and so neatly placed there had to be an intruder, or someone wasn't doing their job!"

"It has to be inefficient cleaning," Moll

insisted. "The place is securely locked."

When Huw told her he had cleaned the floors the previous evening, she still argued that it was the only explanation. A few days later the same thing happened and this time it was Mrs Downs who had dealt with the mop and bucket.

"I'll do it myself tonight," Moll said. "Then I'll believe it's something other than sloppy cleaning. Right?" She and Huw both suspected that the culprit was Mrs Downs, the only non-family member in the café team. The woman did her job but resentment was there. The occasional snide remark showed it. Huw believed the mystery of the litter on the floor was nothing more than Mrs Downs trying to aggravate Moll and Marged, and recommended they forgot it. As usual, they ignored him.

When they left, the floor gleaming with the thorough treatment Moll had given it, Mrs Downs dropped a few matches, throwing them unnoticed behind the door as Marged and Huw locked up. That'll show her, she thought. Accusing me of not washing the floor properly! Well, Moll Piper left herself open for that one! She enjoyed telling Shirley when she got home.

Shirley still worked for the small café in the town, having refused to consider working for the Pipers. But she hoped that the following year she might be offered a full-time summer job now an approach had been made. Freddy would put in a good word for her, she thought with a smile. The beach was a more exciting place to work than a café patronised by the boring and the elderly who came to sit and gossip. She would pick up a nice tan and put on pretty dresses instead of the black dress and white apron she was presently forced to wear.

She met Freddy on the day he finally got his cards from the factory. He had overslept again and when he walked in, to the jeers and cheers of his workmates, his wages were made up and he was told to leave.

Shirley had been sent to the wholesaler to try and buy some tomatoes for the café where she worked, and was carrying the box out of the entrance when Freddy approached.

"Freddy! What a bit of luck. Can you help me to carry this box? It's cutting into my side something chronic."

He walked with her back to the café, then stayed and was rewarded with a cup of tea and a cake.

"What's up?" Shirely asked as she pretended to take his money. "Why aren't you in work? Your papers haven't come already, have they?"

"I was sacked for bad timekeeping. You'd think they needed people desperate enough to overlook a few minutes, wouldn't you?

Where's this war effort we're being told about? A few minutes late and I'm sacked."

"I bet it wasn't the first time." Shirley grinned. "Late nights and early mornings don't go well together, do they? Dancing – pictures..." she teased.

"Fancy going to the dance tonight? There's a live band on."

"And I bet there's not one of them under fifty," she laughed. "Yes, I'll come, Freddy. We won't have many more, will we?"

"Don't say that!"

"I only meant for a while, you daft thing. You'll be home for leaves with stories to make me laugh sooner than you think. And this nuisance of a war won't go on for ever. We'll celebrate every leave, shall we? You and me? And we'll really celebrate when the war ends and you come home for good."

She could see he was still unhappy so she added, "In fact, let's really celebrate tonight, shall we? Just for the practice?"

Promise was in her dark brown eyes and neither of them heard when her employer twice called for her to serve some new-comers who were becoming impatient.

Mrs Downs went in first when they got to the café next morning. She opened the door wide and held it for the others to enter. Moll saw the matches on the floor and looked accusingly at Mrs Downs, who stared at her enigmatically.

"Did you just drop these?" she asked, pointing at the pink-tipped matchsticks.

"How could I? I've just opened the door for you. What are you looking at me like that for? You did the floor. Going to show us all how it should be done, weren't you?"

"You left them there," Moll said. "You dropped them last night as we were leaving."

"Ridiculous!" Mrs Downs replied angrily.

"Look at them. The ends have softened and spread. They were put on a wet floor, wet like when we all went through the door last night."

"You can't accuse me, we all left at the same time."

"But you were expecting me to find them," Moll insisted. "It was written on your face." Taking money from the float she handed Mrs Downs her wages. "I'm not telling you to go because of a few matches, whatever you choose to tell your friends. I can't work with people I don't trust."

"I'll work the day. I'll stay in the kitchen and do the dishes, you'll be hard put to manage on your own." Mrs Downs was beginning to regret her stupid action.

Marged saw this, and also saw the queue already forming. She forestalled Moll's refusal. "She's right, Mam. We're going to be busy today and we'll be glad of your help today, Mrs Downs. Thank you."

How stupid of Moll to sack someone over a bit of nonsense that should have been treated as a joke! Staff were more and more difficult to find, with women being offered good wages in factories and taking jobs previously undertaken by men. They needed to build goodwill, to have people they could call on when the new season began. It seemed a long way off, but it was essential to look forward and plan ahead.

Mrs Downs was smiling when she left. She was leaving sooner than she had hoped, but the scene was set for a revenge for which she had waited a very long time.

Six

"What about painting the helter-skelter and the swingboats red, white and blue?" Huw suggested one morning as they were leaving for the beach.

"That's ridiculous, Huw," was Marged's instant response. "They've always been yellow and red."

"That's no reason not to change them. All the businesses in town are doing something to make people proud of being British, so why shouldn't we?"

"We'll keep them the same, Huw. Mam wouldn't hear of making them so gaudy."

"Gaudy? It's patriotic!"

"Why d'you always want to be different, Huw?" Marged asked in exasperation. "Whatever will you think of next?"

"There was something else," he said, eyeing her to assess his chances.

Marged put down the bag she was filling with the laundry and stared at him, lips tight, a look of irritation on her face. "Look, it's Piper's and we'll keep everything the way it was first planned. Right?" She bustled around gathering everything they needed to take with them. But curiosity got the better of her and she asked, "What was it then, this other fancy idea you had?"

"The Home Guard need somewhere to sit and have a cup of tea during their shift, and the fire-watchers and the wardens pass there often. I thought Bleddyn and I could take it in turns to provide teas and perhaps a cake or sandwich during the evenings. What d'you think?"

"I think we're going to be late, and you and Bleddyn have enough to do helping to keep my business running. Piper's is as much as you can manage without idling your time chatting to the Home Guard and their buddies."

"*Your* business?" He said the words slowly. "Your business is run by me and my brother, and we're Castles, not Pipers. It hasn't been Pipers running things since you married me. Bleddyn and I do most of the work, you run the café. Without us you wouldn't last a month. Yet I can't offer an opinion. The time will come, Marged *Castle*, when Bleddyn and I will have had enough. Right?"

Halfway down the stairs, Beth and Lilly listened in horror. They hated hearing their parents argue. Lately the arguments were increasing and they were always about Piper's.

"Dad's right, mind," Beth said. "Gran and Auntie Audrey are the only Pipers left. The name should be changed. Dad is head of the family. It should be called Castle's."

"You think the man should be in charge whatever the situation?" Lilly sneered. "I don't think so. If our Ronnie and Eynon gave up the beach and I married, there's no chance *my* husband would ever be in charge!"

"I don't think that's right."

"You ought to be thinking the same," Lilly went on. "Imagine if you took over. Your Freddy would never keep his hands out of the till for a start. And as for work, well, it isn't his favourite pastime, is it? No, with Freddy in charge you'd fade to nothing in

196

weeks. Your Freddy hasn't the head for business, he'll never succeed."

Beth continued to defend Freddy but her heart wasn't in it. She had the strongest of feelings that Lilly was right.

In a small town like St David's Well nothing could remain a secret for very long. Several people asked Beth whether she and Freddy had broken off their engagement and more than one commiserated before asking for confirmation, having seen Freddy once or twice with Shirley Downs.

She soon became adept at lying, insisting that she knew and understood about Freddy's addiction to the films and that he occasionally met Shirley, also a film fan, inside.

She told him quite casually what she had been told, and he said apologetically, "Sorry, Beth, but I really enjoy the pictures and, knowing that you aren't so keen, well, I sometimes go on my own."

"That's all right, Freddy, I'm not going to be the jealous girlfriend, just because I'm wearing your ring." She smiled and added, "Just as well you enjoy the pictures. When you're away from home it will be a way of filling in the lonely hours, won't it?"

Freddy hugged her but in his mind he saw crowds of girls filling his hours, drawn to him by his uniform, begging to be taken out to have fun. Not girls like Beth who was his safe, comfortable future, but girls like Shirley Downs offering excitement during his short-lived freedom.

When Moll came to the house to ask for a lift to the café a couple of days after Mrs Downs had left, Beth said, "Granny Moll, all the shops in town are dressing their windows in red, white and blue to show their support for the forces. Couldn't we do the same? Patriotism helps the war effort, doesn't it?"

"Nonsense, girl. Paint to support the war effort ready for next season? The war will be over and done with long before that!"

"You'd better ask her to come back," Huw said when he, Marged and Moll discussed the departure of Mrs Downs.

"Get her back? I thought you didn't want her to work for us in the first place," Moll said irritably. "Worse than a woman for changing your mind you are, Huw Castle!"

"She's a nasty bit of work and you know the way she gossips," he said, "but if we're desperate for help until the end of September, she might be the simplest choice."

It was eight thirty and they were on their way to the café. Beth had said she would catch the bus and join them later. As Marged put the key in the lock and opened the door an unpleasant smell met them.

"What the 'ell—" Huw went into the

198

kitchen, sniffing and pulling faces. "Smells like something's crawled in and died!"

The three of them searched the whole place but found nothing. The smell was strongest in the kitchen and with nothing but fresh air beneath the concrete floor of the café and a solid wooden floor beneath the kitchen area, there didn't seem to be anywhere else to search. Opening the windows and doors as wide as they'd go, they started preparing for the day.

The smell increased as the hours passed. The sun was shining cheerfully and it was one of the hottest days so far that year. Disinfectant was poured everywhere but the smell returned to greet them next morning.

Lilly and Phil were still using the café for their secret meetings but even passion was defeated by the foulness of the air. They dared to leave the door open, hoping no one would walk up the metal steps and come in to request tea and sandwiches. Giggling at the unexpected problem, stretching the joke and laughter to the utmost, they didn't stay long, choosing instead to go separately through the roads and lanes to the park where bushes and trees gave some privacy.

They felt complacent about Phil's deferment from call-up. As the only member of staff able to run both the shop and repair-workshop, he was certain he was safe as, without him, the business would have to close down.

During the last days before Freddy had to report to camp for training, he and Beth saw each other often, but there was a coolness between them that neither mentioned and which Freddy couldn't understand. He thought the explanation about his love of the cinema had satisfied Beth's initial dismay at the rumours about himself and Shirley, and there didn't seem to be anything else amiss.

He came to the beach late in the afternoons, helped the family to clear up and tried, with the rest, to solve the mystery of the dreadful stink. He often went back to Marged's for a late supper but always left early, explaining thoughtfully that he knew Beth rose early and needed her sleep.

Once out of sight of the house in Sidney Street, he hurried to the flat above the newspaper shop and called to see Shirley. Besides the pictures – the town offered a generous choice with three cinemas which all changed their programme halfway through the week – there was also dancing.

Freddy still planned to marry Beth; it was the best way of ensuring a good future. The Pipers and Castles owned entertainments, stalls, cafés and ice-cream and pop factories and their business was sound. He would always have to work, but not too much. He believed that Beth offered him an easy life married to a family who were never likely to be short of the readies. He had to hang on to Beth. He thought he loved her in his own way, but he wanted some fun first.

There was an air of exhilaration about Eynon during those last days on the sands, a hint of a secret about to be told. Blowing up balloons to decorate the stalls to attract the dwindling crowds, he popped one behind Beth, laughing at her alarm. He marked Marged's best mirror with a candle so it looked as though it was cracked, and couldn't contain his laughter when she stared at it in horror before telling her it was a trick. He livened them up with his cheerful presence both on the beach and at home, and nothing was too much trouble. He had never been so helpful or willing. Huw and Marged smiled and put it down to his newly awakening interest in girls. When he asked for a day off Marged didn't hesitate.

"You've worked so hard you deserve it," she smiled, handing him a ten-shilling note. "Take this and give yourself a good time."

Without explanation and also without denying the many hints about a girl that issued from Huw's lips during breakfast, he left early. Long before the post arrived.

It was when they got home from the long

day at the beach that Marged picked up the letter from the doormat.

"Funny," she frowned. "It looks like our Eynon's writing."

"Some joke I'll bet. He's full of nonsense at the moment – in fact, I'm beginning to wonder whether that stink at the café that's beginning to smell fishy isn't down to him. Some stink bomb from the joke shop or something."

The letter with Eynon's handwriting on it was puzzling and Marged stared at it for a while before opening it. She frowned, then glanced at the clock, automatically thinking as a caring mother. "Funny, he didn't say what time he'd be back," she said vaguely. "He'll have to have something cold." She opened the envelope, unfolded the sheet of paper, and screamed.

Huw ran to her and snatched it from her trembling hands. "What does he mean, he's joined the army?" he demanded as though Marged had the answers. "He isn't old enough for call-up till next year!"

"He's volunteered. He's old enough to volunteer," Marged wailed.

Phone calls and visits to the police, the army recruitment office and every other organisation they could think of to demand his return were met with the solid stone walls of officialdom. Eynon was old enough and he was on his way to the camp where

202

initial training would take place. They weren't even told which one. All they could do was wait until he made contact.

"There *is* a war on," the sergeant in the recruitment office reminded them with unnecessary sarcasm.

"So we're short of another pair of hands," was one of Huw's comments the morning following a sleepless night.

"Is that all you can think about?" Marged said unfairly. "Eynon, our youngest, has gone to war!"

"Tomorrow we open the café as usual, and we help others to forget their war for an hour or two. We need someone extra to help on the stalls." He spoke firmly, determined that Marged wouldn't collapse into despair.

"I'll call and ask Mrs Downs to come back, I suppose," she said quietly. "I'll have to grovel a bit, but compared with our Eynon running away, a bit of grovelling isn't important." She looked at the face of her husband, seeing the lines of distress there, she was reminded that for him too this was a difficult situation to deal with; she wasn't alone. "He's only a boy," she said and they hugged, seeking comfort from each other.

A second letter arrived a few days later, a letter full of apologies and cheerful with news of Eynon's first few days as a soldier. He told them he was already making new friends and wondered whether he could bring a couple of the lads home on his first leave, as several had never seen the sea.

"He has the right attitude, our Eynon," Huw said emotionally. "He'll do well, for sure."

"There are a couple of camp beds in the loft." Marged was already planning Eynon's first leave. "And we'll keep that tin of salmon. It's his favourite with a bit of salad."

Eynon was bitterly regretting his decision to join up. Why had he listened to Freddy? The glorified portrayal of adventure and brave acts had stirred his imagination and thrilled his young mind, but the reality was very different from his dreams.

The exercise had been something he had looked forward to with excitement. He considered himself a fit young man, running everywhere and rarely catching a bus. He was sure he'd show the rest how things should be done. He hadn't been prepared for the long hours of marching with heavy kit and little prospect of a rest. Nor had the constant punishments entered into his thoughts. He was there because he had chosen to be, so why punish him for mistakes he couldn't avoid?

His attempts at humour were considered childlike and when he heard the others talking about their lives before they had joined up he realised how sheltered his own life had been. He was smaller than most and that too had been pounced upon as a likely subject for teasing.

Then there was Kipper, so called because of his constant smoking and the fact that he was so dark skinned and thin. He was a sadistic bully and as soon as he saw Eynon, he knew he had found his victim. For a while others took Eynon's side but they quickly realised that if they wanted a reasonably peaceful existence they would have to turn the proverbial blind eye. Kipper tolerated no one else's opinion. After just ten days, Eynon was on his own.

It wasn't the unseen punches and kicks, or the constant "jokes" of making his kit filthy just before inspection, or even the nail that had been driven up inside his boots before a five-mile run. It was the loneliness. He missed his family more than he had imagined. He had no one to talk to and he didn't dare write home complaining.

People walking to the station in a steady stream to see husbands, sons and loved ones off was an almost daily sight. When Beth walked with Freddy one late August morning, her emotions were mixed. In tune with others on the same duty as herself, she looked suitably sad, but inside there was an air of relief. Ashamed of the sensation, she was nevertheless filled with the excitement of being on the verge of something new.

She had been dreading this day, and like many others wondered how she would cope. To her surprise she now knew she would cope very well. She couldn't admit that to Freddy of course and although they said very little, she promised him she would write regularly and would miss him something awful.

Assurances were given that he would miss her too, but to the newly awakened Beth the words had the discordant ring of insincerity. She wondered whether, like herself, he welcomed the break from their very close and long relationship. The saying "absence makes the heart grow fonder" seemed to her at that moment to be wishful thinking.

Their final kiss was less than heartwarming; with others watching and shedding a few tears, she felt uneasy, aware that her falseness matched Freddy's as she clung to him briefly, anxious to be gone.

Mrs Downs returned to help in Piper's Café and the smell lingered in the air for a while but soon faded. She had removed the kipper she had nailed to the back of a drawer and had thrown it into the tide. Huw watched and frowned but said nothing.

"All the place needed was a good scrub," she said with a superior tilt to her head.

Bleddyn lived for letters from his sons. He didn't hear from either of them often, but heard a little news from the letters Taff wrote to Evelyn.

Hannah didn't make many attempts to keep in touch with Bleddyn. Knowing how much he disapproved of his younger son's choice, she didn't know how to be supportive now Johnny was away. She wanted to call, but Bleddyn had made his feelings quite clear on the evening of the farewell party and she was too unsure of her welcome.

She visited Huw and Marged, taking the children and staying for a cup of tea. At these times she was able to impart small items of news, which she hoped would be passed on to Johnny's father. She still continued to help Maude and Myrtle with their reading and Moll was always pleased to see her. The news went in the other direction too. She was able to write to Johnny and tell him of the daily happenings and keep him in touch with the Piper businesses while he was away.

The news of embarkation leave was something Bleddyn was dreading. The night the news had reached him, via a brief letter and a visit from Taff's wife, Evelyn, he was unable to relax. He went for a walk along the edge of the tide, the gentle shushing of the waves soothing his taut nerves. Sitting on the wall, a man's overcoat draped around her, was Olive.

"Can't sleep either?" he asked, sitting beside her and staring out to sea.

"I know it doesn't really make sense, but I feel this is the closest I can get to Ronnie," she said. "He's over there somewhere, beyond that land and over another great stretch of water, but this is the closest I can get."

"I can't explain why I came," Bleddyn said. "I just couldn't sleep and this seemed a good place to come and think back on how good life was until this damned war opened its hungry jaws and took our boys."

"I wish I'd appreciated the happy times more," Olive sighed. "I fought Ronnie, told him I hated working on the beach. I tried so hard to persuade him to leave and get a better job. Now, seeing how people need the nonsense, the laughter and the escape we offer here ... well, I know its value and wish I'd known it before. Ronnie and I would have been happier. I wish I'd helped more and complained less."

"I've been told that both my sons will be coming home on embarkation leave, and you know what that means."

"It means you have to hide your fears and be cheerful and let them be happy." She smiled. "We'll all be accomplished actors by the time this lot is over, won't we?"

"You're right, and they'll go back smiling. Thank you, love, you're a good kid and Ronnie is a lucky devil to be married to you."

"I'll make sure he knows it when he comes on leave." She smiled again. "How are Evelyn and Hannah coping? They must be frightened too. I know; I've been through it, remember."

"Evelyn is putting on a brave face – for my sake, I think – but I don't know about Hannah. She – well, she can't be a serious girlfriend for our Johnny, can she? She so much older and with two children an' all."

"From what I've seen of them it's very serious. Johnny loves her very much, and her children. You should go and see them; it's what Johnny would want, you keeping an eye on them for him."

"I don't think she'd want to see me, I've never been very friendly."

"Then it's time you were." She smiled to ease the criticism and said, "Come on, what about a bag of chips before we go for the bus?"

"Chips? When I run a chip shop most of the year?"

"Why not? You can pretend you're checking on the competition!"

The beach was as full as it could possibly be. Whereas in low season families came and found a circle of sand to call their own, now the tide was high during the afternoon and there were so many trippers flooding into the bay that there wasn't the space to offer any prospect of temporary ownership. Buckets and spades, sun hats and windmills as well as the rest of the paraphernalia of the day out became mingled with the group next along, and cardigans disappeared under sand as people walked past trying to find a place to sit and spread themselves out. The smell of wet sand filled everyone's nostrils and the children glowed with the sun and happiness that only a holiday beach can provide. And still they came. Marged and Beth were serving meals without a moment's rest from the time they opened the café doors.

The wind got up during the afternoons, and Beth ran up and down the steps gathering trays and returning deposits, afraid to leave the trays of china for the users to return, knowing from past experience that some would be lost under the spraying sand or be broken under careless feet. The number of spoons they lost each season was countless, even though the deposit slip clearly marked every item.

Shirley was back working in the paper shop. As with so many other businesses, the men had disappeared and women were in demand. She went back with fewer hours and a ten-shilling increase in wages.

She had worked in the shop for as long as she could remember, standing beside her father and mother, going with her dad to the wholesaler to collect the odd magazine and to pay the weekly account. Helping to carry newspapers out on to the bogie cart her father had made for the paper boys to use on their deliveries was something she had done as soon as she was strong enough, and when she was eight she had been given a round of her own, with money at the end of each week.

She had been only six when her father had left to live somewhere else, and twelve years old when he disappeared from her life completely. She remembered the confusion of her thoughts when she was told he would never come back. For a long time she had looked at people in the street hoping it had been a mistake and he would suddenly appear.

Now she looked at the old bogie cart and wondered whether she could tow it behind her as she had done years ago. Experimentally she pulled it around the small yard behind the shop. If the paper boy let them down again, she might try. Pulling it up Grantly Rise and Channel View Avenue might be less of a struggle than having that heavy bag on her shoulders, she thought with a wry smile.

Shirley was puzzled by her mother's attitude towards the Pipers. She had been told the story about her mother's grandparents losing the business because of Moll Piper's grandparents, but there were stories about lost wealth in every family, apocryphal, the stuff of legends. She had always thought the story about the Pipers was the same. Her mother had hinted about something else, something equally wicked, but Shirley had put that down to a desire to keep the story alive, to continue the hatred, nothing more.

Why was her mother working for the Pipers, whom she insisted she hated? And why, after being dismissed for causing mischief, had she been willing to return?

The Castle family believed that they had lost all their young men and there were no more surprises in store, but Lilly was still to become the final victim of the urgent demands from the government for more soldiers. The shop where Phil worked in apparent safety had been handed over to a fifty-six-year-old man, releasing Phil for call-up. He went just three weeks after being told that the decision on his deferment had been revised.

Lilly was devastated and, because of the situation, couldn't even seek sympathy from friends and family. From being the one member of the Castle team to work hard at avoiding work, she needed to pack as much into her day as possible. She needed to fill the hours and also tire herself for sleep. After only a few days the plan began to work, and she found the untypical enthusiasm exhausted her so much that bed was welcome. In fact she fought against tiredness sometimes during the afternoons.

She interfered with everyone's tasks, disrupting the routines that had been set out at the begining of the season and were working well. She often seemed to be on the verge of tears but Beth, instead of being irritated by her, was patient and understanding. Beth hadn't been told the reason for Lilly's unhappiness but as her sister hadn't been out during the evening for weeks, she guessed that her secret boyfriend had either left her or had been called up.

Lilly was desperate to fill the hours, and even found some extra cleaning to keep herself from grieving. As the secret lover of a married man, she couldn't expect to have news of him, as any letters would go to his wife. Until he was given leave and could slip away for an hour, she wouldn't know where he was or how he was feeling. He had already told her he wouldn't be able to write.

"Everything I write will be read before it's

posted," he had explained, "and I can't risk anyone finding out about us. Not yet, not until I decide the time is right for my wife to accept that our marriage is over. I have to choose my time, love, for your sake. You can see that, can't you?"

Since he had never been so specific before about his intentions to leave his wife, Lilly was deliriously happy. Of course he couldn't write while he was away, she understood that, but as soon as his wife could cope with it she would be told. For herself and Phil, it would mean their love would be out in the open for everyone to see how happy they were. Once the war was over, life would be bliss.

Eynon sat in the lorry that was taking them into mid-Wales for an exercise and listened to the chatter all around him, news and opinions and confidences which he was not allowed to share. His leg ached badly from last night's violent kicking after he had inadvertently touched Kipper's bed. He wondered how he was going to climb mountains and march over rough ground for endless hours and cope with the pain.

The lorry lurched to a stop and they began to jump down.

"Wait there, Titch," Kipper growled as Eynon stood and allowed the others to get down. "Wait there till I say you can jump."

"Why don't you give up this tormenting and leave me alone," Eynon sighed. The response was a punch that sent him reeling, staggering against the sides of the vehicle and making the dark night even blacker.

He was aware of voices, of soft laughter, and then the lorry crunched into gear and began to move. He had to get out. There would be no excuses allowed if he lost contact with the others. He scrambled over the tailgate and, although the lorry had picked up speed, he dropped off. There was a sharp bend at that moment and the driver, with a view hampered by the low lights, didn't see it until he had almost passed it. The resulting swerve as Eynon fell caused him to knock his head on the corner of the lorry, and he fell and rolled until his fall was stopped by a boulder placed to mark the edge of the road.

He wasn't sure how long he had lain there. It was only very slowly that his memory returned. It was still dark. Perhaps it had been no more than a few minutes. He stood, groggily wondering which direction to take, and tried to walk, staggering along holding his head in his hands. He had to find the others. He listened but there was a ringing in his ears that made it impossible to hear anything else. Perhaps he was deaf like Alice Potter's father and would only be able to walk by leaning against a wall? Holding back the need to sob, he made his way back in the direction he thought he had been travelling.

Huw was nervous when Mrs Downs was in the café. He avoided talking to her and when he had any instruction he asked his wife to convey it.

"Come on, our Dad," Beth teased, "she isn't exactly a dangerous woman, is she? Poor dab, she lost her husband in a road accident more than ten years ago and lives in a poky little flat above a newsagent; what can she possibly do to harm you?"

Huw didn't tell her, but he lived with the fear that one day Hetty Downs would tell his family the truth. He watched the woman, convinced that she was planning some disaster in which he would be the central player.

Marged was pleased with the way the woman worked, often staying late when the day had been particularly busy and never complaining about sharing the tedium of washing endless dishes and cleaning the same things day after day until they all felt like robots.

September dragged lazily on and the people who had booked into hotels and boarding houses diminished to the families and couples not tied to school holidays. Fewer children being around changed the mood, but the buses and trains still brought day-trippers. Now the busiest days were at the weekend, when coaches would growl their way into the car parks and trains puffed their fussy way into the railway station, unloading streams of excited hordes set on having a day to remember. By this time, many of the beach traders were weary and longing for a break in the daily round, but none of their tiredness showed in their faces. They all treated the newcomers as they had treated the first to arrive, months before, determinedly making sure their holiday or their day out sent them home with only good memories.

Bleddyn's two sons came home for their embarkation leave and they chose to spend it working on the beach with the rest of the family, insisting that they too needed the memories to see them through whatever lay ahead. Taff's wife, Evelyn, came with him when she could, but working in a factory meant shift work and sleeping at odd times of the day. Hannah was less willing to spend time with the Castles, still afraid of being made to feel unwelcome at this emotional time. But one afternoon, she brought her two girls down and stood with Johnny as he served ice-cream and sold buckets and spades, flags, balloons and windmills and the rest. The day was warm for so late in the season and Josie and Marie stripped their clothes off with her help, giggling behind the stall, and got into their bathers.

"You can't go in the sea, mind," Hannah warned the disappointed girls. "I didn't bring my bathers with me and you can't go in on your own." There were wails of disappointment but she was adamant.

During a lull, Bleddyn left the swingboats to come over and talk to them. He heard of their dismay and said, "I've got my dippers on under these white trousers, I can go in and look after them if you like, Hannah?"

Hannah was about to refuse, belligerent in preparation for the rebuffs she had expected, but seeing the rather anxious expression in his face, she changed her mind, smiled, thanked him and told the girls they could paddle after all.

Taking an inflatable beach ball with them they walked to the water's edge, the girls glancing back occasionally for their mother's encouraging wave. Then they forgot about her as Bleddyn played games and they were soon shrieking with laughter with the rest.

Bleddyn was happier than he had been for a long time during the hour that followed. He lifted the children one after the other and, wading out, allowed them to kick in the waves. He pretended to struggle to blow up the beach ball until the nonsense brought them to their knees laughing at his uselessness.

"Mam can do it easy," they said scornfully when he allowed the air to escape once more. He blew up the ball with their shouted encouragement and threw it for them, fell when he missed it, and generally acted the clown.

Hannah and Johnny were laughing too when the three of them walked back up to the stall.

"Two delightful youngsters you've got there, Hannah," Bleddyn said. "I hope you'll bring them to see me some time."

"Thank you," Hannah said hesitantly. "They'd like that."

"They've just invited themselves to tea in Piper's Café," Bleddyn went on. "And I'm told that it's to be beans on toast with tomato sauce like their Uncle Johnny makes it," he teased, looking at his son.

The nights were drawing in more quickly as summer came to its end but the gloomy evening seemed less so that day as Bleddyn walked home, still smiling at the happiness of his time with Marie and Josie and the glimmer of understanding with their mother and his younger son.

When Johnny was helping at the beach a few days later, Bleddyn decided he would call on Hannah and the girls.

"No, I won't come in," he said when he presented himself at the neat little house near the centre of town. "I just came to tell you that I'm there if you need anything, and if you and Marie and Josie would like to come and spend a little time near the beach, well, I'd like to see you, that's all." He turned and walked away. Hannah had been slow to reply and he didn't want to cause embarrassment to her or himself if she did not want to give him any of her time.

He was closing the gate to the small front garden when she called, "Mr Castle, thank you. That's very kind and, if you like, you can come to tea on Sunday and the girls will make you a cake."

Bleddyn turned and nodded. "Thanks, Hannah. I'll come – when, about four?"

She smiled agreement and he went home proud of his good sense in contacting the little family whom his son loved so much. He had gained three friends where he might have lost a son. He must remember to thank young Olive.

Hannah took a deep breath. Now she had to tell her parents.

Marged and Huw were concerned about Eynon. His letters were short and there was no mention of his having leave. Marged continued to write and one morning she was startled to answer a loud knock at the door to see two military policemen standing there.

She listened in disbelief as they told her

that Eynon was absent without leave.

"He must be hurt. He wouldn't do that without a reason," she said. "What have you done to him? Tell me the truth, where is he? What's happened?"

Coldly, indifferent to her distress, they told her that if he got in touch she must inform the police immediately, and if she did not, she would be committing an offence. Questions tumbled out of her mouth but they walked away as though she hadn't spoken.

In utter panic she ran out of the door, remembering after several seconds that Huw was at the beach and not there to comfort her. When she found him, Huw stared in disbelief. "He must be injured, lost somewhere, he wouldn't run away. Not our Eynon." He tried to picture the happy boy who had left and could only visualise him dead. He said nothing of his fear to Marged.

"He'll get in touch as soon as he's able," he said reassuringly. "It has to be a mistake." But within himself there was a paralysing fear for his son's safety.

Ronnie was in France and his letters were short and heavily blue-pencilled. Olive tried with a magnifying glass to read beneath the heavy pencil in the hope of gleaning more of his thoughts. She wrote to him regularly and hoped that somehow he would receive her letters. But for the past few weeks she hadn't heard from him. She still kept on writing but terror filled her heart and she had to calm herself for fear the worries would reveal themselves in her letters to him.

She said nothing about her fears to his parents, or to Granny Moll. She lied about hearing from him and assured them that everything was all right. She didn't want Marged or Moll worrying him about not hearing from him. She tried not to imagine him in the thick of the fighting. There were plenty of other reasons why he could have been unable to write. She tried to think of some, but her mind was a blank. Best she kept her fears to herself, she realised; she didn't want him upset by the others writing and complaining and telling him how worried they were. However well meant, anxiety from home was something he could do without.

With the season coming to an end, the café was less busy and Marged told Mrs Downs that after the end of the week she wouldn't be needed any longer.

"Haven't you got anything in one of the other businesses?" Hetty asked, glancing at Huw. "There's the fish-and-chip shop and café, couldn't I work there, at least part time?"

Huw turned away after giving Marged a warning stare, and Marged said with regret that there was just enough work for the family. "We usually have to look for winter work ourselves, but with the boys away, we can probably manage without having to," she explained, untruthfully. "There aren't any places to fill, sorry."

The following morning, there was evidence that once more someone was using the café after it closed. A toffee paper was found and a small amount of cigarette ash. Lilly was involved in the discovery, but this time she knew that she and Phil were not the culprits. Phil was a member of His Majesty's forces and couldn't even write to her, she reminded herself sadly.

The mystery was still unsolved by the time October came and they had to close the café for the winter. After a week's rest, the family was kept busy cleaning everything and making sure the building was secure enough to cope with the winter weather.

Phil came home on leave and Lilly expertly escaped from the final cleaning, taking the spare tablecloths and tea-towels home and forgetting to go back.

When she and Phil met it was already dark. They let themselves into the café, which was redolent with the smell of strong carbolic soap, and settled into "their" corner. They laughed about the mystery of the cigarette ash and Phil dropped some more to cause puzzled frowns when Granny Moll and Marged came on one of their weekly checks throughout the winter to ensure there were no leaks or other damage.

Their need for each other was greater because of the weeks they had been apart. They were reluctant to go, knowing it would be several weeks before they could meet again.

"It's past eleven o'clock," Lilly whispered, shining a small torch on to her watch. "What did you tell your wife?"

"I told her it was a friend's stag party. I wish it was mine, the night before our wedding," he said as desire for her grew once more.

Passion spent, they lay together and Lilly asked, "Isn't there a way that I can write to you? I need to tell you things and not being able to write is cruel."

"What things? You can tell me things now, can't you?"

"Special things. I want to write them down as I think of them, so you know what I'm thinking, what's happening to me. And I want to hear the same from you."

She did have something to say but avoided saying it. She knew that a letter, which he could reread and mull over before deciding on a reply, was the best way of telling him.

"I'm cold," she complained as a shiver ran

through her. He wrapped his arms around her once again as they promised themselves just half an hour longer.

Marged and Huw were relaxing, having finished the seemingly endless chores. Huw had changed out of his work trousers and wore grey ones with a V-necked Fair Isle pullover and an open-necked checked shirt underneath it. He puffed slowly on a pipe, his face brown with sunburn which ended at his collar line, his hair slicked back with Brylcreem.

Marged's hair was tightly enclosed in dinkie curlers and she wore a skirt and blouse with fluffy slippers on her feet as she concentrated on finishing the khaki sock she was knitting. She and her daughters and many other enthusiastic people were helping the war effort by knitting socks and scarves for the forces. Clothes factories had been modified and instead of making civilian clothes had been set up for the manufacture of khaki battledress, kit bags, camouflage net, parachute silk, tents, and all the other necessities of war. But there was a shortage of woollen items and women were encouraged to make scarves and socks which were collected at special centres and sent to where they were most needed.

"It's late, Huw, our Lilly should have been in ages ago." Marged looked up from her casting off. "Did she say she'd be late?"

"Probably meeting her secret boyfriend," Beth said. "If he exists. She's invented him if you ask me, as an excuse to get out of work."

The door opened at that moment and Lilly came in, greeted them mournfully and went to the cupboard to take out writing paper. Huw stood up and went to throw the bolt on the front door. "Thank goodness you're in, Lilly," he said. "Now we can go to bed."

Lilly grunted and, with her arm shielding what she was writing, began to scribble on the paper.

"Where's your boyfriend, then?" Beth wanted to know. "Too ashamed to bring him home, are you?"

To everyone's surprise, Lilly burst into tears.

"Whatever is it?" Marged asked, trying to comfort her daughter.

Lilly couldn't explain that Phil was at that moment on his way home to prepare to return to duty after a forty-eight hour leave. Between sobs she explained that she was thinking of Ronnie, Taff and Johnny.

"I was trying to write to our Ronnie but I don't know what to say," she wailed, tearing up the paper and throwing it into the embers, poking it until it flared and blackened.

At that moment there was a loud knock at the door. Puzzled, Huw went to open it, with Marged close behind him. "Bleddyn? What is it?"

"Fire. The café's on fire, you'd better come quick."

By good fortune, a courting couple had passed when the fire near the door of the café was slowly gathering momentum, and they quickly alerted the fire brigade. Their response was fast. Lights had to be extinguished as fast as possible, fires in particular, in case they were intended to be a signal to the Luftwaffe. When Marged, Huw, Bleddyn, Beth and Lilly, who looked decidedly sick, tumbled out of the van, the flames were all but out, but the dining area was a smoking ruin.

The café was made mostly of wood, and they had expected to see nothing left but a pile of smouldering ashes, but from the outside the walls looked undamaged. Inside, however, they saw that the floor, in places, was burnt right through. The sight of the sand and a couple of abandoned deckchairs below, visible with the aid of brief flashes of the firemen's torches, gave them a sick, dizzy sensation akin to vertigo. This was a view they hadn't seen before.

It was difficult to assess the damage to the rest of the place but on inspection with the weak, shaded torches, it appeared that the walls were mostly firm, just blackened, the once neat paint now blistered.

Lilly felt sickness overwhelm her. She and Phil must be responsible for this. They had smoked, left their cigarette ends; they must have forgotten to make sure they were completely out. She tried to think clearly about whether Phil had slipped the evidence of their clandestine visit into a cigarette packet to be thrown away later, as he usually did, but everything was a blur. Her memory jerked from one thing to another and wouldn't settle down. All she could think of was seeing their cigarettes balanced on the edge of a matchbox.

No one else could have started it; there hadn't been time. How could she tell her parents and Granny Moll that she was the cause of this terrible disaster? Just lately it had been one problem after another. In a few hours Phil would be far away and she wouldn't see him for months. She needed to talk to him. He'd help her decide what to do about all this.

A taxi drew up as they were locking up as best they could and preparing to leave. Moll stepped out and stared at the still smoking mess that had been Piper's Café.

"Oh, my God, look at it! Oh, my God, what happened? How will we sort it? Oh, Marged, what will we do? Who did this?"

Lilly was shaking but she went to her

grandmother and hugged her, tears for herself being mistaken for tears for Moll. "Granny Moll, the season's finished. We'll have it sorted long before next year. It isn't as bad as it looks." She held Moll more tightly and said, "I'm so sorry."

"You're sorry? You aren't to blame. But whoever did this will be sorry all right," Moll sobbed. "Piper's, gone. I can't believe it."

"It isn't gone," Lilly soothed. "Dad and Uncle Bleddyn will have it looking better than before in plenty of time for next year's opening."

Marged looked at her elder daughter in surprise. She hadn't expected Lilly to be the one offering sympathy to her grandmother. It would have been more in character for Lilly to cheer to see Piper's go up in smoke. Perhaps she had misjudged the girl.

There was nothing more they could do. They all went back to Sidney Street, Beth and Lilly walking with Uncle Bleddyn, Moll in the van with Marged and Huw. Beth told Bleddyn about the mysterious cigarette ash that had been found several times and the suspicion that someone had been using the place after they had locked up and gone home.

Lilly said nothing. She was still trying to decide what to do. By the time she reached home, she had made up her mind that, having allowed so much time to pass without confessing, the wisest move was to do nothing and say nothing. The moment to confess had passed. Besides, there were other things on her mind – predominantly, Phil Martin.

As the van driven by Huw turned the corner into Sidney Street, Moll lurched against him and at first he thought she had fallen asleep. "Get her off me, Marged, I can't drive with her leaning over me. Poor old girl, she's exhausted. I'd better get her straight home."

Marged tried but couldn't rouse her mother. Standing at their front door was Audrey, with Maude and Myrtle dressed in night-clothes with blankets over their shoulders. Huw stopped and leaned over to open the passenger door, calling for Audrey to, "Come and help your mam, fallen asleep she has. Would you believe it?"

Moll wasn't asleep. The shock of the last few hours had brought on a sudden heart attack which had ended her life. Audrey was now the only Piper left.

Seven

The fire at Piper's Café and the death of Moll Piper caused quite a stir in the town of St David's Well. Moll had been a familiar figure and had been well liked. Her death so quickly after the fire seemed to make it a greater tragedy and people speculating about how the fire had begun suggested reasons that varied from spite for the family's success to enemy action!

A pale Marged seemed suddenly older, supporting her sister Audrey, both of them busy making preparations for the funeral in three days' time. Beth and her father looked stunned. Lilly sat and cried. Maude and Myrtle looked scared.

"We'll have to leave, there's no doubt about it," Maude whispered to her young sister. "Now Granny Moll has gone, the others won't want us hanging around."

"Where will we go?" Myrtle asked as they sat, shivering, in the yard behind Moll's house.

"Don't know, but we'll find somewhere warm for the winter."

"Perhaps they'll let us stay till the spring and we can work on the sands again."

"Maude? Myrtle? Are you out there?" Audrey called and they grabbed each other's hand for comfort and went inside.

"We have to go to the shops, you'll need some dark clothes for the day of the funeral," Audrey told them. "Get your best shoes on and we'll go straight away."

The dresses and cardigans she chose for them were too large and in a style unsuitable for their youth. The clothes made them look smaller and thinner but they didn't care. "It'll be extra layers to wear when we leave," Maude whispered. "Perhaps we'll be able to steal a couple of blankets too. I don't think Granny Moll would mind if we took the spare ones in the old trunk, do you?"

"Why did she have to go an' die?" Myrtle sobbed.

Cards of sympathy arrived for the family, cold, stark white ones with an edging of black. Myrtle was frightened by seeing them standing along the mantelpiece.

"Perhaps we should buy one?" Maude suggested.

"Perhaps." Myrtle didn't look convinced. The sight of them made her shiver.

Marged didn't like the clothes Audrey had bought for the girls. "They're miles too big. They make them look like orphans."

"That's what they are!"

"Just because they're orphans they don't have to look like them!"

"They'll only be worn once, it wasn't worth spending more," Audrey defended her decision.

"Then why did you buy them to fit them in two years' time?"

There wasn't time to go back and change them so they had to suffice. The days went quickly and everyone had jobs to do to ensure the smooth running of the funeral and the gathering afterwards at the house.

They had heard nothing more about Eynon, though there had been several further visits from the military police. Nevertheless, Marged wrote to Eynon at the only address she knew to tell him about the death of his grandmother. "Surely he'll be found and given leave to attend," she said to Huw. Huw nodded agreement, but knew the letter, like all the others, would receive no reply. Wherever Eynon was, he was in a situation in which he couldn't make contact.

Staggering along the unmade road for a few yards, Eynon had known he couldn't hope to catch up with his group. He looked around him, moving his head slowly to avoid the pain such movement produced. There was no light to be seen. Everywhere was blackness and he felt the openness of wild countryside surrounding him. He had to sleep. Taking his groundsheet from his pack took ages but eventually he lay down and, wrapping it around him, slept.

When he woke the day was far from new. He guessed that evening was approaching and he had practically slept the clock around. A wound on his head had bled profusely and was stuck to his great-coat. He stood and looked around. He could hear the trickle of water and made his way to where he could wash the wound. Examining it carefully he felt the damage. It was large and gaping and needed attention, but attention it wouldn't get. He was not going back to accept punishment for Kipper's cruelty. However long this war lasted, he wasn't going back.

The funeral of Moll Piper was a small one. With so many men away fighting the war, and no women allowed at the cemetery for the brief service, the huddle of men surrounding the grave was fewer than a dozen.

Huw and Bleddyn stood together and wished their sons were safe at home and able to stand with them. Neighbours and those who worked the beach were represented although, like the Castles, their numbers were reduced by the call-up.

Bleddyn knew that his sons, Taff and Johnny, would be there had they not been overseas, and Huw thought of Ronnie, from whom they hadn't heard for several weeks. Bleddyn had seen Johnny's girlfriend, Hannah, at the house with the rest of the women, and he had managed to have a word with Marged and Beth to ask them to make her welcome.

Bernard Gregory was there with his son, Peter, who was on leave. Few greetings were exchanged but the young man seemed aloof, as though the death of an old friend was unimportant and he was there under sufferance. At twenty-seven, Peter had already seen so much death he was unaffected by the loss of the old lady, but he comforted his father and made all the right noises to the family. He felt no strong emotion and had no need to hide his tears behind a handkerchief as his father did. He tried to pretend, but could not.

He had been in the army since before war broke out, spending time in France and Holland and Germany and witnessing at first hand atrocities which had not yet come to light. Now he was in the intelligence service, still dropping into enemy-held territory, forming resistance groups, extending his knowledge and, recently, sending others into danger. It was impossible to witness so much without becoming immune to the display of sadness at the death of Granny Molly Piper. He was there solely to support his father, although he had known and liked Moll.

As with many others, the beach had been his playground as a child. He had helped his father as soon as he grew old enough, running with the donkeys, helping to look after them during the winter as well as the summer. Calling into the café or begging sweets from one of the stalls, he had grown up as part of the wider family of beach traders, knowing them all, calling them aunties and uncles, safe under their watchful eyes. Yet seeing the sad faces around the open grave, something in him had hardened. Moll had been nearly seventy-five and she'd had a good life compared with the eighteen-year-old he had seen die two days previously. He felt a surge of impatience and wanted to be gone.

"You'll come back to the house, Peter?" Huw asked. Although he had been about to shake his head, a glance at his father's face told him he would be needed there.

"Just for half an hour," he said, leading them towards the pony and cart waiting at the cemetery gate. "I've no wish to listen to eulogies about a woman who, by dying, has become a saint!"

Bernard was aware of some of his son's experiences and understood his attitude.

"I've known Moll since I was a snotty-nosed kid," Bernard said to his son as the sturdy Welsh cob trotted towards Sidney Street. "Your mam and I did our courting under that café, freezing cold in the winter, or huddled among the rows and rows of deckchairs in the summer. When you were born Moll and her Joseph came to the house and brought us some hand-knitted clothes and a blanket for your cot as though we were both part of her own family. Miss her something awful I will."

"No one likes to lose a friend." Peter was thinking about his young, innocent friend who had died a couple of days before.

"Besides the loss of a friend," his father went on, as the pony walked lazily through the streets, "besides knowing I'll never see old Moll again, it's a warning to get my own life in order. I'm on the front line now, in a row facing the last trumpet."

"Come on, Dad!" Peter turned and smiled with strong affection at his solemn-faced father. "You've got a long way to go yet, and besides, we're supposed to cheer the relatives today, not remind them of their mortality."

"There won't be one around my age who won't be thinking the same," Bernard defended.

When they arrived at the house of Moll and Audrey Piper, there was a knot of neighbours outside, arms folded, leaning towards each other with words of praise for

Moll, sympathy for the family and whispered criticism of the hats. Pushing past them, his tall figure in the smart uniform very impressive, his blue eyes carrying an air of authority, Peter went to find Beth.

The front room, rarely used, which Moll had called the parlour, was full of people, all in dark clothes, moving sluggishly like a tide caught against the sea wall, a seething homogenous mass of humanity. Heads were bowed and voices were slow and low. The curtains across the windows added to the gloom and Peter thought they looked as though they had been drenched in black treacle.

He thought the crowded room smelled of decay, filled as it was with the strong odour of stale clothes, dampness and mothballs. Dull clothes suitable for funerals were kept in the backs of wardrobes; suits and bowler hats for the men and, for the women, ill-fitting black dresses smelling slightly of damp and hats with the greenish tinge of mildew. These had all been brought out, brushed, and worn as a mark of respect for the dead. Tomorrow they would return to their dark places to await the next solemn occasion.

Peter found Beth, her mother and her Auntie Audrey in the kitchen where the air was cleaner, attending to the wants of their guests. Olive had broken down and was talking to Uncle Bleddyn, who was trying to reassure her about Ronnie's lack of letters.

"Never you mind, Olive, love. Ronnie is a thoughtful boy and he'll get a letter to you as fast as he can, but there are bound to be times when it's difficult. He won't be able to trot down to the corner and pop it in the pillar box as easy as you can, will he?"

Peter waved at Beth who looked up in surprise.

"Peter? How kind of you to come." She offered a hand, which he took, pulling her forward and kissing her.

"Beth! How grown up you look. It seems everyone has changed in the time I've been away." His voice was carefully modulated, the accent no longer familiar.

When they had exchanged a few pleasantries, Marged handed Peter two plates of food. "Take these for you and your father in case he can't get to the table, will you, Peter? There's a love."

When Peter had obediently struggled out of the kitchen in search of his father, Auntie Audrey mimicked his voice. "'Beth, how you've grown.' Fancy talk for a boy who ran with the donkeys, eh?"

"None of your, 'Hi yer, how've you bin?'," Marged agreed. "Always fancied himself, that one."

Beth blushed a little, afraid Peter might have heard and been embarrassed. When the food was more or less dealt with, she went to find him. With Freddy so poor at writing letters, she needed to understand something about life in the forces. Through Peter Gregory, she might learn something about the way Freddy lived, even though he was in a different service.

"To say that Freddy is not very good at writing letters is an understatement," she laughingly told Peter. "Three the first week, one the next – and that was to ask for money! And it's now two weeks since I've heard from him. I hear from my brother Ronnie more often than Freddy," she sighed. "Although we haven't heard from him for a while."

"I don't write to Dad as often as I should," Peter confessed. "Walking into the barracks is stepping into a separate world, an alien place where none of the normal rules apply. We cope better by forgetting how things were and concentrating on how they are. I'm part of that different world, Beth, so I can understand how he feels; being taken away from everything familiar, dealing with the day-to-day activities that often make very little sense, pretending the people I share my life with are my friends. It's better to cut yourself off from the real world and accept the artificial one. That way you might survive. So don't be hurt when he doesn't write. He's coping with something he was never prepared for, a way of life he would never have chosen."

He pointed to the corner near the fireplace, now visible as the crowd was thinning. "Who are those girls?"

"Maude and Myrtle, the two girls I found living on the streets and stealing food to survive." She explained about the food left out for them outside Piper's Café, and the devious way she had tracked them down. "Maude was ill and poor little Myrtle was trying to keep them both safe. Granny Moll took them in and, as they refused to go back to the children's home and Granny Moll agreed to be responsible for them, they've stayed with us ever since."

"What's going to happen to them now your grandmother has gone? From the anxious look on their faces, that seems to be their question too." Maude and Myrtle sat huddled together, two pale, thin children dressed in the over-large and sombre clothes, silently watching the people come and go. "Dresses chosen for suitability rather than flattery, by the look of them," Peter whispered.

Beth walked over to the silent girls and Peter followed.

"Has Auntie Audrey spoken to you yet?" Beth asked. "About what's going to happen?"

"No, but we know she'll be telling us to

go," Maude said stiffly. "Stands to reason. Now Auntie Audrey and that Wilf Thomas can get married, they won't want us hanging around, getting in the way, for sure."

"Nonsense! There's no question of you going anywhere. Auntie Audrey needs you for company in that big old house."

"And we'll be staying for ever?" Myrtle said in delight. "Always?"

"For as long as you want to stay," Beth smiled. "But remember your promise to Granny Moll, Myrtle. You're going to work real hard at school."

Myrtle nodded and hid her face. She was not getting on very well, but if it was the only way they could stay and be a part of the Castle family, then she'd have to face it. Young as she was, she knew Maude couldn't cope with another winter on the streets. The only other choice was for her to go back into that home – and without her sister, who was considered old enough to look after herself.

Peter was looking amused. "You don't like school?"

"They tease me because I don't know anything," Myrtle muttered.

"They both missed a lot of school," Beth explained.

"But I can read a bit now," Myrtle told him, "and I can give change for half a crown an' all, mind."

"You'll be fine." Peter delved into his

pocket and brought out a shilling. "Here, take this and buy yourself some sweets."

Beth smiled her thanks for his kindness. "Your father thought he could help us find their family. They must have someone, somewhere." She explained about the old snapshots and Peter turned back to the girls.

"What do you remember about your mam and dad?" he asked.

Myrtle shrugged. "I only know what Maude tells me," she said.

They turned to look at Maude. "I remember they laughed a lot," she said. "Mam used to tease Dad and say he had sticky-outy ears. He pretended to be cross and they chased each other around the room and laughed."

Peter shrugged. "That isn't much to go on," he said, "but you never know. Someone might remember those sticky-outy ears. Lucky you haven't got them too," he teased.

Maude lifted her long hair and said, "But I have, look." She revealed small ears that indeed did not lie flat against her head.

Beth smoothed her hair down and said softly, "Beautiful ears you've got and not at all sticky-outy, I promise."

Peter solemnly agreed.

Lilly had been in the kitchen when the food was being prepared, but after that she had disappeared. Marged asked where she was once or twice, but with all the activity in the house, trying to deal with food and talk to the people who had come to pay their respects, she didn't have time to dwell on her daughter's absence. Lilly had always been adept at avoiding work, she thought to herself grimly. Now, with Granny Moll gone, she would be needed to do her share, but she knew her daughter well enough to know that the extra effort would not be forthcoming voluntarily. If Lilly were to help, it would mean arguments and ultimatums, and Marged knew that life would be easier if they allowed Lilly to go her own way. But that wouldn't be fair on Beth, who had always done more than she was asked.

Marged and Huw had been surprised at the grief Lilly had shown. The depth of feeling had been unexpected. Marged could see by her daughter's eyes that the girl hadn't been sleeping. And her restlessness was apparent by the tangle of sheets and blankets each morning when she went to make the bed. Lilly looked ill and her appetite was no longer enormous; in fact she picked, pulled faces and pushed her plate away barely touched most mealtimes. She had been more fond of her grandmother than Marged had realised.

Lilly was in the park, staring around her

244

but seeing nothing. The October day was drawing to a close, the autumn mist with a hint of bonfire smoke on its breath settling over the trees and bringing a chill to her shoulders. She hadn't bothered to bring a coat. She was responsible for Granny Moll's death and she couldn't talk about it to anyone.

With no one close enough to help her, except her parents to whom she could never confess, she was weighed down with guilt and unable to ease her mind by having someone tell her it was an accident and no one was to blame. She wouldn't believe them if they did, but it would have been soothing to be told. If only Phil were here. He would comfort her, help her to deal with it. An hour with Phil and she would be able to sleep.

A vision of the burnt-out café came to her then. She saw in her mind's eye the corner where she and Phil had sat to tell each other how much they were loved. Because of her carrying on with a married man, meeting him in secret, Granny Moll was dead and the café was a smoking, distorted ruin.

Remorse, shame and the need to tell someone was overwhelming. The café wasn't the only thing to be ruined. If Phil were here, they wouldn't have their secret hideaway any more. It was as though, with the burning of the café, she and Phil and all they had said and done had been destroyed too.

She had been writing long, loving letters to Phil but not posting them. She planned to read them to him when he came home on leave. He had warned her that letters could easily allow their secret to escape. "If people find out before we're ready," he had said, "it will be more difficult for us. And it will delay the time when we can be together all legal, and safe from difficulties. We have to keep our secret until the moment is right for me to ask my wife for a divorce. She mustn't know about you or she'll never agree." She knew he was protecting her, making sure she wasn't shamed by being named in the divorce. She hugged herself. Dear Phil. He was so thoughtful. But now there were things to discuss, urgent things. Surely he wouldn't expect her not to tell him about the fire they had caused? She had to write to him. There was no one else.

She walked down the road, past Granny Moll's house where a few mourners remained with Audrey, who wanted them gone. Her parents looked at her but didn't demand an explanation of her absence. The room was not in its usual state of orderliness. Cups and saucers and plates were piled on the table ready to be returned to the café when it was once again habitable, the burn marks on some of the boxes a stark reminder of her guilt.

Taking out the writing pad, she began again to write to Phil, telling him all her fears and worries: the fire, the death of Granny Moll and all the other things that were on her mind.

Beth had written to Freddy and they walked together to the pillar box and dropped their letters in, both with the fervent hope of a swift reply.

Freddy was on leave but he wasn't sharing it with Beth and he knew nothing about the fire or the death of Granny Moll. Listening to the exploits of others in his group, he wanted some true stories to tell to add to the many untrue ones he had boastfully recited. So he had gone home with a mate and they had gone on the town dressed in uniform and tried their luck at the local dance.

When the last evening of their leave arrived and they were about to give up hope of a flirtation, Freddy caught the train and went to St David's Well to call on Shirley. The dark evenings and the black-out meant there was little chance of them being seen.

She didn't mention the tragedy that had hit the Castles, thinking that there was no point in spoiling the one evening they'd have together, so when Freddy saw the headline in the local paper he didn't at first realise it referred to Beth's family. When he did, he was in a state of shock. He needed to go and see Beth, make sure she was all right, although the article said nothing about anyone being injured. But how could he go? He wasn't supposed to be there. He went back to camp filled with shame at the way he had cheated on her, hiding away and meeting another girl when he should have been with her.

Once the funeral was over, Huw and Marged started making arrangements to repair and redecorate the café.

"Now Moll is gone, and Audrey is the only member of the Piper family left, I think it would be a good time to change the name," Huw said, as they looked at the blackened interior and began to assess the work that needed to be done.

"Of course we won't change the name!" Marged said in surprise. "Piper's it is and always will be."

"But there aren't any Pipers working for the firm. We're all Castles! You and I are Castles. Bleddyn and his sons are Castles. I think it's about time we faced the fact that it's run by Castles. We should make the name match the business. You ashamed of the name you married into or something?"

"Of course I'm not ashamed. I'm always known as Mrs Castle, aren't I? What else

248

would I be called?"

"Then give the café the name of the family who run it."

"No. I'm sorry, Huw, but I can't do that. My great-grandparents started the business and Piper's it will remain."

"Then let the Pipers sort out this little lot!" He left her in the doorway of the damaged café and walked off. At the van he hesitated. He couldn't very well leave her to catch a bus home; she'd be furious with him for days. But he couldn't help her with the plans for reopening either. Castle's it should be and would be before he set foot inside it again. He didn't have a say in anything, yet he and Bleddyn carried most of the responsibility. He wasn't going to put up with it any longer.

"If you want Bleddyn and me to get this place sorted in time for next season, you'll have to change a few things," he called to her.

"You were *glad* when my mother died," she accused as she walked back to the van. "You think that with her out of the way you'll get anything you want. Well, you're wrong!"

"Rubbish, woman. I liked the old girl, but it's time to rethink."

"What a time to choose, when I'm grieving."

"Whatever time I chose it would be

wrong," he muttered. "You never allow me any say. I didn't want you to employ that Hetty Downs, for a start. Went ahead and did it, though, didn't you? And who's to know that it wasn't her who set fire to the place because of some imagined cheating on the part of your great-grandparents about fifty years ago?"

"You don't think she burnt the place for spite, do you?"

"I'm only saying you should have listened to me and not allowed her anywhere near the place. She knew where to go to sort out that disgusting stink that time, didn't she? A bit of rotten fish she found, and she knew exactly where to go to find it. She thinks I didn't see her, but I did. And she blamed our Eynon! I don't trust the woman, she's cracked when it comes to your family, but, as usual, you wouldn't listen to me."

"Perhaps we ought to talk to the police—"

"How can we without evidence?"

Huw drove home in silence, Marged tight lipped and offended, he himself determined not to give in. This was his only chance of succeeding with his plans for the business.

Huw went to see his brother that evening and found him writing letters. "God 'elp, Bleddyn, writing letters is all anyone seems to do these days. Writing letters or knitting socks for soldiers. There's our Beth writing to that Freddy and facing disappointment

250

whenever the postman comes without a reply. There's Marged writing to everyone she's ever known to tell them about Moll, and praying every night for news of our Eynon, and our Lilly is writing to some bloke in secret. A mysterious boyfriend who, like that Freddy Clements, brings nothing but disappointment."

"Let's talk about opening the stalls next spring, shall we?" Bleddyn said, putting the letter aside. "There's plenty to sort out. More restrictions, and ice-cream making is banned. Although I think we might risk a fine or two to give the kids a treat now and then, what d'you say?"

"I told Marged I'm not going to help," Huw told him. "I want to change the name to Castle's. There are more Castles than there'll ever be Pipers. I don't think Audrey will produce an illegitimate son in Moll's memory, do you?" he joked.

"I don't think now is the time," Bleddyn said quietly. "Marged was close to her mother and they've worked together for so long it must be difficult for her to cope with Moll's death, losing her so sudden an' all."

"I still think she should listen to me sometimes," Huw argued.

"I think she will now. After all, there is no one else."

"Thanks. Last-hope Huw, that's me!"

"Come on, let's go and see what we can

salvage. Thank goodness we'd reached the end of the season. Just think how much worse it would have been if this had happened in May."

Peter Gregory called on the Castles to see Beth. He brought the snaps from his father's collection and together they showed them again to the girls, this time with a powerful magnifying glass. Maude, being the oldest, thought she might recognise others in the group photograph but she didn't.

"Can you see your father there?" Peter coaxed.

Maude shook her head. "I look too old. I think this was when we were with Auntie Flossie."

Myrtle stared at the pictures as though begging them to reveal a secret, but it was a waste of time and Peter put them back in his pocket disappointed. As he was leaving, he told Beth, "My father doesn't have a clear memory of the girls, but I suspect there was some scandal attached to them. It's frustrating to have a glimpse of their past and nothing more."

"Thank you for trying to help, Peter. Somewhere someone must have that snippet of information that will set us on the right track. There's nothing more your father can tell us?"

"I'll talk to him again; you never know,

something I say might trigger his memory of that time." He left a card when he went, propped on the mantelpiece with the others, still in its envelope.

Marged opened it and said in surprise, "It's from an old friend of your gran's, she must have just heard."

"Isn't it too late?" Maude asked.

"Never too late for a kind word, fach," Marged smiled.

That afternoon, Maude and Myrtle went to the newsagent above which Mrs Downs lived and chose a sympathy card. "I told you we should have sent one," Maude admonished her sister.

Mrs Downs was in the shop and she saw the two girls giggling as they read some of the words they considered too fancy. Then they looked at postcards and laughed at one which showed a cartoon of a young boy with very large ears.

"Sticky-outy ears just like our Dad had!" Maude said.

Mrs Downs came over and looked at them as though she hadn't seen them before. "What's your name?" she demanded.

"Maude Carpenter, and this is my sister Myrtle."

"How old are you?" They gave her their birthdays and she asked, "Your father, what did you mean about big ears?"

"Our Mam used to tease him and they'd

laugh," Maude said, holding her sister's hand and edging out of the shop away from this angry-looking woman.

"Get out of here! D'you hear me? Get out and don't come back!"

"Mam?" Shirley asked, coming out of the back room. "What is it?"

"These girls, they were giving me cheek."

Maude and Myrtle fled.

Forgetting his ultimatum, over the next few days Huw helped Bleddyn sort out the demolished stalls. Some cafés were still open and they managed to serve a few of the diminishing number of visitors, most now without children, who still found their way by bus and car and train to enjoy the quiet of an autumn break.

The weekend still produced trippers, coaches bringing families on day trips, leaving earlier than in the summer but enjoying themselves just the same. There was lethargy among the few still trading and a false gaiety about the beach, fewer people making more noise to fill the void.

The rock and sweet shop still opened with Alice serving, thankful to get away from her difficult father for a few hours each day. The number of customers dwindled but Audrey kept the shop open for them, glad of the few extra pounds they brought.

Bernard Gregory spent some hours on the

wilder beaches with his pony and flat cart gathering driftwood, which he would saw and chop to sell around the houses now fires had become a necessity once more. The rumours about coal being rationed made him more diligent in his searches and he went further afield than usual, the amiable pony taking him to the less frequented beaches to increase his stock.

While the Castle family gradually recovered from the loss of Moll, and continued to grieve over the disappearance of Eynon, Beth and Lilly each waited for a letter. A postcard came from Freddy addressed to the whole family and containing no words of love. It showed a view of another seaside town, in the west country, and he told them how pretty it was and how much more lively than St David's Well Bay.

Beth read it and reread it, trying to find some comfort hidden in the casual words. Surely he should have received her letter telling him about Granny Moll by now? But then, if he was away from camp on some exercise, he might still not know.

Audrey Piper and Wilf Thomas spent some time clearing out Moll's bedroom. In privacy they put their arms around each other, looked at the huge white-counterpaned bed and dreamed of sharing it as Mr and Mrs Wilfred Thomas.

"I have bouts of guilt about Mam's death," Audrey told him. "All these years we've delayed getting wed, looking after your mother and mine, hoping for a miracle that would make it possible for us to marry, and knowing that the death of one of them was the only hope."

"Now it's too late," Wilf said sadly. "You're free but my mam is too frail to face it."

"There's plenty of room for her here," Audrey suggested. "I have to stay because Maude and Myrtle need a home, and Olive is here of course. But there are spare rooms. We could live on the top floor. Three nice rooms there are up there and we could make them into a beautiful home for the two of us, and I could still run the house. What d'you say?"

"It's too early, love. There's some who'll say we've benefited by poor old Moll's death and that would be hard to live with."

"In a month or so? What about the spring?"

"Well, we could think about it, but d'you think Mam could cope with the upheaval at her time of life?"

"Probably not," Audrey sighed, content to continue as they had done for so many years, unable to relish the idea of upheaval herself but unwilling to admit it. Pretence was kinder for them both, she thought philosophically.

They put aside some of Moll's jewellery for Beth, and for Ronnie's wife Olive. Some of the best pieces went to Lilly – who cried as loudly as she had when Moll had passed away.

Beth was surprised at the regret Lilly had displayed. Her sister hadn't been particularly fond of Granny Moll when she was alive, had often moaned when told to do something to help her, yet since her death Lilly seemed to be continually weeping.

With the approach of winter, and with the café in the hands of builders, the Castle family were taking on work for the winter months. Lilly went back to the café at the back of the fish-and-chip shop run by Bleddyn, but after two weeks she admitted that she no longer wanted to work there for six months of the year.

"I need something out in the open," she explained. "The smell of that fish makes me feel quite ill."

"You've done it every winter for years," Beth protested. "Why suddenly is the job beneath you?"

"If you must know I've never liked working there, coming home with the stink of fish and fat in my hair! I did it because I had to. It's a family business and I'm family!"

"When it suits you!" Beth retorted.

"Stop it, you two," Marged sighed. "If Lilly doesn't want to work in the café, we'll find someone who does. What about you, Beth, fancy giving it a try?"

"All right, I'll try," Beth said, relieved that she didn't have to take a job in one of the cold, open-fronted greengrocers like she had the winter before.

"Jump in my coffin so quick, would you?" Lilly snapped. "I haven't decided no for definite yet!"

Before Beth could retaliate and start a serious quarrel, Marged raised a hand and told them to hush.

"What would Granny Moll think of you two arguing all the time like a couple of kids?" she demanded and Lilly, predictably, collapsed once more into tears.

Lilly made little effort to find work. She made no comment when Beth started in the job that she had always considered her own at Uncle Bleddyn's café. She rose late and went to bed early, and, in between, did as little as she could get away with. Marged threatened her with a visit to the doctor, thinking that the mourning and grieving had gone on too long for a healthy young woman, and were now simply an excuse to be idle.

Letters were eagerly awaited by most families, and friends and neighbours shared what little news they had with others. Beth received a short note from Freddy, full of what he had done and making it seem that life was one long, laugh-filled pub crawl. He taught her a new word, "skiving", which was an essential skill for survival, he told her. He then asked whether she could send him some money as he was finding it difficult to manage. She threw it down in disgust. Why hadn't he responded to the news about the fire and Granny Moll? Her letter must have reached him by now!

The following day she received a second letter, this one full of remorse at his previous one. He told her the letter had been mislaid and he'd just read it. He explained that he wrote all that nonsense as a way to fill the pages, because life was really very dull and he missed her and longed to be home once again. He was sympathetic, concerned and as loving as she could wish. Saying nothing to her parents, she went to the post office, took out ten shillings and popped it into her next letter.

Thoughts of money made her decide to check on their savings. Freddy had taken it out of the bank and had told her it was safe in National Savings. A word with his mother, a hint that she intended to surprise Freddy by adding to it, and the book was in her hands. It contained only three shillings. Once again he had spent all they had saved. It was no more than she had suspected.

Marged picked up a letter from the doormat

one morning and puzzled over the writing. It wasn't a hand she recognised. Fear clutched her heart. It was Eynon. Someone was writing to tell her he was dead! Audrey was there and Marged handed it to her; she was unable to open it and her hands shook as she waited for her sister to tell her what it contained.

"It's from someone calling himself Ross, but I think it's Eynon."

Marged snatched it back and read, "Dear Auntie Marged, Just to let you know I'm all right and will get in touch soon."

"You'll have to take it to the police, Marged. The boy has to be found for his own safety."

"They can put me in prison first! If he comes here I'll do everything to make sure he doesn't go back."

The long-awaited letter from Ronnie arrived and Olive was told that he was injured and would be coming home. She ran to tell Marged and Huw.

"What happened?" they demanded in unison. Handing them the letter, she said breathlessly, "An injury to his knee, apparently, but he's alive and he's coming home!"

One morning, as her father and Uncle Bleddyn were setting off to begin to grease the joints of the dismantled stalls and put them away for the winter, Beth received two letters. One was the usual brief note from

Freddy with a PS thanking her for the money. The other envelope was addressed in handwriting she didn't recognise.

She sat down in surprise when she unsealed it. It was from Peter Gregory. Very different from Freddy's hastily scrawled note, it was full of amusing observations about people he remembered from when they were children. He asked about the two girls, Maude and Myrtle, and remembered to ask about Freddy, Eynon and Ronnie too, something Freddy never did. His PS was to hope she was well and had found interesting work for the winter.

Feeling a bit guilty at the comparisons she was making, she handed it to her mother and father then said, "I might go and see Mr Gregory. I expect he'd like to read it too. Can't have too many letters at a time like this."

"I wonder why he wrote to you?" Marged said, hope of a separation from Freddy Clements adding a sparkle to her eyes.

"I think they like to keep in touch with home. Writing is a way of making contact." Beth's tone was casual, but she was already mentally composing her reply.

The stalls were taken apart and cleaned before being stored in their winter premises, a barn on a farm a few miles out of town. They would be repainted in the spring, and

Huw was determined they would be a patriotic red, white and blue.

Bernard Gregory's donkeys had been taken to their winter home, where they had two large fields and comfortable stables. As Beth was working in Bleddyn's fish-and-chip shop, she was free during the afternoons. She took the letter and cycled to the house in Goose Lane where Bernard Gregory lived.

She found him in a large shed at the back of the premises, cleaning the saddles ready for waxing. The donkeys all had names and holidaying children grew to know each one. Dolly, Bertha, Pat, Hazel, Charlie, Bertie, Clifford: the names were brightly painted on the headbands. Without their name plates Beth was never sure which was which, but Bernard knew the names and characters of every one.

"Dolly is as gentle as you could wish, but Hazel, she has to be treated with caution. Anyone too heavy and she won't move, and she has been known to tip a persistent rider off! Charlie has to be leader, or he kicks..." He laughed affectionately as he remembered.

Beth handed him the letter and his eyes filled with tears as he read it. "Thanks for bringing it down, lovely girl. Peter writes as often as he can, but it's difficult at times. This is a bonus."

"Will it be all right if I write back?" she asked.

"Good heavens, why not? Love to hear from home, they do."

"I only thought that he might not want to bother writing to me again. It's more important that you get letters, after all, but if I write and tell him I don't expect a reply—"

"If you have the time to tell him about what's happening here, it would help him. Just casual chat about home, that's all they want, everyday things. A reminder about the sanity of home."

Talking to Peter's father she picked up on several things to tell him in her letter and as she cycled home she felt excited at the prospect of another letter in response. Writing to Freddy wasn't much fun, she had to admit, and his replies were hardly worth the cost of the stamps – which she had paid for anyway, stamps she sent him to encourage him to write.

In defiance of his wishes, Lilly had written several times to Phil but every day the postman passed without bringing her a reply, until one day she lost her temper and wrote a fiercely angry letter, threatening to go and see his wife if she didn't get a response in two weeks. At last, in November, the long-awaited letter arrived.

With trembling hands she opened it, and burst into tears.

"What's the matter with the girl?" Huw demanded irritably. "Waiting for the postman with more interest than that snappy terrier on the corner and when he finally brings her a letter what does she do? She cries! God 'elp, Marged, the girl is beyond me."

Lilly looked up and in a low voice said, "Mam, Dad, I'm expecting and the father is married and won't leave his wife. He refuses to help in any way, says it can't be his."

Eight

Marged stared at Huw and they both stared at Lilly as though waiting for her to explain her words, tell them she had been joking, that they hadn't heard properly, anything other than face the situation with which she had presented them.

"It's true," she said harshly. "I'm expecting and there's no one to help me. There'll be no hasty marriage to try and make this respectable, Mam. I'm on my own."

"Just tell us who the father is and I'll see if you're on your own," Huw growled.

She looked at him contemptuously. "Don't you listen? There is no father. This baby will just have me. No one else, understand, Dad? No need for you to flex your muscles and start playing the outraged Victorian parent. This baby has no father. Right?"

Too shocked to complain at her rudeness, Huw looked at his wife for support.

"We have to do something, Lilly," Marged said. "There's more than you involved here, whatever you say."

Lilly shook her head, screwing up Phil's letter and throwing it into the flames of the fire so nothing could be gleaned from it. Cajoling, threatening, pleading, nothing did any good. On the matter of the baby's father, Lilly would not budge.

As though she was not there, Marged and Huw discussed the possibility of sending Lilly away, having the baby adopted. Lilly refused to consider it.

"I'm having this baby, Mam, and if you don't want me, then I'll find somewhere else to live." She had no idea how she could possibly cope on her own, but was determined not to give in to threats.

Marged looked at Huw and said softly, "How are we going to tell Audrey?"

Beth was the next to be told and it was Lilly who told her when they were alone and she could put her case to her sister for having the child, without her parents adding their opinions.

"I'm convinced that when – my boyfriend – sees the beautiful baby he'll love her and want us both," Lilly told Beth, looking at her for reassurance.

"Have you written to him since he told you he wouldn't help?" Beth asked, avoiding a reply. "Perhaps when he's had time to think, he'll at least help financially."

"Yes, I wrote back, not angry, not pleading and helpless either, mind. I just stated the facts, and reminded him that the baby is his, and he'll regret it if he abandons her."

As the sisters sat and talked, all previous antagonism faded. Beth felt a strong need to defend her sister and take care of her through the difficult weeks ahead.

"If it's a daughter, he'll definitely want her then. Fathers are notoriously soft when it comes to daughters," Lilly went on. "Remember how we used to run to our Dad when Mam told us off?" They both smiled at the memories of Huw's spoiling.

"I'll stay with you when you tell Auntie Audrey, shall I?" Beth offered. "You're not alone, Lilly, we're all here and the baby won't lack love." She hugged her sister and was surprised to feel a painful tinge of envy.

Audrey told her much the same as Beth. She didn't mention the baby's father, but she could guess who it was. She would help in any way she could and heaven help anyone she heard gossiping about Lilly. "Put them to rights straight off I will," she promised.

Wilf nodded tacit agreement, but his eyes and his tightly clenched mouth told a different story. Disapproval was clear and as soon as they were on their own, he told Audrey so.

"Why is everything being made so easy for her?" he asked.

"Times change, Wilf. You wouldn't have our Lilly treated like a criminal, would you?"

"No, but it's so unfair."

"I know, dear, but when is life ever fair?"

"It certainly wasn't for us, was it?" he said, taking her hand and holding it tight.

Uncle Bleddyn was philosophical about it. "I don't think you'll be the only young woman in this situation, fach," he said hugging her. "Men away from home month after month, women tempted by men who are available, stands to reason, we'll soon have a whole flock of 'em."

"No more knitting for soldiers," Marged said. "I'll be knitting for my grandchild, won't I?"

Huw remained determined to find out who the man was, and make him pay.

A visit to the doctor confirmed Lilly's fears and she was told the baby would be born early in May. Quickly working it out in her head, she realised that their visits to the café after closing had made hers and Phil's love-making too easy. The dark, cosy privacy had relaxed them, made them forget the danger of their growing desire. If they had stuck to the park and back lanes she might have been saved this distress, but somehow, even with Phil's refusal to become involved, she wasn't sorry.

It was unlikely she would marry. She loved Phil and because of his determination to remain married, he had made love to her, told her how much he cared, then let her down in the worst possible way. She would never feel the same way about anyone else, so this baby would be all she had to fill her life. While her mother and father continued to discuss ways of finding out who the father was, she gently dreamed of girls' names and boys' names and wondered if she might be the first in the family to produce twins.

"So I have to plan for May," Lilly said one day as she and her mother were washing up after supper. "I'll have the winter to get everything ready, won't I?" She sighed happily. "A spring baby will be lovely."

"Typical!" Huw grumbled. "Right at the start of the season. It couldn't be worse."

Beth silently thought that Lilly being unable to work wouldn't change much; she never had been too keen to do her share.

"Don't worry, Dad," she said. "With Freddy away, I'll have plenty of spare time."

"And besides," Huw went on, glaring at his daughter, "what's lovely about having a baby and everyone knowing you haven't been churched? No engagement ring or even a visible boyfriend. People'll think you're a tart, that's what they'll think, mind. Carrying on like a tart. What's lovely about that, eh?"

"That's enough, Huw," Marged warned, and Huw stomped off to look at the garden to cool his anger.

Apart from Beth, it was Hannah who helped Lilly the most. Bleddyn had told her about the pregnancy when she visited him with her two girls to share one of Johnny's letters with him.

"D'you think I could call on Lilly?" she asked, and Bleddyn walked up to Sidney Street with her and Marged invited them in. While Bleddyn and his brother went out to look at the garden, a euphemism for talking in private, Lilly and her mother went to make tea. Leaving Josie and Marie listening to the wireless, Hannah followed them into the kitchen.

"Johnny's dad has told me about the baby," she said hesitantly to Lilly. "I wondered whether you'd like to borrow my pram? It's in Mam's loft and it's been well polished and covered against dust, so it should look smart enough."

"Thanks, that's kind of you, Hannah." Lilly was delighted with this positive response to her news. "I'd be glad to borrow it. There's so much to get, isn't there, and me without a husband." She lowered her eyes, expecting sympathy, but Hannah's reaction surprised her.

"You're on your own, but at least you know it. Some mothers think they're safe and secure in a marriage and find they are not. That's worse. Forget looking for sympathy, face the facts and get on with it, that's my advice."

Shock and the beginnings of anger showed in Lilly's face but then she relaxed and smiled. "Thanks again, I think I needed that."

"Sorry if I was rude," Hannah apologised.

"No, not rude, just reminding me that I've got myself into this mess and I have to – as you put it – face facts."

"Married, was he?" Hannah asked, thinking of her own ex-husband's games.

"I don't want to talk about him," Lilly said quietly.

"If ever you do, then come and see me. I've had plenty of disasters in my life and it's taught me, among other things, to be discreet. And I love Johnny and would never do anything to hurt his family."

They arranged to meet at the weekend,

when Hannah would help her make lists of what she would need. "I might even find a few baby nightgowns and a cardigan or two. I don't think I'll be needing them any more," Hannah told her.

When Ronnie was released from hospital, Olive went to the station to meet his train. She stood on the platform, watching the few passengers wandering about, some carrying shopping bags and others with briefcases and a newspaper. It was all so different from the day Ronnie had left. The platform had been crowded then, groups surrounding young men as they left to join their training camp, travel warrant ready to show the inspector, small suitcases with all they were allowed to take held tightly in one hand, the other in most cases around a mother or a sister, a wife or a lover.

It had been quiet then as now, in spite of the crowd; the departing ones having nothing left to say, wanting to be gone, to get the painful parting over with. Those staying behind had given up repeating the same clichés about taking care, avoiding damp socks and eating well, and there were no more promises from both sides to write regularly. It had all been said. Now, waiting for the train to bring Ronnie back, Olive couldn't help feeling relief and gladness that her husband was coming home safe and relatively sound.

As the train puffed importantly into the station and squealed to a stop, she looked up and down the train as doors opened and people stepped out. Not so many. At three in the afternoon few people travelled. He came out backwards, awkward on his crutches, an elderly woman helping him, much to his embarrassment. Olive ran to him, thanked the lady and hugged Ronnie, almost falling against the train as she did so.

She was glad to hide her shock and distress from him by burying her face against his shoulder. He looked thin and so very, very pale. No sign of the suntan that darkened his face in the summer months. He looked as though he hadn't seen the sun in years. His hair was unbelievably short and a bandage was visible under his hat. She felt his bony body and wondered how she could hide her alarm.

After a moment, composing herself, she eased away from him, a smile fixed on her face, and stared into his eyes. Although they were more deeply set in his wasted face it was Ronnie she saw there and she knew it was up to her to make the rest of him strong again.

The lady who helped him was standing there, obviously with something to say.

"I hope you'll be going back when your wounds have healed, young man," she said warningly. "Hitler won't be beaten if we shirk our duty."

"Of course," Ronnie said, then, in a whisper, he added, "Not it I can help it!" making Olive laugh.

Linking arms, Ronnie using two sticks, they made their way to the exit where a taxi was found to take them back to their two rooms in Moll's house in Sidney Street. After greeting Auntie Audrey and assuring her he was really quite well, Ronnie went upstairs. Refusing Olive's assistance, he sat on the bottom step and went up backwards.

"Perhaps you'd better have a bed downstairs," Audrey said. "I can get it ready in no time."

Ronnie refused. "Thanks, Auntie Audrey, but I have a goal in mind. I'm going to get up and down stairs without sticks before the end of the month. I can't give up that easy."

The war news was becoming serious and very frightening with stories of air raids and threats that the bombing campaign would get far worse as Hitler tried to destroy cities and lower morale to the point where Britain would surrender. But for Olive that day, looking across the fireside at her husband, the war belonged to other people. Sympathy was there for the families who had lost their homes through the fierce bombing, and the hundreds who had lost their loved ones, but it was lessened by her relief that for Ronnie, the war was as good as over.

Beth had an occasional note from Freddy and on almost every occasion there was an accompanying letter from Peter. She always gave Peter's letter to her parents to read as there was nothing more than casual friendship displayed. He wrote amusing descriptions of the people he met, and his observations were real enough for Beth to see them clearly. He wrote of his own mistakes and foolishness, and Beth began to look for his letters with more enthusiasm than for Freddy's.

Freddy usually filled the short page with complaints, wanting sympathy for his boredom, and often asking for money to help him afford the pictures when a rare pass enabled him to go into the town near which he was based. She wondered whether he had a girl to take. Freddy had never minded going alone, but he preferred someone beside him to share the laughter and the fear and all the other illusory emotions the film world offered him.

Beth hadn't mentioned the disappearance of their savings. He was a man who had to have money to spend, she knew that. The temptation of knowing money was available was too much for him when there was something he needed or just wanted. In future, any saving would have to be done in her name. She already had twenty-two pounds put aside but she said nothing about it to Freddy.

She knew that both Johnny and Taff both sent money home for Hannah and Evelyn to save for them. It wasn't much, just a gesture to remind them they were together and planning for the future. She didn't think Freddy would send money to his mother and he certainly wouldn't think of adding to their savings. No, Freddy liked money to spend. He had no thought of looking further than today. Looking into the future and planning a home was for her to deal with. Like Lilly with her baby, she was on her own. But she bought a five-shilling postal order and put it in with her reply.

She had continued to take Peter's letters to his father. Bernard Gregory was always very pleased to see her and sometimes she stayed a while and helped him feed the chickens, stack the firewood he sold or fill barrels with seaweed gathered from the beach, which he sold further inland as manure for allotments and gardens. He was always busy, making a few shillings in one of many ways, occasionally using the donkeys to bring seaweed and wood along the narrow paths from the beach, but whenever possible taking the larger cart and the pony. He delivered for a few shops too, when they lost their drivers to the army, and transported furniture when required. Anything that would bring in a few shillings, providing for himself and the animals by his efforts.

A procession was arranged by the local churches and the donkeys were employed to take part, although this was voluntary. It was to raise money for the Red Cross. Beth went along to help with the costumes, enjoying the unexpected activity when winter and the black-out brought its gloom.

One mid-November evening Marged gave her a cake to take to the old man. She was hoping that Peter would be a greater attraction than Freddy, she admitted to her sister Audrey as they watched Beth set off for Goose Lane.

"Selfish and greedy, that's what Freddy Clements is, and I'd be delighted if she gave him the push and married Peter Gregory instead."

"We all make our own choices," Audrey said. "Beth would find someone else if she thought Freddy's selfishness was going to be a problem. Some women like a man to have faults, it makes them feel needed. People say that Mam was selfish, stopping Wilf and me from marrying," Audrey went on. "And that's true, she was." Her eyes went misty as she thought back to those difficult times. The memories were still painful. "She did it because it suited her. No other reason. Wilf and I wanted to marry but once the problems we had were sorted, there was never any great urgency after a while. I began to think she had been right, but she wasn't, she was just selfish."

"Beth wouldn't marry him if she wasn't sure he'd change. It isn't down to us to tell her how to live her life."

"Freddy is cheating on her and he used money that was for their future. Yet she still plans to marry him." Audrey stared at her sister with a quizzical tilt of her head.

"What are you saying? Beth wants to look after Freddy and feels the need to accept him faults and all?"

"Some women like that, enjoy being a bit of a martyr. Although with Freddy it might be different. Perhaps Freddy doesn't want to get married but hangs on to Beth in case he doesn't get a better offer, and he wants to make sure there's someone to look after him."

"Audrey! That doesn't say much for our Beth!"

"It says even less for Freddy," Audrey retorted.

When Beth arrived at the cottage on Goose Lane there was no sign of Mr Gregory. The door was never locked and she went inside, intending to leave the cake, the letter and a note for him. She was stepping into the kitchen when she heard voices. Calling to let Mr Gregory know she was there, she stepped out into the back garden, still bright with fuchsia bushes, dahlias and a few late roses, and saw Mr Gregory walking up from the beach with Peter. A sudden shyness overwhelmed her and she darted back into the kitchen, hoping to avoid being seen.

"Beth?" Peter called. "Is that you?"

"I only brought a cake for your father," she said shyly. "Mam sent it. Not much fat in it, rationing, see, but I hope you'll enjoy it," she prattled on, backing away as though in a hurry.

"How kind," Peter said, running forward and taking both of her hands in his. "I hope you aren't dashing back home? You must stay and taste it with us. Dad?" he called back to where Mr Gregory was putting the harness away in the shed, which he rather grandly called the tack room. "The kettle is as good as on, don't delay."

He busied himself in the kitchen, putting china and cutlery on a tray, which he carried to the table. Beth felt the need to help, but having had no female to run the house in the past ten years, she could see that setting tables and the tasks usually dealt with by the woman of the house came easily to him.

She usually cycled to call on Mr Gregory but today she had chosen to walk, so Peter offered her a lift home.

"No need," she said, longing to accept. The prospect of another half an hour in Peter's company was alarmingly tempting, but she had to refuse. "I can easily walk," she assured him. "You need to spend as much time as possible with your father. He looks forward so much to your visits."

"He values your visits too," he said. "Thank you so much for being kind to him. I really appreciate it. I'm very fond of the old boy, you know."

She hesitated so long about how to reply that she ended up saying nothing and felt silly for being so unaccomplished a conversationalist. She imagined that Peter's girlfriends would always know exactly what to say.

He handed her her coat and as she put it on she felt a wave of disappointment flood over her. Why hadn't she said yes, she would like him to walk home with her? Why hadn't she acted the helpless woman and told him she was nervous out alone in case there were parachutes falling out of enemy planes and ... She knew she couldn't act the helpless woman and she'd make a mess of it if she tried.

Turning to call goodnight to Mr Gregory, she saw that Peter was putting on his overcoat. A repeat protest almost reached her lips, but not quite.

The night was clear, the moon a Chinese lantern floating in a velvet sky, large and bright as though lit from within. The lights from the town were blocked by the black-out curtaining and wardens stalked the streets warning people to "put that light out!" if a glimmer were allowed to escape. Peter took her hand and tucked it under his arm companionably.

"I'd hate to lose you," he teased. As they walked, they talked about their plans for the future. Peter wanted to move to Cardiff and run an agency finding work for people, covering all occupations.

"I have some qualifications in running a business," he explained. "Accountancy and other aspects of the day-to-day running of a business of my own. And I have a theory that once this war is over, nothing will be the same and, among other things, employment will change dramatically. Women are beginning to realise that they needn't stay at home all day every day to run a home. Until they have children and when the children are grown, or even when the children are at school, they can spare a few hours a day to earn some extra money. I want to expand on that."

"I can't imagine working anywhere else but the beach," Beth told him. "Mam and Dad have always worked there with Granny Moll. Even when we were small we went over to the sands with them. I can't imagine doing anything different. I work in town in the winter, of course, but there's always the beach to come back to."

"I think you're very fortunate to have a dream and be able to live it. So few of us manage that." He squeezed her arm against him and smiled down at her, and in the intimacy of the darkness his nearness was as exciting as a kiss.

"I should be doing more to help, but Dad says what I do on the sands is part of the war effort, helping people to relax and have fun and pretend for a while. So my conscience isn't too troubled."

She asked him about his occupation in the forces but he told her it was secret work and it would be tantamount to treason if he revealed the details of what he was doing.

It wasn't until they were almost there that Beth realised she had been talking about herself and not her and Freddy. She thought perhaps she was guilty of a different kind of treason for enjoying Peter's company so much. Again an explanation almost reached her lips, but not quite.

"Come again tomorrow," Peter suggested. "We can go and see the donkeys in their winter quarters."

"Love to," she said at once, willingly pushing thoughts of Freddy Clements from her mind.

Investigations into the cause of the fire had ended with the conclusion that the fire had begun near the door, but there was no evidence about how it had started. Anything combustible that might have been either thrown behind the door or pushed through the letter box had been swallowed in the flames.

Whatever the cause, Marged and Huw decided that there would be no letter box on the new door. It had never been needed and people had been known to push rubbish through. Perhaps a cigarette end had been included with an empty packet or matchbox, they suggested to the investigators.

Both really believed that the fire was a deliberate act, perpetrated by a resentful Mrs Downs, and Huw constantly reminded Marged of his suspicions about the woman and of how his warnings about her had been ignored.

Beth returned to Goose Lane the following day, the last day of Peter's leave. She should have cycled, but the thought of Peter walking her home again made her decide to walk.

They sat and talked for a while, Mr Gregory smiling, puffing on his old pipe, contented it seemed to see the young couple enjoying each other's company. He knew Peter had plans for when the war ended, plans that would take him far away from St David's Well, but he hoped that, with a local girl stealing his heart, he might change his mind and stay closer to home.

He didn't go with them when they went to see the donkeys. "I'll be going up later with the food," he said. In the summer the donkeys managed with grass and an occasional treat, but as winter approached their feed increased and they were given mash each evening before being locked into their stables.

Peter didn't walk Beth home that evening. Instead he used the pony and flat cart and they clip-clopped slowly around the lanes, in no hurry to reach their destination. As the streets with their darkened windows were reached, he stopped the pony, turned to Beth, and kissed her.

"There, complain if you must, but I've been wanting to do that for so long."

"Why should I complain?" She leaned towards him and they kissed again.

"Please write often," he whispered, his breath feather light on her cheek. "I look forward to your letters more than you can imagine."

"Kiss me again," she replied, "in case I forget how it feels."

"I'll never forget our first kiss. Never," he said drawing her close to him.

"I'll remember every moment," she whispered, before being silenced once again by his lips.

Lilly was still up when Beth went in and a glance told her that Beth had done more than walk down to Goose Lane. "Peter home, was he?" she asked.

"Peter was there, yes, but he's going back tomorrow."

"He didn't make you forget you're engaged to Freddy Clements, did he?"

"Of course not," Beth said, too quickly.

"Oh, like that, is it? Absence makes the heart grow fonder? Don't make me laugh! Plenty of men will come home to disappointment after this war."

"Oh, Lilly, he's so nice. We talked so easily and about everything. I don't remember enjoying myself so much in ages. I like him so much I feel" – the word came back to her – "like a traitor, forgetting all about Freddy while I was with Peter."

"How d'you think *I* feel? I encouraged – him – and I feel traitorous when I think about his wife. It wasn't just a nice chat and a casual kiss." She patted her slightly extended belly. "This isn't a pimple, is it!"

Work on restoring the café on the cliffs

284

above the beach began in earnest once the insurance company were satisfied that no further investigation was required. Bleddyn and Huw had to do much of the work themselves as so many builders had left to serve in the forces. Finances were another consideration. They were worried that they might no longer be able to depend on a good summer season to boost their income. They had to conserve as much of their savings as possible in case the worst happened and the beach had to close.

The framework of the building was metal and the wooden floor was made of thick timbers, which in most areas were scorched rather than seriously damaged. So apart from cleaning, sanding and replacing the windows and some of the furniture, decoration was the biggest task.

Huw and Bleddyn left the choice of colour to Marged, but when she chose what he considered a rather dull yellow and a dark blue, he ignored her and bought white.

"Now and then I have to remind her who's boss," he joked to his brother, but he made sure Bleddyn wasn't there when Marged saw their effort for the first time.

Expecting a row, he was relieved when she agreed with his choice. "Practical having all one colour, and cleaner looking too," she said. "We'll stick to blue for the curtains and tablecloths, shall we?"

Huw frowned. Why was she asking his opinion – was she building up to ask a favour? Something he wouldn't like?

Huw found work for the winter in a factory, and was alarmed when given a reminder that when the new season began he might not be able to leave. War work was increasingly important and more and more people were having to accept work in stores or factories. There were dozens of items needed to keep the army supplied: uniforms, kit bags, metal tools, cooking equipment, cutlery and survival gear, besides the many and varied weapons.

Beth, Audrey, Marged and Lilly went on knitting, sometimes for the soldiers and sometimes for the baby. Olive helped when she wasn't attending to Ronnie, who walked with difficulty, was easily exhausted and still needed constant attention. Living with Audrey and Maude and Myrtle meant she had help and someone with whom to discuss the future.

"Ronnie won't ever be strong on that leg," Audrey said one morning when the five of them were finishing breakfast. "I don't think he'll be able to manage a long day on the beach with Huw and Bleddyn and the others."

"What will he do? He loved the beach," Olive said, looking sadly at Ronnie who sat half smiling, amused at being talked over as though he were a helpless and not very bright child.

"I've thought of that and I've decided what we'll do, if you agree, Olive," he said, and the others stared at him in surprise. "I want us, you and me, Olive, to take a market stall."

"A market stall?"

"Selling vegetables, fruit when we can get it, and perhaps fish."

"Fish?"

"Stop behaving like a parrot and listen," he teased. "The stall at the back of the market, near the door into Frog Street, has had to close as the man who ran it has joined up, so I suggest we reopen it. I'm sure the previous owner would help us with suppliers and all that. I could sit down for a lot of the time. It would be perfect. What d'you think?"

Olive's first instinct was to say no, but she remembered how happily Ronnie dealt with the crowds on the beach. He liked people, he enjoyed working with them. A market stall would suit him perfectly. For herself she had doubts, but she smiled at him, her eyes shining, and said, "Ronnie, love, I think it's a wonderful idea."

During November and December people began to hoard what they could, and save from their rations to prepare for Christmas.

Besides trying to work up excitement for the celebration, every household seemed to live for the postman's visits, longing for news while avoiding thinking about the visits of the telegram boys who brought the worst news of all. Every day, Marged looked out and watched as the postman approached, praying for a letter to tell her Eynon was coming home. He hadn't been home once since joining up and now she didn't even know whether he was alive or dead. She was convinced that he must have refused the offer of leave initially, afraid for some reason to face them all. Now the only news of him was the negative kind, when army representatives called to ask if he had made contact.

The last time she had shouted at them, "I had him for seventeen years without a problem. You had him five minutes and you lost him!" Stony faced as always, the men left with a repeat of the warning about informing the authorities the moment she heard from him.

She took out the pathetically few letters and cards he had sent. In the first ones he had told them he was enjoying his training. Then one told her he wouldn't be coming home on his leave because a friend from Yorkshire had invited him there. Marged relived the disappointment of those words. She remembered how she had forced a smile and said to Huw, "Grown up he is and

288

able to choose his friends. He'll be home next time for sure."

She now knew there had been other reasons for not coming home. Had he been in trouble? What trouble could there be that he couldn't tell her about? He must have been desperate if he'd run away. Was he regretting signing up for five years? Had he been wishing he could come home but was afraid of breaking down when he saw all the familiar places and faces?

She still wrote to him almost daily; cheerful letters, full of reminders about the summers to come when he could decide for himself whether or not he would work on the sands.

"We'll be so used to managing without you, me and your dad and Uncle Bleddyn, Beth and Lilly, and Ronnie too when he's well enough, that we won't have to press-gang you into service," she joked.

She had told him about Lilly and teased him about being an uncle. The bulk of her letters were about the family and the people he knew, giving details about them, about where they had been and what they had been doing, telling him that the beach was still attracting visitors this late, and about the stalwarts who swam in the cold months of the year "like Bleddyn used to do".

"It's as though he's in prison with no hope of getting out ever again," Marged said to

Huw after her most recent letter to him had been returned. "So homesick he must be."

"At least the occasional card tells us he's alive, and that's all he can tell us until he decides to give himself up. Once he decides to face it, he'll settle down to army life. He must have had a bad start. I don't think it's easy for some. Got to be a part of it, see, be thought of as a character, one of the lads. He won't be down for long, not our Eynon."

Eynon was washing the gash on his head and wondering if it would ever heal properly. The bruises from the kicking and beatings from Kipper had faded to yellow and they would be gone soon.

For the past week he had been sleeping in a barn about five miles outside Aberystwyth. He had been found on the third night huddled in the hayloft with chickens and dogs below, dogs who were friendly and shared his supper of chips, bought in the town with money he had stolen and eaten in the solitude of the barn cold and greasy but sufficient to ease the pangs of hunger. He could have eaten them hot, straight from the shop, but there was a need to pretend he was going home, and the dogs were there waiting for him, a substitute family.

It was when they were sharing the last of the chips that a man appeared in the doorway. Eynon didn't see him at first, but the dogs wagged their tails and looked towards the door and he knew he had been discovered. He felt a flash of relief that it was over and he could return to something like normal, then the instinct to run.

"I'm not doing any harm, mister," he said softly.

"Runaway, are you?"

"I just couldn't resist the chance when it came. Ashamed I am, but I couldn't take it."

The man came in and Eynon was alarmed to see a shotgun over the man's arm. He foolishly grabbed one of the dogs and held it close to him. He hadn't suffered all this to be shot in a farmer's barn, had he?

The man broke the gun and laid it down. "Thought you might be a Jerry parachutist," he explained.

To Eynon's relief he was offered a bath and some food before going on his way. The wound on his head was dressed and the farmer told him it wouldn't heal until it was stitched into place; the lip of it would constantly pull away and start the bleeding until the flap was secured properly. Eynon thanked him but knew he wouldn't try to see a doctor; not yet. Not until he was ready.

While he was washing the filth of weeks from his skin he listened anxiously, half expecting the police to arrive, but he was allowed to sleep peacefully until the following morning then sent on his way with his pockets filled with food.

The coming of autumn heralded the start of a more intense bombing campaign on London and other major cities. The Luftwaffe seemed in control of people's lives, forcing thousands of Londoners to pack their most valued possessions and hurry underground night after night in the hope of evading the bombs. It was a campaign with which Hitler hoped to destroy the capital's commercial centre.

A new menace increased the danger to shipping and warnings of even greater shortages of food were announced. The war was being fought a long way from St David's Well but it was involving every man, woman and child in the fight.

Freddy had written to tell Beth he was coming home for three days, and like Olive when she had gone to meet Ronnie after his injury, Beth waited at the railway station and compared the calm of his return with the chaos of his departure.

The train was full with office workers and shop assistants coming home at the end of their day, and she stood near the ticket-office wall looking anxiously around, afraid they would miss each other in the crush.

Freddy stepped out on to the platform

right in front of her, and he turned to help a trim little WAAF girl, who clearly didn't need it, putting his arms around her and lifting her down from the step. Beth looked away, wanting to hide so she could pretend not to have seen the incident. Glancing back she saw they were kissing.

She backed towards the fence, urgently needing to run away, but there wasn't time. Freddy waved and blew another kiss as the girl hurried away through the barrier, where the ticket collector stood checking everyone who went through.

The platform had almost cleared before Freddy saw her. He looked fit and confident and, after a brief hug, immediately asked her if she had any money to spare. "For a taxi, see, I haven't any change," he explained as she stared at him in surprise.

"Freddy," she laughed dryly, "at least wait until you've said hello before you ask for money!"

She handed him a few shillings and they climbed into the back of the Austin, where he immediately put his arms around her and kissed her – a surprisingly passionate kiss, and from the way he looked at her, she knew he wanted more. This was a very different Freddy from the one revealed in his scrappy letters. He missed her, wanted her, and actions were more his way of telling her than writing letters, she thought as the taxi wound its way through the streets of the town.

"Who was the girl?" she asked.

"The WAAF girl? Oh, no one; she'd hurt her arm and I helped her, that's all."

Beth wondered how many other girls he had been kind to in such an affectionate way.

There was no one in the house and he coaxed her upstairs under the pretext of wanting to look at the view.

"Freddy, when were you interested in a view from a window?" she laughed as he pulled her up the lino-covered stairs behind him.

"Who said anything about looking out of a window?" he said, pushing her jacket off her shoulders and kissing her neck, his lips moving lower until they reached the swelling of her breast. "I love you, Beth, and I've been dreaming of this moment."

Alarmed, tempted, afraid of discovery, imprisoned by desire and frightened by what was happening to her, she tried to push him away. His hands were everywhere and eventually fear blocked out desire and she hit him hard, on the side of his face.

Shocked, he stared at her and in a bewildered, little-boy voice said, "Beth, the way you kissed me in the taxi, I thought you wanted me as badly as I want you. Come on; I have to have something to keep me going while I'm away. I might not come back, Beth; you know that, don't you? Hundreds are dying and I could easily be one of them. This is embarkation leave. This could be our last chance."

The dreaded word "embarkation" almost persuaded her, but not quite. It was a vision of Peter that kept appearing in her head that prevented her from succumbing to desire and blackmail, so that she did refuse and allowed her anger to show.

"Stop it! What have you been up to, Freddy Clements? What makes you think you can come back here and treat me like some common tart?"

"I love you, Beth. I'm going a long way from home and I want memories to take with me. What's wicked about that, eh?"

"Three days? I thought embarkation leave was longer?" she said as he sat and stared at her.

"It's all I've got, then I'll be sent abroad and I won't get any home leave then. Please, Beth." He stood and walked towards her, his arms spread wide, but she slipped past him and ran down the stairs.

Whenever they were alone he tried to persuade her to make love, and it was becoming increasingly difficult to refuse. But refuse she would. She didn't want to be in the same position as Lilly. Freddy might tell her how much he loved her, but she had a thinly veiled conviction that his love wasn't strong enough to cope with her having his child. However passionately he loved her, she didn't think Freddy was ready for marriage and responsibility. That brought a shadow of sadness to the three days he was home.

Freddy didn't spend the whole time with Beth. She thought her refusal was the reason for his disappearances but he explained that, faced with a long absence, he wanted to say cheerio to his friends. In fact the only friend he saw was Shirley Downs, and although his leave was actually seven days, he had kept the other four days free. He didn't want to spend it all here, where, besides being uncooperative, Beth restricted his activities. He had grown away from all that. He had quickly discovered that not all girls were like Beth. With the girls who were attracted to the uniform, there wasn't much persuasion needed before moral stands were abandoned.

On the last of his three days he and Beth walked over to St David's Well Bay to the now empty sands. There was no sign now of what had been a holiday beach. The stalls had long gone, and only a few people strolled, perhaps remembering the frenzied activity of the past summer, when the clean golden sands, the varied stalls and amusements had attracted hundreds of families to come and have fun.

Seeing the café with its boarded-up windows shocked him.

"I'd forgotten about the fire," he said. "Did you find out who started it?"

"Not really. But Mam and Dad are convinced that Mrs Downs was responsible," she said.

"What d'you mean, responsible? Was she careless about things? Like leaving the gas burning?"

"No, worse than that. They think she burnt it down deliberately. She hates my parents and accused Granny Moll of stealing her grandfather's business or something. I don't remember the facts, although it's a regularly told story."

"That's a lot of rubbish!" Freddy said angrily. "Mrs Downs wouldn't do anything like that! They shouldn't say such things."

"Mrs Downs accused Granny Moll's grandparents of cheating, of stealing the business from her family."

"Who told you that? Granny Moll, I'll bet! Her grandparents bought it from Mrs Downs's grandparents. How can Mrs Downs resent that? It's all in Granny Moll's head. She made it up!"

"Freddy, it's true, you know it is!" Beth was alarmed at his anger and his refusal to support her.

"Damn it all, Mrs Downs worked for

them, didn't she? If they really believed she hated them enough to burn the place, would they have employed her? Just using her as a scapegoat they are, and you're as bad for repeating it. What's Shirley or her mam ever done to you, eh?"

His anger frightened her and she backed away from the furious expression on his face. He ran off then and after a moment's hesitation she hurried after him. A bus came around the corner and was moving off as he reached the bus stop. She slowed down in disbelief as he jumped on it and left her standing there.

She was furious about the way he had treated her, accusing her of lying about Mrs Downs, walking off and leaving her to walk home alone like an abandoned puppy. She walked fast, releasing her anger, but slowed as outrage left her. By the time she had reached home she had calmed down and was able to put his unexpected outburst down to his stress at the end of his leave, and having to go back and face the dangers of the front line. But she did wonder why he was quite so vehement in his protection of Shirley's mother, a woman he barely knew. Unless, as many hinted, Shirley Downs really was more than a girl he occasionally bumped into at the pictures.

Nine

Ronnie and Olive's market stall idea was under way by the end of November, but it was a bad time to begin. Seasonal fruits were finished, apart from a few scruffy apples, the import of bananas and oranges had all but finished permanently, and there were few vegetables to be found.

Leeks and cabbages and carrots and swedes were the mainstay, with potatoes being the most important item they offered. The government was beginning to suggest more ways of using the vegetables that were available, to make them more interesting, but sales were poor and Ronnie and Olive were afraid the stall would only support itself until the spring. Profit was an unlikely outcome.

Olive continued to work at the factory, but helped out on the stall when she could and, to her surprise, began to enjoy it. The bustling market with its hordes of busy shoppers looking for bargains or a commodity in short supply gave her an excitement she had never found on the beach. There were no frantic crowds fooling about and looking for excuses to laugh and shout, just people quietly searching for ways to feed their families. The place hummed with activity whereas the beach had shrieked.

They were situated close to the back entrance to the market hall and close by there were shoe stalls selling bargain-priced footwear and handbags and purses. Another vendor offered remnants of floor covering, mostly linoleum and cheaper imitation, and rugs of various sizes. On occasion there would be a few pieces of carpet at very low prices and, as though by bush telegraph, the news went out and a queue would quickly form.

"If only we were in the other entrance, catching the customers as they come in," Ronnie sighed as a couple of chattering women walked past with their baskets packed high. "I hope we didn't make a mistake."

Olive looked around them.

"No, Ronnie love, I don't believe we did."

"You like working here, don't you?" Ronnie asked her later as she took the money for a few tired-looking tomatoes they had bought from Mr Gregory.

"Yes, I do. I didn't think I would. I imagined the market would be the same as the stalls on the sand, but it isn't. The customers here are more inclined to stop and chat for one thing. When we're busy on the beach I seem to do nothing more than look at their hands, take the money and return the change. I often stop and realise that I haven't looked at a face for ages. And" – she looked at Ronnie, touching his arm, hoping he wouldn't be offended – "I think part of the reason I'm so happy is that it's ours, yours and mine, and we don't have to do what others tell us."

Ronnie had to sit on a high stool for much of the day, but his cheerfulness and ready wit attracted customers and they were soon recognising the same people returning once or twice each week. Their names were unknown and they began to give them nicknames, which they would whisper to each other. One elderly lady always wore a startlingly bright green hat; another carried a basket made from raffia-covered milk-bottle tops sewn together, in which a tiny Pekinese puppy travelled. These women received polite names, but others did not. Adenoids, Woodbine Winnie, Big Nose and Slipper Feet were some of the names they would whisper. Others were named for the words they always used, like "What you got then?" and "Too dear" and, one of their fav-ourites, known to every stall-holder selling food in the hall, "Any throw-outs I can use to make a soup?" These and many others became regulars. Then there were the wounded men who came past on crutches or with a sleeve folded and pinned, and the sad-faced women who looked as though everything it was possible for them to bear had already weighted down their shoulders. There were those with children being carried or walking holding their mothers' skirts for fear of being lost. To these Ronnie and Olive were generous, even though their profits were almost nil.

The war raged on, the bombing killing hundreds and making thousands homeless, far from the boundaries of St David's Well, but touching them all the same.

One lady, whom they had seen passing on several occasions, a fair-haired woman of about twenty, surprised them one day by bringing them a cup of tea each from the café at the entrance where she worked.

"There's cold you look," she said handing them the cups and saucers over the piled-up vegetables. "Have these on me and if you want the same tomorrow I'll bring them over and you can pay at the end of the week. Eleven a.m. and three in the afternoon all right, is it?"

Olive and Ronnie thanked her and the cups of tea and a brief chat were a welcome break in their morning and afternoon. The woman, who was unmarried, was called Janet Copp, and she managed the small market café. She told them some of her story over the first few days.

"I haven't got no family. But," she said thoughtfully, "I suppose I might have cousins somewhere. Mam never said much about them, mind. They moved away years ago. But neighbours hinted at some dark secret. Perhaps Mam did something shameful and was cut off from the rest of the family. Exciting, eh? Just think, they might be rich enough to save me from the boring ol' café. There's lovely that would be."

Olive and Ronnie told her about Lilly expecting a child without naming the father, who was married to someone else.

"Mam and Dad wouldn't dream of refusing help, or cutting her off from the family like that," Ronnie said. "Our Lilly's a part of the family and nothing would be allowed to separate us."

"Ronnie's mother is so kind, even to strangers. She even took in a couple of children who were living rough. They hadn't been abandoned, though. Their parents are dead and they had run away from a children's orphange," Olive explained.

"Thank goodness I was too old to go through that. I'd have hated being cared for with dozens of others in a place like that." She grinned at Ronnie as she collected their empty cups. "Their name isn't Copp, is it?"

"Sorry, but life isn't that tidy I'm afraid," Ronnie smiled. "Carpenter they are and, like you, they'd love to find their family. Not much hope though. They do talk about a sister-in-law and a brother, but we've never been able to find them."

"Pity," Janet sniffed. "I'd like a couple of sisters."

Bleddyn's daughter-in-law, Evelyn, didn't call on him very often. With the work she did involving odd hours, and Bleddyn's house a long way off her regular route, she rarely found herself in that part of town. In his letters, Taff often asked whether she had seen his father but she evaded replying.

Like many others, she was beginning to find the restrictions of wartime life tedious. With Taff away she wouldn't go dancing like many of her friends did; she didn't want even a whisper of trouble to reach him. So there was only the pictures where she went sometimes with Maude and Myrtle and on rare occasions with Audrey and Wilf too. The girls with whom she worked came in most mornings full of the fun they'd had the night before and, although not envious, she felt dull being unable to join in. Listening to the wireless, doing the week's ironing, racing home to catch the shop, it was hardly riveting. There were the letters from Taff of course, but unlike some of the others she didn't want to read out his words to have them mulled over and laughed at.

When one of the girls was celebrating her birthday and asked her to join them, she agreed, and wondered afterwards where her common sense had been at the time. Before the planned night out, she went on one of her rare visits to Bleddyn and found Hannah and her two girls there. Shame, jealousy and embarrassment made her abrupt with her greeting and Hannah stood at once to leave.

"Well, Mr Castle, I'll leave you to talk to Evelyn, shall I? We'll all be down to see you on Sunday, unless you'd like to have tea with us?"

Evelyn stood with a look of impatience on her face as Hannah dressed the children against the cold, discussed final arrangements for Sunday and left.

"Why did you do that? Is there anything wrong?" Bleddyn asked when they were alone.

"Do what?"

"Rush Hannah away like that. What is it you have to tell me that she can't hear?" His voice was slow and soft, but Evelyn sensed the anger.

"Sorry, Dad, but I was disappointed to find her here. She works a few hours in the mornings and evenings, she has plenty of time to visit you. I have to come when I can and I hoped you'd be alone."

"She's very kind and calls often, sometimes bringing me a letter she's had from Johnny."

"Dad, I'm going out tomorrow night, with the girls from the factory. One of them is eighteen and she's going to join up, so it's a celebration and a farewell."

"Good, you shouldn't be stuck in night after night. Taff wouldn't want that."

"It's only a drink. I wanted to tell you, so you know it's nothing more."

"I hope you enjoy yourself," Bleddyn assured her, forcing a smile. When she left, the smile changed to a frown as he stared at the closing door. He hoped this was not the beginning of trouble. Women who went out without a man, especially in a group, might be tempted to stray out of boredom. Perhaps he ought to visit her more often, make sure everything was still all right.

Maude and Myrtle were intrigued by the story of Janet Copp who, like themselves, had no family. They made Olive and Ronnie repeat it several times, like the children they still were. Although the story had nothing in it to offer them hope, it cheered them to know there were others in a similar state to themselves.

Coming out of the pictures a few days later, standing still to accustom their eyes to the darkness, they heard a voice call, "Hey, Mrs Carpenter, over here!"

The two girls reacted as though in shock. They stared, trying to pierce the darkness and by force of will trying to see the woman who was referred to by their name. Gripping each other's gloved hands, they pushed through the crowd to where they had heard the voice. Fortunately the woman called again, "Mrs Carpenter, yoo hoo!" The two women were all but concealed in the blackness, but they made out the figure of a young woman pushing herself through the closely gathered bodies, making for the person who had called and who was now waving her hands in encouragement.

"She might be our sister-in-law," Myrtle breathed.

Maude dragged Myrtle behind her and followed as the two women set off along the street.

The two women, one of whom was wearing a fur coat, went through the doorway of a public house, the sounds from within bursting forth as people chattered, shouted and laughed. Tinny notes from a piano were heard, and a few were singing a sad song tunelessly. The girls grinned. The discordant, harsh sounds swelled up then stopped abruptly as the doors swung behind them.

The black-out arrangement involved two doors positioned at either end of an angled, covered passageway. Still holding hands, the sisters crept in through the first door and pushed the second open to look into the bar room. They looked around and eventually recognised the two women they had followed. They were at the bar trying to get served by a barman who was determined to serve all the men first. He didn't approve of unaccompanied women in his pub.

"Shall we wait?" Maude suggested, and in the darkness she felt her sister nod her head.

Still looking through the slit, Myrtle gasped and told Maude to look in the corner close to the fire. Around a table about eight women and two soldiers were sitting, and one of the women was Evelyn.

The group were giggling and rosy faced and they saw that one of the soldiers had his arm around Evelyn's shoulder. They couldn't hear what was being said as she tried to move away, but guessed that the others were encouraging Evelyn to have some fun.

The two girls stepped backwards and out into the dark night. They didn't want to see any more, but eventually couldn't resist one more peep. Evelyn was now looking angry and they saw her take a glass of beer belonging to one of the soldiers and pour it over the head of the one who was annoying her. Helpless with laughter, the girls ran out once more into the night.

It was tempting to run home and tell Auntie Audrey what they had seen, but the need to talk to someone bearing their name was too strong. Hiding in the shadows, stifling giggles, they didn't have to wait long. The two women, easily recognised by their voices and the fur coat, came out and they followed.

Having to keep back and occasionally hide, they lost their quarry after a few short cuts through lanes, but found them again waiting at a bus stop. It was almost half-past ten by now and they both knew they should really be going home.

"If we can find out where she lives, we can go back another day," Maude said when Myrtle became worried. "We won't talk to her tonight."

At home Audrey was knitting, stopping every few rows to stand on the front doorstep and listen for sounds of them coming. They had never been this late before. She wished her mother was there. She wouldn't dither, she'd do something. She gave herself another fifteen minutes before going to tell Marged and Huw that they hadn't returned.

The girls followed the two women on to the bus and asked for the terminus. When the women alighted near a row of small terraced houses outside the town, still apparently oblivious of the girls trotting along behind them, they followed.

The inadequately lit bus lumbered off and

before Maude could reach for her sister's hand, they were grabbed roughly. Amid their screams of fright, the women demanded, "What are you doing following us? If my husband has asked you to see what I'm up to, you can tell him—"

Swearing their innocence, the girls cried and promised that they hadn't been sent by anyone.

"We're looking for our brother, and we heard someone call you Mrs Carpenter and we thought—" Maude's voice faded as the woman began to laugh.

"Carpenter? My name isn't Carpenter, it's Callender."

The girls waited for a long time but no bus appeared to take them home, so with only a vague idea of where they were, they set off to walk home. Myrtle was dragging her feet and complaining and Maude tried to carry her so that both girls were exhausted when they eventually turned into Sidney Street.

Something was wrong. There were voices shouting, asking questions, making suggestions, someone was crying and, most remarkable of all, lights were escaping from doorways and streaking across the street. Slowing to a hesitant crawl, they soon realised that every house was open, the neighbours were out in force, some in groups talking, others with torches stabbing the ground in front of them. Everywhere men and women were hurrying around. In a doorway they saw two wardens, who seemed oblivious of the black-out regulation being flouted. Cups of tea were being handed out and men with torches were approaching from a different direction from those setting off.

"God 'elp, Myrtle, they're all looking for us. Auntie Audrey'll kill us!"

It was one a.m. before their story was told and everyone was settled, and Audrey had relieved her fears by telling them off. The last thing they heard before going to sleep was the warden shouting for someone to "put that light out", adding, "You needn't think you can make an 'abit of this, mind!"

Peter continued to write regularly to Beth, but it was two weeks before Beth heard from Freddy. Then it was a picture postcard and the frank told her it was posted in Blackpool. She wondered what he was doing there. It was a long way from his barracks. The note was the usual scrawl, casual, friendly, with no mention of missing her or with any reference to their brief time together. He didn't refer to his imminent departure either and she began to wonder whether his words were prevarications when he wrote later, this time from his usual address, and told her that another leave might be possible very soon.

Was it loyalty that kept her pretending he was the man she loved? Or was the war a pause in in her life, a time that was not real, a time to hold back and not think too deeply about what was happening to closeness, love and trust? When the world returned to normal, she would remember how much she loved Freddy, wouldn't she? She wouldn't think about Peter every moment. Everything would be fine.

Once the soldiers began training for their posting overseas, they weren't allowed out of camp: she had learned that much by talking to friends. There was the danger of spies learning of their possible movements and passing on information to the enemy. She thought of asking Peter if he knew what might be happening but decided not. Talking about Freddy would be an intrusion, an unwanted, jarring note in their happy hours together.

She and Peter never did anything that Freddy would consider very exciting when Peter managed a few days' leave. When he was free on one of Beth's days off, they walked in the gradually fading colours of autumn, talking, stopping sometimes for refreshment at an inn or café, or taking a picnic and finding a sheltered corner of a local beach. Between times they wrote long, chatty letters, broadening their knowledge of each other, growing closer, but without the complications of love. They kissed on meeting and when they parted, but rarely did more than hold hands otherwise. Beth knew it was because of the engagement ring she wore and foolishly began to feel irritation with Freddy: resentment, too, for being there, clearly visible on her finger, while he was unlabelled and free to do what he wanted.

She remembered with surprisingly little pain the kiss he had given the WAAF girl on the train, and the way he had leapt to the defence of Shirley's mother, Mrs Downs. He was not being faithful, something deep inside her told her that.

She talked to Lilly about her doubts and Lilly advised her to tell him goodbye.

"I can't, Lilly. Not when he's on the point of going overseas. I'd feel so guilty, him not having anyone to write to him. They all need someone at home who cares for them. It gives them hope, being able to plan for when the war's over."

"And you've just told me you suspect there's someone else he's seeing!" Lilly said in exasperation. "Why pretend you're the only one who'll write to him? Are you the only one to help him spend his leave? I doubt it, and so do you if you're honest. Why don't you face facts, Beth? Freddy's seeking pastures new in more ways than one and only bothering to write when he wants money. Peter is here, asking nothing of you, writing to you, and spending every moment he can with you. How much more do you need before you stop kidding yourself that Freddy loves you?"

Using her pregnancy as an excuse, Lilly rarely worked. She appeared to be busy helping Marged in the house, but in fact did very little. Every afternoon she insisted she needed a rest, and most evenings she either went to the pictures or visited friends. One of her friends was Hannah, for a while at least.

Hannah worked longer hours now Josie was back at school and Marie was at nursery school, but she welcomed Lilly whenever she called, even though she was usually very busy. At first they talked happily about the birth of Lilly's baby and discussed ideas for making and knitting the little garments she would need, but Hannah began to lose patience when she realised that although they talked, nothing was ever achieved by Lilly, only by others doing things for her. Time, she thought, for some serious discussion.

"When are you going to stop feeling sorry for yourself and get organised?" Hannah asked when Lilly had sat in her room all afternoon drinking tea and talking about the unfairness of life, that she had chosen to fall in love with a married man.

"I'm not sorry for myself, I don't go screaming to his wife do I? I'm sorting myself out without causing trouble like some would in my situation," Lilly protested.

"Sorting yourself out does not mean leaning heavily on your mother. Sorting yourself out is getting up and doing what you can to prepare for this baby! How are you going to support it? Have you thought of a job? You should be using these months to train or at least decide what you'll do."

"I can work on the beach in the summer like always," Lilly defended.

"That isn't a job. You take the wage, but from what I understand, you don't do much to earn it."

"Why are you being so unkind? I thought you were my friend," Lilly said tearfully.

"I am, and I hope you value my friendship enough to listen to what I'm saying. I do like you, I would like you to be my friend, my real friend, but you aren't even a friend to yourself, living like you do."

"I dream of having a decent job sometimes," Lilly said. "But working on the beach year after year with Mam and Dad has made me think of work as boredom. How would you like it, doing the same thing day after day?"

"I clean up after other people, the same old chores, day after day after day," Hannah said softly. "Boredom? You don't know what boredom is until you've cleaned floors and walls and lavatories, with the only variety being the different sorts of litter or the colour of the soap."

"Lavatories? Ugh! How can you do it, Hannah?"

"Because of my girls. I do whatever is necessary to keep them fed, clothed and happy." Hannah spoke softly and stared at Lilly, allowing the words to sink in. "They are my responsibility, my joy, my life and I'll do anything for them."

"Having parents who can afford to keep me makes all that noble stuff unnecessary," Lilly replied.

"Until you develop some pride."

"Fat lot of pride in cleaning lavatories!" she retorted as she flounced off.

With Hannah's words ringing in her head, Lilly went for a long walk, through the park, passing places where she and Phil had stopped to kiss, remembering how wonderful it had been. Overwhelming self-pity enveloped her. She hadn't needed Hannah's words to tell her how lazy she was. All her other friends had work, many of them in munitions factories or other work that contributed to the war effort. Even Auntie Audrey went around collecting money for National Savings and was a volunteer fire-watcher, besides running the big house where Granny Moll had lived all her married life.

The baby wasn't due until May. She could work through the winter, and suddenly she knew she wanted to. She had to put aside her easy acceptance of idleness, using the excuse that she was different, that it was her basic character. The question was, with the fish-and-chip shop shop still making her feel queasy, what could she do?

It was the beach, the place she said she hated, that gave her employment. Two of the cafés remained open during the winter. They had small rooms which offered teas and snacks during the summer, but in the winter they made a reasonable living by opening the top room, which was enormous, for dances, tea dances and, on occasion, celebration dinners for various firms. Lilly went there and offered her services as waitress and occasional kitchen hand.

The wages were small, but there was the promise of tips, which appealed. She would be so charming that the tips would give her baby all he or she needed. But she would have to avoid mention of that or she wouldn't get the job in the first place!

Hannah loved Johnny Castle but she still had no illusions about him marrying her. Although he had declared his love for her and had told her he wanted them to marry, he had also said he wanted to delay the announcement in case people thought he was marrying her on the rebound from his broken engagement to Eirlys Price.

Eirlys had been in London for almost a year and he still hadn't made the announcement. With two children and him being so much younger, she had to settle for friendship. Johnny was a good friend. From the morning they had met outside the greengrocer when her paper carrier bag had collapsed and sent all her vegetables rolling down the street and he had stopped to help her, they had been friends.

He had walked home with her to the house where she lived with her parents, using two rooms and with restricted use of the kitchen. He didn't need any explanation of their attitude. Their disapproval showed on their faces and in the way they spoke to her and the little girls, their granddaughters. They were embarrassed and angry at having a daughter who was divorced and bringing up children without the father's presence or help.

"Shamed they are," she had told Johnny one day, when she had been forbidden to allow the girls to play in the garden. Johnny had asked her to explain.

"I had a husband who refused to work," she began. "He spent most of his time in the snooker hall, or in friends' houses playing

318

cards. At other times, when he could find the money, he was in the pubs, or at dances, and..." She hesitated before he nodded for her to tell him more. "There were other women, and he didn't even try to hide them from me." She avoided telling him the full story of how he had hit her in drunken rages, and how her parents refused to support her.

"When I sued for divorce, he forced himself on me one day and, well, the result was Josie. Another time, when he was really angry with me for the statement I'd made, he did it again and I had Marie. Born out of fear and anger they were, yet they're the sweetest, gentlest of girls."

"Poor love," Johnny had said. "But I don't understand why your parents aren't more helpful. Surely they love their grand-daughters?"

"They reckon they were born out of wedlock, as, officially, we were separated. So that makes me a loose woman. They don't believe rape is possible between husband and wife, even in those circumstances."

Hannah thought of that terrible confession as she opened one of Johnny's letters. In it, he asked whether the garden was still out of bounds. Holding the letter, she went through to the kitchen and asked her mother if the girls could play outside for a while before supper.

Tight-lipped, her mother shook her head. "I don't want you flaunting your shame for all the neighbours to see."

She wrote a cheerful letter to Johnny, ignoring his question and giving him details of a trip the three of them had made to see his father, followed by a fish-and-chip supper for herself and the girls, served by Beth. "Your father is so kind to me; I can't tell you how much it means to be able to talk and laugh, without feeling ashamed of showing happiness," she wrote. Then she tore that piece off. She didn't want to sound even slightly dejected. She wanted to visualise him reading the letter and smiling. Instead she wrote about something amusing that Josie had told her and ended on a happy note, before signing it "your loving friend, Hannah".

To make extra money, she did sewing for various people. She had worked as an alteration hand in one of the larger gown shops before her marriage, but with the two girls she couldn't return to the shop and they weren't willing for her to do the work on their very expensive gowns at home, in case of accidents.

She had promised to finish a dress for one of Josie's friends and it had taken much longer than she had expected. Already late with some other work she had promised for the following week, she was sitting near the window, concentrating on the smocking that would decorate the front of the pretty yellow party dress for the six-year-old, when there was a knock at the door.

Johnny was home on leave and after seeing his father and changing his clothes, he had come straight away to see Hannah. The door was answered by her mother, who left him waiting on the doorstep while she told Hannah he was there.

"Johnny! I didn't know you were coming home!" She smiled and hugged him as her mother quickly pushed the door shut so no one could see them.

"Can you get out for an hour?" he asked. "You don't have to meet the girls until half-past three, do you?"

"I have some sewing to finish by tomorrow, but, yes, of course I can spare an hour!" She collected a coat and looked at the dress with its half-finished smocking. She would have to work half the night to finish it anyway.

They walked hand in hand through the small park, where, wrapped up against the autumn chill, children played and mothers stood in groups.

"Dad said you go down and show him my letters," he said. "Best I just write the one and you can share it." He grinned to show he was teasing.

"Oh, no. Don't stop writing to me, please!

I look forward to your letters so much, and besides, your father likes to have a second news report to know you're safe and well."

"He likes you calling to see him too."

"Does he? I hope so."

"Thanks, Hannah. He's very much alone these days, with Taff and me in the army and the beach no longer filling his time. He has the fish-and-chip shop, but the clientele isn't the same. At the beach everyone is out for a good time, there's laughter and nonsense as they forget the tragedy of the war and have fun. The people who queue for their supper talk about nothing else but the latest war news and who is dead or injured. He finds it very depressing."

"Thank goodness he has Evelyn. Taff's wife calls often, doesn't she?"

"She used to, but this winter the war seems to have changed everything. She works in a factory and goes out with the girls a couple of times a week, and just calls on Dad when she happens to be passing."

After that brief walk before rushing back to meet the girls, Hannah felt more secure in her relationship with Johnny. Nothing important had been said, but his fondness for her was more apparent, and when they parted, his kiss was more than the usual affectionate salute of friends, containing the promise of something more.

She felt more secure, but as she allowed

her imagination to roam, also more afraid. She didn't know how she would cope with a relationship with Johnny, or anyone else, once they reached the stage of making love. Her experience of love-making had been so unhappy. But she pushed the thought aside, her emotions like a switchback ride.

How could she imagine Johnny loving her? She was older by eight years and she had nothing to offer. Johnny was living far away from home, in an artificial situation with men from every strata of life teaching him things he would never have learned if life had remained normal. He needed her, but only while he was living away from home, afraid and lonely, where contact from the real world was desperately needed. Any day he could meet someone younger and without the trappings of children, an ex-husband and difficult parents, someone young and trouble free with whom he could live happily ever after.

The thought wouldn't go away as she sat into the early hours finishing the smocking. Ever afterwards, smocking on a yellow dress reminded her of that solemn night when she faced the fact that Johnny was unlikely to ever be more than a loving friend.

She finished the dress and took the small payment, wondering why people refused to pay a reasonable portion of the money charged by a shop when the same work was done in the back room of a terraced house. War changed many things, but not attitudes like that, she thought wryly.

Lilly started work at the café at nine thirty the following Monday. She was half an hour late but this was excused, she thought, by the fact she was unused to finding a moment to wash with the rest of the family already in their routine. She smilingly told her boss that once the family had accepted that she was a working girl too, things would improve.

After telling her three times to hurry and constantly having to remind her to go at once when someone entered and sat at a table, she was told, not very politely, that she would not be needed the following day.

She smiled without rancour and told the boss it was for the best. She wasn't used to having to rush. She then told her parents that someone else had applied and been given the job and they had forgotten to tell her she wasn't needed. Then she happily settled to read the magazines she had bought and asked Beth to make her a cup of tea. Her burst of heroic industry had fizzled out like the proverbial damp squib.

Freddy managed to get a weekend pass but he didn't write to tell Beth. Instead he telephoned the paper shop and told Shirley.

"I can't meet you in St David's Well, mind," he said conspiratorially. "You'll have to meet me somewhere out of town."

Boldly, Shirley suggested the Grantham, a rather run-down hotel that had once been as grand as its name implied.

"It's a hell of a long way out," he said.

"We could stay overnight," she said as the pips went. She stood by the phone, ignoring the customers that were patiently waiting to be served and, as she expected, the phone rang again and a breathless Freddy said, "Did you mean it?"

"Of course. I'll book for us, shall I? Friday till Sunday?"

"Well, yes, but—"

He didn't have the chance to say more, as Shirley interrupted him with, "Meet you there then." She smilingly replaced the receiver and went to serve her customers.

Serve Beth right, she thought as she looked up the number of the Grantham to arrange the booking. If she doesn't know how to keep someone like Freddy Clements happy, she can move over for someone who does!

Myrtle was slowly making progress in school and, to her surprise, became a bit of a celebrity, once her story about living off her wits and sleeping in an abandoned stable rippled through the classrooms. She began to use her experiences during the writing lesson, impressing her classmates by asking the teacher how to spell "orphan", "abandoned" and "deprived", all words she had overheard Granny Moll and Auntie Audrey whisper when they were talking about her and Maude. Her writing was still large and untidy, but she began to practice after school and Audrey took great pleasure in helping her.

"Why are you so determined to write well?" Audrey asked one day. "You never practice your sums like you used to, and they're equally important."

"I want to put a letter in the paper when I'm old enough, asking if anyone knows where our brother and sister-in-law are," Myrtle explained.

Audrey hugged her and told her that if she thought it would do any good she would do that for her at once.

"Then will you, please? They could be living near and not know how to find us."

A letter to the editor of the local paper resulted in a photograph of both girls appearing in the paper with an article explaining how they had come to live in Sidney Street with the Pipers.

"Damn me," Huw grumbled. "When will I be allowed to use my own name? We're the Castles. And I'd like people to know it, right?"

The argument about the name of Piper's Café wouldn't go away. Marged insisted that the tradition was important, and it was such a well-known name that it would cause confusion to change it, but Huw argued that no one called Piper worked the stalls and cafés any more. "Castle's, it should be," he insisted with increasing frustration over his wife's stubbornness.

"Castle's Café," Marged sneered. "It sounds like something from Comic Cuts!"

"Then call it just Castle's."

"On a beach? It's so daft it'll seem like a joke!"

The café was almost back to normal now. The building work was completed and a new fridge and a larger cooker had been installed. This had caused another argument, but one which Huw had won.

"There'll be more and more visitors now travel is restricted, what with petrol getting scarce and the trains being needed for the transport of soldiers and the rest," he prophesied. "There's this meeting in town of all the people involved with holidays, not just us café owners but landladies and that newly formed entertainment committee. Rumour has it that the government is already talking about big campaigns to persuade people to spend their holidays at home. We've got to be prepared for the opening next May. Really prepared. It's no good waiting till then and finding we need a bigger cooker." So Marged had agreed.

"I miss your Granny Moll," Marged told Beth when they went to see the newly restored café. "She always had the last word and it made everything easier. However seriously your father and I disagreed, we both had to accept her final word. Now we seem to disagree on everything and there's no one to help us settle it."

"The new sign isn't up yet," Beth remarked, looking up at the front.

"That's something else we can't agree on," Marged said. "It's always been Piper's and your father wants to change it to Castle's."

Looking down at the deserted sands below, Beth grinned and said, "Castles in the air, eh?"

"Daft name, Castle's."

"You're Mrs Castle, I'm Bethan Castle, you aren't ashamed of it are you?"

"Of course not! What an idea."

"Dad probably thinks you are."

"Don't be silly," Marged said dismissively, but Beth continued to look at her.

"There's only Auntie Audrey and if she eventually marries Wilf ... Why don't you do it as a surprise, Mam? I think Dad's right, Castle's it should be."

"No!"

That evening the subject of the new name

came up again and to Beth and Audrey's alarm the argument was louder and more unpleasant than ever before.

"You've already ordered it?" Huw said angrily. "You've no right, Marged. This is a family business. It belongs to Bleddyn as well as the rest of us. We all contribute and we all have a say. We're supposed to talk about things, not watch you go out and do what you want."

"Forget it, Huw, the sign's going up and that's the end of it."

"Don't do it," Huw warned. "Or I won't wait for Mrs Downs to burn it down again, I'll damned well burn it down myself!"

"It's Piper's. That's final."

"Then you work it without me. You never listen to me, do you? If you hadn't employed that Downs woman against my wishes this wouldn't have happened and we wouldn't be arguing like this. Damn it all, I might just do it, too," he said, staring at her and striking his thumb against the wheel of his lighter. "Down to you the fire was, and I'll never let you forget it."

Lilly, who was struggling to knit a pair of tiny socks, burst into tears.

"What now?" Huw said, exasperated.

"Don't argue about burning the place down," Lilly sobbed.

"Joking he was, girl. As if one of us Pipers would burn down our own place," Marged soothed, at which point Lilly cried even louder.

"It was me," she wailed. "I went to the café and – the man I was with – left a cigarette burning, I know he did and that was how it was burnt down and it's all my fault."

Beth and Marged stared at her in disbelief. Only Huw spoke.

"Thank God you didn't own up before the insurance paid out!"

Lilly took a lot of calming as she went on to tell them she felt responsible for Granny Moll's heart attack and death.

"I'm not thrilled to be told that you and this man, whoever he is, crept into the café and—" Huw couldn't finish the sentence. "But I still think that Mrs Downs had something to do with it. There was something about her face, the smirk she wore like a badge."

"It started in the corner behind the door where we used to sit," wailed Lilly.

"Just near the letter box," he pointed out.

"Yes."

"Where people were in the habit of pushing rubbish through."

"Yes," she said again.

"Then that's most likely what happened," Marged said, guessing Huw's intention of exonerating their distressed daughter.

In Beth's next letter to Freddy she told him

that Lilly thought she might have been responsible for the fire and that they were all sorry that they had accused Mrs Downs. She also told Peter's father when she went to Goose Lane.

"Don't tell anyone else," Mr Gregory warned. "You could get your father into real trouble if the insurance people think there's been intent to defraud."

"It isn't certain," Beth told him. "She only told us that she and this mystery man used to go into the café after hours and sometimes smoke a cigarette. Dad still believes it was Mrs Downs, because of her grudge against the Castles."

"Best if you think so too. Saves complications."

They walked over to see the donkeys in Sally Gough's field and Beth helped give them their bran and potatoes. She watched while Mr Gregory examined each one, talking to them as though they were friends.

"I saw Mrs Downs's daughter last week – Shirley, isn't it?" Mr Gregory said as they walked back to Goose Lane.

"She works in the paper shop," Beth explained, "and they live above the shop."

"She was a long way from home then! I was delivering a new farm gate in one of the villages and she was coming out of the Grantham. I thought I saw Freddy with her, but I must have been mistaken; so many men are in uniform it's easy to make a mistake."

"What would Freddy be doing at the Grantham?" Beth laughed. "If he had some leave he'd come home."

"Of course he would, home as fast as he could with a pretty girl like you waiting for him." He spoke brightly but he wore a frown. It had been Freddy. He had been too close for him to have made a mistake. And he could guess why he and Shirley Downs had been there. No mistake about that either.

Beth sensed Mr Gregory's unease and that evening she wrote to Freddy asking why he hadn't come home when he had had leave. She also asked what he had been doing in the Grantham in the village of Gorsebank. She didn't mention Shirley Downs. She waited with something bordering on detached amusement for his reply, vaguely wondering why his behaviour was no longer capable of hurting her.

Freddy received her letter and thought carefully about how to handle it. He eventually decided on a devious plan. Basically, he would write as though he had not yet received her letter.

"Dear Beth," he began.

I was sent out for some extra training last weekend and we were staying in digs with some of the locals in the village called Gorsebank. You'll never guess who I bumped into? Mrs Downs's daughter Shirley! We had a drink in some pub there, a bit scruffy it was, mind, but the beer was welcome.

He signed it just "Freddy" and Beth put it on the table for the family to see. Lilly picked it up and said, "D'you still think you're the only one to write to him? They must have arranged it somehow!"

Beth didn't reply, but she knew Lilly was right. Freddy was a cheat and an accomplished liar, but she still felt unable to tell him goodbye. It was the war, the knowledge that tomorrow you might be dead, that was why he was cheating on her. Once the war was over, everything would be fine.

She kept telling herself this and at times almost believed it. But as she tried to envisage a future with Freddy she knew she was lying to herself. She was not so feeble that she could pretend to feel the same about him. When he was home and safe, she knew they were unlikely to stay together. Too much had happened to them both. The idea of telling Freddy goodbye no longer gave her pain, just sadness, and guilt at the way she felt about Peter Gregory.

She settled down to write to him. She would keep writing, keep up the pretence. She would post it when she went to start her lunchtime shift at the fish-and-chip shop. Still called Piper's, the name was still a contentious issue between her parents. It was unlikely that she would change her own name from Castle to Clements. Her eyes blurred with tears as she thought defiantly that she didn't like the name anyway. Bethan Castle was good enough for her. And Mrs Freddy Clements was not.

Ten

Winter slowly drifted in, dusk settling in over the town a little sooner each day, filling the corners with shadows, making silhouettes of the once vibrant trees. Spiky remnants of flowers gave gardens a neglected look, a devastation that had taken only weeks to achieve yet had the appearance of age-old abandonment.

Children no longer pleaded to be taken to the beach, and street games came into their own. Hopscotch numbers were drawn on pavements, skipping ropes were unearthed and long lengths were held across the road in deep loops for children to jump in and out, counting and chanting well-known rhymes. Home-made whips sent coloured tops spinning, hoops made from wheel rims were bowled along with small sticks, and bogie carts were already doing the rounds, their owners begging rubbish for the bonfire that, this year, would not be allowed, though the children hoped to sneak away into the fields, defy the ban and outrun the wardens.

Fire-watchers and wardens were on patrol each evening and Audrey went around the streets selling National Savings and collecting for a Christmas savings scheme she and Marged had always organised for the neighbours. She was out very late one evening, and she was alarmed when she realised that it was past nine o'clock and she hadn't given Myrtle and Maude their supper.

At fifteen, Maude was quite capable of finding food for herself and Myrtle, but she never did. With food rationed, she was well aware of how carefully the day-to-day use of commodities like butter and sugar and meats were apportioned. Audrey organised the food strictly, and only she knew what they could use each day. Over-generous help-yourself was not possible; it could make the time spent waiting for Friday, which was ration day, seem very long.

She dashed into the house apologising for making them wait, but when she pushed open the door to the living room, where there was always a fire burning, the room was empty. Filled with remorse now, she ran up to their bedroom, ashamed that they had put themselves to bed hungry. The beds were neatly made and empty.

"Oh no," she murmured, "surely they haven't gone off again to look for that brother!"

A search of the house, a hasty visit to Marged and Huw, even a foolish run around the street calling their names produced no response. She was convinced that this time they had run away.

Ronnie and Olive told her not to worry.

"Why should they leave a comfortable home, Auntie Audrey? It isn't as though they have anywhere else to go. They'll be back soon." They went back to their card game unconcerned.

"Of course they haven't run away! They haven't taken anything with them, for a start," Huw said, to calm everyone down. "I bet they heard something that they thought would lead them to this fictional brother and sister-in-law, and they took off, too impatient to wait for you."

"More likely they've gone to look for you, Audrey," Marged offered.

"I was out so late," Audrey wailed. "Where will they be?"

"They were talking to Olive and our

Ronnie earlier when we went up to borrow a candle for the outside lav," Huw offered. "Perhaps they'll know something."

"I've already asked and they said not to worry."

"Go and ask them again," Marged suggested.

Back to the house, and a knock on the door of Olive and Ronnie's room resulted in the information that the girls had been interested in Olive's talk about Janet Copp, the lady who worked in the market café, and had learnt that, like them, she was without a family. "I bet they've gone to see her."

"Poor little kids," Marged sighed. "Desperate they are for this sister-in-law."

They were standing at the gate of Audrey's front garden when they heard the sound of singing, punctuated by footsteps. Hope brought them all out on to the pavement in time to see Janet Copp arm in arm with Myrtle and Maude dancing and singing, "Show me the way to go home".

"I hope you weren't worried," Janet called cheerfully, "only we had a bit of a chat. They told me about their name and we compared what we knew of our families, but found no connection. Then we walked over to your Bleddyn's chip shop. Hungry they were."

When the girls were in bed, Janet explained.

"They thought that as I had no family and

had narrowly escaped being sent to a home, I might be their sister-in-law, or know something of her and their brother," she said sadly. "Desperate they are and me unable to help."

"Thanks for talking to them. I think they both know it's hopeless but a dream is hard to discard," Audrey said. "They don't even know his name, this brother they want to find. I don't know whether he really exists."

"They seem convinced about having a sister-in-law, mind. But even the name they were given could be wrong. Things get muddled so easily. A spelling mistake perhaps, then someone else thinking to correct it and filling in a different name altogether. I'm called Cope sometimes and have to point it out."

The fortune teller, who had a stall on the beach until the end of summer, continued to trade. Sarah lived in two rooms on Sunnyside Road, and her living-cum-consulting room was bedecked with scarves and shawls and sparkling mirrors, and stars and moons and many other mysterious symbols. Low-wattage light bulbs draped with thin veils of cloth added to the mood and people who came quickly absorbed the atmosphere and were ready to believe anything.

Sarah was standing on her front doorstep

one evening when Maude and Myrtle passed on their way home from the pictures. A glimpse of the interior made Myrtle want to hurry past, but Maude held her back.

"Can you help us find our sister-in-law and our brother?" she asked, her heart racing with her own temerity.

"Come with money and your friend, Audrey Piper, and I'll seek knowledge from within the crystal ball," the woman said, before Myrtle grabbed her sister's arm and pulled her away.

"You'll never guess what Maude did," Myrtle said as they burst through the door and greeted Audrey. "She went up to that gypsy woman and asked her to find our sister-in-law."

"Oh? What did she say?" Audrey asked, smiling at Wilf who was chuckling at their story.

"She said we have to go with you and take some money, and she'd insult the crystal. What d'you think she means? Will she help us?" Myrtle asked in a hushed voice. "Will she find them, d'you think? If we pay her?"

"It's *consult* the crystal," Maude said scathingly, "and of course she will. You only have to look at her to know she's clever about such things."

"Then why didn't we ask her before?" Myrtle demanded.

"Don't get your hopes up, girls," Wilf said.

"She might have the gift of seeing, I'm sure some have, but there are also those who are cheats and just take your money, talk a lot and tell you nothing."

"But we'll try?" Maude asked hopefully.

"We'll see what Auntie Marged has to say."

Maude's shoulders drooped. "She'll tell us no," she said sadly.

Surprisingly, Marged, again defying Huw's common sense, agreed.

"Where's your sense, woman?" Huw protested. "Gullible they are – like you and your Audrey – and they'll believe everything the woman says and expect miraculous results. We don't want them upset for nothing. Best they forget they ever had a sister-in-law. We don't even know if that's true, do we?"

"It won't do any harm. We have to show the poor dears we're willing to help."

"Daft nonsense. I should have said yes, shouldn't I? You'd have been sure to say no then, contrary woman that you are," Huw muttered.

Freddy came home on a "forty-eight" and Beth dreaded his arrival. She didn't know what to say to him. Should she mention Shirley Downs again? Or just pretend she hadn't given her a thought since Freddy was last home?

It was Freddy who broached the subject.

"Would you mind if Shirley came to the pictures with us tonight?" he asked.

"The pictures? Why are we going to the pictures? You've only got a few hours before going back to barracks. I thought we'd go somewhere where we can talk." She didn't see the pained expression on Freddy's face at the prospect of "talk". "And why should Shirley Downs want to tag along? She has friends of her own, surely?"

"You don't like Shirley, do you? And your father hates her mam. Have you ever wondered why?" Freddy asked.

"I suppose it was the story about Granny Moll's grandfather buying Piper's from Shirley's great-grandfather. The place being a mess and Piper's working the business up from nothing."

"That isn't what I've been told. The Downs were cheated."

"Granny Moll said the place was run down and filthy, and her grandfather bought it from Mrs Downs's grandfather and built it up. Mrs Downs and her daughter are talking rubbish. Piper's Café's success is due to my family's hard work, not robbery."

"And there's nothing else?"

"I haven't heard anything more, but I think my father upset her again somehow. No one will talk about it. Mam gets all tight-lipped if I ask, so I've given up being

341

curious about it all. They dislike each other, that's plain to see. And, at first, Mam and Dad believed Mrs Downs set fire to the café as some sort of revenge. That's all I know."

"There is something else, but Shirley doesn't know the story either."

"Talk about us often, do you? Is that why you go out with her?" she asked. "So you can solve the mystery and get hold of some sordid gossip about the Pipers and the Castles?"

"I don't 'go out' with her!" he protested. "We've met by accident once or twice, that's all."

She tried, but couldn't believe him. "I don't think I want to go to the pictures tonight," she said, "but you can go if you like. It's rare for me to have a Saturday off; Uncle Bleddyn only agreed because you were coming home. I'd rather spend it somewhere else. A walk perhaps?"

She was horrified when he accepted her invitation for him to go without her.

"You wouldn't mind?" he asked cheerfully. "Only I promised Shirley that we'd go. Come on, love, come with us. You'll enjoy it. We can have some chips after, and—" He grinned as he realised what he'd said. "No, not chips; you see enough of them, don't you?"

"Quite enough."

"All right, then," he retorted. "and remember I get enough of walking, usually wearing heavy boots and weighed down with kit."

They went to the pictures.

"Why don't you tell him goodbye?" Lilly asked when a despondent Beth came in. "He doesn't even try to hide the fact that he's more interested in Shirley, does he? Give him more than you do, does she?" she asked coarsely.

"Freddy is sorry for her; she doesn't have much of a life, living in that flat with her mother, working all hours selling papers, up at the crack of every dawn and delivering them too when the boys don't turn up."

"Aw! Pity for her too," Lilly mocked. "What about the long hours we work over the beach week after week in the summer?"

Beth declined to argue about just how much of that work involved Lilly.

"I bet she sees more of his money than you do too," Lilly went on. "In fact, I bet you paid for the pictures and for the sweets he bought her."

"Don't be daft," Beth protested.

Lilly grinned. "I've seen you putting postal orders into the letters you write."

Eynon was still on the run. Since leaving the farmer's house near Aberystwyth, he had continued to sleep rough, staying away from habitation except at night, when he would go searching for food.

The closest he'd been to home was when a lorry driver offered him a lift one evening. He had approached as close as he dared to Sidney Street and had stood for long hours, just watching the comings and goings of his family.

He saw Mam and Dad, arguing as usual, go in with some shopping. He watched as Audrey and Maude and Myrtle set off to collect National Savings, smiled at the warden's "put that light out" and marvelled at the ordinariness of it all.

Later he dared to walk through the streets, half hoping, half dreading being seen by someone he knew. He knew he was reaching the stage when to be caught would be a relief. He couldn't walk into a police station and give himself up, but knew he would be relieved to be caught and taken back.

The only person he met that he knew was Mrs Downs. She stared at him and said clearly, "Well, if it isn't Eynon Castle."

Panic overwhelmed him and he said quickly, "No, I'm not, I'm Frankie Davies." He tried to walk away but she caught hold of his overcoat and pulled him towards her. It was then that he realised that she was drunk.

"Frankie Davies I am and I've never heard

of this Evan, or whatever you called him."

Confused, the woman released her hold and wandered away. Lowering his head, Eynon went through the lanes intent on putting as much distance as he could between himself and St David's Well. It had answered one question for him. He might be a bit low, but he was not ready yet to give himself up!

He had regretted joining up before he was made to, and now he regretted even more the foolish impulse that had led to his absence without leave. "AWOL", it sounded daring and a bit of fun, but he knew the punishment he would receive if he were caught would be far from funny.

Turning off the quiet road as the sillhouette of buildings appeared in the distance, he walked along the hedgerow and found the bedraggled remnants of a haystack. This would have to do for a resting place until the early hours, when he would be able to wander around and find something to eat undetected. He was lucky, there was a piece of tattered tarpaulin which had kept a section of the rotting hay relatively dry. Luxury indeed, he thought sadly, as he curled up and settled to sleep.

His head throbbed alarmingly, the wound still refusing to heal properly due to the knocks it received when he went in and out of his various shelters. He'd get it seen to one day, when he was ready to face up to the punishment that awaited him.

Maude and Myrtle looked eagerly at the local paper, read the letter they had submitted and waited hopefully for a response. None came. A week later, Audrey took them to see Sarah.

The late autumn day was bright, with a watery sun creating shadows reminiscent of summer. Walking into the overheated and dark room was unnerving.

The old woman looked into their palms for a long time, glancing up, dark intelligent eyes twinkling, smiling at them as if highly amused at their nervousness. She told them only good things about their future. "Love and laughter, comfort and ease," was her summing up. "A very good reading, the best I've seen all this week. Go, children, and be happy." Then she removed the black velvet cover from her crystal ball and stared into its depths for a long time.

"You will find the answer to your question in the grave," she said briefly as she held out her hand and stood, dismissing them. Audrey placed the coins on the outstretched hand and, thanking Sarah, led the girls out again into the bright sun.

"Did she mean we won't know till we're dead?" a frightened Myrtle asked.

"I thought she'd be able to tell us," Maude

said sadly. "Uncle Huw said she'd talk a lot and say nothing; I know what he meant now!"

"Why didn't she tell us?" Myrtle asked Beth when they returned home and told her about their expedition.

"Perhaps she did," Beth said. "I think she meant that you'll have to search in the cemetery, you know, look at the names on the graves."

Accepting that the cemetery was where they would find the graves of their parents they pleaded with Audrey to take them. She adamantly refused.

"No! I will never set foot in the place, now or ever! So don't you dare ask me again."

The girls were surprised at her implacability. She rarely refused to help. But on this she remained firm. They put it down to the fact that as she was quite old, she had a fear of the place where she would certainly end up.

Huw promised to take them, but when Marged heard of their plan she persuaded him not to go. Eventually it was Beth who set off one Sunday afternoon for the cemetery with two subdued and anxious girls, without telling either Marged or Audrey where they were heading.

A horse and cart approached as they walked hand in hand, arms swinging, along the road towards the cemetery gates, and

Beth was delighted to see Peter and his father riding on the pony and cart, waving to them enthusiastically. The cart was filled with bales of hay which they were taking up to the donkeys' winter home.

"Climb up if you can and we'll give you a lift," Mr Gregory called. And with some apprehension regarding their Sunday best dress and coat and shoes, Beth sat between Peter and his father on the board seat and the girls laughingly found places for themselves between the hay bales.

"Which first, cemetery or donkeys?" Peter asked, when told of their destination.

"Donkeys," Myrtle said at once. She was afraid of the gloomy place visible over the wall from their high perch, and besides, if yet another disappointment was in store for them, she wanted to delay it.

A chill wind blew as they left the houses and rode out to the field where the donkeys lived. They were in a huddle, heads together, backsides to the wind. "Like a group of gossiping women," Peter said, making the girls laugh.

While Bernard Gregory attended to the daily feed of hot bran and potatoes, Myrtle and Maude admired the donkeys and Beth and Peter talked.

"Heard from Freddy lately?" Peter asked.

"Just the usual scribbled note, nothing of interest," she replied.

"How much longer are you going to put up with him making a fool of you, Beth?" he asked softly.

"He's so far away from home, how do I know how he's coping with it all? How can I judge when I've no idea what's happening to him? We aren't all natural letter writers like you are, Peter."

"You say that as though I should be ashamed of my ability to write when life is difficult."

"Peter, I love your letters. I read them again and again, they're full of interest, amusement and – and—"

"Affection?" he offered.

"And affection," she agreed with a smile. "Please don't stop writing."

"But it's Freddy from whom you want to hear, isn't it?"

"Freddy isn't the most thoughtful of men, I know that, but we've been together all our life and I can't abandon him at a time when he's unable to defend himself against my decision, can I?"

"Does he correspond with anyone else?" He meant Shirley Downs but it would have been indelicate to name her.

Beth smiled to herself. "Correspond" indeed. She would have said "write".

"Why are you smiling?" he asked.

"I like the way you say things," she replied.

"And does he? Keep in touch with anyone else?"

"His mother and father of course, and I think he might write to Shirley Downs. He feels sorry for her. Her mother is deeply unhappy, mixed up, disappointed with life, and she sometimes drinks heavily. It's difficult for Shirley to cope with it."

"Freddy can be thoughtful at times, then," Peter said pointedly. "Look, I know I haven't the right to say anything, to interfere in your private life, but don't let him make a fool of you, Beth. You're worth more than that."

Before she could reply, the girls shouted with laughter and, turning, they saw that Mr Gregory's arm had been knocked by an enthusiastic animal and the food he was carrying had spilled on the grass.

"Damn and blast it, Dorothy, when will you learn to wait for it?" Mr Gregory said as the donkeys pushed him aside and began to eat.

Beth and Peter said very little as the now empty cart wended its way slowly back to the ornate gates of the cemetery. Mr Gregory tied the pony to a convenient post and they all went in, without any set plan, to read the inscriptions on the gravestones.

"Wait a minute," Peter said, waving them back to where he stood. "Let's do this military style. You two look on the left, and

Dad, you look on the right. Beth and I will take the next path."

Beth had brought a notebook and with Peter searching one side of the path, she bent to examine every inscription, looking for some name that might tie in with the little they knew about the girls.

The name given to the home had been Carpenter and this was the name they hoped to find. They found several, but none were the right time or the right age to have been Myrtle and Maude's parents. Nevertheless Beth wrote the details meticulously into her notebook in case something fitted into the information they already had, limited as it was. Any entry might be the clue that would lead them, eventually, to the answer they sought.

Mr Gregory called urgently to Beth and his son, signalling them not to alert the girls.

"This is strange, Beth; is this one of yours?"

A small tombstone, barely visible amid ivy, brambles and nettles in a neglected corner, had been partially cleared by Mr Gregory's rough hand. A small bunch of roses, faded and brittle, falling into fragments, lay across it, and at one side another bouquet, brown and even older than the roses, was half pressed into the earth. Mr Gregory rubbed his hand across the lettering to reveal the legend:

Bobbie Piper
Born September 1910
died November 1910
Greatly missed by his mother

"Could it have been a brother?" Beth wondered as she wrote the information down with a trembling hand. "A baby born to my mother before she married my father?" She felt a sense of guilt, as though she had been caught prying into someone else's business.

"Your mother?" Mr Gregory said, staring at her strangely. "Why not your Auntie Audrey? She's a Piper too, isn't she?"

"But she couldn't have—"

"Couldn't have what, loved someone when she was a young woman?" Mr Gregory said.

"I don't know." Beth shook her dark head in confusion. "I can't imagine her in that situation, I suppose."

Mr Gregory smiled sadly. "Why are the young incapable of seeing the older generation as anything but ancient? Why do they never accept that we were once young and capable of love?"

A shout of excitement came from a short distance away, in a section that, though newer, was almost as neglected.

"Beth, come quick. I think we've found something," Maude was calling.

The three left the mysterious and uncommunicative grave and went to where the girls were dancing up and down and pointing to an ivy-covered gravestone.

Peter and Beth knelt down, scraped away more of the moss and pulled at the persistent ivy, and Peter read:

In memory of Martha Maude Copp
mother of Maude and Myrtle Copp
died 1931

"If that's us, then our name isn't Carpenter, it's Copp. Janet Copp must be a relation," Maude said.

"No, I don't think so. Don't get your hopes up," Beth told them. "This can't be your mother. It's just a coincidence."

"But it says 1931, that's when Mam and Dad died," Maude argued.

"Then why isn't your father buried here too?" Peter asked softly.

Frantic now to prove the connection, Maude and Myrtle sobbed as they read the stones nearby. The others helped but without much enthusiasm.

"I know this was our mam," Maude said, "I can't explain the name, but I'm sure it's our mam." She hugged her sister and they stared, white faced, at the neglected grave.

"Why did Mam tell everyone we were

called Carpenter, then?" Myrtle wanted to know.

"I don't understand why," Maude said tearfully, "but it's her, I'm sure of that."

"Perhaps she was ashamed of us," Myrtle said, also on the edge of tears. "Mam hated us and pretended we weren't her daughters, that's why."

Ashen faced, the two girls were led from the gloomy grounds and helped back on to the cart.

Peter told them silly stories in an attempt to cheer them and Beth started singing one of their favourite songs, "When Father Papered the Parlour". Mr Gregory joined in, but the girls remained silent and tense, each wrapped in their own thoughts, trying to come to terms with what they had learnt.

"I really don't think that grave was anything to do with you," Peter said, "but perhaps you could write to the paper again, this time in the name of Copp?"

Beth agreed with forced enthusiasm, but the gloomy expression of the girls' faces didn't change.

When Olive and Ronnie were told the outcome of the search, they explained it all to Janet Copp when she brought tea to them on their stall at the market. When she heard the story, she promised to befriend the girls and help them to gradually accept that they were on their own.

"They'll soon realise how lucky they are to have found the Castles and been given a ready-made family. Just think of what might have happened to them if Beth hadn't been curious about young Myrtle. For one thing, Maude might not have survived the winter."

Hannah continued to visit Bleddyn and give him news of his son Johnny whenever she received a letter. Then she had a letter that made her hesitate. In it, Johnny asked her to marry him.

I love you more than I can tell, and I want to be with you for always. Marry me, darling Hannah, and I'll ask nothing more of life. I love you and I adore Josie and Marie, and I know we can create a happy home for them to grow up in. On my next leave – heaven alone knows when that will be – we can make plans. I want us to get married as soon as we can arrange it. Don't let's wait, this is a precarious life and I don't want to waste another moment of it.

There were more endearments and pledges and promises and as a PS he had written, "I bet this is one letter you won't show my Dad!"

She was smiling as she handed it to

Bleddyn, watching his face for his first reaction: a reaction on which her answer would depend.

"Darling girl, I'm delighted. I couldn't wish for a better daughter-in-law." He hugged her and handed back the letter. "Thanks for showing me. I don't think Johnny expected you to, mind! That PS wasn't a joke, it was a plea, so if you don't tell him, then I won't."

"Thank you. I was going to ask you not to say anything; I'd hate him to be embarrassed – although, why is it, d'you think, that love and affection and caring for someone other than ourselves causes embarrassment? More than some crimes cause, it seems to me."

"When will you tell the girls?" Bleddyn asked.

"As soon as I've posted my reply" – she patted her pocket – "and told the rest of your family. There's your Taff, and Evelyn. Perhaps I could write to Taff, if Evelyn doesn't mind? Then Beth and the others, quite an ordeal."

"I'll come with you to see Evelyn if you like. She'll be pleased, as we all will."

"Perhaps."

"Why are you so worried? Is it because you were married before?"

"That and the children, and the fact I'm eight years older than Johnny. It's a big

356

difference."

"Rubbish! You and our Johnny are perfect together. Come on, let's go straight away. Evelyn'll be back from the factory about now."

Evelyn was abrupt in her congratulations. "Although," she pointed out rather coldly, "it isn't official yet, is it? You haven't replied and Johnny hasn't asked you face to face. It might have been a moment's loneliness that made him write that letter and afterwards regretted it. I'd wait before you tell everyone, in case it falls through."

"Evelyn!" Bleddyn said. "What an odd way of greeting the news. Of course Johnny meant it. He's already spoken to me about how he feels about Hannah and her girls." He glanced at Hannah and added, "It wasn't such a surprise as you thought, but I didn't want to spoil your telling me, unlike some!"

"Sorry. Well then, congratulations, Hannah." The words had softened but not the coldness of Evelyn's expression. "Will you marry soon?"

"Johnny is somewhere in Europe so far as we know so it's impossible to answer that. But it will be as soon as we can arrange it – if that's what Johnny really wants," Hannah couldn't help adding.

"Wouldn't it be wiser to wait until the war's over?" Evelyn persisted.

"I don't think either of us wants to wait that long. It could go on for another year or more."

Telling the rest of the Castle family was easier. Beth hugged her and Marged too. Huw shook her hand and asked when she was going to bring the children to see them again.

Lilly looked up from the magazine she was reading and asked, "Will you want the baby clothes back in case you and Johnny have another, then?"

"Of course not," Hannah said, her face reddening in embarrassment in case they thought she was expecting a child. "That isn't the reason Johnny wants to marry so soon. It's the war and the uncertainty of everything. If he manages to get home he'll certainly be sent abroad again, he could be away for a very long time the way things are going, and he wants to know we're there, building a home for when he comes back."

"Where will you live?" Beth wanted to know.

Hannah laughed breathlessly. "I haven't given it a thought. This is all so new. I'm so excited about his proposal. I won't be able to stay with Mam and Dad, that much is certain. When he gets his next leave we'll plan everything and hopefully book the wedding date."

When she walked back to collect the girls

whom she had left playing with friends at a neighbour's house, she felt a sudden draining of confidence and began to feel that she had spoken too soon. When another letter appeared the following day, repeating his proposal and threatening to ask her every day until she said yes, she was relieved. That one was more loving than the last and it was one she didn't show to Bleddyn.

A meeting was called by the entertainments officer for the town. He asked that everyone connected with holiday-making attend. Beth went along with her parents and Uncle Bleddyn, anxious to know what was being planned for the following year, now that there were so many restrictions on everything they had previously taken for granted.

A gloomy audience awaited the speakers, expecting to be told that, like so many other places, St David's Well Bay would be sealed off from the public for fear of invasion. In fact the opposite was true.

"With fuel in short supply, and transport needed for our servicemen and their needs, the call is on for people to forget travelling to other towns for their holidays, and the slogan is 'Holidays at Home'," the chairman announced. "Every town in the country is asked to make plans for next year's season, and make sure no one wants to go anywhere else but the area in which they live. We have to do everything we can to persuade the local people that the best holiday they can have is right here. In St David's Well we are fortunate. We have the beach, numerous parks and many other attractions and we have to make sure everyone knows it. This means starting now, to plan for the summer."

The first business was to find a representative for each of the the various groups involved: landladies, hoteliers, café owners and of course the beach stall-holders, who voted for Huw to stand as their representative.

Once this was acomplished, and some shuffling had taken place to allow the various delegates to sit together, the chairman asked for suggestions. The other two speakers on the platform started it off by giving their ideas for entertainments that would involve the whole town.

A carnival with floats representing every organisation, a choir chosen from the schools to sing in the parks, brass bands, dancing, sandcastle competitions and a donkey derby were all proposed. The list went on until the noise in the hall was deafening. People forgot about addressing the chair and spoke to their neighbours, sharing ideas and forgetting the speakers completely.

Shouting for order, the chairman smiled, said he considered the meeting a rousing success and suggested they all stood to sing the national anthem before leaving to continue with the discussions in the newly formed individual groups.

While the meeting went on, Johnny was on a ship making his way home across the channel. The darkness hid the small ship from some dangers but others lurked below and he stood on deck wondering whether he would survive the perilous journey and see Hannah again, or whether one of the unseen U-boats would destroy the ship and the men whom it carried.

He knew that even if he did survive this journey, he wouldn't be home for more than a few days. He was being sent to Scotland for more training before being sent to Italy – or at least that was the whispered rumour surmised from the snippets of unreliable information they had received.

He arrived safely and after leaving his kit with his father and quickly eating a meal while catching up on the news, he went to see Hannah. The following day they arranged a marriage by special license.

With no time for the niceties, it would be a small affair, with only the family, including her still disapproving parents, and the girls, for whom she had promised to make very special dresses. Hannah's parents refused to discuss it. All they did was remind her that in the eyes of the church she was still a married woman and what she was doing was a sin.

Slowly Hannah rolled up her sleeve to reveal the scar left by one of her husband's drunken rages.

"Where were the eyes of the church then, Mam?" she asked.

"You're married. What you're doing is not right and you'll never be happy until you tell this Johnny Castle goodbye and return to your rightful husband. You can't build happiness on the destruction of someone else's."

Their remarks were hurtful but with so much to do to arrange the wedding in so short a time, she pushed her parents' attitude aside and concentrated on the list of things she had to do.

Inexplicably, the news of the wedding upset Marged. It was the thought of having a family celebration without Eynon being present. She looked at the calendar and counted the days since she had last seen her son. It seemed like a lifetime.

Marged and Bleddyn, like most others in the town, spent a lot of time writing letters. Marged told herself that this was something cheerful to report. Bleddyn wrote to Taff, told him about the wedding and enclosed the note Hannah had written. And Marged wrote to Eynon.

She wrote every week. But the letters always came back, having been read, and with a note reminding her that if he should turn up, then it was her duty to inform the authorities. She ignored the warning, stacked them away for Eynon to read when he came back, pretended he was replying and wrote again, telling him that everything was all right.

She did receive an occasional card, signed in strange handwriting as though from a cousin, Ross, or a friend called Reginald, and even on one occasion from a girl called Bessie. She tried writing with her left hand, to see whether that explained the unusual writing. There was no news, just a sentence telling her he was all right and not to worry. After showing them to Huw, she hid them upstairs in the back of the wardrobe. One day he would be home and able to tell her everything that had happened. For now she would write and tell him about Johnny's wedding, and pretend that he would soon be reading about it.

Johnny would be married in uniform and Hannah, defeated in her effort to treat the day as being in any way joyful by her mother's constant reminders of her wrong-doing, decided on a brown dress and coat with a handbag rather than flowers or a prayer book.

Beth quickly persuaded her to change her mind and, with Marged a willing supporter, the three of them went shopping and bought her a pale blue dress worn with a silk scarf. Hannah also borrowed one of Lilly's hats, which she decorated in the same trailing silk. She looked lovely and they all knew how thrilled Johnny would be when he met her at the register office. Flowers were ordered and Cyril the Snap promised to give them some photographs to treasure, which were paid for by Bleddyn.

"You're all so kind. You shouldn't be doing all this," Hannah protested as Bleddyn gave her money to buy a gift for each of the girls.

"You're a Castle now," Bleddyn told her fondly. "And you'll do us proud."

The day was dry and bright and they walked to and from the register office along the busy roads past the shops, where shoppers stopped to look and admire the little girls following their mother and their new stepfather. Some clapped and Bleddyn hid a tear, and Johnny looked as proud as proud, and after a few yards walking with her head down, Hannah looked at him and smiled, forgot her mother's bitter words and raised her head proudly, looking forward to a happy future as Mrs Johnny Castle.

There was no cake apart from a small

sponge Marged and Audrey had swopped various rationed goods to make. A couple of ounces of tea for some sugar, a piece of bacon in exchange for some margarine. It somehow made everyone appreciate the spread more and several admitted that the wedding was happier than many they had attended in the past.

Lilly cried, of course, but no one was surprised. This was a moment she still dreamed about, and one that most knew would never happen, not with the child growing within her and no man willing to accept responsibility for it. Hannah left Johnny's side for a moment and sat with her.

"We're cousins now, Lilly. I hope you're as happy about that as I am. The girls are a part of your family and if you're willing, I'd like them to call you Auntie Lilly."

Bleddyn heard her and smiled. Hannah was an asset to the Castle family, he thought proudly. No mistake about that.

"Johnny," he said to his son. "You're a lucky devil and don't forget it."

"How could I?" Johnny smiled, putting an arm around his glowingly beautiful bride.

Eleven

"We aren't the only family of Pipers, for heaven's sake!" Marged said impatiently. Ever since Beth and the two girls had returned from the cemetery, the questions had come at her from all sides.

"At least come and see it, Mam," Beth pleaded. "It could be a distant cousin. Families never keep in touch after the cousins grow up, do they?"

"I haven't the time to go off wandering around the cemetery to look at the grave of a stranger!"

"You know something about it, don't you?" Huw accused. "Why else are you so angry?"

"I'm not angry," she protested. "I just don't want to give Myrtle and Maude any hope of finding their family. Too much time has passed and looking at gravestones isn't the occupation for young girls."

"We're talking about the child's grave, someone called Piper." Beth frowned. "Nothing to do with Copp."

"You know what I mean. We'll go exploring and they'll be searching for some family that might not even belong to Myrtle and Maude. Plenty of families could be using those names."

Beth knew her mother was deliberately misunderstanding her, trying to edge the discussion away from the Piper child and confusing her with talk about the Copp burial. Abandoning the attempt to get some information from her mother, she asked her father to go with her.

"Why bother?" he asked. "Your mother won't help us solve the mystery even if we do go. What'll be achieved, besides another argument with your mam?"

She decided to go alone. She still worked most lunchtimes and evenings at the chip shop, however, and with the days so brief and so dark, there wouldn't be much time to go and examine the grave during the afternoon. With the weather a mixture of gusty wind, short showers and dark clouds, the prospect of visiting the eerie place without company was not very cheering.

The heavy clouds that day prevented anything resembling daylight. From the almost indistinguishable dawn, the sky was hidden, the houses were wrapped in heavy mist and there was only a sort of twilight that was uneased by shop or street lighting.

The hedges bordering the pavements as she approached the cemetery were dripping with moisture and there were few people around. Her footsteps echoed back at her, and at times it sounded as though there was someone following her, as she forced herself to go on. She glanced around nervously, peering uselessly through the threatening gloom.

She almost turned back; the heavily ornamented iron gates and the rows of solemn graves were daunting in the semi-darkness. She walked briskly, purposefully, and headed straight for the area where the small grave lay, half hidden by the overgrown hedge.

To her surprise she saw fresh flowers there, bright in the surrounding gloom. She stopped and looked around, half expecting to see the person who had placed them there. But nothing stirred except the trees, moving in the wind, shedding the remnants of the recent shower.

Curious, she didn't approach the grave but instead ran back to the main path where she saw a figure in the distance, a figure she knew.

"Auntie Audrey," she called, running to join her. "What are you doing here?"

"Oh, I suppose it was the thought of that poor little grave you told us about, neglected, no one to remember, so I took some flowers."

"Why didn't you say? We could have come together," Beth said.

"You know what your mam's like. If she said we shouldn't bother it's best not to tell her."

Beth laughed. "Not scared of our Mam, are you?"

"Best to avoid arguments, don't you think?"

"Will you come back with me? I thought I'd look around the area in case there are other Pipers buried there. Families are buried together when possible."

"I'll come back with you, dear, but I don't think you'll find any other family near by."

"You've looked, have you?"

"Yes, I've looked."

They cleaned the stone and pulled some more of the stubborn ivy off the small plot, and Beth suggested they came again, this time armed with scissors and a sharp knife, so they could cut back some of the brambles and make the memorial more visible.

That evening, when Beth and her parents were finishing their meal, Audrey came with Myrtle and Maude, and Olive and Ronnie.

"We have news for you," Ronnie said, limping in and sitting beside his father. "Tell them, Olive, love."

"I – we – we're going to have a baby," Olive said shyly. "Some time in July."

"Bang slam in the middle of the busiest month!" Huw said, smiling to show he was teasing.

"That's what Ronnie said!" Olive laughed.

"Congratulations, to both of you," Marged said, hugging them.

"Yes, well done," Huw added.

Audrey said nothing, remembering the tiny grave and the tragedy of that birth.

"Such a happy occasion, a time to celebrate," Marged went on, unaware of her sister's distress.

"Yes," Audrey said quietly, "a happy time, isn't it, Marged, except when a baby is born out of wedlock. Then it's a different story, isn't it?"

"What d'you mean?" Huw asked. "These two have been married for ages, there's no problem there."

"That little grave the girls found—"

"Not now, Audrey," Marged interrupted quickly. "Talk about someone else's problems another time, not now when we're celebrating Olive and Ronnie's news."

She spoke sharply in a tone that would normally have silenced Audrey, but Huw said, "No, don't let's forget it. There's no harm in reminding ourselves that we're the lucky ones and others don't have such fortunate lives."

"Not *now*," Marged almost shouted, but Huw looked at Audrey with a determined frown.

"You know something about the grave of that child, don't you?"

"The grave is that of my son. Ten weeks and two days he lived. Wilf and I were to have married that year but Mam forbade it, insisting that Wilf, being a bank official, wouldn't help in the family business and I couldn't be spared."

Utter silence greeted her words. Beth went over and put her arms around her aunt. No one else moved. Huw stared at Marged and waited for her to speak. But it was Beth who broke the painful silence.

"Why didn't you tell us before, Auntie Audrey? You shouldn't have kept it to yourself. We all lost the baby, he was a cousin for me and Lilly and Ronnie and our Eynon."

"I couldn't tell you because I was constantly reminded of how I had disgraced the family name," Audrey said harshly. "The neighbours were told that I was looking after the baby because his mother had died. Wilf wasn't allowed to see him, not once. And it was not until after little Bobbie died that we were allowed to meet. Then it was only when we had a chaperone, usually Mam."

"You knew?" Huw asked Marged, who looked away, up into the corner of the room, refusing to comment.

"Yes, Marged knew," Audrey answered for her. "She supported Mam and Dad at the time and has since refused to discuss it. I needed to grieve. But they wouldn't even allow me to do that."

Beth stared at her aunt, seeing the coldness, the bitterness in her usually gentle face, the dry eyes that sparkled, not with tears, but with the pain of the memories.

"Damn me, Moll has a lot to answer for," Huw muttered. "Giving out that she was so kind and caring, yet she could do that to her own daughter."

"I can still remember the sigh of relief she uttered when poor little Bobbie died," Audrey whispered.

"Why didn't you and Wilf marry?" Beth asked softly.

"I was told I must never marry him because of what he'd done. Punishment was always Mam's first thought. And although we planned to run away and defy them, first Dad died, then Wilf's mother became ill, and slowly the years passed, and we drifted into middle age and the urgency was gone. Poor little Bobbie. When he caught pneumonia everyone was happy. Except Wilf and me."

Marged stood up, still unable to look at them. Red faced, she stared unseeingly through the doorway to the kitchen, longing to escape but unable to. She knew that if she ran from this now, she would never be able to face any of them again. Yet how could she turn and face the accusation in every eye?

"You should never have told them,

Audrey. How could they understand?" she said finally, her voice harsh, defensive. "Mam did what she did because she thought it was for the best."

"Best for her but not for her daughter! Plenty of people marry just in time for the birth," Huw said.

"Not the Pipers."

"Damn it all, Marged, it's not a criminal act, it's an act of love!"

Maude and Myrtle hugged each other and stared, white faced, at Audrey.

"Do you have a photograph?" Olive asked, reaching out and touching Audrey's arm.

"Your Granny Moll burnt them all. At least, she thought she had." Taking a wallet out of her handbag, Audrey pulled out a faded, dog-eared snap showing her with the baby in her arms. It was passed around without comment. No one knew what to say. There were no words that would offer comfort.

Olive and Ronnie left soon after, with Audrey and the two girls. Beth hugged Olive and said enthusiastically, "There's thrilled I am to be an auntie. Auntie Beth, how does that sound?" The telling of their glad news had been marred by Audrey's revelations and Beth knew how disappointing that must have been. She smiled until they were at their door, then her face collapsed from the false smile as thoughts of Auntie Audrey's tragedy hit her once again.

She stood on the doorstep long after they had disappeared through their front door a few yards up the street. The revelations of the evening had distressed her, partly for the grief her gentle aunt had suffered, and also for the realisation that although she had loved Granny Moll, she had not really known her at all.

She went to bed without any further discussion, leaving her father and mother in a silence that was prickling with words waiting to be said, and for most of the night she was disturbed by arguments and shouting. The argument ended with her father slamming the front door and walking with swift, angry strides up the road.

With the approach of Christmas, women prowled the streets looking for anything that would help make the season a cheerful one. It threatened to be the oddest one in most people's memory, with shortages making it impossible to plan for the usual overeating and the generous welcomes in every home. The government had announced that the ration would include an extra four ounces of sugar and an extra two ounces of tea.

"How will that help us make a Christmas cake?" grumbled Marged. "It's fat we want and some good dried fruit and fresh oranges and lemons for the juice and peel."

"Carrots, that's what Lord Woolton recommends!" Beth laughed. "It'll be interesting to see what sort of a cake you make with carrots."

Huw said nothing. He rarely spoke these days and Beth knew that her parents were sleeping in separate bedrooms. She discussed it with Lilly, who had not been present when Audrey told her story, and Lilly said she thought it was their mother keeping the truth from him that had upset him. "When you've been married as long as they have I don't think you'd expect any surprises like that one," she said, adding with a laugh, "I bet Granny Moll would have had something to say to Auntie Audrey for spilling it out like that, just when Olive and Ronnie announced their news of a baby due to be born all respectable, in wedlock!"

"It isn't funny. Poor Aunt Audrey."

"Poor Olive too, having that reception when she told the family their news."

"It was us finding the grave."

"You aren't sorry, are you? At least Auntie Audrey can share her sadness. It is sad. Losing a baby must be the very worst. No replacing it, is there?" She frowned and added thoughtfully, "And when you think of how many parents are having to face that terrible loss every day, it's hard to imagine how they must feel. Just when their children have grown up and they think they're safe from childhood illnesses and accidents, this war comes to threaten them."

Beth was surprised at her sister's compassion. Expecting a child had made her a nicer person.

She had written to Peter telling him the outcome of their sad discovery and he had written back, promising to go with her and her aunt and clean up the site when he was next home, "which won't be until after Christmas," he added.

When she had a letter a few days later telling her that Freddy would be unable to get home for Christmas, it was less of a disappointment. He still wrote occasionally, and she had developed the habit of sending him ten shillings every two weeks, for which he thanked her.

She saw Peter's father often. He called sometimes to see whether they needed fresh vegetables and when he had a few rows of young leeks which he wanted to clear so he could plant broad beans, he offered them to Olive and Ronnie for their market stall. This had led to them buying and selling on other things, including rabbits, which were a popular addition to the meat supply.

Towards Christmas he began taking orders for chickens, which so far were not included in the weekly meat allowance.

"Got a couple of geese too, mind," he said when he called into the bustling, noisy market. He wrote their order in his scruffy notebook, which he kept tucked inside the lining of his hat.

"Never cooked a goose," Olive said. Mr Gregory enjoyed a few moments telling them the best way of putting it in the oven, hanging it above a drip tray to remove much of the grease.

"And keep the goose grease, mind," Janet Copp said as she arrived with their morning tea. "Good for rubbing on chests when you've got a cold, mind."

"Thanks, Janet," Olive laughed. "But I think I'd rather have a cold!"

Between dealing with the occasional customer, they watched as the Christmas decorations went up. There was such a happy atmosphere they were unaware of the time passing. It was a surprise when the inspector came out of his cubby-hole of an office to remind them it was time to close.

"Tomorrow we'd better do something to add to the rest," Ronnie said as they set off for home. "I bet Auntie Audrey will have some trimmings tucked away. She's sure to find a few streamers and baubles we can borrow."

As the next day was Sunday the market was closed. On Monday, Ronnie tried to deal with the complicated task of fixing the trimmings, but he didn't get very far. Besides the impossibility of bending his injured knee, his fear of climbing too high in case of falling and damaging it further thwarted him. Exasperated by his uselessness he sat on his stool and resigned himself to waiting for Olive to help.

"Stuck for a bit of help, is it?" the woman on the other fruit and veg stall called. Ronnie shrugged expressively and she gave her husband a nudge. "Go on, Arthur, give the poor lad a bit of a hand."

Arthur came across smiling cheerfully and, with his wife shouting instructions and Ronnie helping where he could, the stall was soon as brightly decorated as the rest, right down to the sprays of holly, which Arthur sold on his stall, and the strategically placed bough of mistletoe.

Ronnie was as pleased with the Christmas display as he remembered feeling as a child. Every year about this time he had come downstairs one morning with Beth and Lilly and Eynon to find the tree sparkling and the room filled with streamers that dipped down from the centre light to the corners and along the walls to the door. Magic. The stall was almost as good; he couldn't wait for Olive to see it.

Olive declared it "wonderful", and went straight away to thank the couple for their help. Arthur and Sally told her it was a pleasure.

When the market closed and everyone had

finished packing their stalls away for the night, Olive called to Janet and told her about the discovery of the grave of Ronnie's baby cousin and the distress it had caused in the family. Inevitably the conversation then returned to the discovery of that other grave, Myrtle and Maude's mother, a few weeks previously. "Copp she was called, like you. Strange, isn't it?"

"I don't think it's any relation of mine, though," Janet said. "Pity, mind; I'd have liked a couple of long-lost sisters. But so far as I know I don't have any other relations. Certainly not round here. From Birmingham my family were, not South Wales. But, tell you what, I'll wrap up a parcel for each of them girls for you to put under the tree, and tell them that having the same name is sure to make us friends. How will that be?"

Lilly's pregnancy progressed easily. She did less and less around the house, insisting that she needed fresh air every day and had to avoid any heavy work. As "heavy work" included practically every type of housework, she found very little to tax her energy.

She daydreamed a lot, imagining seeing Phil on the day he was demobbed and presenting him with the beautiful child and him falling in love with them both and leave his wife and – There the dream ended every time, bringing her down to earth with a jolt.

She had never discovered exactly where he lived or she would have paraded up and down from time to time hoping to catch him on one of his leaves and persuade him to at least help her. When she had asked about his home he had been evasive and the only clues she had were that he came from the direction of the beach when he walked up to meet her. She had also seen him on one occasion walking along one of the roads not far from the promenade, with a slim, fair young woman carrying shopping. Lilly presumed she was his wife.

She had walked along that road once or twice but hadn't seen Phil or the woman he had been with that day. So she enjoyed a dramatic few moments every day wondering if he was safe or injured, or perhaps a prisoner of war in some dreadful camp. If only she had news of him. Perhaps his wife didn't write very often. He might be glad of more letters from home. If only there was some way of finding out what was happening to him.

She found out in the harshest way possible. Each week the local paper listed the reported deaths and there was his photograph and his name, Philip Martin Denver. Not Philip Martin, the name he had given her, but there was no doubt about the picture. It was Phil, and while she had been daydreaming about a joyous reunion and being happy ever after, he had been killed.

Surprisingly she didn't burst into noisy tears. She was stunned by the news; her head hurt as though from a blow and was filled with a kind of pressure that blocked out all sensation and all thought. As the shock slowly receded she was calm and controlled. There was absolutely nothing that she could do. Nothing at all. She couldn't tell anyone and she couldn't be seen to grieve.

She knew that even at a moment like this she couldn't tell anyone. Selfish as she often was, she couldn't distress his wife more by letting her know that her husband had been unfaithful. She grieved silently, seeing before her a future empty of love. In the privacy of her room she hugged herself, seeking comfort from her unborn child who was unequivocally without a father, even an absent one.

Marged and Huw noticed how quiet she was, how less inclined to argue, but they decided there was no serious problem.

"Nothing to be alarmed about," Marged said, and Huw agreed.

"Our Lilly's always been moody."

The shops lacked their usual displays. They all had black-out material over their windows, so instead of the usual glitter of

Christmas cheer, with grocers and butchers and toy shops, making a walk through the main shopping streets an exciting event for the town's children, everything became dark as soon as the day ended. No coloured lights enticed window-shopping children with bright eyes, marvelling at the magic, to wander and hope and dream.

Once darkness fell, most people stayed home and listened to the wireless, where news came of waves of German aircraft filling the skies night after night, many of them to be destroyed, but others coming in their place, relentlessly continuing to bomb the larger cities, leaving them wondering how anything could survive. Pity for the victims was mixed with relief that St David's Well had nothing of strategic importance to the enemy.

Eynon gravitated towards St David's Well as Christmas drew closer. He didn't know what to do to extricate himself from the mess he had made. One evening, he walked along the promenade where the silent shops gave no sign of the bright days of summer. Some were boarded up against the winter gales, others still showed posters advertising the ice-creams that were no longer allowed to be sold. Leaves and piles of sand filled the once neat doorways and everywhere was a travesty of the golden days of the past summer.

At the rock and sweet shop he stopped and thought of Alice. Where was she now – still looking after her sick and foul-tempered father? He smiled sadly as he remembered his plans to save her from that, dreams in which he would flirt a little and perhaps become seriously involved. Then he had been ready for fun and adventure, now he would settle for having a friend.

Footsteps approached, running, accompanied by soft laughter. They slowed to a walk, then were running again. There was a shout of anger, then more running.

He stepped into the doorway of the rock and sweet shop and hoped the shadows would hide him. His eyes were used to the dark, living as he had far from towns and people for the past months, so as the girl and the dog who was causing the trouble passed the doorway, he recognised her.

"Alice!" The word was out before he thought of the risk he was taking. Appearing like that so soon after she had filled his thoughts, he was unable to help himself.

"Eynon? But I thought – I thought you were missing," she said, grasping the dog's collar in an effort to hold him still.

"I shouldn't have spoken," Eynon said. "Please, Alice, please forget you've seen me."

"Is it true then? You did run away?" she gasped.

"I ran away from a situation that I thought couldn't get worse, and I was wrong. Now I don't know what to do."

"Everyone thinks you're missing, or a prisoner of war."

"That's what I am, but I'm in a prison without walls."

"Dad'll be asleep; will you come back and have a bath and some food? I can cook you something."

"I can't do that. If you're seen to be helping me, you'd be in serious trouble."

She stepped into the doorway beside him. "I'll risk it. Come on, I'll tell them I was trying to persuade you to give yourself up." Then she saw the unsightly scar on his head and asked, "What's that? It looks painful."

"I did it when I fell from the lorry on manoeuvres, the day I ran away. I was knocked out for a few minutes. That was weeks ago and it just won't heal. It's a bit sore at times because I keep knocking it."

"You needed a few stitches, that's why it won't heal."

"I know, but it's too late now," he shrugged.

With Alice's father asleep upstairs, Eynon went into the kitchen and filled the galvanised bath with warm water and soaked luxuriously for a while. Beside him, half shielded by a curtain, Alice prepared eggs on toast, planning to tell her father that she had dropped them while cleaning the cupboard.

Daringly, she led him upstairs after he had eaten and showed him the spare room. There was a gas lamp on the wall and the curtains were open.

"Don't light that, whatever you do," Alice whispered.

He opened the window and stared out. The sky was clear and a moon shone over the town. Roofs were touched with its silver light and the street below, sharply etched, looked unreal.

Homesickness overwhelmed him and Alice held him as he took deep breaths to contain his grief. Then he slipped under the sweet-smelling sheets and was asleep within minutes. Alice watched for a while, thinking about how young he looked, in spite of a roughly chopped beard, and of how unfair life could be.

The next morning she called him early and he left with pockets filled with bread and her ration of cheese, promising he'd be back as soon as he had sorted everything out.

"Write to me," were her last words before he slipped out of the back gate and hurried away in the early dawn.

Two weeks after the death of Phil had been reported, Lilly was idly looking through her

"treasure box", a chocolate box with a sentimental picture of kittens on the front, in
which she kept her private memorabilia. She
found the only photograph she had of Phil,
taken when the beach photographer had
snapped them unaware. If he'd thought
about it at all, he would have presumed the
negative had been destroyed without a copy
being made, but he would have been wrong.
She had kept it hidden in her treasure box,
to take out occasionally and relive some
precious moments. She had hoped that one
day, when they were together and their love
was no longer a secret, she would show him
and they would laugh at her mild deception.

Now she wondered whether she should
give it to Phil's wife. She needn't tell her the
truth, just that she knew Phil from the
repair shop. She could say that the photographer had taken the snap when they had
met by accident, and that she had kept it as
it was a flattering one of herself. It was a
plausible story and to add to its authenti-
city, she would wear a wedding ring to
reassure the poor widow that she was no
threat. Granny Moll's ring was in the house
and would fit well enough.

Most people managed to decorate their
rooms with either home-made streamers or
ones saved from previous Christmases, but
for Beth, any attempt at adding the usual

trimmings came to nothing. Every time she painstakingly put something up, her father frustrated her by pulling it down.

"What is it, Dad?" she asked when the artificial tree she had found in a cupboard had been thrown into the ashbin. "You might be angry about something, but for the rest of us, it's Christmas and we want to enjoy it."

"No cheek from you!" he snapped and she sat down, the crêpe-paper streamers she had made resting on her lap.

"Dad, why are you so angry? It's been ever since Auntie Audrey told us about the baby. Why has that upset you?"

"I can't talk to you about something like that, girl!"

"Why not? Our Ronnie's wife is expecting and I do have an idea of how that happens, Dad!"

"None of your impertinence, right?"

"Cheek, impertinence, there's a terrible daughter I am," she teased, hoping to coax a smile.

"All right, it isn't about the baby, it's about your Granny Moll. She ruled this family, insisting on having the last say in everything."

"Piper's was her business, and her father's before her. I suppose she thought she had the right."

"It was me and your Uncle Bleddyn who

ran it, and we ran it in spite of her inter-
ference not because of her help. Lazy sod
her old man Joseph Piper was. Never did a
stroke of work unless he was forced.
Bleddyn and I came into the firm when we
were still at school, working dawn till dark.
We worked full time, and I mean full time,
when we were only fourteen and slaved like
fools all these years with neither praise nor
credit. And all the time Granny Moll was
telling everyone how her grandfather Joseph
brought the business round after he took
over from Mrs Downs's grandparents."

Beth only half believed what her father
was saying. Anger and disappointment can
easily distort the truth in the most honest
people.

"But why are you suddenly angry about
this now?" she asked.

"Because of what she did to your Auntie
Audrey. She was a bully, her righteousness
was a hammer which she wielded on us all,
me, Bleddyn, your mother, poor inoffensive
Audrey, and even you, Lilly, Ronnie and our
Eynon, insisting that you worked on the
beach even though you might have wanted
something different."

"I didn't, though," she protested.

"How do you know? Ever since you were
born, you and Lilly and Ronnie and little
Eynon weren't given the choice. You were
told by devoted Granny Moll that your

future was Piper's. Damn it all, it's a couple of cafés and stalls, not a flamin' dynasty!"

He went out soon after and later Beth learned that he had gone to the fish-and-chip café, after collecting the sign he had ordered some days before – which had been changed to "Castle's".

Huw was still sufficiently angry to relish the moment when Marged first saw it, and he smiled in anticipation. He was determined it would stay if he had to sit up on the roof all night and guard it!

Lilly made up her mind. With the item in the newspaper giving her sufficient clues, she would find Phil's wife and give her the photograph. It was the last thing she could do for him. He had let her down when he learned about the baby she was carrying, but she still loved him and knew that he had loved her, at least a little. Not enough to behave honourably, but she could hardly blame him for that. Every family had its secrets, she knew that, particularly now, since the truth had come out about Auntie Audrey's lost child. It had made her feel less alone, knowing poor Auntie Audrey had been through something similar although with a far less happy outcome.

She searched through her mother's small collection of jewellery and slipped her Granny Moll's ring on her wedding finger.

Tomorrow she would go to Queen Street and knock doors until she found her.

The road was a long, stone-built terrace, one of three closely arranged rows climbing, one behind the other, up a steep hill from one of the town's busy shopping areas. She went to the first house and asked for the family of Denver and was directed to the house at the far end. She knocked and waited apprehensively for the woman who was Phil's wife to answer.

Suddenly she was afraid, and wanted to run away. How could she face the woman she had cheated on in the most degrading way? What had happened to Auntie Audrey could have happened to her: Mam and Dad could have forbidden her to keep the child. Then she might have been forced to tell the truth about its father. How could she stand here so blatantly and face the woman and pretend she was on an errand of kindness and friendship?

Her heart was racing and she had begun to move away when the door was opened and a rosy-faced woman of about fifty stood there. Her arms covered in flour, her apron folded up and held to save spilling more flour on to the shining doorstep, she stood there smiling. The appetising smell of apples cooking issued forth around her.

"I hope you're not selling nothing, love. Broke I am," she said at once.

"I heard about the death of Phil, I knew him from taking things to be repaired in his shop. I have a photograph, taken when we met by accident over the beach last summer. Cyril the Snap took it, thinking we knew each other, and I was curious to see how I looked so I bought it." She held out the rather tatty snap. "I thought his wife might like it, see, and as it's no real use to me as I didn't know him, I thought I'd bring it for her."

"For who, love?"

"Like I said, for his wife."

"Phil wasn't married, never had been. Plenty of women, mind, never no shortage of women with my Phil, but never no wife."

The street seemed to spin, the houses dancing as though in some crazy dream. Lilly reached out to grab the door frame for support and instead found herself held in the woman's arms and being guided inside the house. The once delicious smell from the apples began to make her nauseous. She thought she might be sick. She also thought that the sharp scent of apples cooking would always bring back memories of that moment.

"Is it Phil's child you're carrying?" Mrs Denver asked in a matter-of-fact tone as she helped her visitor to drink some hot, sweet tea. "Told the tale of being married regular he did, so's not to be expected to marry them."

"Them?" Lilly asked, her voice slurred, her mouth dry.

"Two children he's got and I never see a hair of either of them. I know they're both boys, but I don't even know their names. Sad it is, not even being able to send them a card on their birthdays or a present at Christmas."

She saw the ring on Lilly's finger then and hurriedly apologised. "Oh, you're married. Sorry, I thought – oh dear, I've really said the wrong things. Just a friend, are you, genuine friend and nothing more?"

Lilly took off the ring and placed it on the plush-covered table. "It was my gran's," she explained. "I thought Phil's wife would believe the story of us hardly knowing each other if I pretended to be a married woman. I didn't want to distress her with the truth."

"Such a kind girl you are. Here, let me get you another cup of tea – and a piece of my tart wouldn't go amiss, I'll be bound. Sugar for shock don't they say? And I put half my extra Christmas ration in that tart!"

Lilly was trembling and Mrs Denver sat and talked to her, coaxing her to drink the tea. She urged her to eat the oversweet tart on to which she had sprinkled even more sugar.

As Lilly calmed down they talked, Lilly

explaining that she had kept Phil's identity a secret in respect for his non-existent wife. Phil's mother told her of her disappointment over her son's behaviour.

"Now he's gone and I've no real family left," Mrs Denver said sadly. "Only a sister who lives in London who I never see, and two grandchildren I'll never be allowed to meet." She looked at the distraught girl sitting huddled close to the fire trying in vain to warm away the chill within her, and said, "Will you come and see me? When the baby's born, I mean? I know I can't be a real grandmother, you and Phil not being wed and all, but I could be a sort of friend, couldn't I?"

Looking up into the round, motherly face, Lilly smiled shakily and said, "I'd like that. I've a feeling I'll need a few friends once the secret is out."

"When is she due?" Mrs Denver asked, her deep blue eyes shining with happiness. "I'll be able to start counting the weeks."

"Some time in May, early in the month I think."

"Perfect."

"Mam and Dad don't think so," Lilly grumbled, then, having explained about Piper's Café and the stalls, she added, "I'll be expected to work on the beach or the chip shop as soon as I'm out of bed!"

"Then stay there for an extra week or so!"

Mrs Denver said with a laugh. "Men don't like to ask questions when it's to do with women's problems, do they?"

"To be honest, I've worked that out myself." Lilly gave a tentative smile. "I haven't done much work since I knew this little one was on the way."

"Good on you. Take advantage of it. We don't get many opportunities in life!"

Like two conspirators they talked about the beach and how it would not be good for the baby, at least for the first two years.

"I'll have to find some way of earning money, though," Lilly said. "I don't want to lean on Mam and Dad for ever."

"Plenty of work about with this war on," Mrs Denver said confidently. "Factory work pays well and you can easily find someone to look after the little girl."

"You said 'she' and now 'little girl'; are you so sure?" Lilly asked curiously.

"Never been wrong yet. The others were boys," she added sadly.

Lilly walked to the bus stop with her new friend and felt happier about the forthcoming birth than at any time since it had been confirmed.

Huw was disappointed by Marged's reaction to the new sign above the chip shop and café. Although he hung around as often as he could, she saw it for the first time when he was not there. She went to speak to Bleddyn about something and walked in without noticing it. As she was on the way out, Beth called, "Hello, Mam. What d'you think of the new sign, then?"

It took a split second for Marged to realise what had happened and, having her back to Beth and Bleddyn as she pushed her way through the queue of customers, she was able to hide her initial fury. She walked on through the shop and out on to the pavement, then looked up at the brand new sign and nodded casually at them.

"Very nice," was all she said before walking on.

"She took that well," was Beth's comment.

"I wouldn't fancy being in your Dad's shoes, all the same," Bleddyn laughed as he shook salt and vinegar on to a bag of chips.

Marged didn't go straight home. She went to the sign-writing business, which was now run by the once retired father and uncle of the owner, who was now painting camouflage on army lorries, guns and tanks.

"There's been a terrible mistake, Mr Morton. The sign was ordered and paid for by Mr Castle, but the sign should have read 'Piper's'."

She spoke briskly and with an edge of irritation at their incompetence, so that they hovered over their order book and both agreed that they could see how easily the mistake could have been made.

"I'll be generous, considering the mistake was yours," she told them, and offered to pay a small sum for the correct sign – the old one repainted, for quickness – to be erected on the following Sunday.

"Sunday? We don't usually work on a Sunday, Mrs Castle."

"No? But then, I don't suppose you usually make a mistake and paint the wrong name on a sign for a long-established business, do you?"

They agreed to fix the old sign, repainted, on Sunday morning.

Lilly went to see Mrs Denver a week after her first visit and once again the lady was baking.

Lilly wondered where she found the ingredients and Mrs Denver smiled as though reading her thoughts.

"I do a bit of cooking for the café down the road," she explained. "Get an allowance they do and I'm good at ekeing out the stuff and making more for them to sell. Tell the truth, Lilly, love, I use smaller tins too and a slice of cake is a slice of cake, eh? Nobody bothers to measure it, do they?"

It was obvious from her home that Mrs Denver was far from wealthy, but one day she insisted on going shopping to buy what they could for the baby.

After an initial refusal, Lilly agreed. She could see that Mrs Denver wanted to be a part of the baby's life and with her only son dead, there was no other family for her to cherish, so she agreed.

As she explained to Beth a few weeks later, "I can always find ways of repaying her, give her things she needs and won't be able to buy."

Beth went to see Freddy's parents one morning and when she went into the living room she was instantly aware of an atmosphere. Then she saw a forage cap on the arm of the sofa.

"Is that Freddy's? Is he here?" she asked, excitement mixed with confusion. "He didn't tell me he was coming on leave."

"Well, I—"

Mrs Clements seemed unable to decide what to say and suspicion coloured Beth's face as she began to walk towards the door. "He told you not to tell me, didn't he?" Then there was the sound of feet running down the stairs and Freddy burst in.

"Beth, love. How did you know I was home? It was meant to be a surprise!"

She wasn't sure she believed him, but it was easier to pretend so she joined in the joke, telling Mrs Clements she wasn't a very convincing liar and telling Freddy he was a dreadful tease.

"Back to camp tomorrow, mind. This was so short it was hardly worth the fare, except that I had to see you," he told her when his mother had left the room.

"What d'you want to do, then?" she asked, expecting him to say, "the pictures", as usual.

"I want to walk in the dark and kiss you and tell you how much I love you," he said.

"I did have something arranged for this afternoon but it's easily cancelled. And I'll go and see Uncle Bleddyn; I'm sure he'll find someone else to take my place lunchtime and tonight," Beth responded, pleasantly surprised.

"No, love, it's impossible. That's what I *want* to do, but it isn't what I have to do. Special leave this is. I have to go and see the wife of a chap who was killed a week ago. I promised him that if he – you know – if he didn't come back, I would go and see his wife and children. Take the letter he left with me."

"Oh Freddy, not even an hour?"

"Hell of a war, this, isn't it, love? I want to be with my girl but I can't even spend an afternoon telling her how much I miss her."

"You were going to call, though?" she asked doubtfully.

"On the way back to the station, yes. Just time to tell you how much I love you and miss you." They kissed and hugged each other but it was clear that Freddy wanted her to go and disconsolately she walked back to Sidney Street and changed out of her best clothes for the two hours serving fish and chips and the ever more mysterious rissoles.

When she finished clearing up after the lunchtime session, she didn't go home. Instead she walked to Goose Lane. She supposed she might as well keep the arrangement she had made. The disappointment with Freddy was something she was becoming used to.

Peter had an unexpected pre-Christmas leave. He wasn't able to tell her why, but she gathered that there was a meeting he'd had to attend. She knew from a few things he had let slip that he was involved with codes and cyphers and she wondered whether he was involved with men working behind enemy lines. She wondered, but didn't ask. Peter was easy to talk to and open about everything else, but his work was a strictly forbidden subject.

He and Beth had planned to spend an hour or two cleaning up the small grave. She walked up and he was waiting for her at the gates, with a few tools in a bag beside him. Audrey and a slightly embarrassed Wilf met them there and, armed with their selection of assorted tools, they began to clean the stone and make the inscription easy to read.

It was cold, frosty and damp, and as soon as they broke through the soil they were surrounded by an unpleasant earthy smell which seemed to permeate their clothes. They were soon scratched and bleeding from the determination of the brambles to defy their efforts to remove them, and Peter and Wilf, who was now fully involved, tried to persuade the two women to leave it to them.

They organised a rota with each man taking it in turns digging out a root and passing it to the other to be cut and packed for removal. When the pathetically small grave was cleared, a rose bush planted and seeds of forget-me-nots scattered, Beth and Peter walked away leaving Audrey and Wilf to remember and grieve.

"It was so cruel for Auntie Audrey to have to grieve alone, and for Wilf never to have been allowed to see their child."

"It was considered to be such a disgrace, wasn't it?"

"I suppose Granny Moll thought she was doing the best thing."

"I would never have allowed anything like that to happen to you, Beth. I would have fought and fought for you, whatever the family thought."

"Would you, Peter?"

"I care for you, Beth, you know that, and I'd never let anything bad happen to you."

He put an arm around her and pulled her against him. She relaxed against the strength of him, knowing she only had to raise her head to share the kiss that was waiting for her. The moment was fraught with longing, and slowly Beth moved closer. A flash of Freddy's face drifted across her mind and was discarded together with his lies and cheating. This was now, and Peter was showing her a different future. Why should she hesitate?

Then over Peter's shoulder she saw Audrey and Wilf, and the sight of them, familiar, a part of the real world, the world in which she had promised Freddy she'd be his wife, brought her down to earth. Moving reluctantly away from Peter, her hand grasping his as if through the door of a prison, her inside and him unattainable on the outside, she called to the other couple, "Peter's father has invited us back for a cup of tea. All right?"

They all went back to the house on Goose Lane and took the smell of the dank graveside with them. Mr Gregory offered tea and as darkness brought an end to the day, Peter took them all back to Sidney Street on the cart. He looked at Beth longingly as she stepped down and she felt aching regret as, with tears welling, she turned away.

Twelve

Shirley's mother was beginning to wish she had not encouraged her daughter to befriend Freddy Clements. All she had hoped for was to separate the boy from Beth to spite the Castles and give them some grief. Now it seemed that her daughter Shirley was more involved that she had intended. Freddy was a nice enough boy, she mused, and while he had worked for the gents' outfitters, a likely prospect as a husband. But now he was in the army as a regular, and that meant absences and opportunities to seek the company of other women. Nice he might be, but trustworthy he was not, she decided. She knew from bitterly learnt lessons that most men were weak when faced with temptation or the demands of a strongly sexual woman. She didn't want Shirley to have the same disappointments as herself. Freddy Clements was vain, and the type of man who'd be as easily flattered as her husband Paul had been.

"Don't you think you could do better than Freddy?" she asked her daughter one morning as she was getting her coat on ready to go to work. "You won't see much of him, even after this war is over, him being a regular."

"Five years he's signed for, not life. He'll be out when he's twenty-three, Mam. He could go back to the shop – or perhaps he'll learn a trade while he's in the army and come out qualified to do something better."

"You've talked about it, then? You and him, after the war?"

"Talked about it, yes, but not him and me. He's engaged to Beth Castle, isn't he? I just provide a bit of company now and then."

"As long as that's all you're providing!"

"I don't think he and Beth are all that well suited, mind," Shirley replied, ignoring her mother's remark. "A bit boring she is. Doesn't like dancing and Freddy loves it. She won't go into a café because she would rather eat at home."

"Not surprising she won't eat in cafés, she works in them most of the year!"

"She doesn't like the pictures, she only goes to please him – and I bet she makes sure he knows it, too!"

"And you're better suited, you and Freddy?"

"I think so. He just got trapped with Beth Castle. They started off at infant school and it's nothing more than habit that kept them together all this time."

"Be warned that if he's unfaithful to Beth,

he could be the same with you. I know what it's like living with a man who doesn't remain faithful. Laughing at me he was, your father."

"Just friends we are, Mam, that's all."

"Them Castles are no better than they should be," Hetty Downs sniffed, wrapping a thick scarf around her head. "Lilly expecting and not saying – perhaps not even knowing – who the father is!"

"Lilly's all right. It's Beth I don't like. At least Lilly's ready for a bit of fun."

"And she's got a souvenir of some man's 'fun', hasn't she? Don't make the same mistake, Shirley. A man doesn't respect women who're easy."

Shirley smiled to herself. What made people think sex was a chore for women and only fun for a man? She knew better than that!

Hetty dragged on her short, fur-lined boots and picked up her handbag and umbrella. "Got to go. It's mornings like this when I wish I still worked in the shop below. At least you haven't got to face the icy cold weather and walk to that icy cold factory."

"You've forgotten quick! The shop door open all the time, and only a small electric fire for a few hours? Frozen stiff I am, long before you get to your factory!"

They both thought about Freddy during the morning, Shirley wondering how soon

404

she could suggest to him that he broke off his engagement to Beth, and Hetty wondering how she could break them apart. Neither was concerned about Beth. If they considered her at all, it was with the casual attitude that she deserved to be abandoned by Freddy because she did nothing to try and keep him.

In Audrey's house the post arrived and was casually put on a small table to be inspected later. When Ronnie came down he saw that one of the letters was headed OHMS and he opened it to learn that he was to attend a medical examination to see whether he was fit to return to active service.

Olive ran down and read the letter and, trying to stop him worrying, said cheerfully, "Don't worry, love. You'd be a liability to anyone except me!"

"It'll be routine, won't it? They can't send me back, not like this." Unconvinced, he added, "I'll go this morning to see if Mr Gregory has any ideas where we can get a few Christmas trees to sell on the stall, shall I?"

In Sidney Street, at both Audrey's house and Huw and Marged's further down the road, the day had begun slowly. Long after Shirley and her mother had started work, Marged was cooking breakfast for Lilly, Beth and herself while they all tried to persuade Beth to leave Freddy.

"Face up to the facts," Marged said, slapping a plate of toast and one of Mr Gregory's hard-boiled duck eggs in front of her. "You know he's been coming home on leave and not telling you. You suspect he's seeing more of Shirley Downs than he's telling you. There's certainly a lot he isn't telling you! What more do you need to be convinced?"

"I'd know what he's up to if he was my fiancé," Lilly said. "You wouldn't catch me playing second fiddle."

"You what?" Beth laughed. "What's that lump then, if it isn't second fiddle?"

"Enough," Huw said. "Lilly's only trying to make you see sense, like the rest of us."

"Let her try and sort herself out," Beth retorted. "Why doesn't she go and see the man and tell him he has to help?"

"Because he's dead, that's why." In the silence that followed, Lilly told them that the man had been killed in combat. Then she decided to tell them the rest. "I had a photograph of him and I put on Granny Moll's wedding ring so she wouldn't be upset, and went to give it to his wife."

"You met her?" Beth sat down and stared at her sister. "That was brave – or stupid; I don't know which."

"Stupid as it happens. He wasn't married after all, he'd only told me that so I couldn't expect him to marry me. It was his mother

I saw." Lilly glared at her sister and went on, "So you're right, I don't have the sense I was born with, and shouldn't be trying to tell you what you should do about that waster of yours. At least Freddy isn't very good at covering up."

No one knew what to say. Beth hugged Lilly and Marged stared at Huw, urging him to say something, anything, to make Lilly feel better.

"Glad we are that you won't have to marry him," Huw said gruffly. "I don't want to lose either of my girls just yet and I certainly won't want to lose this baby of yours. He's a next-generation Castle, and we'll love him, won't we, Marged?"

"Mrs Denver thinks it might be a girl," Lilly said, attempting to laugh.

"Then she'll have to keep her name when she marries, eh?"

"Denver?" Marged frowned. "Not Phil Denver, him who calls himself Phil Martin?" She stared at her daughter in disbelief. "But everyone knows about him telling that old story! It's been a joke for years!"

Lilly lifted her head, her face pale and taut with dismay. "Everyone knew, did they? Then why didn't someone tell me?"

Ronnie still limped badly and the doctor told him that he would not improve much further when he was called back for another medical to see if he was fit enough to return to his unit. He and Olive waited nervously for the decision. He knew it was unlikely that he would have to go back – even with a desk job he would be a liability if his unit was sent to the front line – but with more and more men, and women, being called to register every week, nothing was certain.

When the letter came, he and Olive looked at it together.

"No return to active service," they read aloud.

"That's such a relief," Olive said. Then she looked at her husband's serious face as he read further. "Ronnie? What is it?"

"I have to work in a munitions factory, reporting in two weeks' time, unless there are extenuating circumstances for which a waiver might be granted."

They wrote straight away, pointing out that without his help, as his wife and partner in business was expecting their first child, the market stall, their only source of income, would have to be closed. The reply came almost by return post; their request was denied.

Another form was filled in explaining their need to keep the business intact, this time with a word from Ronnie's own doctor to add weight to the plea.

With the war changing everything and many

families in mourning, the town had an air of false gaiety as December speeded up, heading for the celebration. Cakes concocted with the most unlikely ingredients were made and were the cause of much laughter. Flagons of beer were carried back home to be stored until Christmas Day with a bottle of port or sherry, which for most was as much as they could afford.

The shops quickly emptied of anything that could be considered seasonal, queues forming when anything in short supply was rumoured to be available. Chickens and rabbits were snapped up by those who had the money to buy them and the bacon ration was saved for several weeks so a small joint could give the illusion of extravagance.

Marged couldn't think of Christmas with her usual enthusiasm. How could she when she didn't know where Eynon was? A couple of cards arrived purporting to come from Auntie Ethel and a Mrs William, a sentence to let them know he was well and hoping to see them soon. Although the writing was a scrawl, Marged knew the cards had been sent by Eynon. William was his second name. But she was unable to discuss them with anyone except Huw, and there was also the fear that something had happened since they were written and now, this moment, he could be far from well, all alone and in serious trouble.

The military police still called on occasion, starting by warning her of the seriousness of keeping his whereabouts from them, but as she didn't know where he was, and the postcards wouldn't have helped anyway, she said nothing. Now, with this everlasting disagreement between her and Huw, she grieved for him in lonely silence.

Beth didn't relish the thought of the holiday. With her parents hardly speaking to each other, Audrey and Wilf grieving anew for the child lost so many years before, and Lilly insisting on being spoilt, it was only the thought that it was Maude and Myrtle's first Christmas as a part of the family that made her do what she could to add some festivities to the house on Sidney Street.

Mr Gregory had promised them a chicken so it was with some surprise that she saw one arrive, in a box, well and truly alive.

"He wouldn't send it for us to kill!" Beth said, reaching for her coat, intending to go to Goose Lane.

Huw came in just as she was leaving and said, "Oh, it's arrived then."

"And I'm just off to tell him he can come and take it back!" she said.

"What's the matter with it? I won it fair and square, I did."

"Won it?"

"In a raffle at the pub. With the one we've ordered from old Gregory we'll have enough to invite the whole family around."

Thankfully, Beth removed her coat and sat down. "What will you do with it, Dad? You can't kill it."

"Who can't? Of course I'll kill it. What d'you expect me to do, buy it a present for under the tree?"

Beth reached for her coat again. She had kept well away from Mr Gregory's while the slaughtering was going on, but she had to stop this situation at once. He would give the poor thing a home. What was her father thinking of?

"I'm going to see Mr Gregory. And," she told her father, "I'm not going to let you kill that poor little creature, whatever you say. Even if I never have a Christmas dinner ever again!"

Huw watched his daughter leave then picked up the beautiful speckled hen. He went into the yard and with feet wide apart took hold of the hen's body in one hand and its head in the other. Then a scream rent the air and he dropped it. The hen ran off and hid behind the shed. Maude and Myrtle stood at the door with such an expression of horror on their faces Huw felt like a man caught about to commit a murder.

"Murderer," Myrtle choked, confirming his thought.

"How can you, Uncle Huw?" Maude said, sobbing loudly.

The chicken came out from behind the shed pecking the ground, aimlessly searching for edible morsels, apparently unharmed and unfazed by her narrow escape.

"What d'you want me to do with it?" Huw asked irritably. "Keep her as a pet?"

"Oh, Uncle Huw, thanks," Maude said.

"This is the best Christmas present we've ever had," Myrtle echoed.

Leaving the girls to decide on a name, Huw chuckled as he went back inside. Thank goodness they had ordered one from Mr Gregory. At least they wouldn't recognise that as anything more than a few slices of meat. Then he crossed his fingers. He didn't want them refusing to eat the meat they had spent so much money on, or spoiling his own appetite by making him feel guilty! He sighed, a mixture of irritation and amusement. "I suppose I'd better build the thing a coop," he shouted after the girls.

Later he sat listening to the wireless and wondering how he could prevent Christmas being spoilt for the rest of the family by Marged's attitude. They tried to keep it from the family, but they hardly spoke to each other and continued to sleep in separate rooms.

Beth, Lilly and Ronnie knew that their parents were having difficulties and Lilly was worried. It is frightening to realise that your parents, on whom you rely for security and comfort and advice, aren't getting on. In a rare fit of willingness, Lilly was helping Beth wash up after supper when she voiced her worries.

"What will become of us if they decide to leave each other?" she whispered to Beth. "Our Dad's gone to meet friends and colleagues from the beach this evening, and Mam refused to go with him."

Peeping through the door, they looked at Marged sitting in her usual chair at the side of the fireplace, knitting furiously and saying nothing, anger apparent in her expression and in the speed of the flashing needles.

"It was a meeting about next season, and the restrictions on catering and all that. Important enough for her to want to be there, don't you think? Running the stalls and the cafés is her life. It must be serious if she's refused to go."

"Mam? Why didn't you go with Dad?" Beth asked. "The new season is going to be difficult with the new regulations and all. You have to know what's happening."

"I don't need to go to listen to a lot of gossiping old men trying to tell me what to do. I know how to deal with the beach trade. I'm a Piper and I've done it all my life."

"At least Dad and Uncle Bleddyn have gone."

"And they needn't think they can come

413

back here and tell me what I must do," Marged warned.

"It's their business too, Mam," Lilly dared to say. "God 'elp, they've been involved since they were about eight!"

"None of your cheek! And I get enough of that talk from your father. It's Piper's, and your father won't change that."

"But we're Castles. Dad and Uncle Bleddyn run it now Granny Moll is dead."

"And we've run it since we were children!" Huw had walked in and stood, glaring at their mother.

The two girls backed away into the kitchen and continued to discuss the rift in whispers. They finished clearing up and got into bed while below them the row still rumbled on.

"What will we do?" Lilly said. "I can't bear it, Beth. If only Granny Moll was here none of this would be happening. Talk some sense into them she would."

"I think it's Granny Moll that's the trouble," Beth told her. "Ever since Dad found out about Auntie Audrey and the punishment she suffered – Granny Moll not allowing her to marry, treating her and Uncle Wilf like criminals – Dad's been angry. Mam obviously supported Granny Moll, didn't she? The worst bit of all for Dad was being married to our Mam all these years and not being told. Since then they haven't spent an hour in each other's company without rowing, have they?"

"I still don't understand why."

"Neither do I. It must be something to do with Granny Moll being so hard. I think Dad and Uncle Bleddyn want some recognition of the work they've done to keep the business running. The story of Auntie Audrey just made him realise how much she needed her own way in everything."

Lilly shrugged. "It still doesn't make sense."

The bedroom door opened and their father stood there.

"Sorry I am that you've heard all this. But your Mam and I don't seem able to sort this out. I'm going to stay with Uncle Bleddyn for a while, until she accepts that we're a partnership, all equal. Me and your mam and Uncle Bleddyn. All of us Castles."

They stared at the closing door, their hearts racing with fear. What would happen to them now? Predictably, Lilly began to cry.

They heard the front door close and their father's footsteps fading as he walked up the street to where he parked the van. They heard the van drive away and a few minutes later, in the silence of the night, they heard the water drawn to fill the kettle and the fire being poked to boil it.

"Come on, Lilly. I think we're entitled to

hear Mam's side of things, don't you?" Together, they went down the stairs to face her.

Huw went into his brother's house and Bleddyn saw at once that something serious had happened. Evelyn was there and Hannah was ironing in the kitchen.

"How are those girls of yours?" Huw asked Hannah after greeting the others. "Looking forward to Father Christmas's visit? I'm hoping for a new razor; I think Marged trimmed the oilcloth with mine," he joked.

Evelyn went out into the kitchen and closed the door, guessing that the brothers needed to talk in private.

"Can I stay a couple of nights?"

"Stay here? Why?" Bleddyn asked.

"Marged and I've had a row and until she sees sense I'm not going back," Huw replied. "I can't get her to see that this business wouldn't be here at all if it wasn't for you and me. Moll did all the shouting, but we did all the work. Wicked she was, treating us like idiots and poor Audrey like a criminal. I can't really explain why, but it was the last straw for me, her treating her own daughter so badly and Audrey still doing penance all these years after."

"You won't get anywhere by staying away, not talking to Marged. Go home and insist

416

on her listening to what you have to say. That's my advice."

"She never listens. As soon as I start talking, her ears close and you can see her about to explode with the need to say her piece. No matter what I said, the answer would be no."

"Shall I try?"

"If you want to, but I don't think it'll do any good. Moll trained her well. Thinks she's the top of the heap because she's a Piper. Being married to me all these years hasn't altered that!"

"You've seen the chip shop then?"

"She never changed the sign back!"

"She did. Got Will Morton to take down the new one and put the old one back."

"Well, tomorrow it's coming down again. No sign at all it'll be, just an empty board, until she agrees to it being called Castle's. Right?"

"Right. Er – I think. What will we do if she refuses right up to the new season?"

"Then there won't be a season, will there? If it's Piper's she wants, then she and Audrey can run it and see how well they do. Now, have you got a bed I could use? I'm worn out with all this wrangling, and that's a fact."

They talked a while longer. Evelyn and Hannah and the two sleepy girls said good-night and left, with Bleddyn and Huw walking them home to where they all now lived, as the night was so dark. When they returned, Bleddyn settled Huw into a single bed in his own room, as it had been simplest for both of them to use the room in which there was a heater, and lay there wondering what would become of them.

Huw also lay with his eyes open, sleep a vague hope. He thought about Lilly and her baby, about Beth and that pain in the arse Freddy, Marged and her stubborn righteousness – inherited from the other pain in the arse, Moll.

"Damn it all, Moll wasn't a Piper anyway until she married that useless Joseph! She was a Jones!" Huw said in exasperation.

"Shut up and go to sleep," growled Bleddyn.

"Made me suffer all these years because of—"

"Shut up!"

Beth and Lilly tried to persuade their mother to talk about what had happened between her and their father but Marged refused. She made tea, gave them a cup and sent them back to bed.

"It looks serious," Beth whispered, "our Dad walking out like that. What will happen, d'you think?"

"Mam won't let the café go, whatever happens she'll open that next year."

"She can't do it all on her own though."

"We'll have to help as much as we can."

"I can't!" Lilly said at once. "I'll have a baby to look after."

"So did our Mam when we were small, remember. She still managed to keep everything going, didn't she?"

"I'm not like Mam. I couldn't do it," Lilly admitted as she drained her cup. "But I can't see any other way of earning my keep and with our Dad gone, I suppose I'll be expected to, won't I?" On that sad note, she turned over and tried to sleep.

Christmas was the happiest time but it could also be the loneliest, Eynon thought as he trudged along an empty country road on Christmas Eve. He thought longingly about the Christmas dinners he'd enjoyed at home, and the games they had played after tea. Hot and tired and overfed he'd been, and so happy that laughter came without the need of an excuse.

In his pockets now he carried a couple of maggotty apples and a bar of chocolate stolen from a shop when he went to ask the time. Both had been saved for the day when the celebrations would be under way. He would pretend to be sharing Christmas day with his family. And Alice.

He was so deep in thought he wasn't aware of the rumbling sound that seemed to make the road on which he walked vibrate. It gradually entered into his consciousness and looking back he could see a great cloud of dust where the mud on the road had been disturbed by many wheels. There was a convoy, an army convoy coming his way.

Cutting across a field, he ran hurriedly to where a secondary road, little more than a track, emerged. He didn't bother to look either way as he clambered over the hedge and slid down on the other side. The armoured car was almost upon him and he tried to get back up and over the hedge, but because the bank was steep and very slippery after a succession of frosty nights he found himself sliding, unable to gain purchase with his worn shoes, and he was soon out of control, falling inexorably into the path of the vehicle.

The driver stopped the car but not soon enough. Eynon felt a blow and then waves of darkness, but he didn't quite lose consciousness. He was aware of footsteps crunching towards him. The pain in his head was severe and he felt the unmistakable sensation of blood running down his face.

He came to fully with a voice asking his name and whether he was all right. Then a hand was slapping him gently on his cheek, and he looked up into the rugged features of a man wearing a forage cap. An army uniform appeared below the face and his brain cleared in seconds. He opened his eyes wide and recited his name and army number clearly and confidently.

"Where are you from, son?" the man asked.

At this Eynon frowned and looked frightened. "I don't know, sergeant. I can't remember." Then acting for all he was worth, he sat up and began to behave in an agitated manner. "I should be back there with – the lorry. It's gone." He repeated the same words several times in a variety of ways, acted confused and recited his name and number again, and was eventually taken back to camp.

There he underwent severe questioning and he told most of the truth, just adding that since the fall from the lorry he had been confused about where he should be and how he could get back there. He hid his excitement. Soon he would be able to receive letters and find out how his brother Ronnie was, and Johnny and Taff.

On Christmas Eve, two military policemen knocked loudly on the door of Marged's house and told her that Eynon had been found and was in hospital. "Private Eynon William Castle is accused of absconding," they told her in their cold indifferent manner. "If it is proved, he will be sent to a military prison before being returned to his unit for further punishment."

Laughing between tears, Marged's only thought was that he was safe, and that their news was the best Christmas gift she had ever had. Then she sent Beth down to tell Huw. This must surely bring him home.

Christmas Eve brought news for Ronnie too. Their second appeal had been successful. He would be allowed to continue working at the market stall. He and Olive hugged each other and, like Marged, thought this was the best news they could receive now they knew Eynon was safe.

Ronnie handed the letter to Olive and said, "Don't forget to read the last bit." He was warned that should his situation be changed, then he had to let them know.

"That's all right; we don't plan a return to the beach next summer, do we?" Olive spoke the words lightly but she held her breath for Ronnie's reply.

"No, love. I think we'll stay on the stall. There are plenty of Castles and hangers-on to run the rest of it, eh?"

Olive thought she couldn't be happier. She had found her niche and was sharing it with Ronnie.

Christmas morning was the strangest one Beth could remember. Their father was still sleeping at Bleddyn's and presumably he would eat Christmas dinner there too. Mam was busy in the kitchen, throwing pots and pans about, the noise and the muttering revealing the extent of her frustration. After unpacking the presents that had been displayed under the tree, except the four awaiting Huw's return, and those for Audrey and Maude and Myrtle who were coming later with Ronnie and Olive, Beth suggested a walk.

"If you aren't going too far, I might come with you," Lilly said.

"Call for the girls, they might like to get out for an hour," Marged suggested.

"Why don't you come too, Mam?"

"Christmas morning? Don't be ridiculous, there's far too much to do!"

"The chicken is cooking, the pudding's simmering nicely, it's too soon for the vegetables and we'll only be half an hour."

Marged finally agreed in the hope that Huw would call and find them all out. Dressed in their warmest coats and wearing the new scarves and hats and gloves Marged had given them, the five of them set off through the town, intending to go to the park and feed the ducks, something Myrtle particularly enjoyed.

At the park gates they came face to face with Mrs Downs and her daughter Shirley, who had been on a similar errand, Shirley celebrating one of only two mornings in the year when there were no morning papers to deal with.

Beth was embarrassed, having to speak politely to the girl she suspected of seeing Freddy. Wishing Shirley and her mother a Happy Christmas stuck in her throat.

"Pity your Freddy couldn't get home for Christmas, eh?" Shirley said. "Send you a card, did he? I had a big-huge one a week ago."

"Kind of him," Beth said stiffly.

Although they had all spoken to Mrs Downs, she had said nothing. She was staring at Maude and Myrtle.

The shy girls backed away from her nervously, remembering the woman's anger when she had chased them out of the shop. She took a step towards them.

"So you're Maude and Myrtle," she said, and her eyes were filled with pain. "Not much like your father, are you?"

From Maude came a deep intake of breath. "You know him?"

"Knew him more like! He's dead. And it's all because of your husband, Mrs High and Mighty Castle! He was responsible, your Huw. For that and all the rest!"

It was only then that they realised that the unhappy woman had been drinking.

"Come on, Mam." Shirley put an arm around her mother and tried to lead her away.

"Please, tell us who he was," Maude begged. "We want to find our sister-in-law. We might have a brother, see."

"What are you talking about? You haven't got a brother, you stupid girl." Pulling away from Shirley, Mrs Downs lurched towards Marged and said, "Killed in an accident he was, when your husband got him drunk and left him and that woman of his to find their way home."

"What is this to do with Maude and Myrtle?" Marged asked, looking at Shirley for the answer. Shirley said nothing, concentrating on getting her mother to move away.

Mrs Downs shrugged herself away from her daughter's grip and said belligerently, "He was their father, wasn't he? Your Huw introduced my husband to Martha Copp, and he left me for her. Even that wasn't enough. Oh no! No, he left them drunk, in a strange town and they were killed on the road. All down to your husband, Mrs High and Mighty Castle. Proud of him now, are you?"

Shirley apologised and succeeded in guiding her tearful mother away from them. "Always bad at Christmastime, she is. It was this time of year that Dad died, see."

The questions came in a torrent from the girls and Marged tried to answer evasively, unsure of how much of the woman's outpourings were fact and how much was fiction, a fantasy built over the years to pass the blame on to someone else, excusing her husband for his infidelity and abandonment and making it easier to bear.

When they got back to the house, Marged put the vegetables on, following the routine like an automaton, unaware of what she was doing. When she did remember it was Christmas dinner she was cooking she wondered, as she had no appetite and the others were silently lost in their own thoughts, who was going to bother to eat it.

In the flat above the paper shop Hetty Downs had calmed down a little. Shirley took the opportunity to learn a few facts before her mother sobered completely and refused to discuss it.

"Strange, wasn't it, Beth finding Maude and Myrtle and then discovering they were Dad's daughters?"

"Illegitimate they are. Nothing to do with us. At least your father had the decency not to give them his name."

"Decency? What's decency? Whatever you feel about Dad, they are his children and my half-sisters. I don't think I can ignore that, Mam."

"Just remember that I had to face the shame of living with a man who was unfaithful, who left me for another woman and gave her the children that I was denied. Oh yes, everyone will know and once this gets out – and it will – memories will be uncovered and I'll have to live it all over again."

"I'll be here, Mam. I'll help you deal with it."

Hetty seemed not to hear. "How can you think of marrying when you could be facing something like that?"

"D'you think she called them Carpenter so the secret would be safe?"

"How do I know how her mind worked?"

"If so, it might have been to protect you," Shirley said, but her mother didn't answer. Hate was a habit and she wasn't ready to give up on it yet.

The girls went several times to the grave of their mother over the Christmas period. Now they knew the truth, they also found the burial plot of Paul Downs, their father. Both of their parents had been killed in December. That seemed more poignant, as they had found him so close to the anniversary.

Maude and Myrtle went with Beth and knocked on the door of Hetty Downs. There were a multitude of questions the girls needed to ask, but Mrs Downs refused to open the door.

"Is Shirley really our half-sister?" Myrtle asked.

"Yes," Beth told her. "You had a half-sister, not a sister-in-law, so no brother I'm afraid. But when things have settled, I think you might be able to talk to Shirley and learn something about your father."

Audrey and Wilf were married quietly in January 1941. They said nothing to Marged. When Wilf's mother passed away two weeks later, Wilf moved his belongings into the house that had been Moll's home. The move was accomplished quietly and without fuss, and Wilf's house was sold in the same way.

Since the revelation about their child had been aired, Wilf had spent more and more time with Audrey. They had arranged for a retired nurse to look after his mother, who by that time no longer knew whether he was there or not, or even who he was. So slowly did the change take place, it wasn't noticeable enough for Maude or Myrtle to mention it with any degree of importance when he moved in altogether.

Although tradition in the town disapproved of women attending an interment, there were so few mourners that Marged went to Wilf's mother's funeral and stood beside Huw and Bleddyn silently, as though they were all strangers. They both knew that they would have to discuss what was happening with regard to the stalls and the café before the new season, but neither of them felt able to make the first move. Huw was still angry and determined that the business should be renamed Castle's, Marged was equally determined that it remain Piper's, and Bleddyn thought it politic to stay out of it until the couple had at least reached the stage at which they were willing to discuss the situation without quarrelling. All they did at this stage was repeat recriminations with tedious regularity.

During the time following the funeral of Wilf's mother, Marged was aware of Audrey spending time helping Wilf to sort out Mrs Thomas's possessions but took little interest. Time was passing and she was becoming more and more worried about the approaching season.

"Uncle Wilf is here," Myrtle told Marged one afternoon when she called with some shopping.

"That's nice," Marged said casually. "Company for you and your sister as well as Audrey."

"Staying for supper, as well, mind," Myrtle insisted, but Marged only smiled. She was too wrapped up in worries about what would happen to her and Huw and Piper's for her to show any concern about her sister.

Eynon had recovered his health rapidly

once he had been taken to the military hospital. The wound on his head which had taken so long to heal had needed a small operation and was now settling down to what he thought would be an interesting scar around which to weave stories to tease his friends and family.

He stuck to his story of being unaware of what had happened to him and where he had been during the months of his absence, and his word was finally accepted. One day he wrote home joyously to tell his family that leave had been granted and he would be home to see them very soon.

Marged immediately began to think about the food she would prepare for him, and insisted that his bedroom was freshly decorated. "It's like Christmas all over again," she said as she began to reply to his letter. She thought of all the letters she had written and which had been returned. He would be able to read them now and know just how much they had all missed him. Huw was as excited as she, but he still didn't return home.

It wasn't until Audrey invited Marged for supper one day in late January that Marged was finally faced with the fact of her sister's marriage. She walked into the house just a few doors from her own and was surprised to see balloons decorating the walls and a slab of fruit cake sprinkled with icing sugar on the table, amid sandwiches and pasties, garlands of evergreens and even a few coloured candles.

"What's this?" Marged asked. "I haven't forgotten a birthday, have I?" She began to smile but the movement froze on her face as Huw stood up from the couch and stared at her.

"A celebration, Marged. A celebration of a wedding that should have taken place years ago." He picked up a glass containing a small serving of port. "A toast, to Audrey and Wilf, Mr and Mrs Wilfred Thomas. Married a couple of weeks ago. Aren't you going to congratulate them?"

The room went out of focus as a shocked Marged took in what he was telling her.

"Married? You and Wilf are married? But when did this happen? Why wasn't I told?"

"We wanted it to be our day, no one else's," Audrey said quietly.

"We had to wait a very long time for it," Wilf added, "and we were determined to make it special."

Marged felt anger rising. She looked around the room for a sign of support but although all the family were there, including Bleddyn, Evelyn and Hannah with Josie and Marie, no one looked anything but delighted. Only Huw's face showed disapproval but that was for her, a silent warning for her not to spoil this moment.

To hide her face and give herself a chance to recover, she hugged her sister and wished her luck. Then the room was filled with noise and laughter as everyone relaxed now the possibility of argument was gone. The food was dispensed by Beth and Lilly, helped by the kindly Hannah.

Later, Marged was glad to immerse herself in clearing up and washing dishes, away from the rest, remembering the day she had told her sister's secret and persuaded her mother that she should work at the beach café and Audrey should be punished for the shame she had brought on them by being made to run Moll's house, away from the fun and prying eyes.

Marged had always behaved herself and didn't see why she should be the one stuck at home doing housework. Now there was a chance to put that right.

As they were about to leave, Audrey took out the wedding photographs. She had worn a dress made by Hannah from delicate lace and lawn which had been dyed a pale primrose colour and decorated with embroidery in pearls and gold thread. Marged stared at her sister's smiling face. She was too old to be a sparkling bride yet she did sparkle. And Wilf made a handsome enough bridegroom. Then, as she was about to remark on the charming picture they made, she looked at the rest of the group and gasped.

Beth was bridesmaid, Ronnie was best man. Huw was there too. She later discovered he had given the bride away. They all knew but had kept it from her. Her gentle sister had taken her revenge.

"Why? Why didn't you tell me?" she asked, her voice low with pain.

"You spoilt everything for them once; we were determined you wouldn't do it again," Huw said. "Ambition is all right, but not when it makes one person consider themselves more important than the rest."

"I didn't see why I should have to to run the house. I wanted to work on the beach," Marged explained. She realised how bad the words sounded as soon as they were spoken.

"So did I," Audrey said softly. "But only one of us could. One had to stay home."

"And you made sure it wasn't you," Huw said to Marged, bitterly.

Marged kissed her sister and Wilf, who had remained silent throughout. "I'll go now," she said, forcing a smile. "I'll come and see you tomorrow, shall I? We can talk about what we all want to do."

"I don't want to change anything," Audrey said. "Not now. It's too late. Wilf and I will live here and do what's necessary to help. I'll organise the rock and sweet shop. Alice will probably help me again. Glad to get away from that foul-tempered father of hers she is."

"I admire a strong woman," Huw told Marged in one of their rare quiet moments together, "and there's no doubt a strong woman was needed to run Piper's. But there's never any need for greed and ruthlessness, and determination to get your own way whatever the cost."

"I'm not like that!" she said horrified. "Huw, you can't see me like that?"

"You were willingly led by Moll, weren't you? She pulled all the switches and made certain we understood who was boss, and she could always rely on you for support. But it can't go on. Not now. It's caused too much unhappiness."

Marged had to agree. "I was young, outraged morality was a wonderful feeling. At the time Mam was very convincing."

"That was her biggest and most dangerous fault. She was always convincing."

Beth was happy that her aunt had married at last, but she was less happy about her own marriage plans. Freddy was unreliable and he was hopeless with money. But true love had no boundaries and she supposed she had to accept him with all his faults, as she expected him to accept her. Occasionally she felt a stabbing fear when she thought about the future, imagining sitting at home wondering whether Freddy was being unfaithful. She was ashamed to realise that these thoughts were greater worries than concern for his safety.

There were stories in the newspapers of men being let down by women while they fought the enemy and she determined that, whatever her doubts, she would remain loyal and support Freddy until the fighting stopped. Then Peter came home on leave and her strength was sorely tested.

She went for a walk one Sunday morning in February when the sun was beginning to spread its warmth, with a promise of the better days to come. Before she reached Goose Lane she met Mr Gregory and his flock of donkeys heading for the cliffs. Bernard was walking beside a small cart being pulled by the donkey known as Gus and the cart was loaded with hay bales and the drum of food for the donkeys' evening feed.

Mr Gregory knew the story about Paul Downs and his affair with Martha Copp, and he filled in a few gaps. "Things aren't ever forgotten, Beth, my dear. The gossip dies down but the facts lie dormant, simmering beneath the surface, and ready to pop up and start all over again. Remember that it's the girls who are the victims in all this. The less they hear of the worst side of the story the better. They should know only that their father and mother loved them dearly."

"I agree," Beth said. "I've told them that already. And that their father loved their mother so much he gave up a great deal to be with her."

"Good girl," he said approvingly, puffing fiercely on his pipe. "I knew you'd say the right things." He smiled at her proudly and tilted his head as a salute. "Now why don't you come with me to Sally Gough's field, then we'll go back for a cup of tea."

Enjoying the slow, unhurried pace of the donkeys, Beth walked beside the cart with him, one of them on either side of Gus, through the lanes.

"Peter's due home tomorrow," Bernard told her. "Will you be able to get off for an hour or so? It being a Monday, you don't open the chip shop, do you?"

"I might," she told him. "Although Mam is already getting started on the café over the beach. With Dad not willing to help, and Uncle Bleddyn keeping away afraid of being involved, there's a lot to do before the May opening."

"Peter'll be disappointed not to see you," Mr Gregory said. "He loves your letters and looks forward to seeing you when he gets home. He reckons his leaves will be few and far between from now on. He can't tell me

436

of course, but I think there's something serious in the offing."

"I'm not promising," she said, her heart racing as she tried to speak the words she didn't want to say. "It's Freddy, see. I'm not sure, but perhaps he'll be home and I won't be free."

"You and this Freddy, still engaged, are you?"

"Still engaged. This isn't the time to break off engagements, is it, with the men likely to go out to France or further afield, facing danger at any moment."

"You know he sees Shirley Downs and writes to her and you don't mind?" the old man asked curiously. "You modern women mystify me and that's a fact!"

"He feels sorry for her, that's all. She'll find herself a real boyfriend soon and then Freddy will forget her. Men and women can be friends without it developing into – you know – something deeper," she admonished.

"Oh, can they?" Mr Gregory didn't sound convinced. "The back row of the picture house wasn't for innocent friendships in my memory."

She didn't ask if he had seen Freddy with Shirley recently. She didn't want to know. Just get the war over, she told herself, and then they would sort their lives out. Now, she owed Freddy loyalty and support, whatever he felt about Shirley Downs.

They sat in the field that sloped down to the rocky edge of the sea for a while as the donkeys explored their temporary home. The sea was empty of boats. The restrictions on their movement meant that the all-important fishing went on within a rigid timetable or they risked being shot out of the water by patrols.

There was no sound apart from the waves dashing against the rocks. Whereas the regular movement of the sea would normally have relaxed her, Beth felt an increasing restlessness that was nothing to do with the sea and everything to do with Peter, who was coming home tomorrow.

"I can't be more than a friend to Peter," she said sadly. "Tomorrow I'll tell him so."

"Sure about that, are you?"

When they left the cliffs, having settled the donkeys in and seen to their feeding, she didn't go back to the friendly cottage in Goose Lane. Instead she went back home to write to Freddy and Peter and Johnny and Taff. It was her war effort and a very important weekly chore, she told herself. Nothing to do with the aching need to see Peter, and feel his arms around her, have her lips touch his, telling him how much he was loved. She wrote Peter's letter first, describing the peace and beauty of the cliffs and the contentment of his father. She mentioned in a casual way that she and Freddy would probably marry the moment he was demobbed. She read the lines that were filled with untruths in writing that was decidedly wobbly and told him nothing of how she really felt, and kissed the pages before putting them into the envelope, imagining him kissing them too.

Eynon came home for a forty-eight hour visit and the family celebrated with a party. No one outside the family was invited but that didn't stop them coming. From every house neighbours poured, most bringing something to add to the feast. Bottles left over from Christmas, food stored for that special occasion.

The scar was admired as though it had been earned in an honourable battle and even when he told people he'd done it falling from a lorry, no one believed him. There was a war on, they wanted a hero, and he was it!

He invited Alice but she didn't stay long, afraid of her father's wrath if she wasn' there when he looked for her. She promisec to write, though, to his delight. He returned to camp to a different group of boys, stronger and with no fear of bullying, prepared to do what had to be done, older than his years and more sure of himself than ever before.

Shirley Downs called at Audrey and Wilf's house and was made welcome. She spent time with Maude and Myrtle, filling in gaps and talking about their father. She was surprisingly happy as she remembered incidents involving her father when she was young. Her stories were soaked up like a sponge by the girls as they built up a picture of Paul Downs, their father, who was buried not far from their mother.

During March, which came in like a lamb and therefore threatened to go out like a lion, Huw still lived at his brother's house. They did nothing towards preparing for the new season at the beach and if Bleddyn thought Huw and Marged were stupid, he kept it to himself.

Bleddyn continued to run the fish-and-chip café and he occasionally asked Beth how Marged was, but it never went further than the kind of brief, polite remark that warranted nothing more than a brief, polite reply. Both were determined not to become involved in taking sides. Mostly they talked about the latest letters from Johnny and Taff, and now Eynon too.

Beth kept away from Goose Lane while Peter's leave progressed. It would be a forty-eight, Mr Gregory had told her, so she felt safe to go there the following weekend. As she touched the gate she heard laughter and saw Peter coming around the corner arm in arm with a pretty girl of about her own age. She stopped and looked around as though preparing to run, but Peter had seen her, called to her and she was rooted to the spot.

"Beth, how wonderful. I thought you weren't going to visit us this week. Do come and meet Diana. Diana, this is Beth about whom you have heard so much."

Taking in the small neat figure, the pale baby-pink skin enhanced with rouge and lipstick, and the fair hair with its bow of ribbon tying back curls, Beth felt untidy and wished she had bothered to change out of the casual clothes she habitually wore when visiting Mr Gregory and his donkeys. She felt sick with jealousy, frighteningly, horrifyingly sick, afraid that if she didn't get away from this happy-looking couple she would almost certainly throw up on Mr Gregory's neat garden.

"I was on my way to the cliffs," she said. "Can I use your lavatory?"

Why had she said that? Why ask to use the lavatory before even responding to Peter's introduction to his friend? What a stupid remark! How embarrassing! Why couldn't she be self-assured like Diana obviously was? Then she thought, Why does it matter? I'm going to marry Freddy Clements. But even to her, that sounded more stupid than asking to use the lavatory.

She didn't stay. She went into the garden behind the house and walked down to the euphemistically named ty bach – little house – and stayed a moment, combing her hair and wishing it was fair and curly instead of straight and black. She examined her face in the speckly mirror and pretended the freckles were in fact marks on the glass, wishing she had bothered to smear a little lipstick on her lips.

When she came out, the girl was talking to Peter's father over near the chicken house and Peter was waiting for her in the kitchen.

"Peter," she said, wrapping her scarf tightly around her head. "I don't think I should write to you any more. Freddy doesn't like it and as I've asked him not to write to Shirley, who was only a friend, it seems only fair," she lied.

"What harm were we doing, getting to know each other better?"

"You know how painful jealousy can be," she said, glancing towards the pretty young girl.

"I understand jealousy," he said slowly. "I'm extremely jealous of the time you spend writing to Freddy. Are you sure you want to stop writing to me? I don't know how I'll bear it, Bethan."

"It's the best thing to do," she said, with

the conviction that she was being more stupid than at any time during her life.

Her dismay gave her face an expression of stubbornness and Peter stared at her for long moments before saying, "Of course. I understand. You love Freddy and I have to accept that. I'll miss your letters enormously. They were the highlight of my week." He stepped towards her but she moved away, unable to trust herself. She was afraid to look at him; he would surely see in her face the tumult of her emotions.

"Goodbye," she said, stepping towards the door.

"If you should change your mind, Beth, I'd be so happy," he replied.

She hadn't realised just how strong an emotion jealousy could be. Beside the sick feeling that hadn't gone away, she felt as though her racing heart would explode with the agony of it. Peter and that fairy doll of a girl. Imagine her feeding the donkeys on a wet and windy hillside, Beth thought. She'd still manage to look beautiful.

There was a letter waiting for her when she reached home, and she recognised the writing as Freddy's. It was longer than usual and she took it to her room to sit in privacy and read it. It said he thought they should end their engagement, as he was seeing rather a lot of Shirley and thought he and she were better suited.

Beth was still staring at the words when there was a knock at the door. Shirley Downs stood there.

"I think we ought to talk about Freddy," Shirley said.

"Don't worry, Shirley. I've had a letter that makes everything clear. He's right, you'll make him happier than I ever would," Beth said, trying to keep her voice steady.

"I don't suppose you'll ever like me, but I hope we can be friends, if only for Maude and Myrtle's sake," Shirley went on. "They aren't guilty of any of what went on between my family and yours. Even Mam can see that, and I think she'll be able to get to know them once the pain of finding them has eased."

"Let's meet in a day or so and take the girls somewhere where we can talk," Beth suggested, forcing a smile.

There was nothing to be gained by being bitter. The end of her engagement to Freddy was completely painless. At least, it would have been if she hadn't been so determined to tell Peter goodbye, she thought sadly as Shirley left.

She had to get out of the house so she went to talk to the girls. When she got back her father was there. She went straight to the kitchen and shut herself in, afraid of interrupting what might be an attempt at reconciliation.

Marged and Huw at last began to talk to each other. With so much to do before the opening of the new season, common sense had prevailed. Marged's first act of surrender was to arrange for the new signs. The Pipers were all gone; even Audrey was now Mrs Wilf Thomas. The new name would show proudly above each of their businesses.

Lilly was given the task of dealing with the laundry and the daily ordering of fresh food, a side of the business previously dealt with by Moll. She agreed, but hoped that the baby would excuse her from most of it by being born so conveniently in May when the season started.

Beth had watched through a crack in the door with her fingers crossed that first day when her parents had begun to communicate, and heard her father say, "Most importantly, we'll listen to each other, won't we, Marged?" He was smiling but there was a threat in his glinting eyes and the stiffness of his lips. "All of us. We'll all have our say; the Castle family is a strong, unbeatable team."

A rota was arranged for washing woodwork and painting, especially the helter-skelter, which would proudly bear the colours red, white and blue. The new season was rapidly approaching, but although relieved that her parents were talking again, Beth was unable to involve herself in the excitement.

She had told Peter she didn't love him out of misplaced loyalty. Now it was up to her to try to put things right.

She met Mr Gregory, who told her that Peter was leaving on the nine o'clock train the following morning, and she decided to try and see him. If she could just write to him again, and continue to watch for the postman with such hope, that would be better than nothing. She stood at the station, trying to decide what she would say and how she would say it. She remembered Freddy's first departure and his first leave and wondered how this railway station meeting would end.

Peter came on his father's cart, his father driving, while Peter sat beside him writing something on a pad of paper.

"I just wanted to say goodbye properly, Peter," she told him when, with a great smile, he jumped off the cart and ran to where she was waiting. "I will still write, if you want me to, and if Diana doesn't mind. I wouldn't want to do anything to spoil things."

"Diana? She's a customer of Dad's, Beth! There's nothing there to spoil, and as for writing, I've just started a letter to you, begging you not to abandon me." He handed her the piece of paper on which he had written, "Darling Beth, please tell Freddy goodbye, and marry me."

With only a few moments before the train was due to leave, they hugged and kissed and promised to write every day. Peter said, "We'll marry as soon as the war is over and I've set up my employment agency."

"Not before? But what if things change?"

"If I die, you mean? You'd rather be my widow than my loving friend?"

"Oh Peter, I didn't mean that! Please, don't die. I meant that you'll be away from me and might meet someone else."

"I don't need anyone else. All I need is to imagine you on the beach, helping everyone suffering because of this terrible war to relax and have a good time."

Their parting was swift and painful, the kiss harsh and greedy and they were breathless as Peter turned and waved to his father who was waiting with the pony and cart to take Beth home.

"Peter and I—" she began to explain.

He interrupted with, "An' about time too."